W9-BKF-522

the greatest thing

Sarah Winifred Searle

:01
First Second
New York

First Second

Published by First Second
First Second is an imprint of Roaring Brook Press,
a division of Holtzbrinck Publishing Holdings Limited Partnership
120 Broadway, New York, NY 10271
firstsecondbooks.com

No references in this book to real organizations are intended to suggest any authorization, endorsement, or sponsorship by such organizations.

Library of Congress Control Number: 2021909951

Our books may be purchased in bulk for promotional, educational, or business use.
Please contact your local bookseller or the Macmillan Corporate and Premium Sales Department
at (800) 221-7945 ext. 5442 or by email at MacmillanSpecialMarkets@macmillan.com.

FIRST

EDITION

First edition, 2022
Edited by Robyn Chapman and Hazel Newlevant
Cover and interior book design by Molly Johanson
Authenticity readers: Gia Drew, Melanie Gillman, and Mey Rude
With special thanks to Janina Scarlet, PhD

Drawn and colored in Clip Studio Paint on an iPad.

Printed in China

ISBN 978-1-250-29723-5 (paperback)
10 9 8 7 6 5 4 3 2 1

ISBN 978-1-250-29722-8 (hardcover)
10 9 8 7 6 5 4 3 2 1

Don't miss your next favorite book from First Second!
For the latest updates go to firstsecondnewsletter.com and sign up for our enewsletter.

BY ART
WE LIVE

For Adam
and Matthew

Content Note:
This book contains depictions
of self-harm and disordered eating.

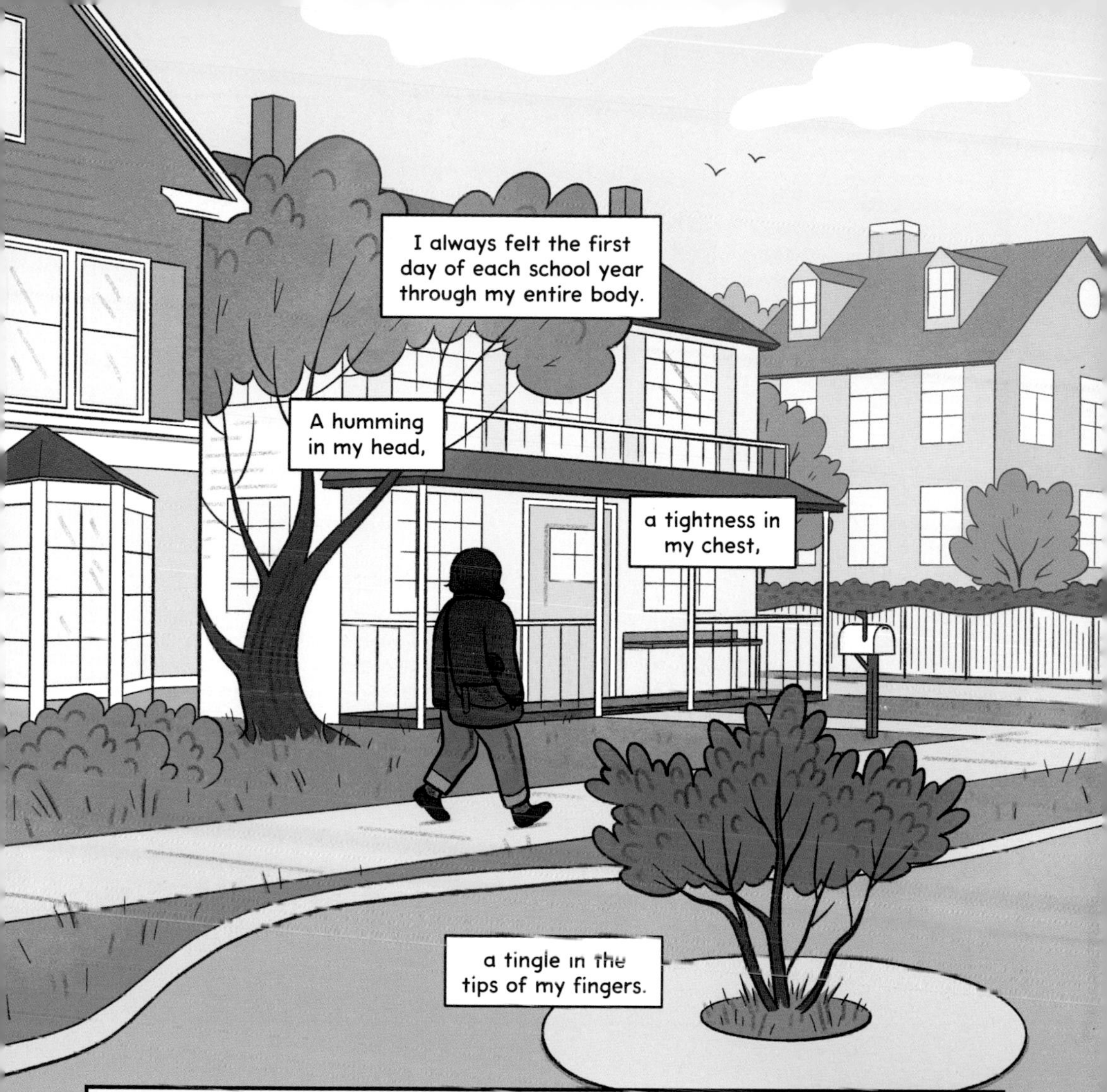
I always felt the first day of each school year through my entire body.
A humming in my head,
a tightness in my chest,
a tingle in the tips of my fingers.

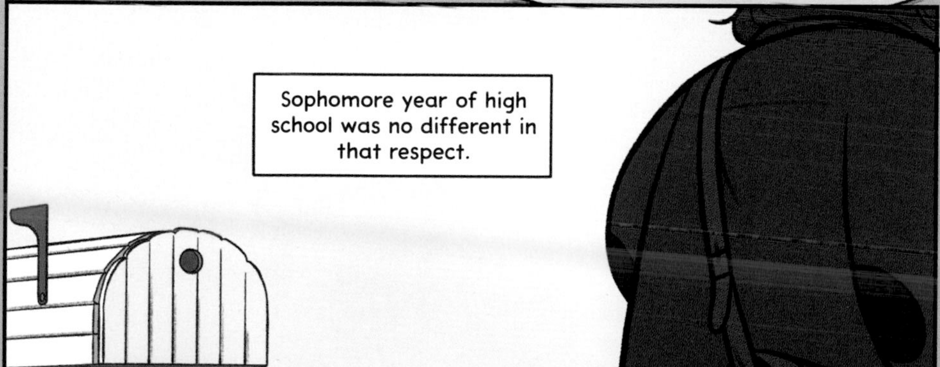
Sophomore year of high school was no different in that respect.

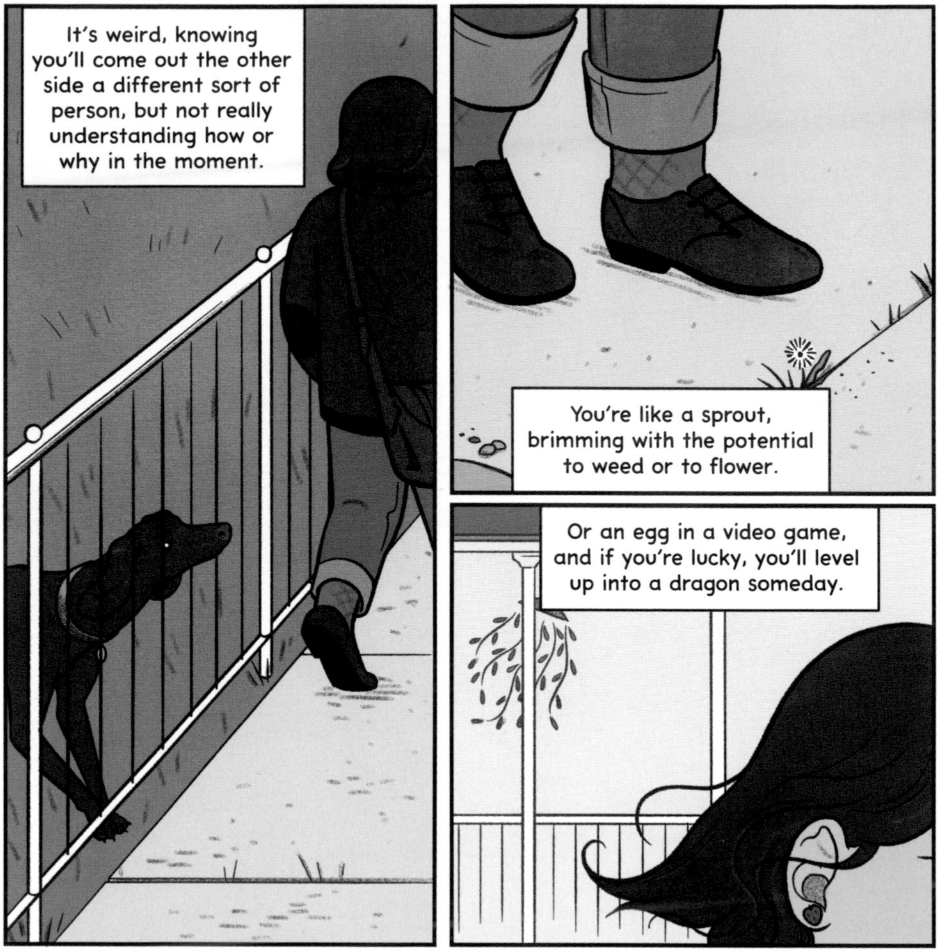
It's weird, knowing you'll come out the other side a different sort of person, but not really understanding how or why in the moment.
You're like a sprout, brimming with the potential to weed or to flower.
Or an egg in a video game, and if you're lucky, you'll level up into a dragon someday.

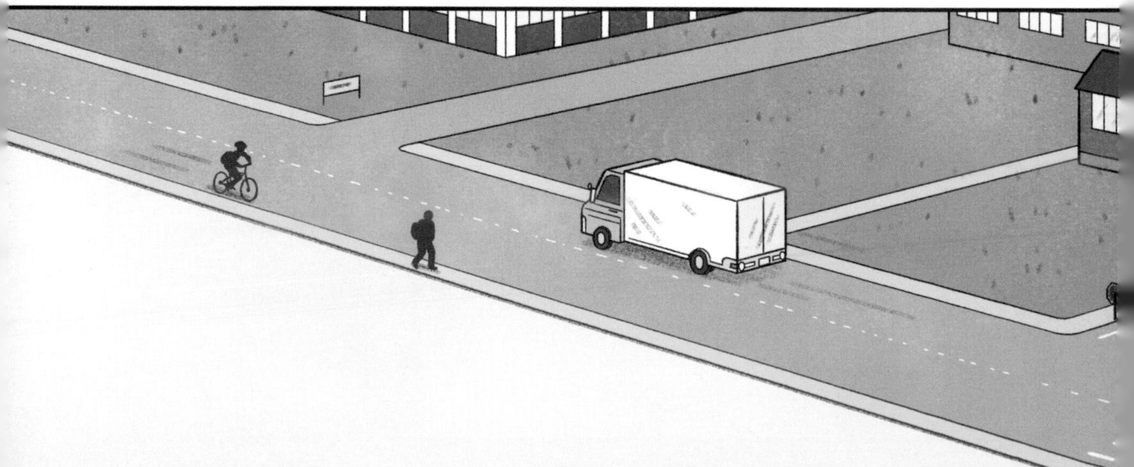

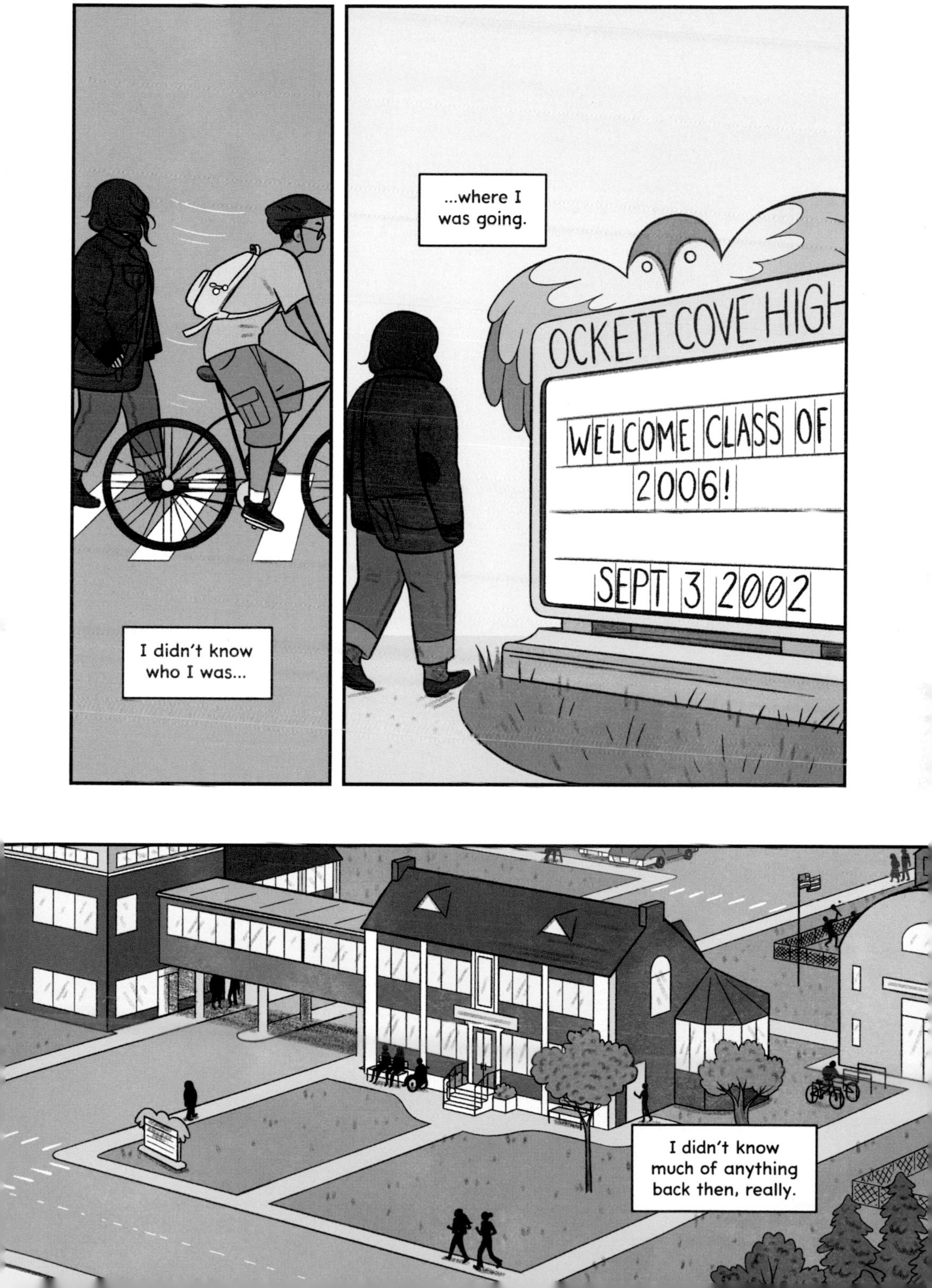
I didn't know who I was...
...where I was going.
OCKETT COVE HIGH
WELCOME CLASS OF 2006!
SEPT 3 2002
I didn't know much of anything back then, really.

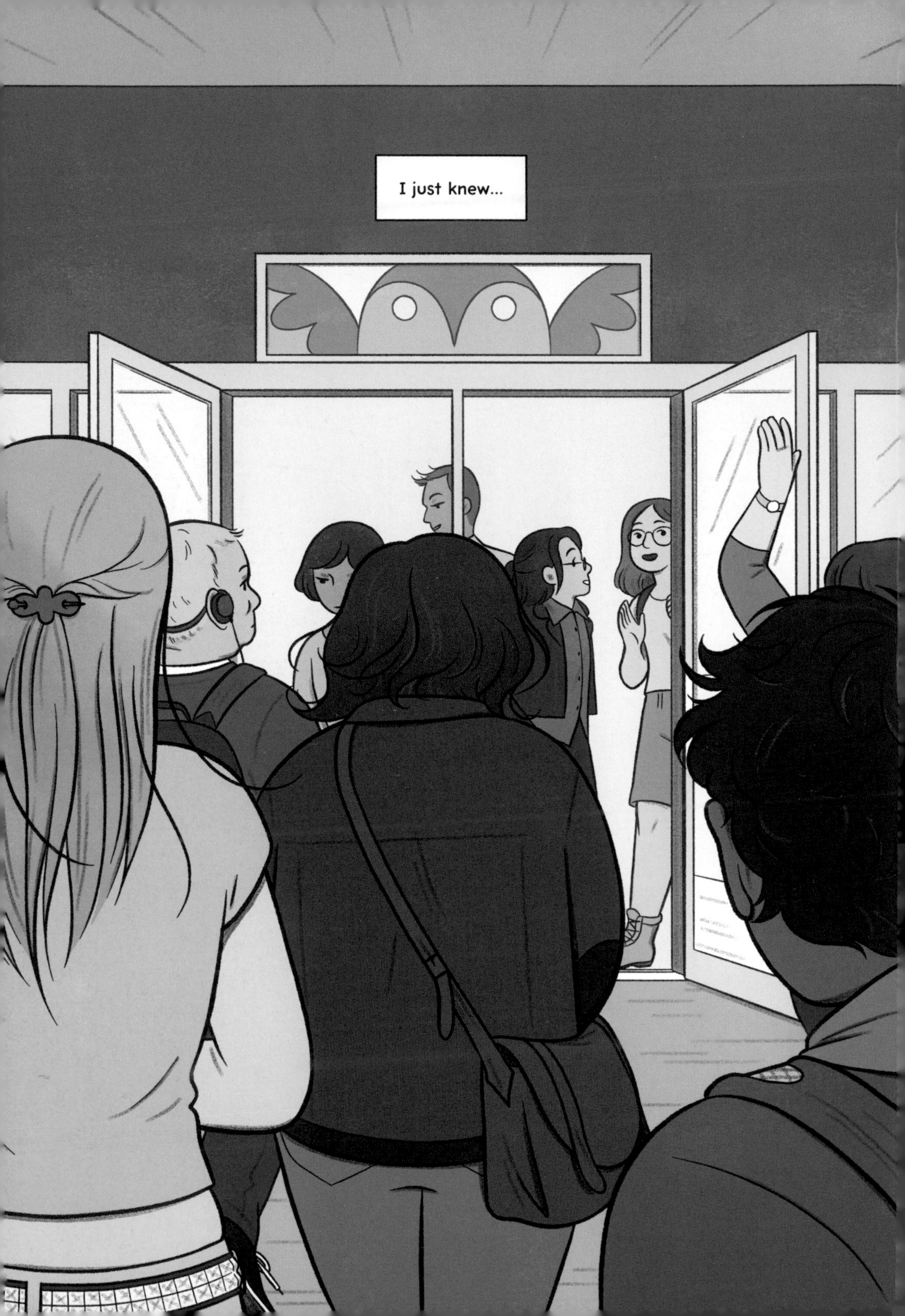
I just knew...

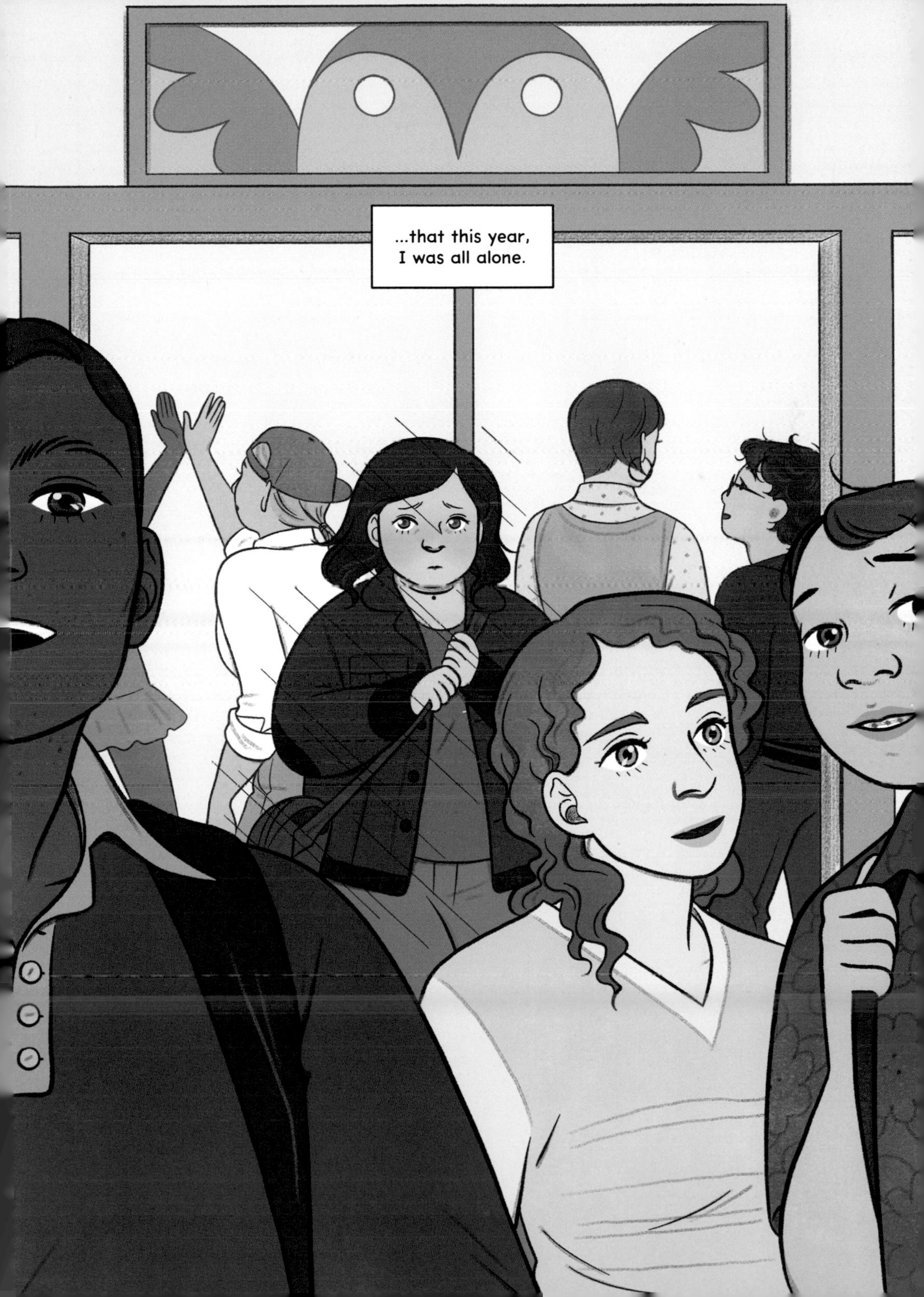
...that this year,
I was all alone.

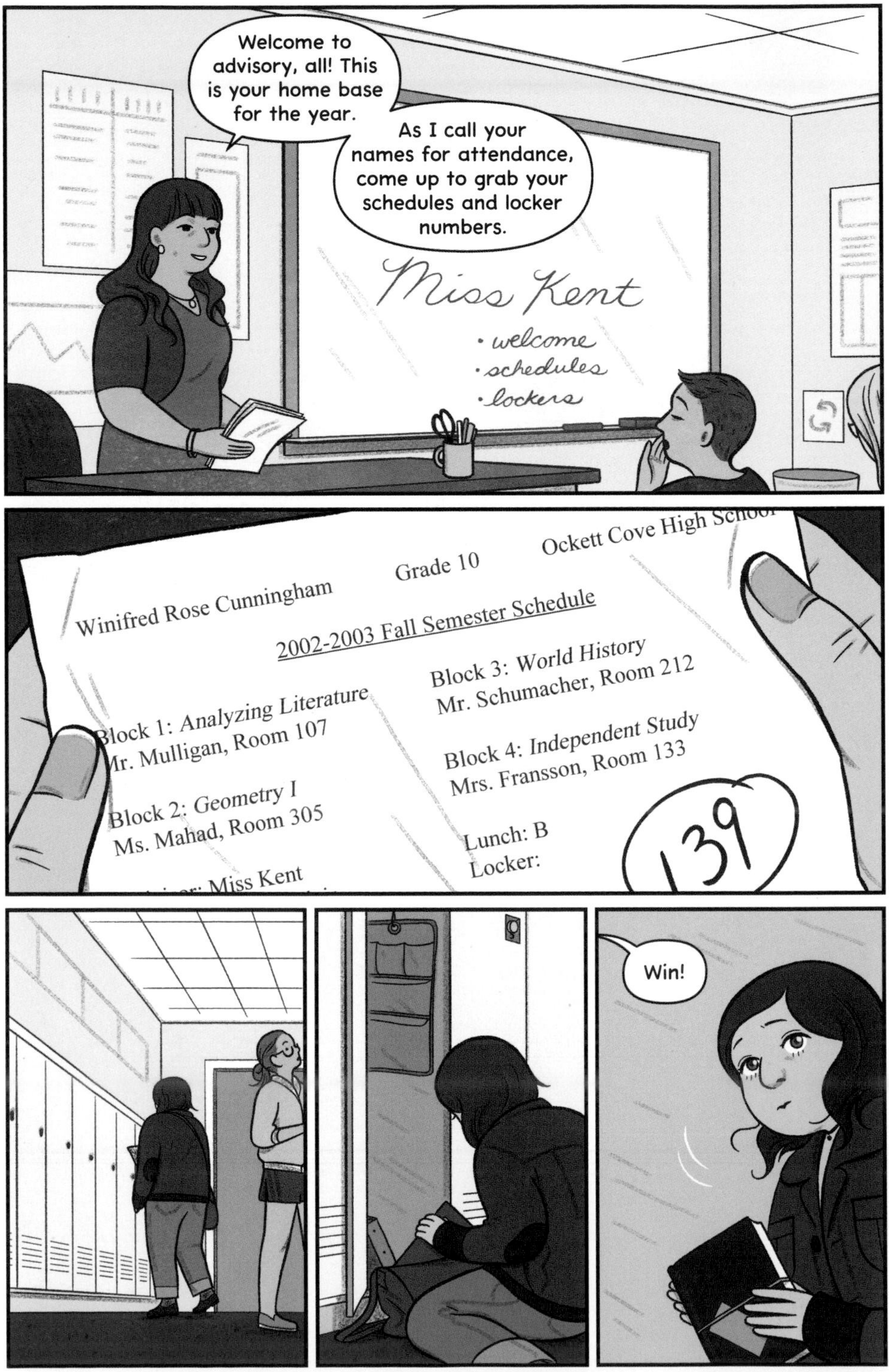

Welcome to advisory, all! This is your home base for the year.
As I call your names for attendance, come up to grab your schedules and locker numbers.
Miss Kent
• welcome
• schedules
• lockers
Ockett Cove High School
Grade 10
Winifred Rose Cunningham
2002-2003 Fall Semester Schedule
lock 1: Analyzing Literature
r. Mulligan, Room 107
Block 2: Geometry I
Ms. Mahad, Room 305
Miss Kent
Block 3: World History
Mr. Schumacher, Room 212
Block 4: Independent Study
Mrs. Fransson, Room 133
Lunch: B
Locker:
139
Win!

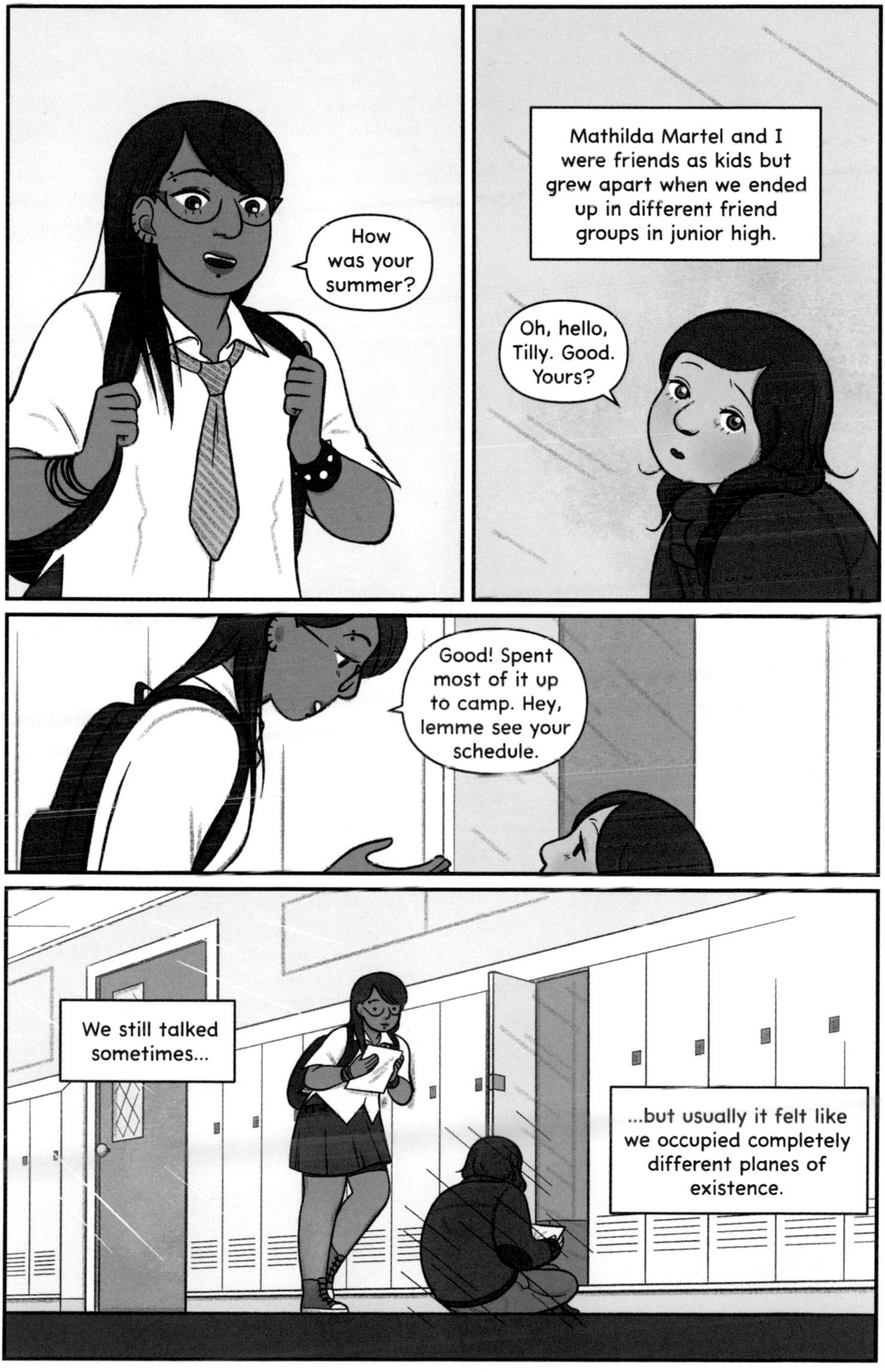
How was your summer?
Mathilda Martel and I were friends as kids but grew apart when we ended up in different friend groups in junior high.
Oh, hello, Tilly. Good. Yours?
Good! Spent most of it up to camp. Hey, lemme see your schedule.
We still talked sometimes...
...but usually it felt like we occupied completely different planes of existence.

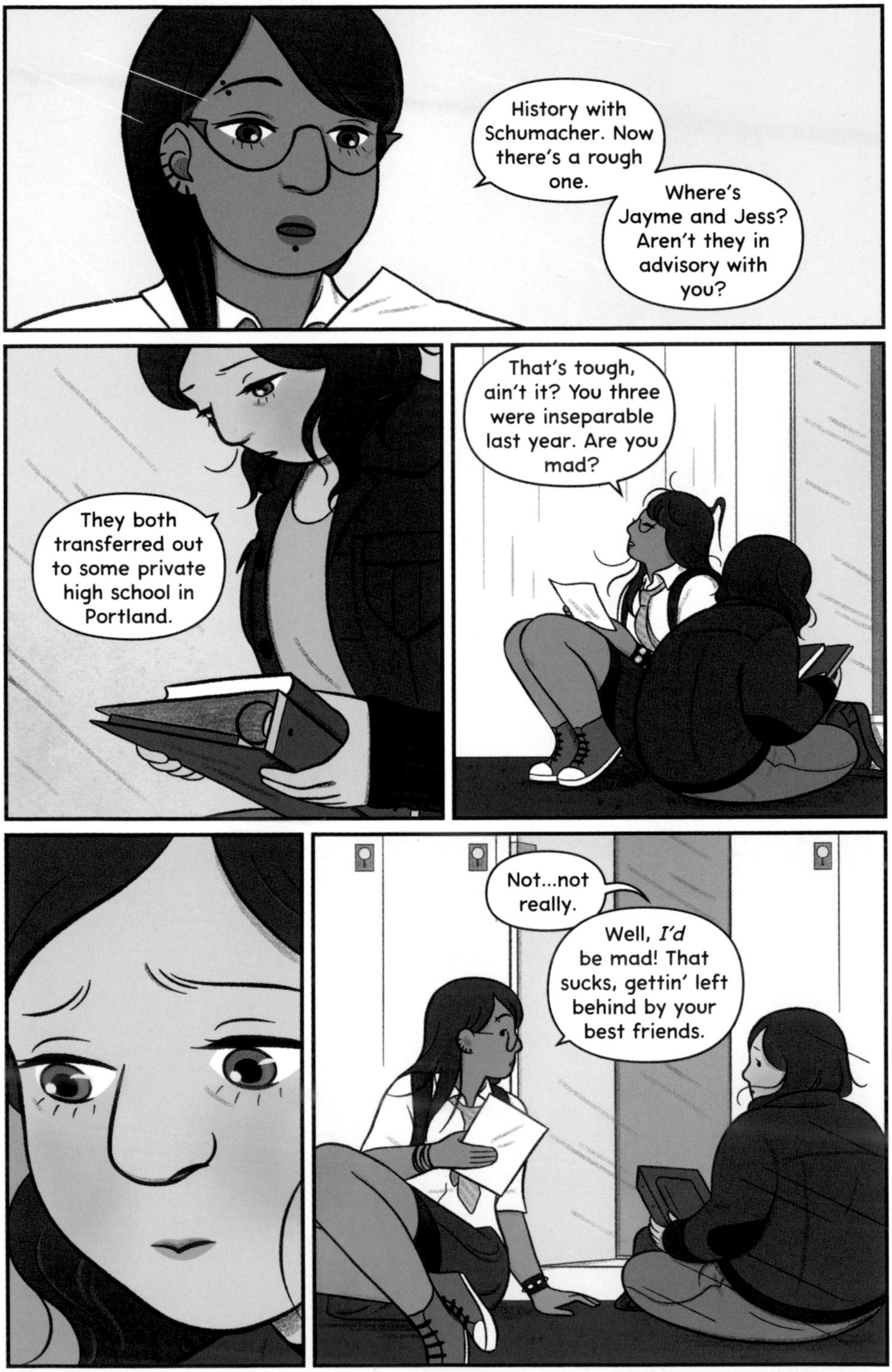
History with Schumacher. Now there's a rough one.
Where's Jayme and Jess? Aren't they in advisory with you?
They both transferred out to some private high school in Portland.
That's tough, ain't it? You three were inseparable last year. Are you mad?
Not...not really.
Well, *I'd* be mad! That sucks, gettin' left behind by your best friends.

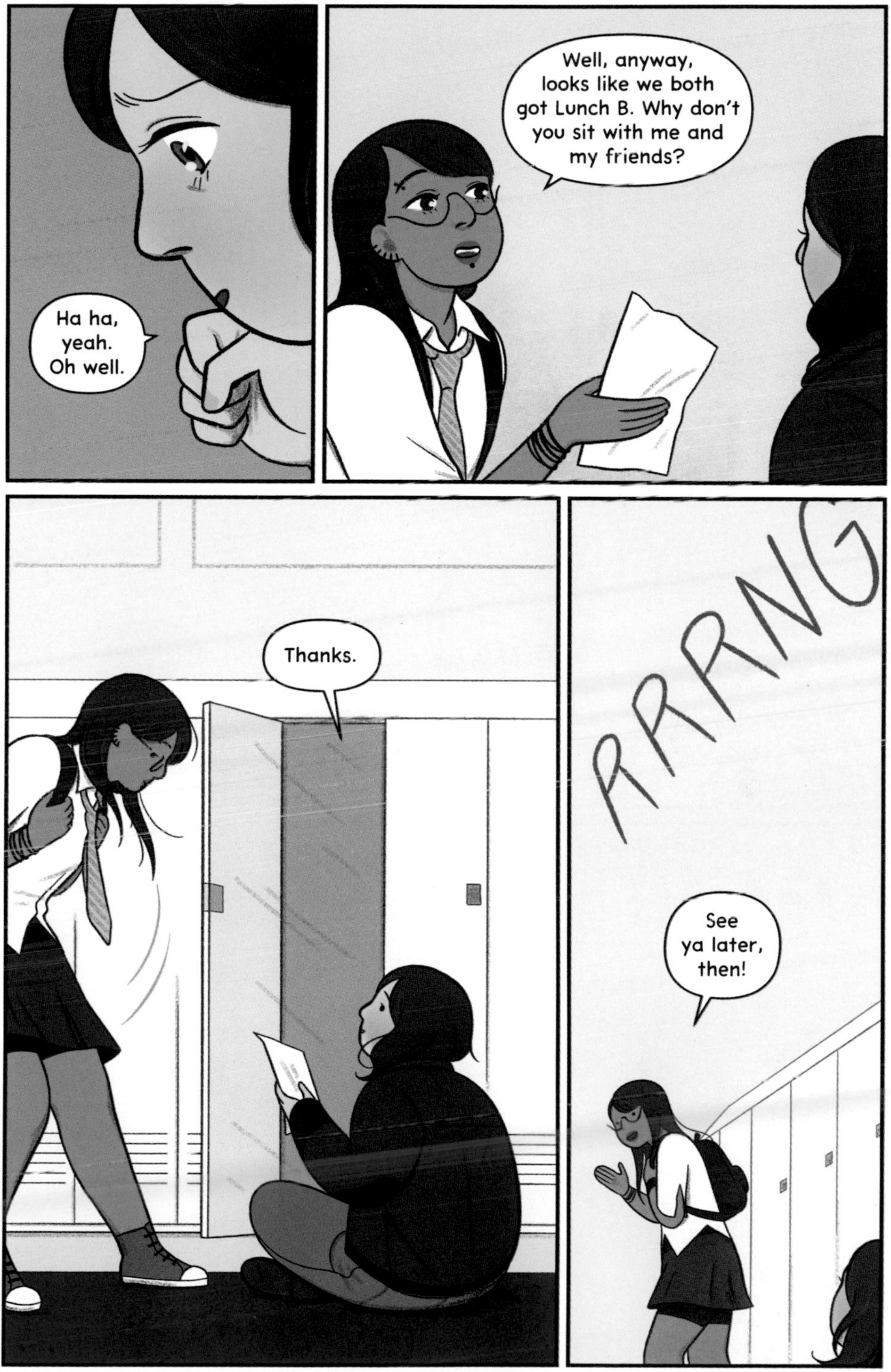
Ha ha, yeah. Oh well.
Well, anyway, looks like we both got Lunch B. Why don't you sit with me and my friends?
Thanks.
RRRNG
See ya later, then!

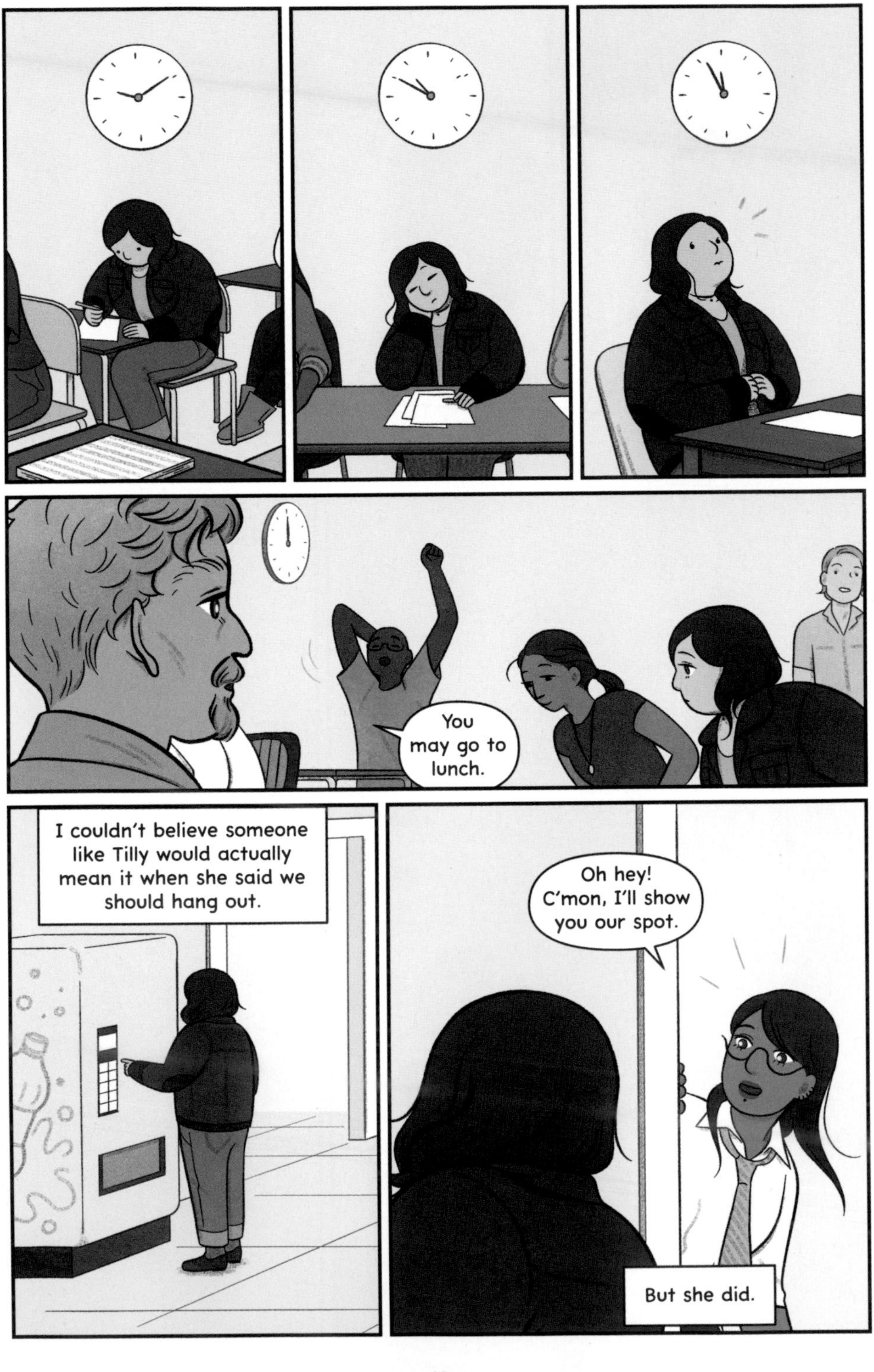
You may go to lunch.
I couldn't believe someone like Tilly would actually mean it when she said we should hang out.
Oh hey! C'mon, I'll show you our spot.
But she did.

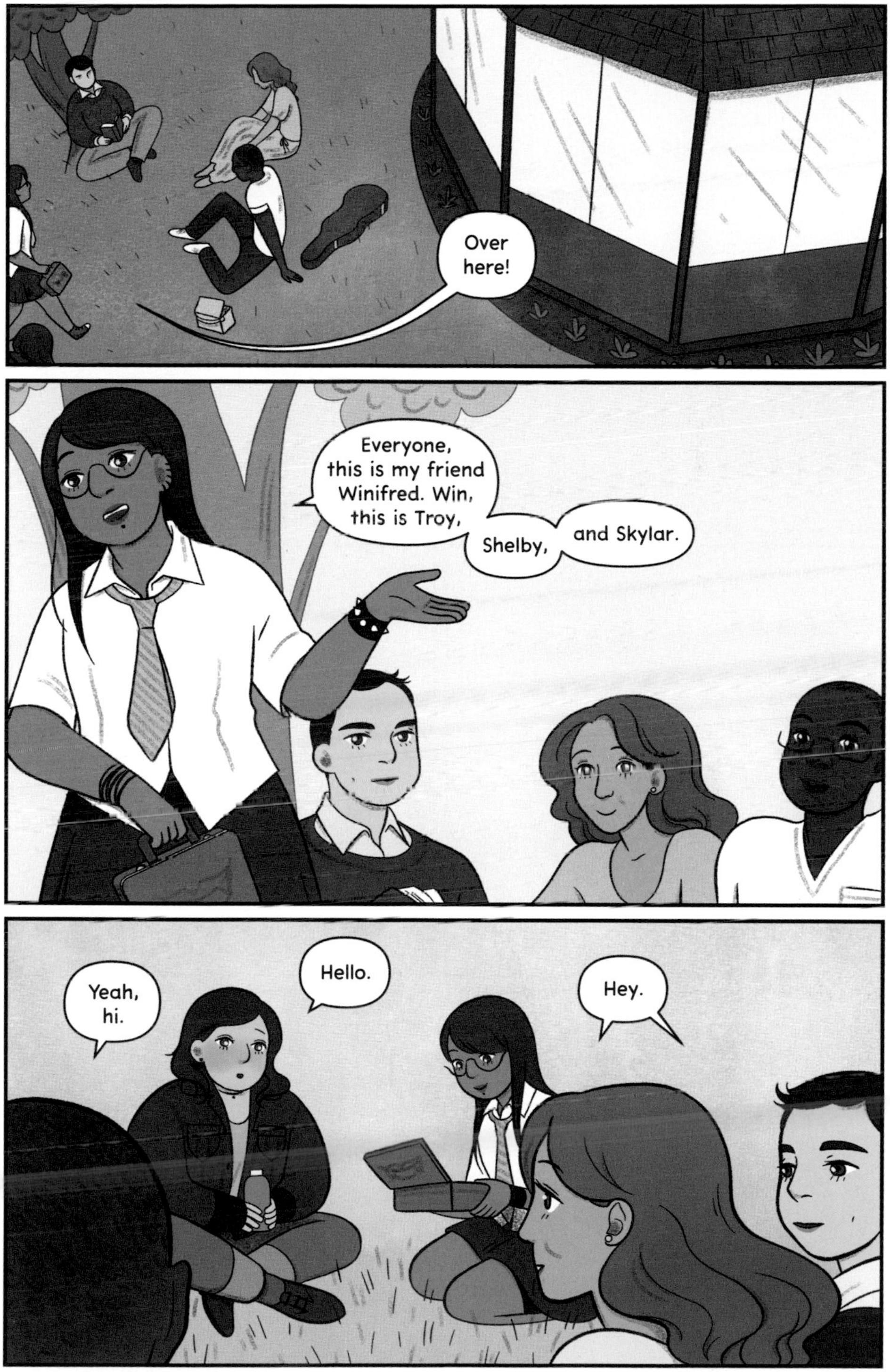
Over here!
Everyone, this is my friend Winifred. Win, this is Troy,
Shelby,
and Skylar.
Yeah, hi.
Hello.
Hey.

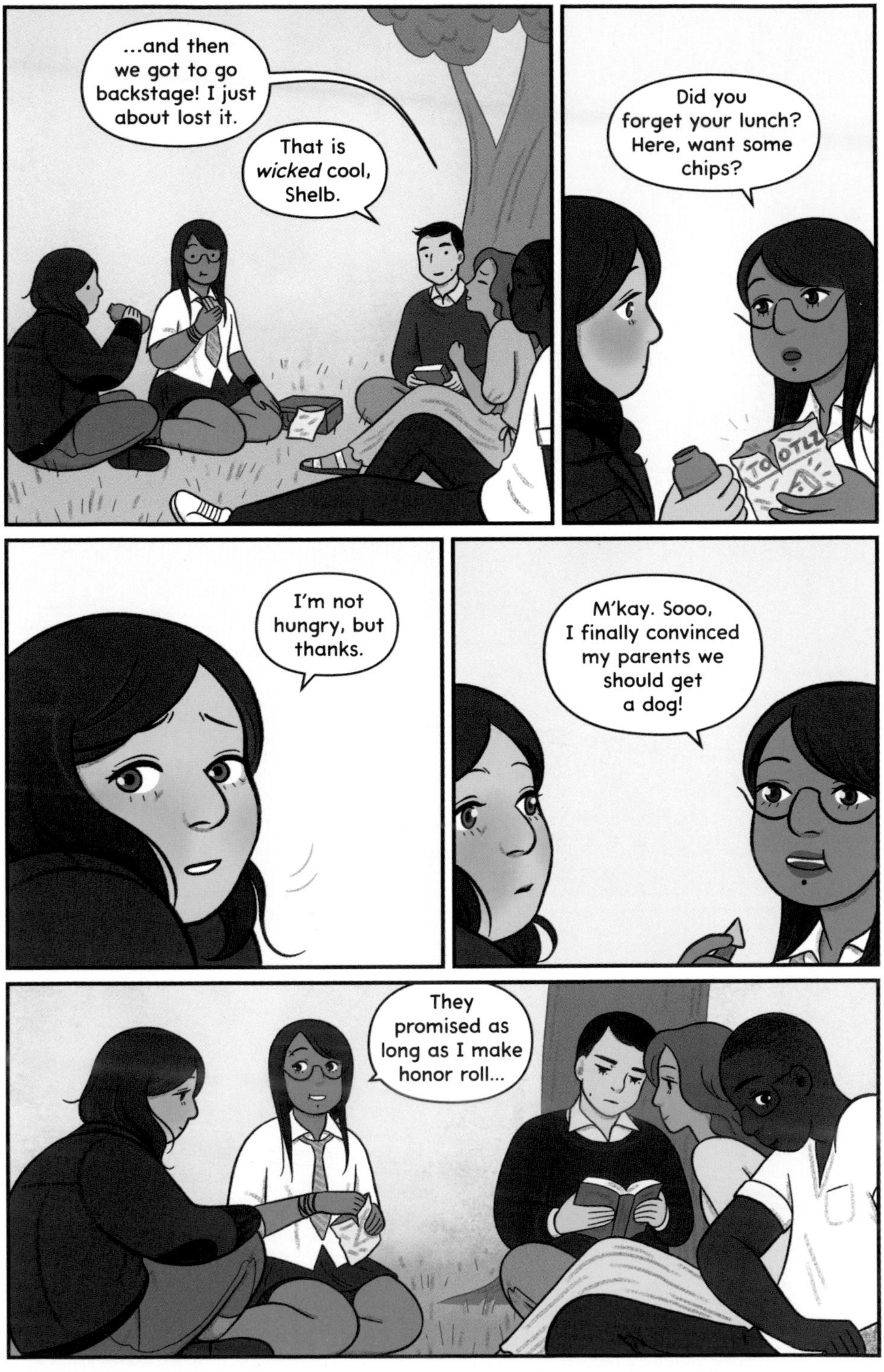
...and then we got to go backstage! I just about lost it.
That is *wicked* cool, Shelb.
Did you forget your lunch? Here, want some chips?
TOOTLZ
I'm not hungry, but thanks.
M'kay. Sooo, I finally convinced my parents we should get a dog!
They promised as long as I make honor roll...

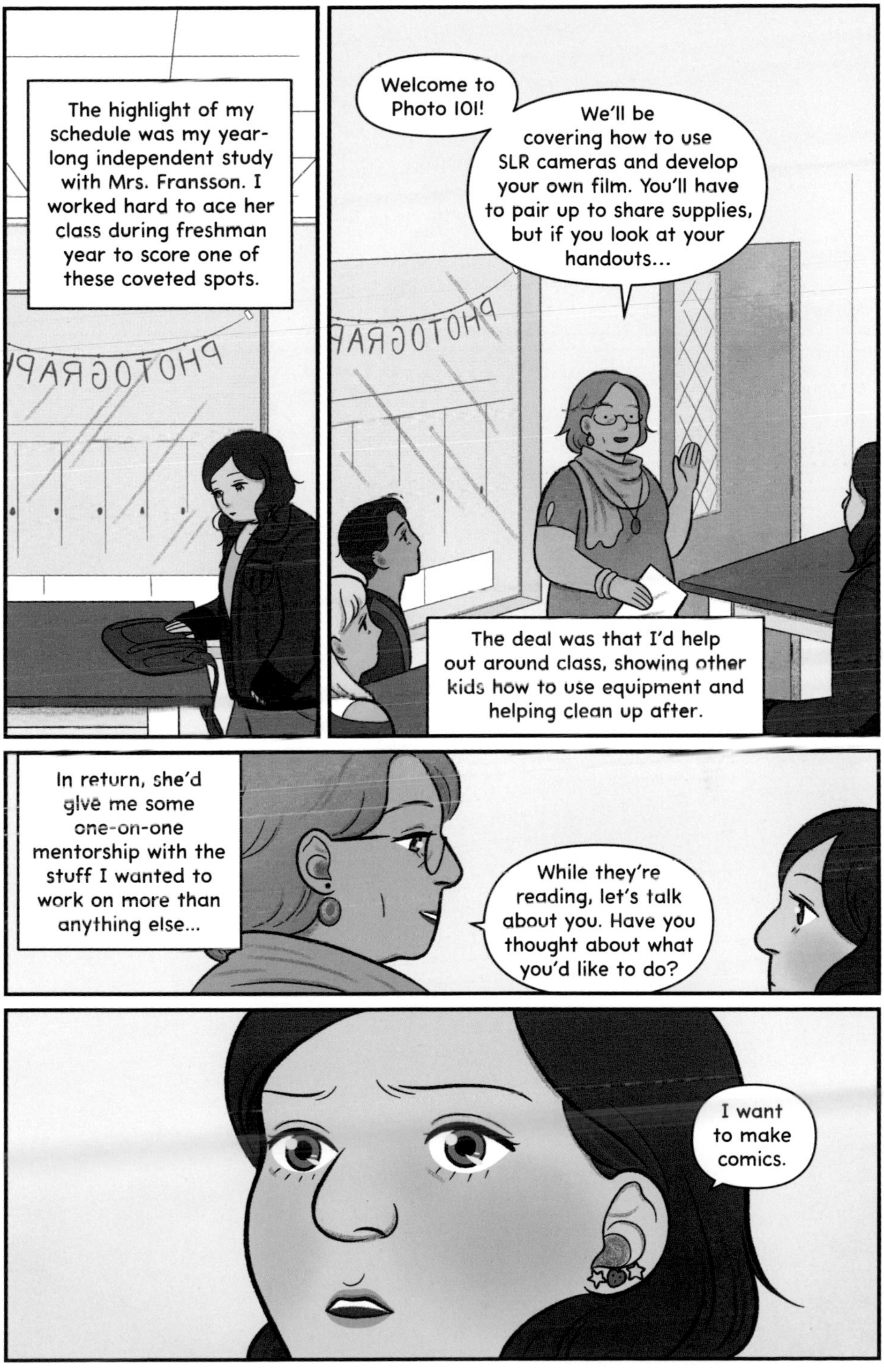
The highlight of my schedule was my year-long independent study with Mrs. Fransson. I worked hard to ace her class during freshman year to score one of these coveted spots.
PHOTOGRAPH
Welcome to Photo 101!
We'll be covering how to use SLR cameras and develop your own film. You'll have to pair up to share supplies, but if you look at your handouts...
The deal was that I'd help out around class, showing other kids how to use equipment and helping clean up after.
In return, she'd give me some one-on-one mentorship with the stuff I wanted to work on more than anything else...
While they're reading, let's talk about you. Have you thought about what you'd like to do?
I want to make comics.

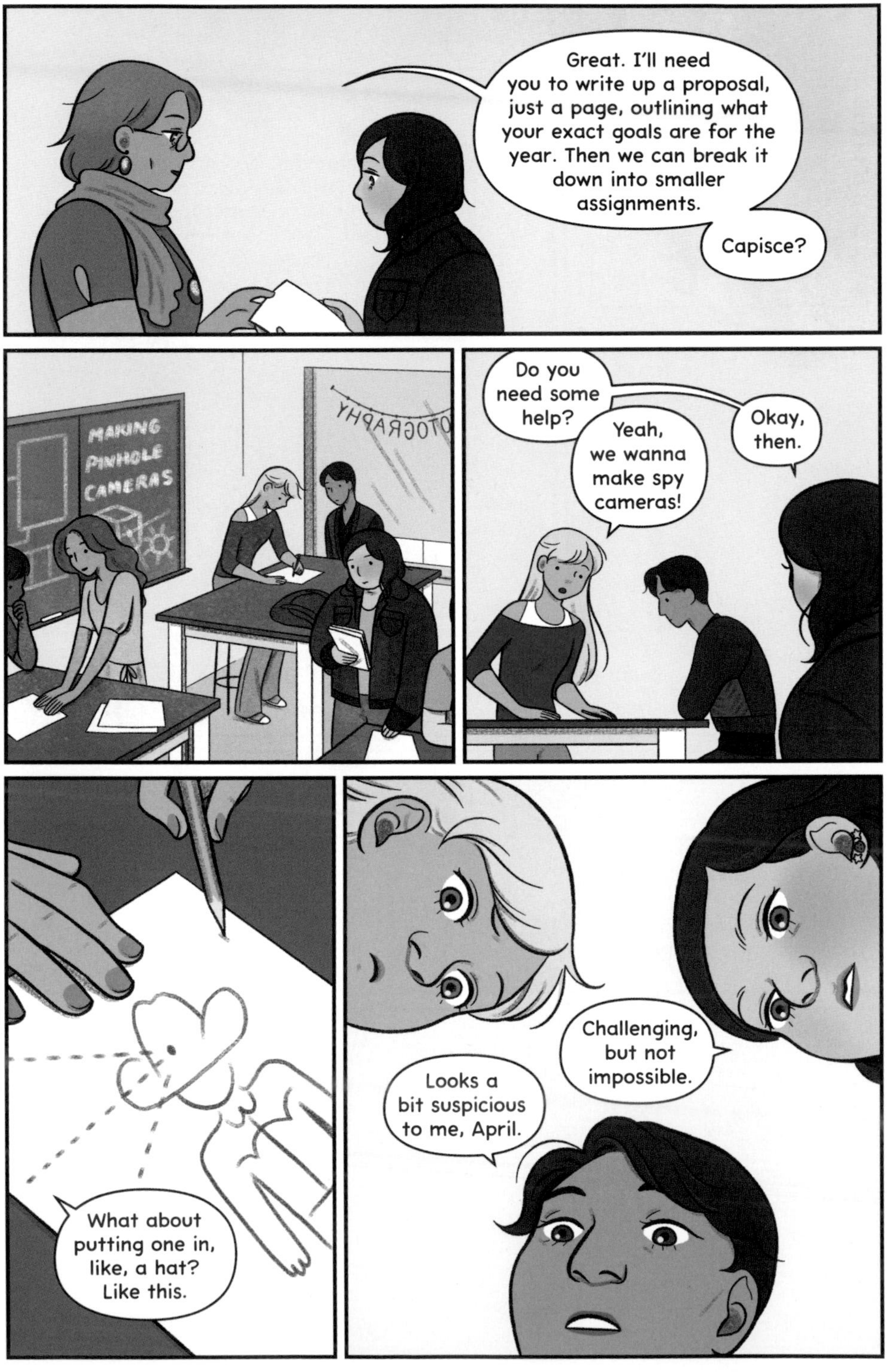
Great. I'll need you to write up a proposal, just a page, outlining what your exact goals are for the year. Then we can break it down into smaller assignments.
Capisce?
MAKING PINHOLE CAMERAS
OTOGRAPHY
Do you need some help?
Yeah, we wanna make spy cameras!
Okay, then.
What about putting one in, like, a hat? Like this.
Looks a bit suspicious to me, April.
Challenging, but not impossible.

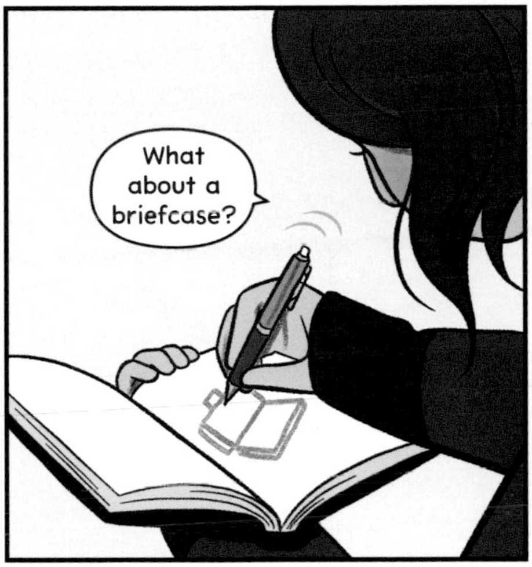
What about a briefcase?

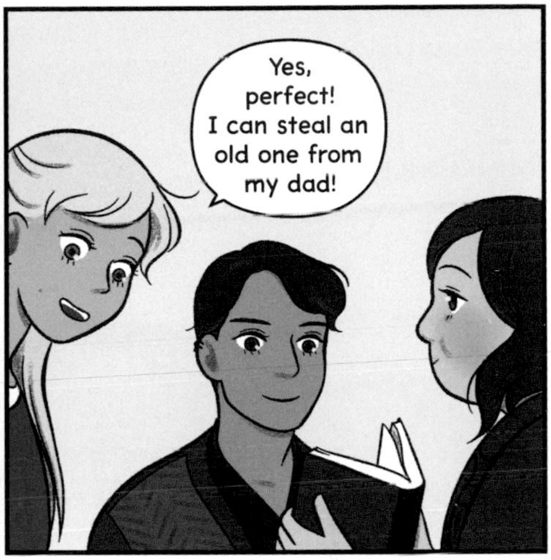
Yes, perfect! I can steal an old one from my dad!

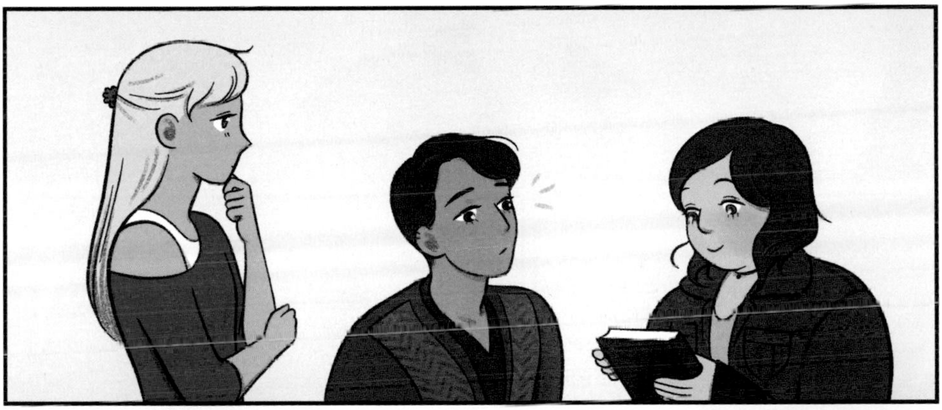

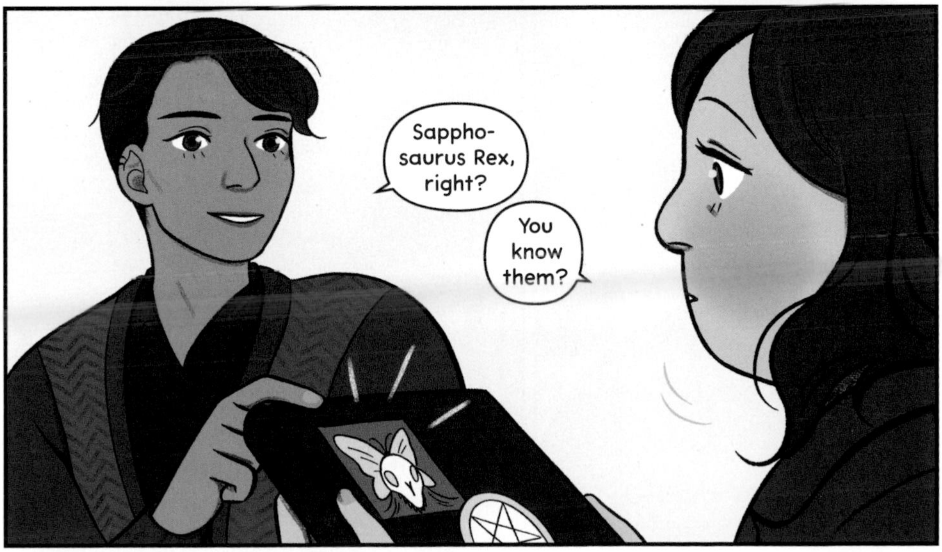
Sappho-saurus Rex, right?
You know them?

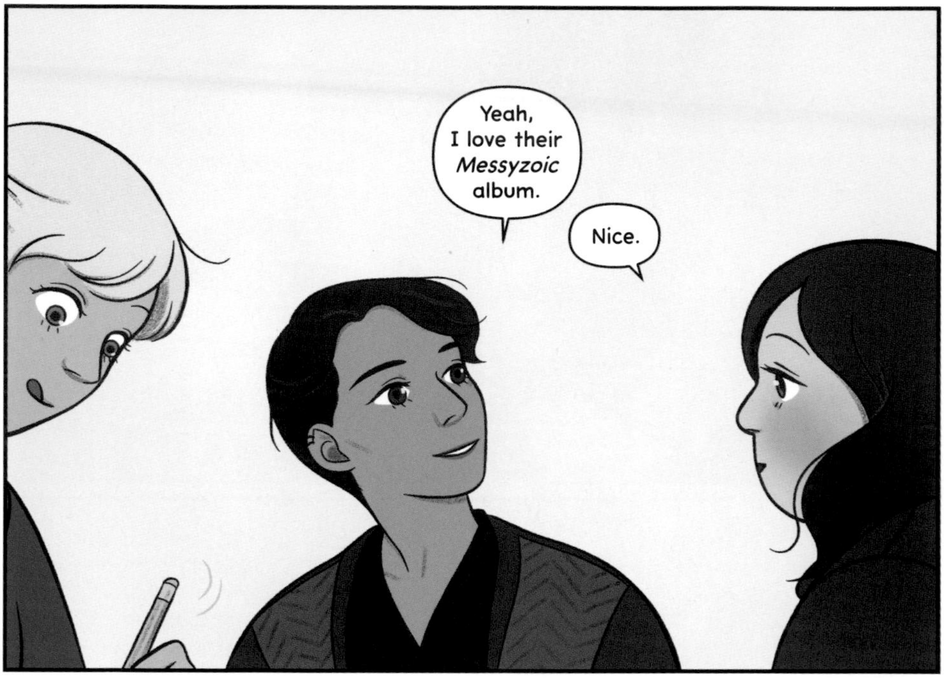
Yeah,
I love their
Messyzoic
album.
Nice.

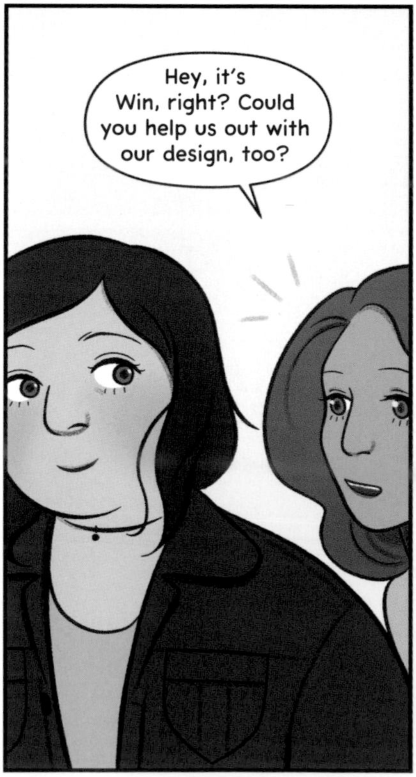
Hey, it's
Win, right? Could
you help us out with
our design, too?

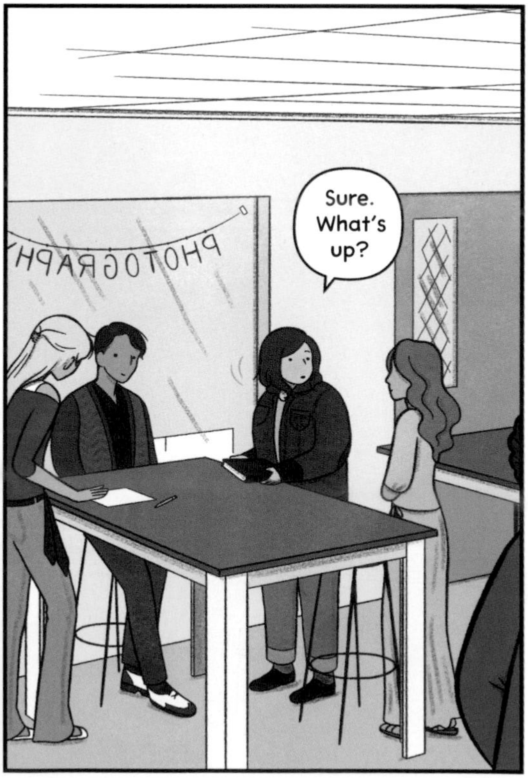
PHOTOGRAPHY
Sure.
What's
up?

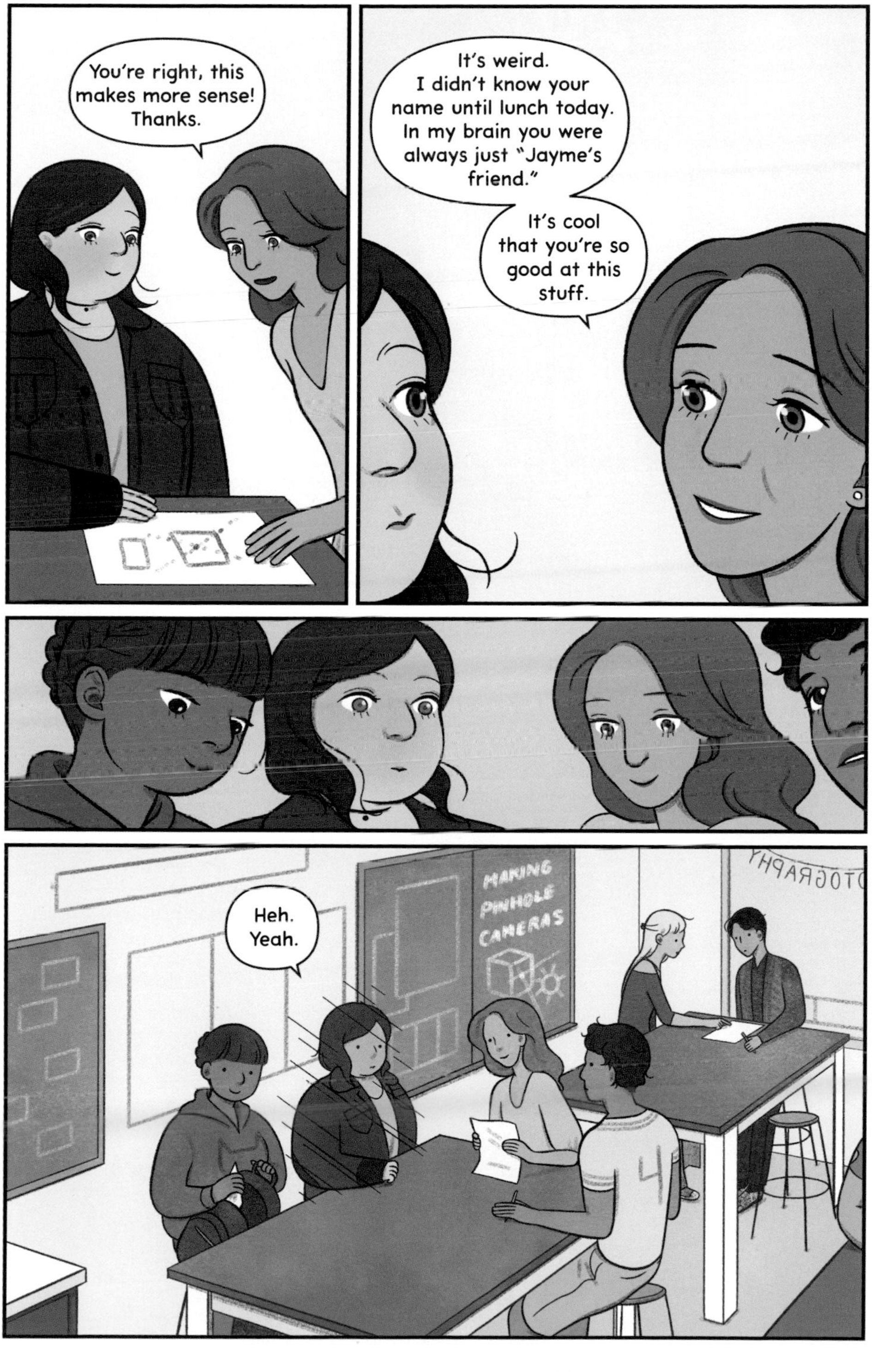
You're right, this makes more sense! Thanks.
It's weird. I didn't know your name until lunch today. In my brain you were always just "Jayme's friend."
It's cool that you're so good at this stuff.
MAKING PINHOLE CAMERAS
OTOGRAPHY
Heh. Yeah.

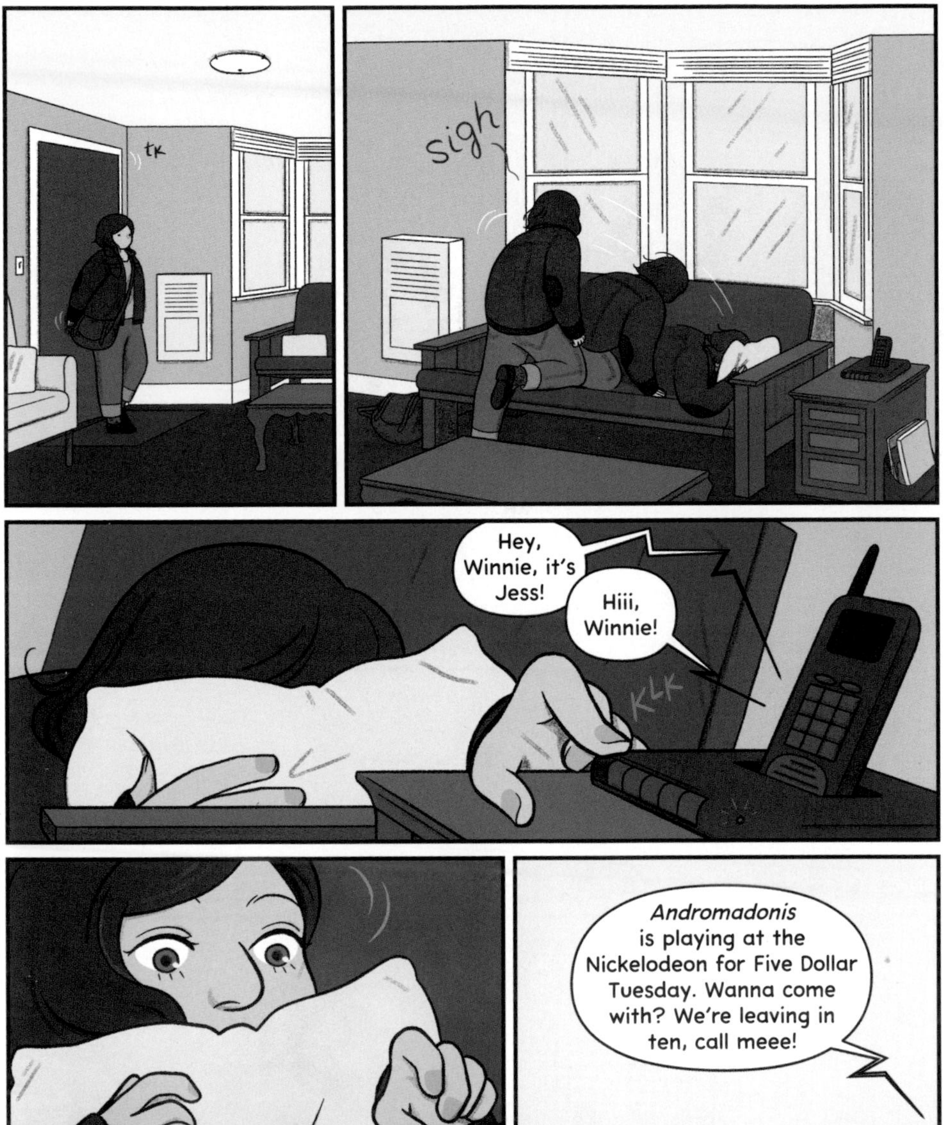
tk
sigh
Hey, Winnie, it's Jess!
Hiii, Winnie!
KLK
Ha ha, shut up, Jayme, I'm leaving a message!
Hee hee!
Andromadonis is playing at the Nickelodeon for Five Dollar Tuesday. Wanna come with? We're leaving in ten, call meee!

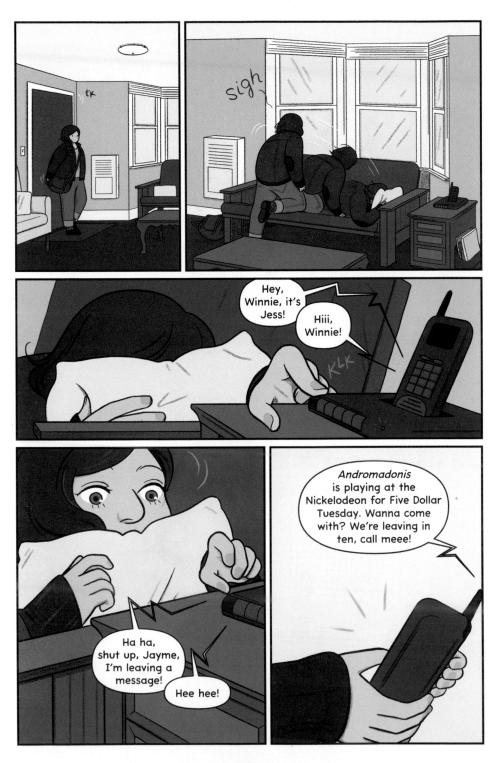

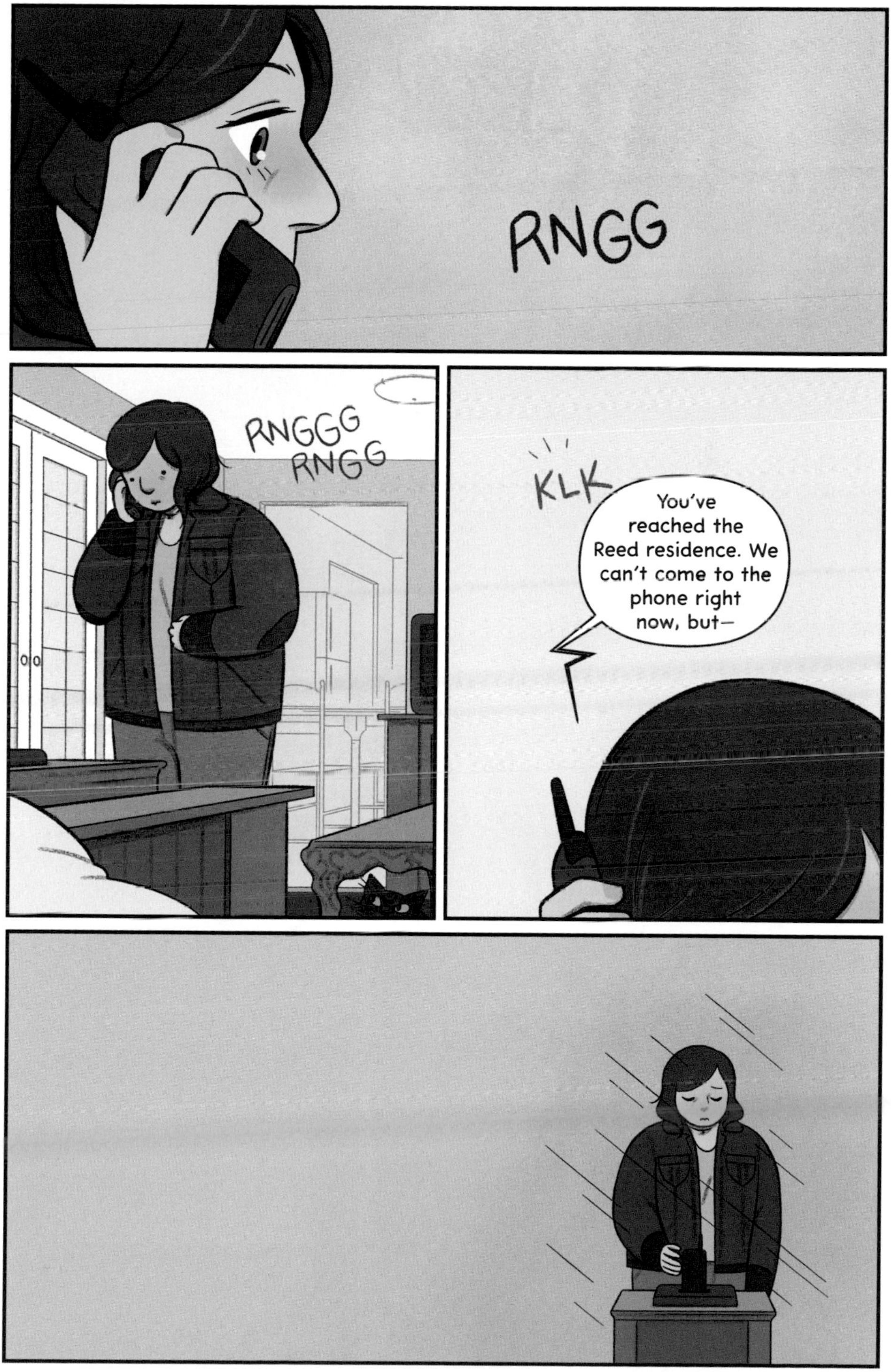
RNGG
RNGGG
RNGG
KLK
You've reached the Reed residence. We can't come to the phone right now, but—

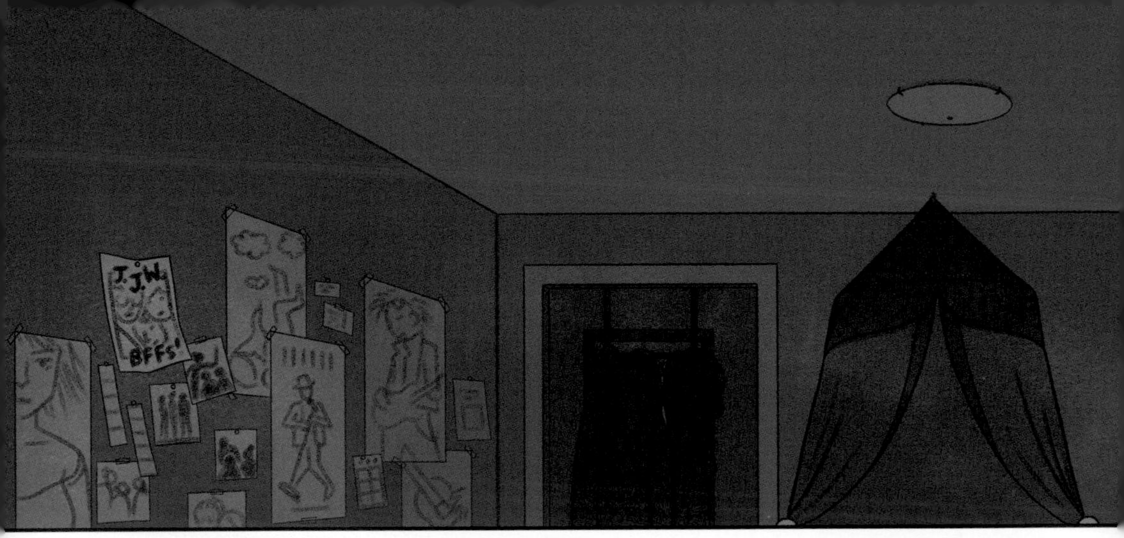

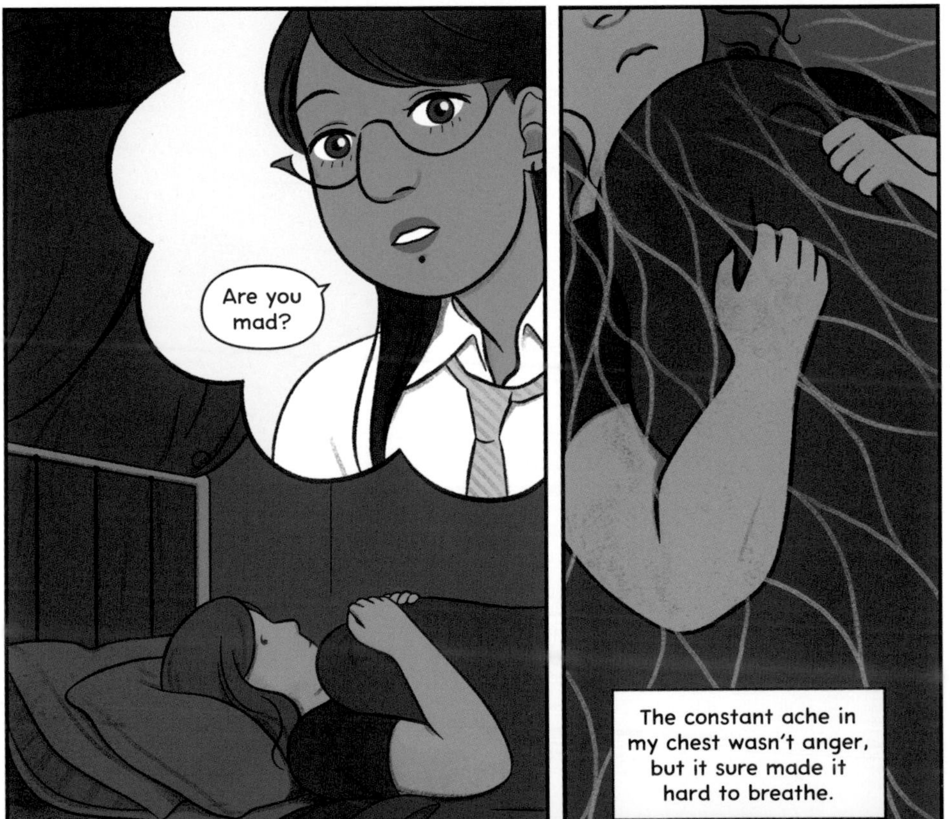
Are you mad?
The constant ache in my chest wasn't anger, but it sure made it hard to breathe.

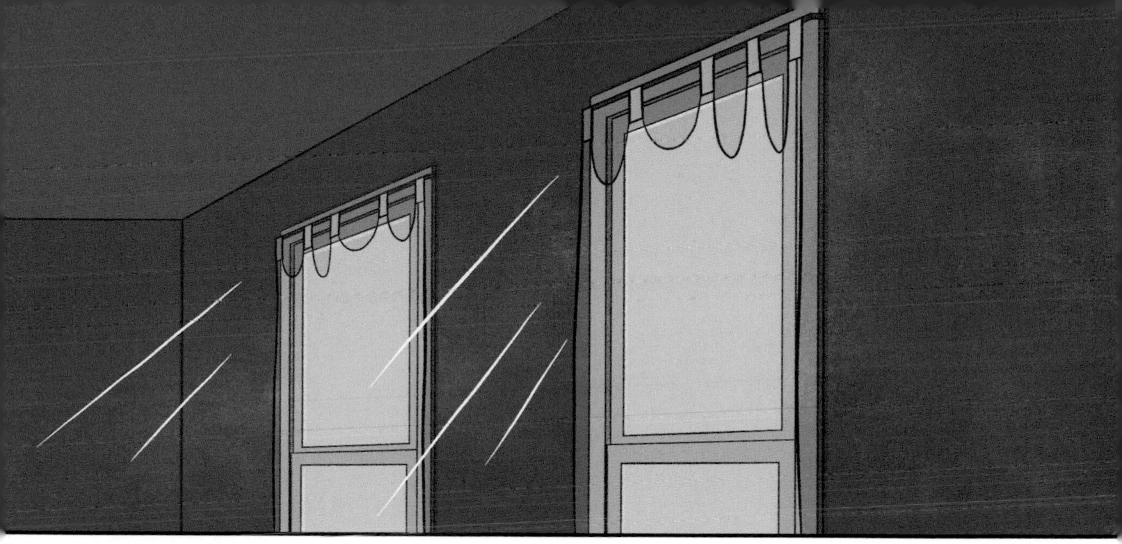

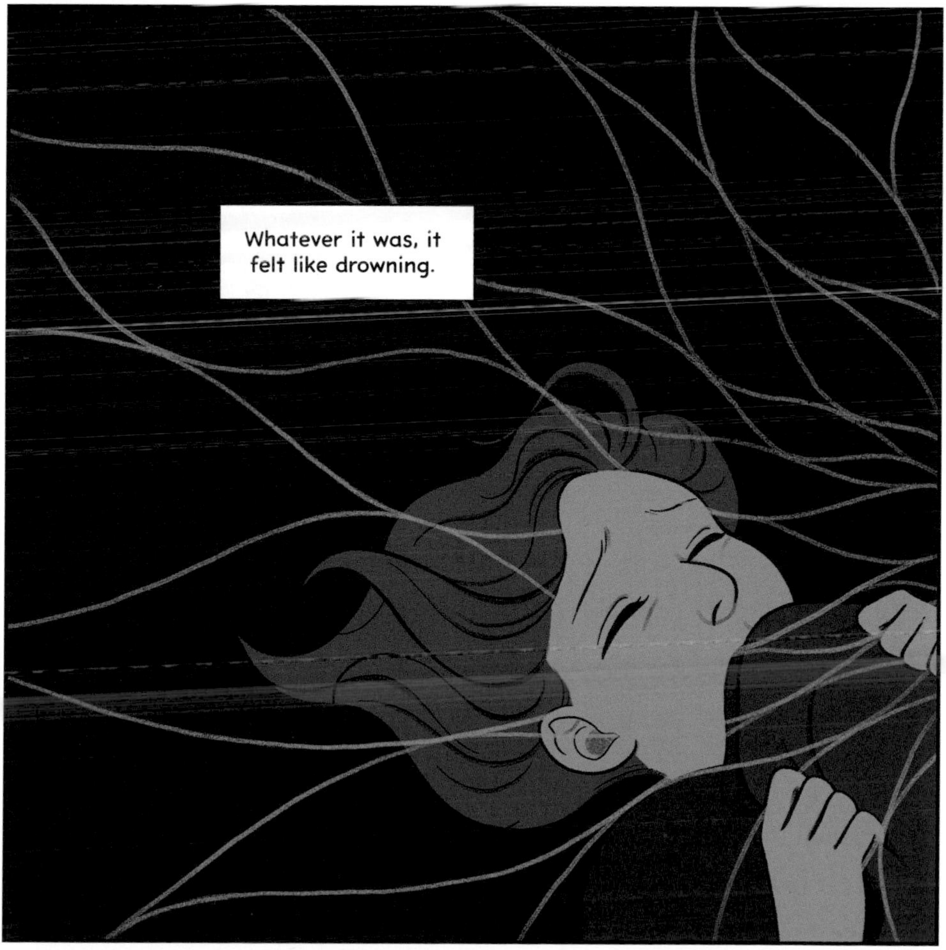
Whatever it was, it
felt like drowning.

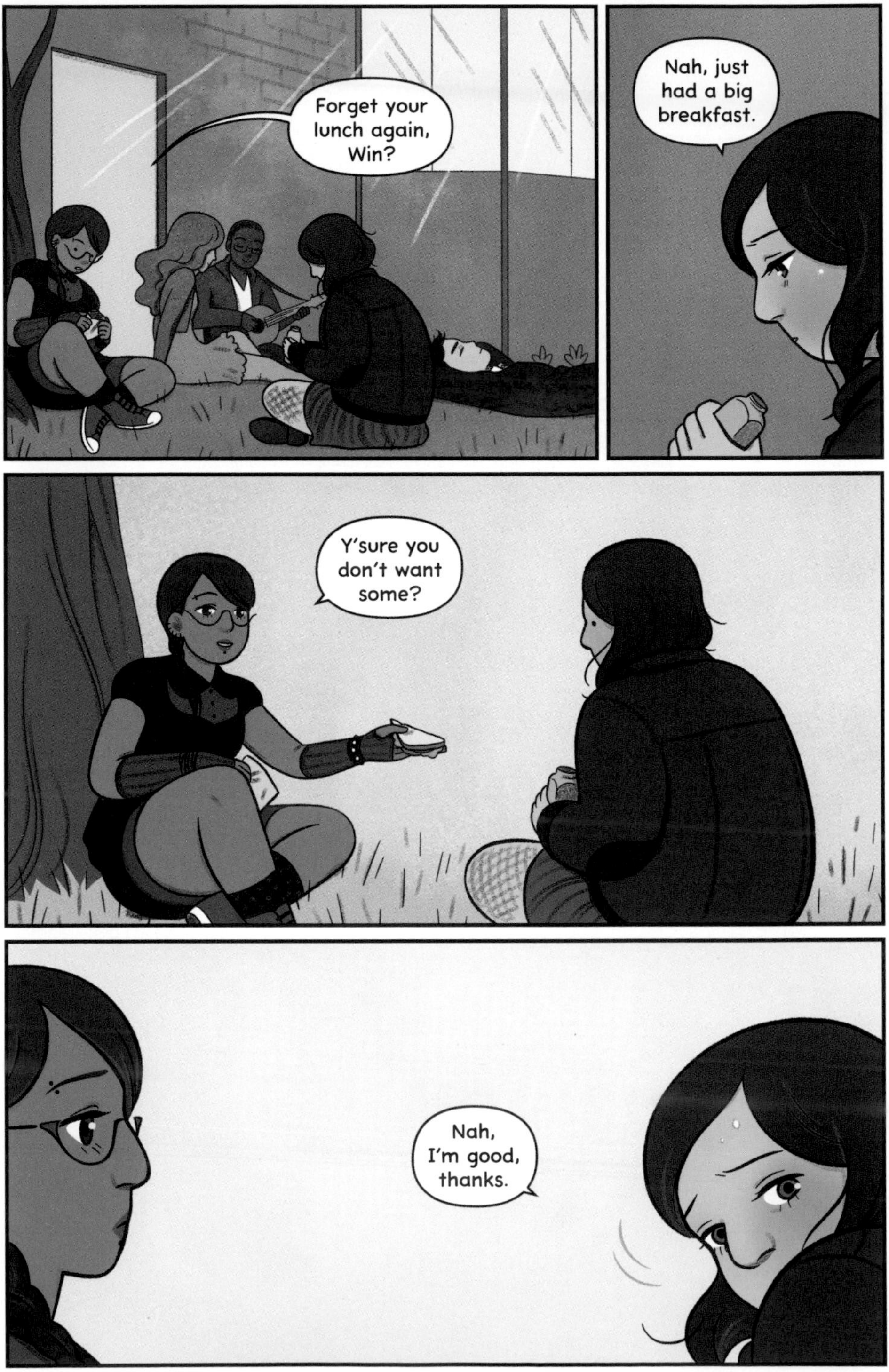
Forget your lunch again, Win?
Nah, just had a big breakfast.
Y'sure you don't want some?
Nah, I'm good, thanks.

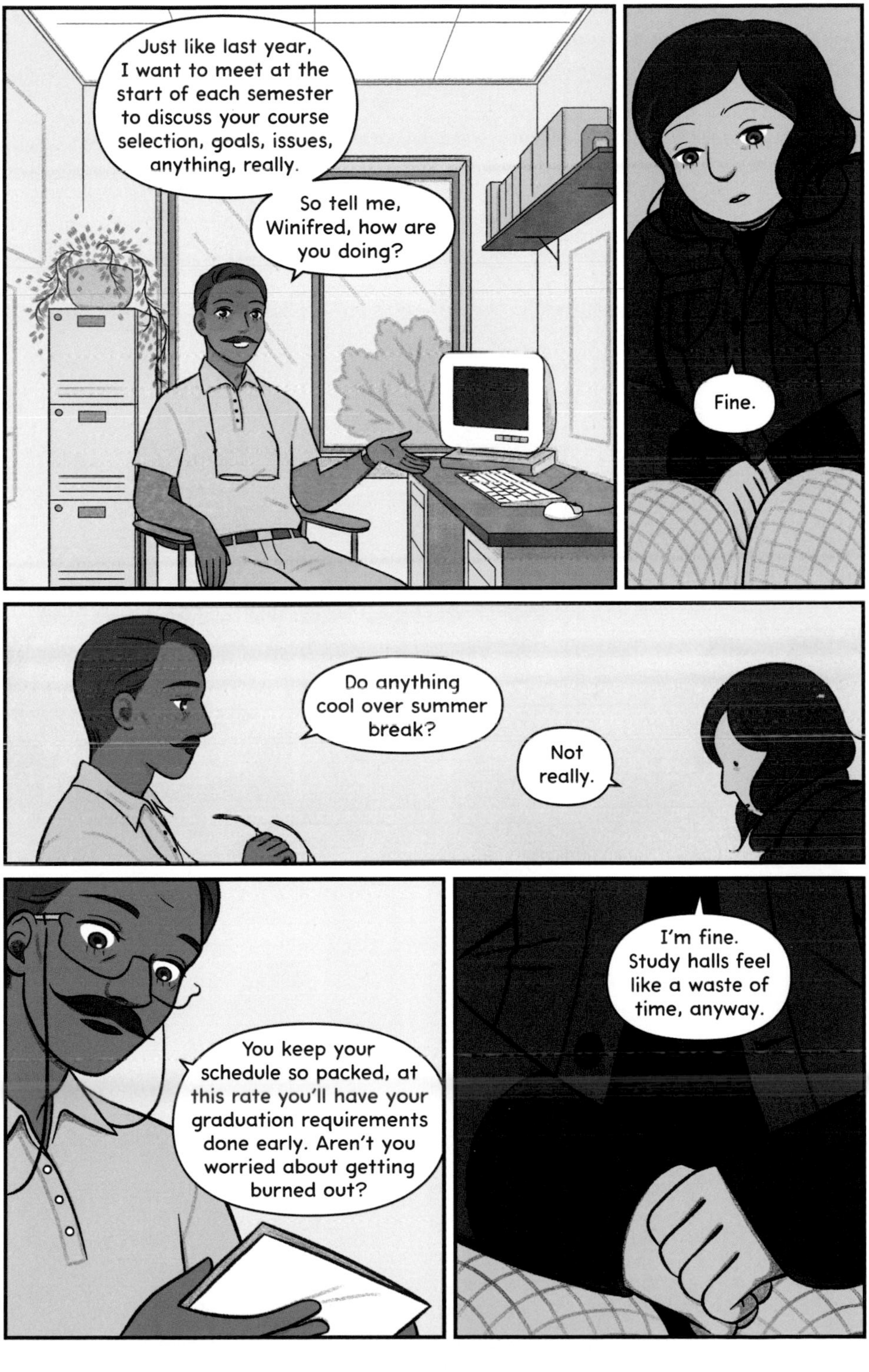
Just like last year, I want to meet at the start of each semester to discuss your course selection, goals, issues, anything, really.
So tell me, Winifred, how are you doing?
Fine.
Do anything cool over summer break?
Not really.
You keep your schedule so packed, at this rate you'll have your graduation requirements done early. Aren't you worried about getting burned out?
I'm fine. Study halls feel like a waste of time, anyway.

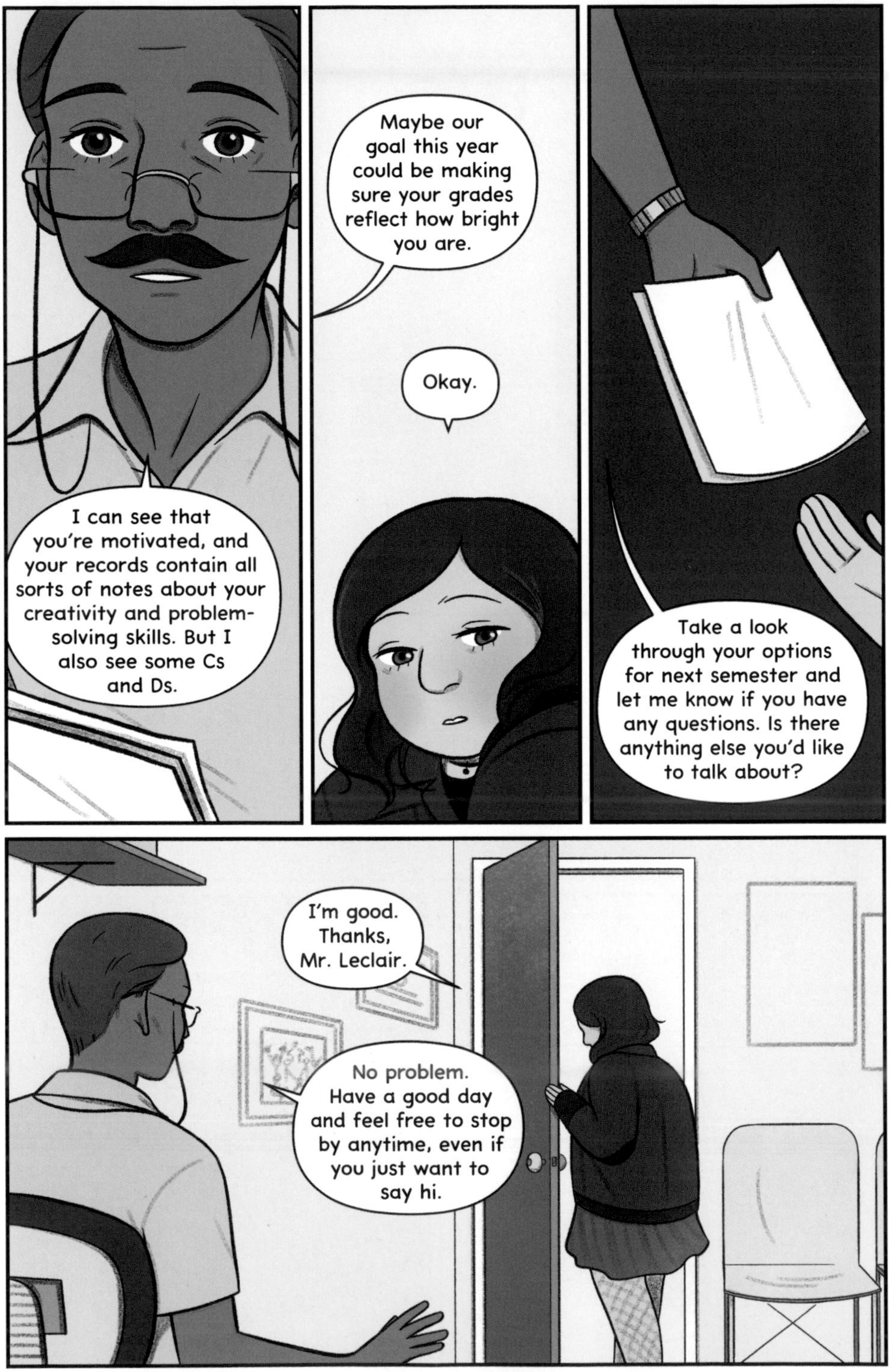
I can see that you're motivated, and your records contain all sorts of notes about your creativity and problem-solving skills. But I also see some Cs and Ds.
Maybe our goal this year could be making sure your grades reflect how bright you are.
Okay.
Take a look through your options for next semester and let me know if you have any questions. Is there anything else you'd like to talk about?
I'm good. Thanks, Mr. Leclair.
No problem. Have a good day and feel free to stop by anytime, even if you just want to say hi.

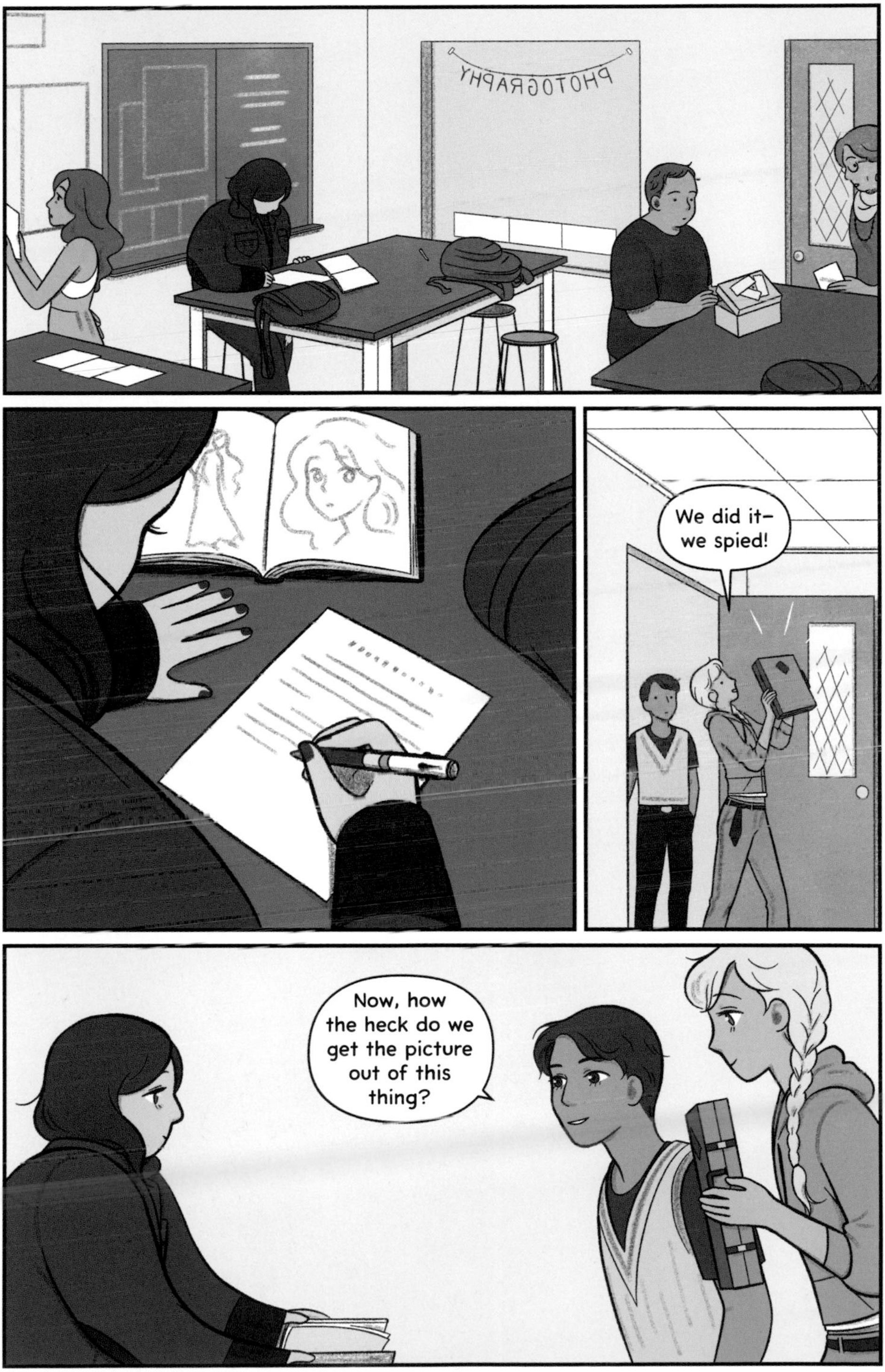
PHOTOGRAPHY
We did it—we spied!
Now, how the heck do we get the picture out of this thing?

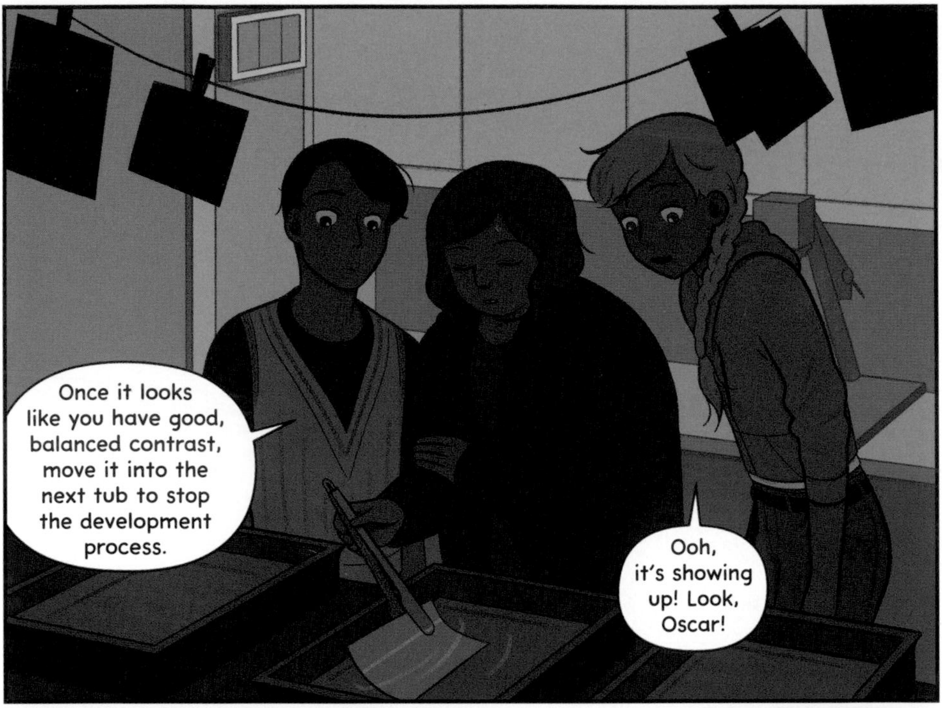
Once it looks like you have good, balanced contrast, move it into the next tub to stop the development process.
Ooh, it's showing up! Look, Oscar!

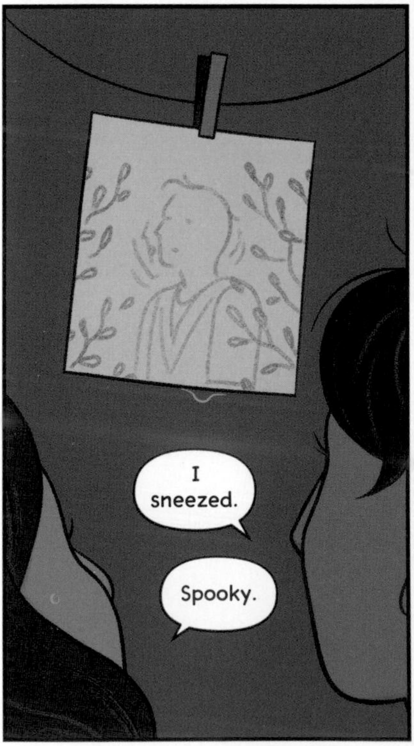
I sneezed.
Spooky.

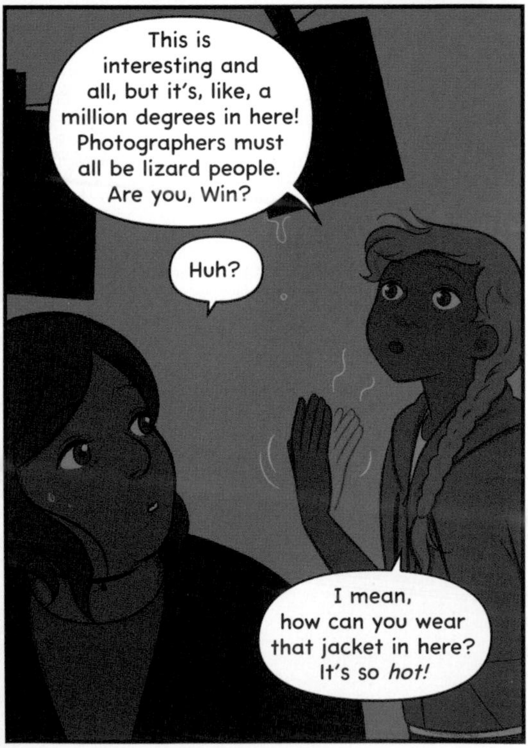
This is interesting and all, but it's, like, a million degrees in here! Photographers must all be lizard people. Are you, Win?
Huh?
I mean, how can you wear that jacket in here? It's so *hot!*

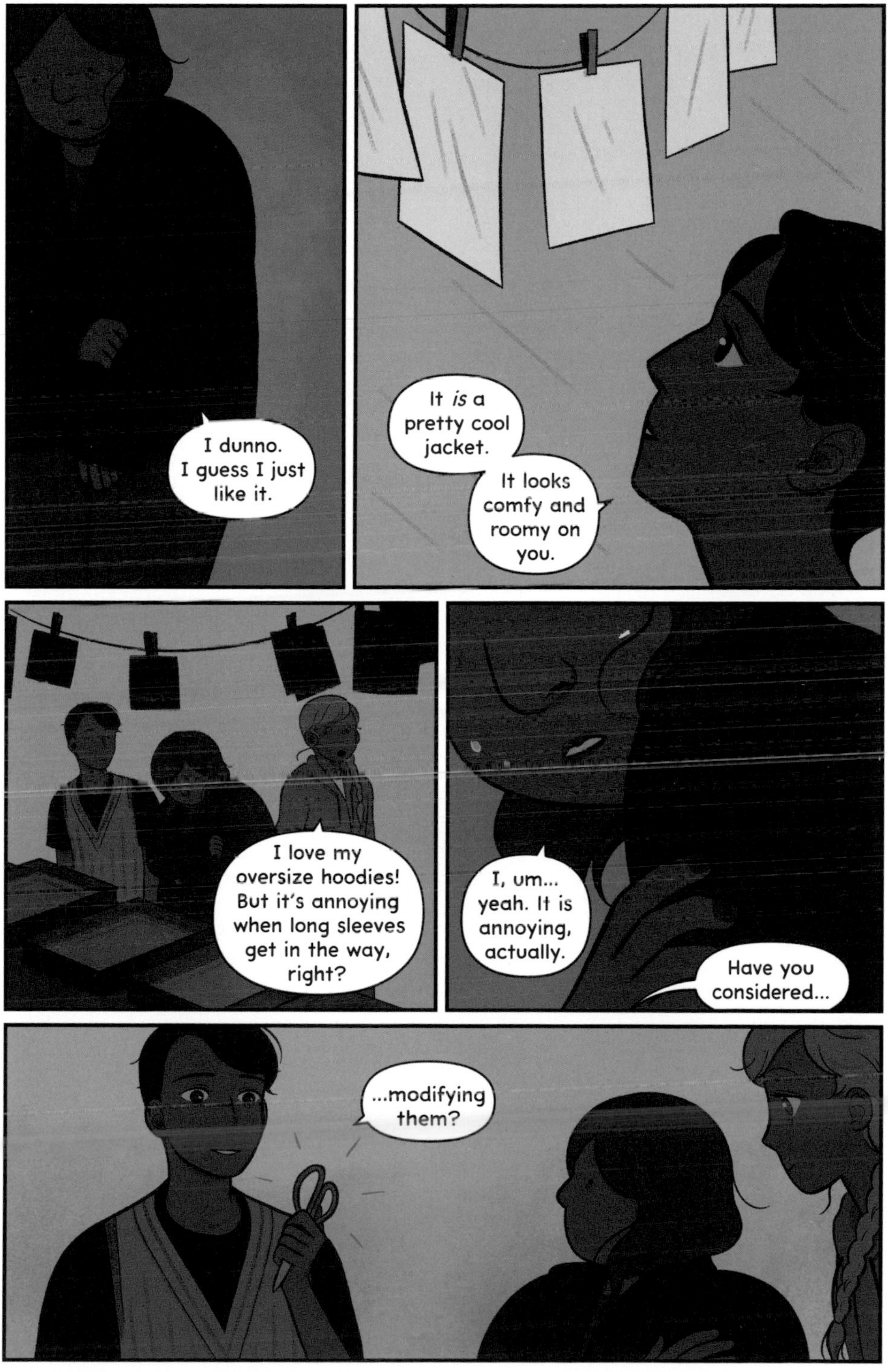
I dunno. I guess I just like it.
It *is* a pretty cool jacket.
It looks comfy and roomy on you.
I love my oversize hoodies! But it's annoying when long sleeves get in the way, right?
I, um... yeah. It is annoying, actually.
Have you considered...
...modifying them?

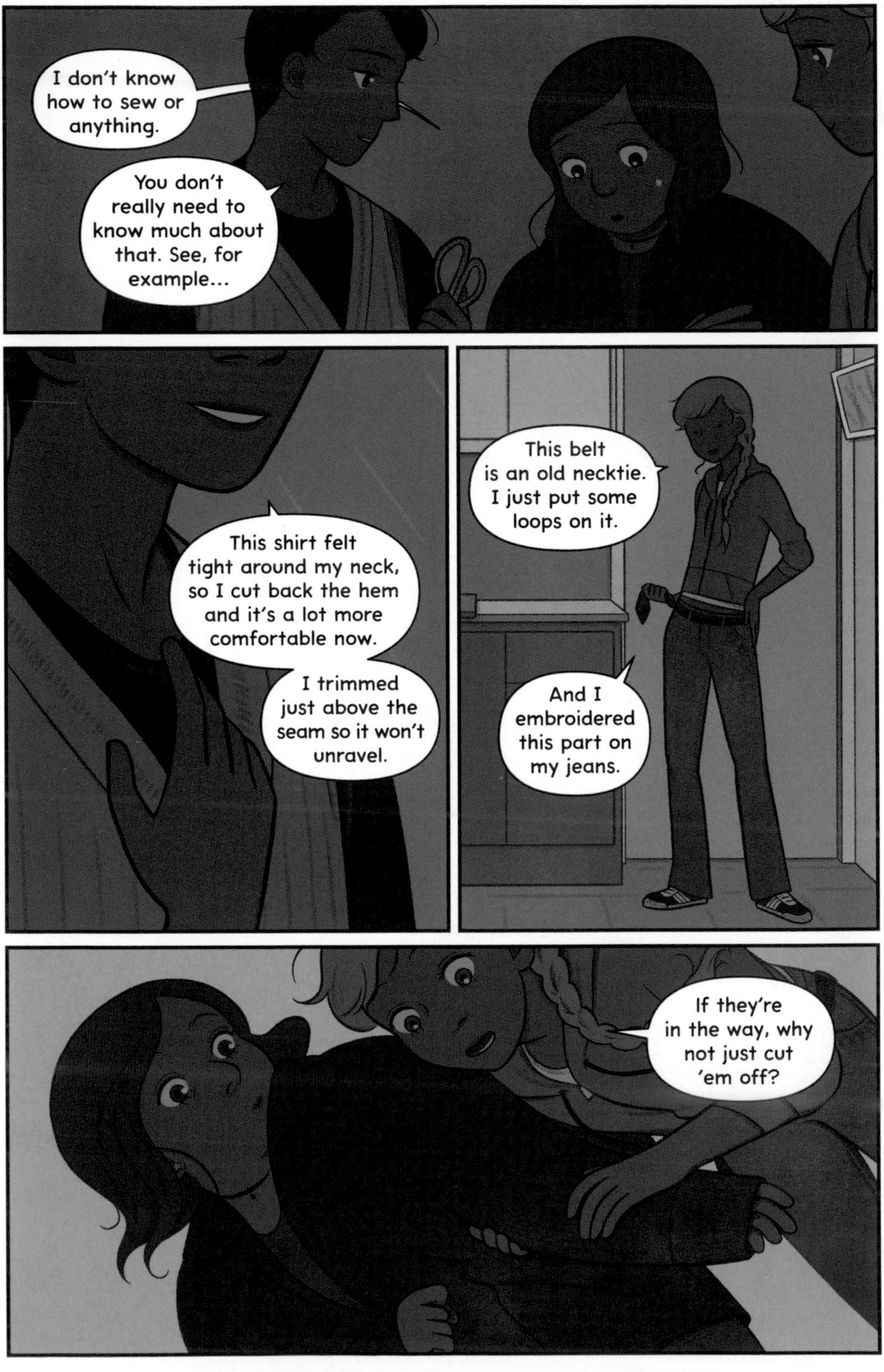
I don't know how to sew or anything.
You don't really need to know much about that. See, for example...
This shirt felt tight around my neck, so I cut back the hem and it's a lot more comfortable now.
I trimmed just above the seam so it won't unravel.
This belt is an old necktie. I just put some loops on it.
And I embroidered this part on my jeans.
If they're in the way, why not just cut 'em off?

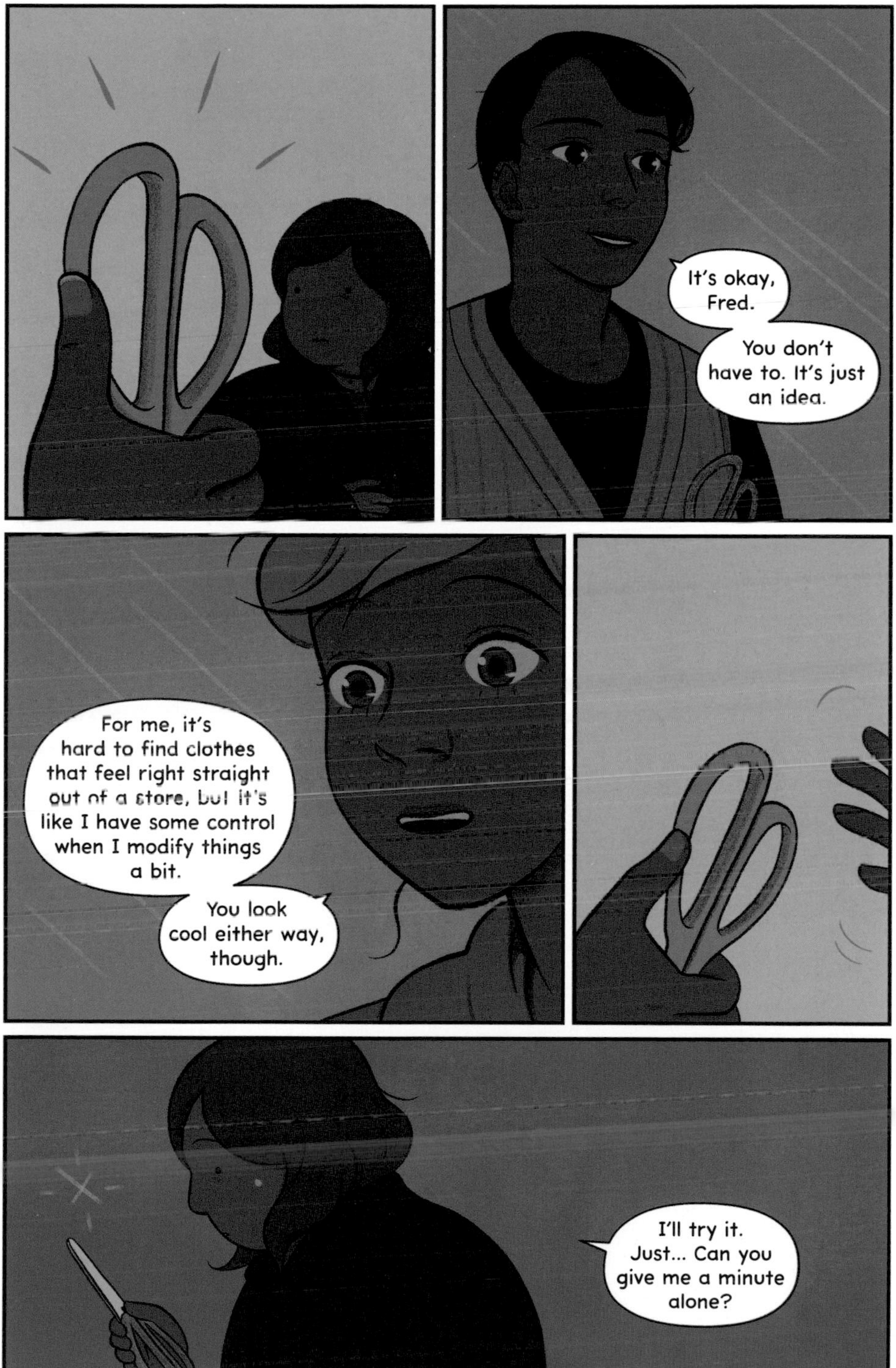
It's okay, Fred.
You don't have to. It's just an idea.
For me, it's hard to find clothes that feel right straight out of a store, but it's like I have some control when I modify things a bit.
You look cool either way, though.
I'll try it. Just... Can you give me a minute alone?

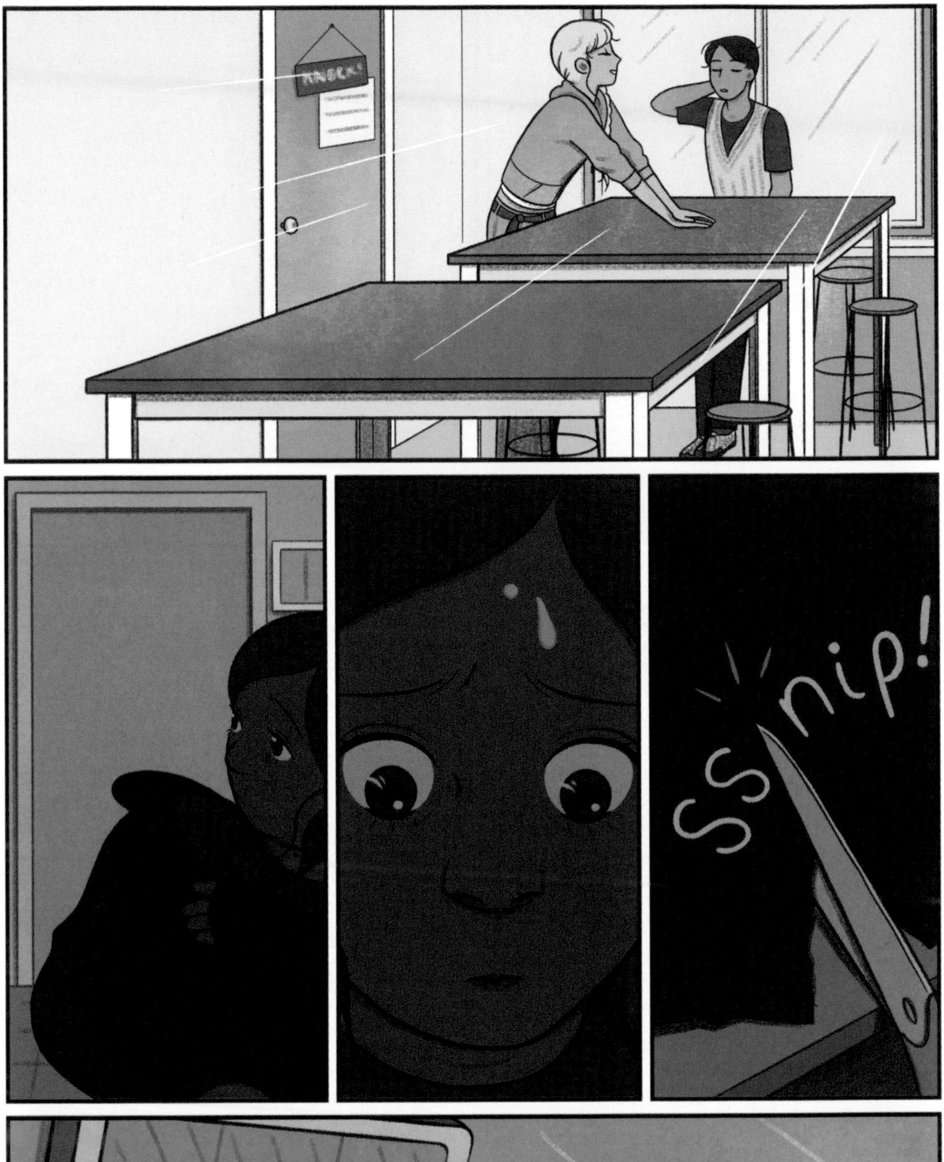
SSnip!
snp
snp

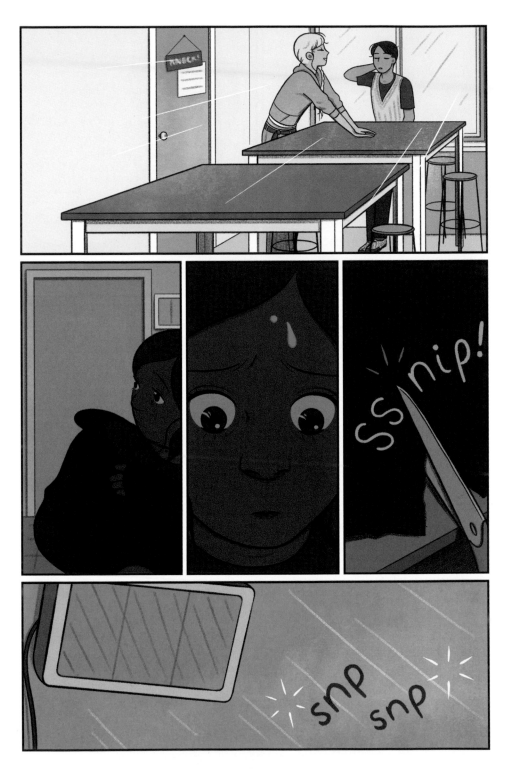

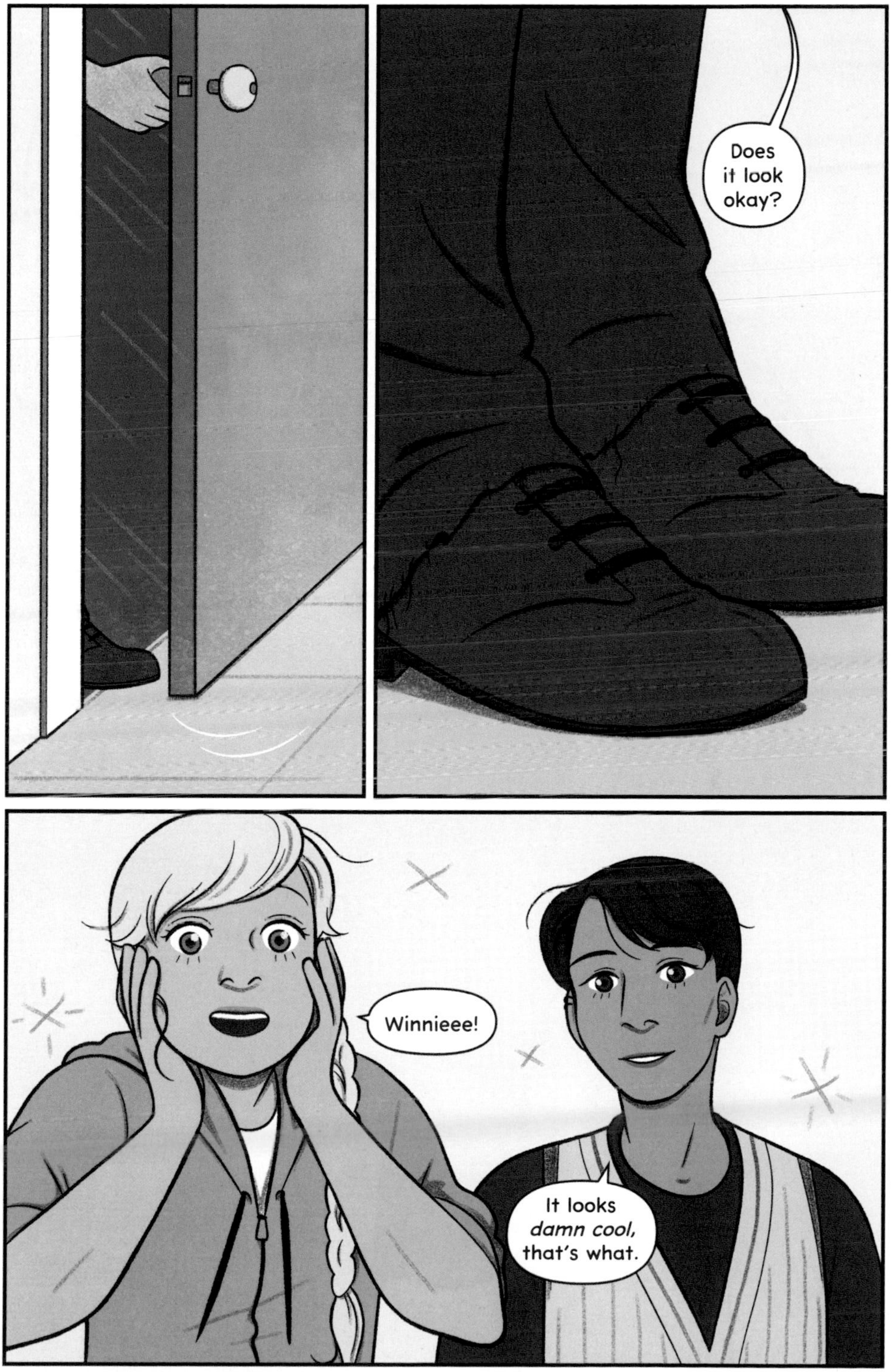

Does it look okay?
Winnieee!
It looks *damn cool,* that's what.

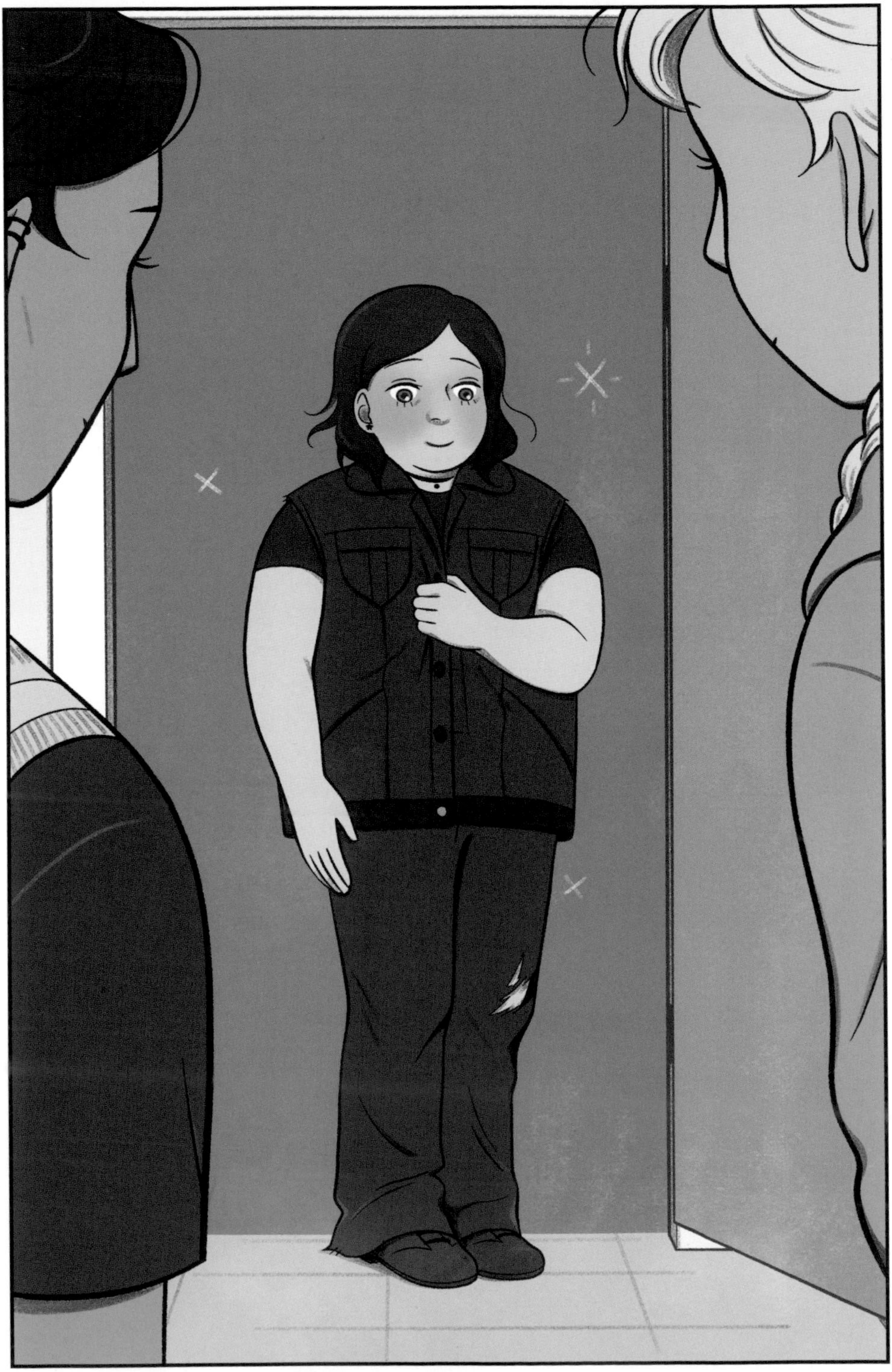

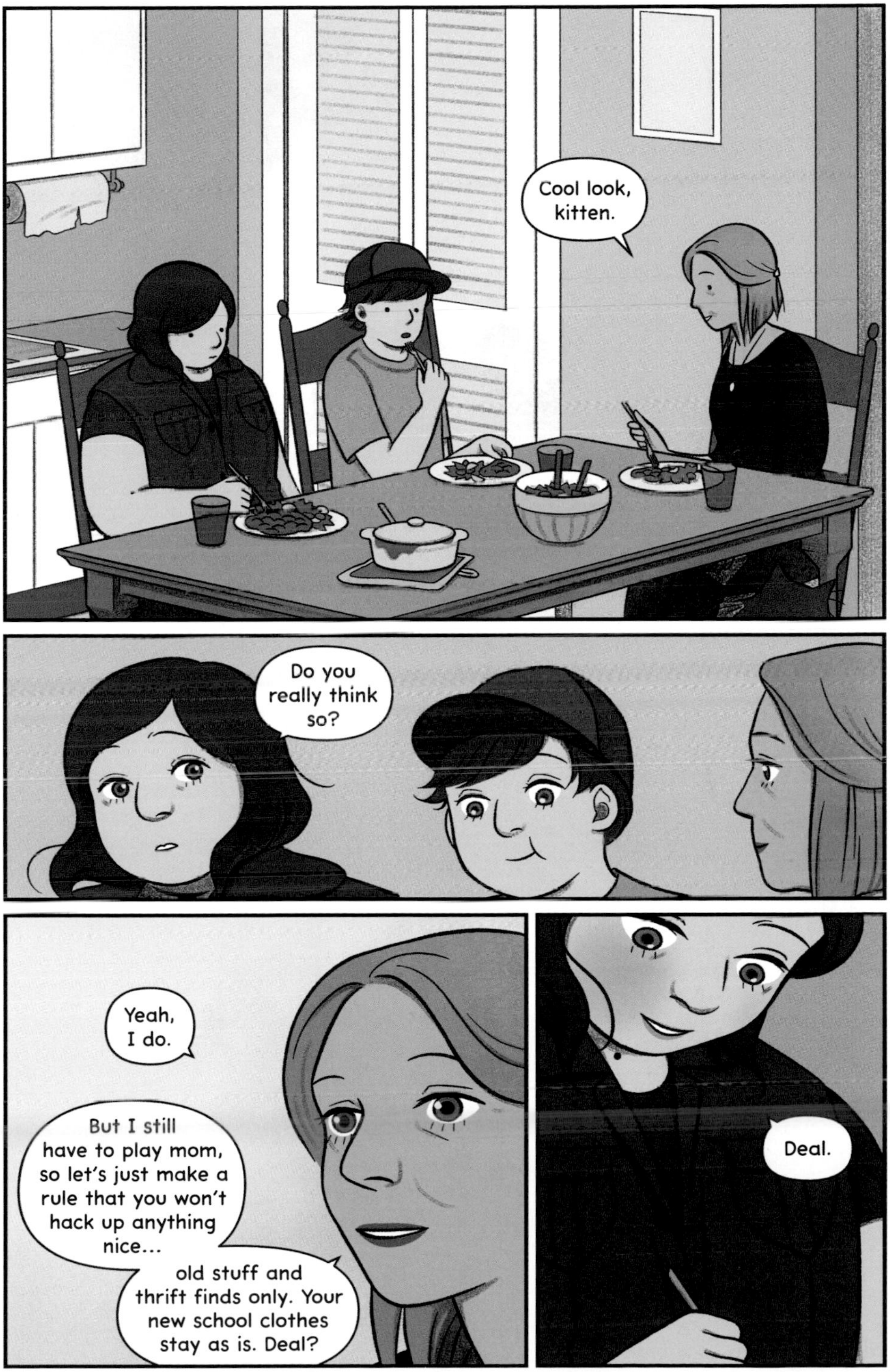
Cool look, kitten.
Do you really think so?
Yeah, I do.
But I still have to play mom, so let's just make a rule that you won't hack up anything nice...
old stuff and thrift finds only. Your new school clothes stay as is. Deal?
Deal.

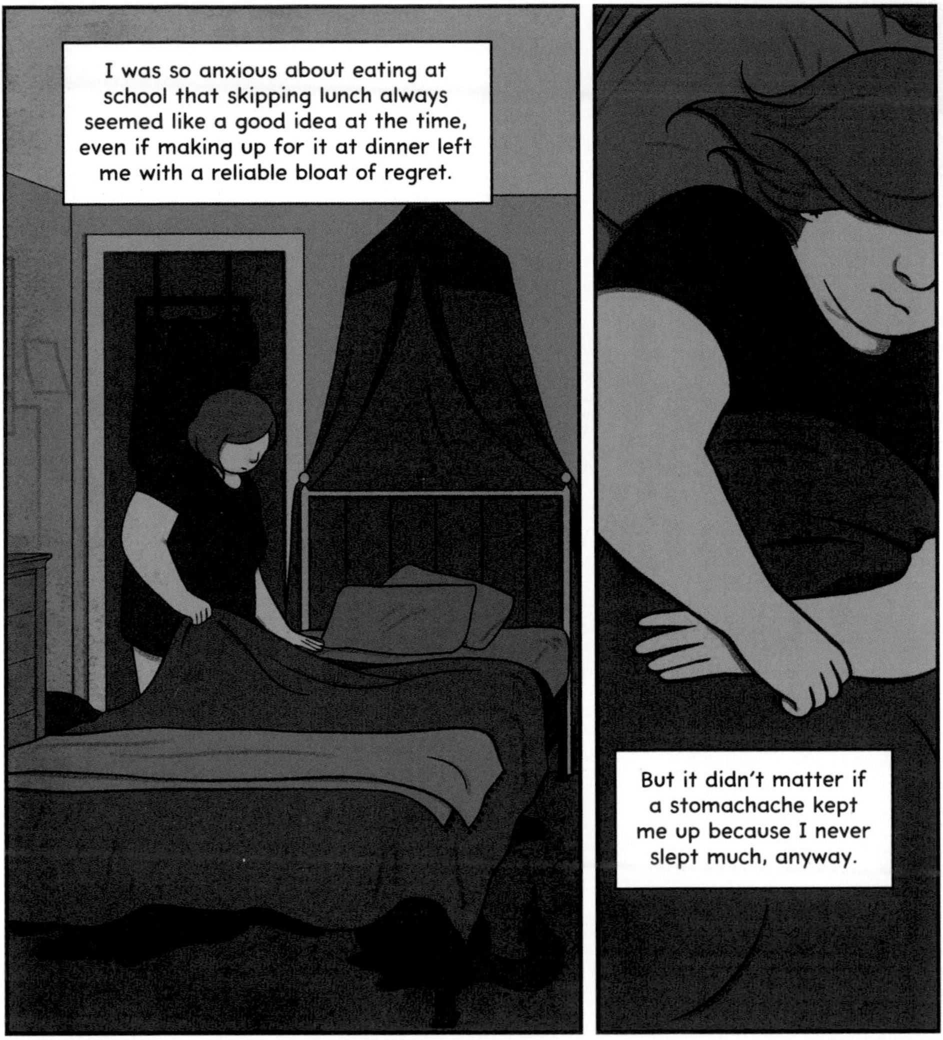
I was so anxious about eating at school that skipping lunch always seemed like a good idea at the time, even if making up for it at dinner left me with a reliable bloat of regret.
But it didn't matter if a stomachache kept me up because I never slept much, anyway.
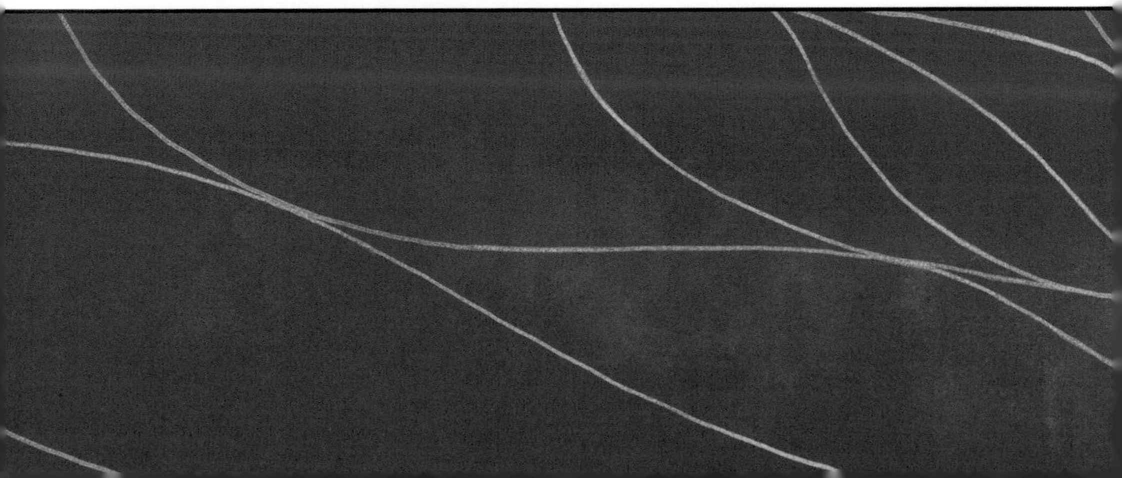

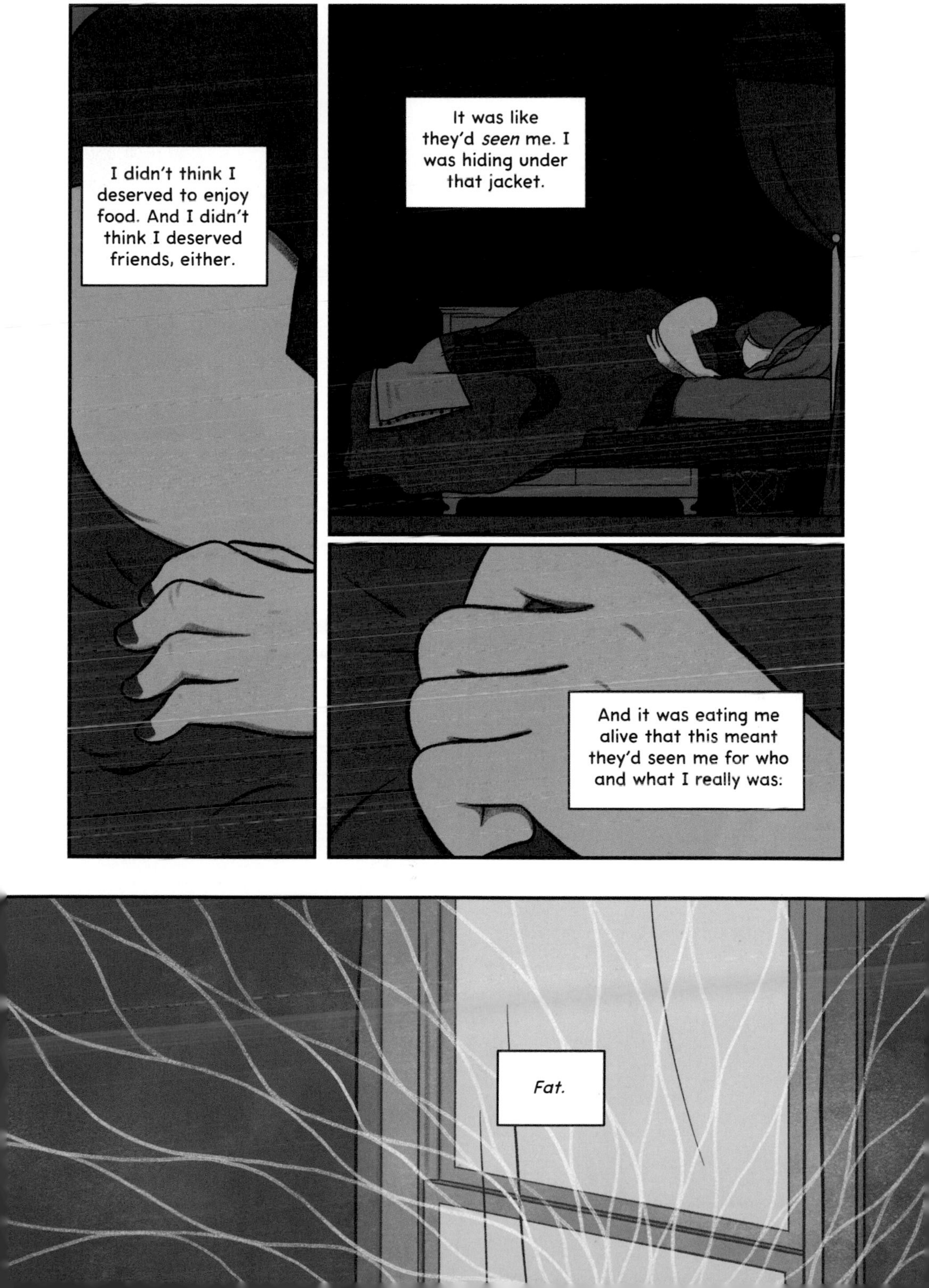
I didn't think I deserved to enjoy food. And I didn't think I deserved friends, either.
It was like they'd *seen* me. I was hiding under that jacket.
And it was eating me alive that this meant they'd seen me for who and what I really was:
Fat.

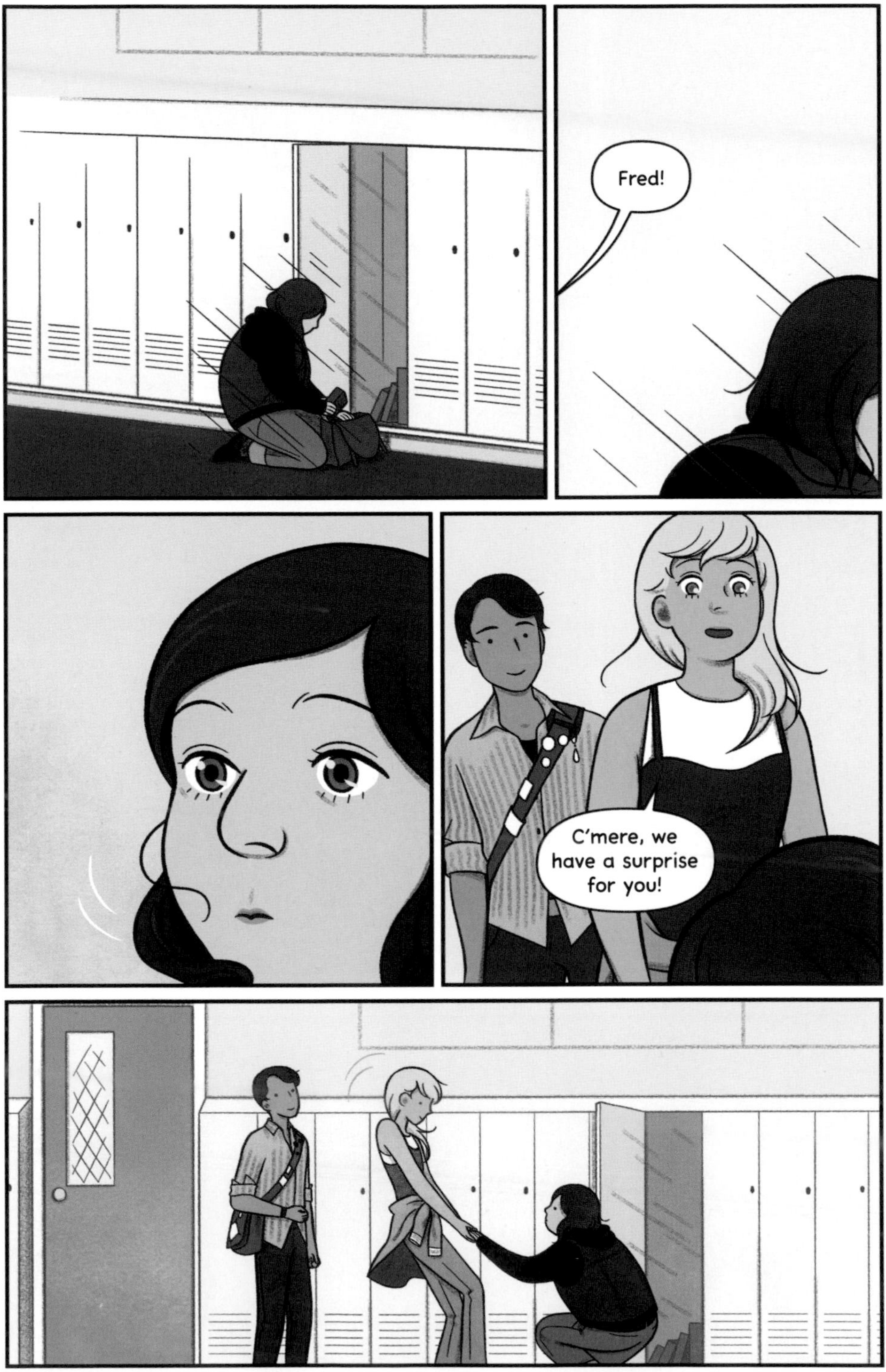
Fred!
C'mere, we have a surprise for you!

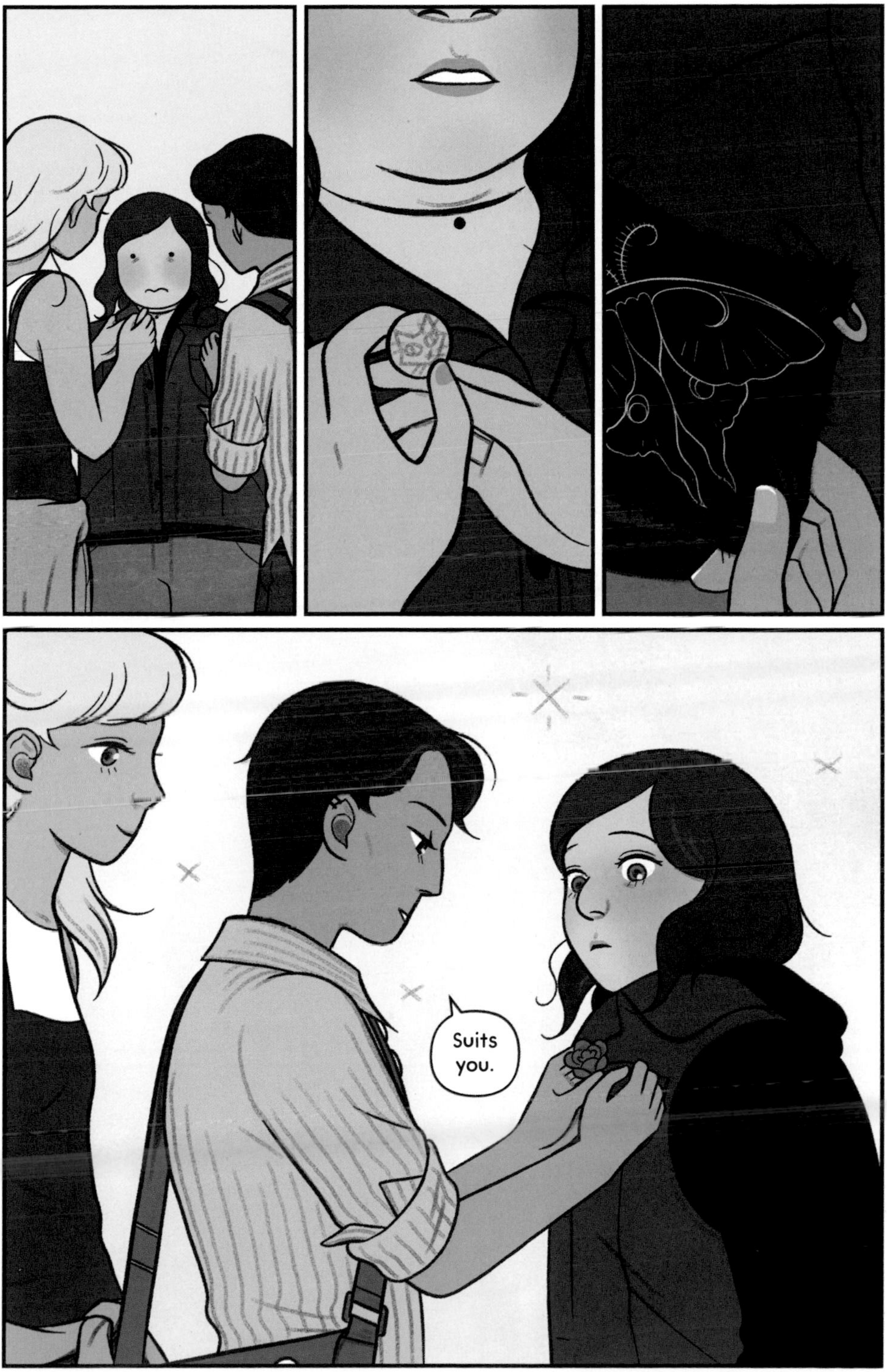
Suits you.

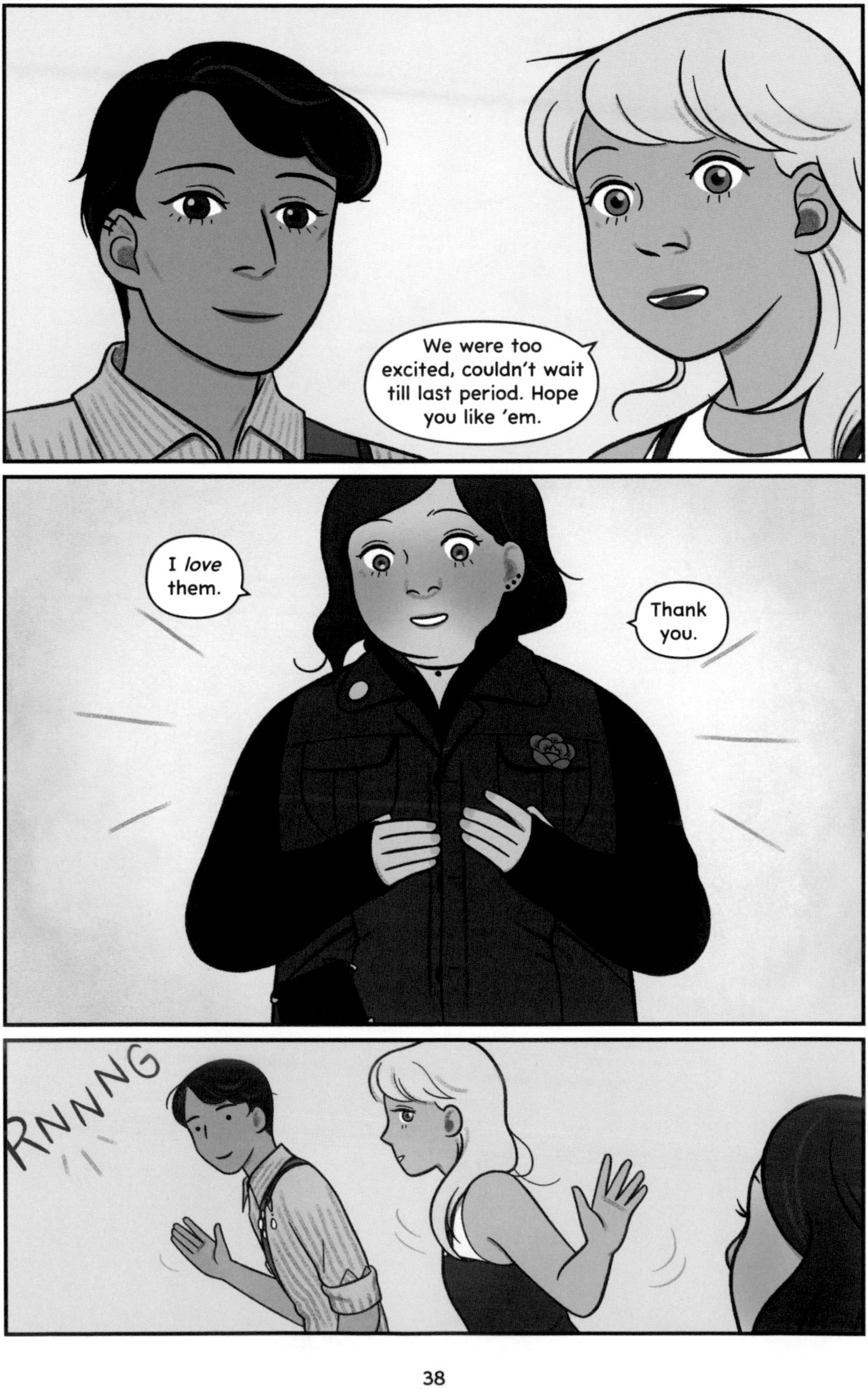
We were too excited, couldn't wait till last period. Hope you like 'em.
I *love* them.
Thank you.
RNNNG

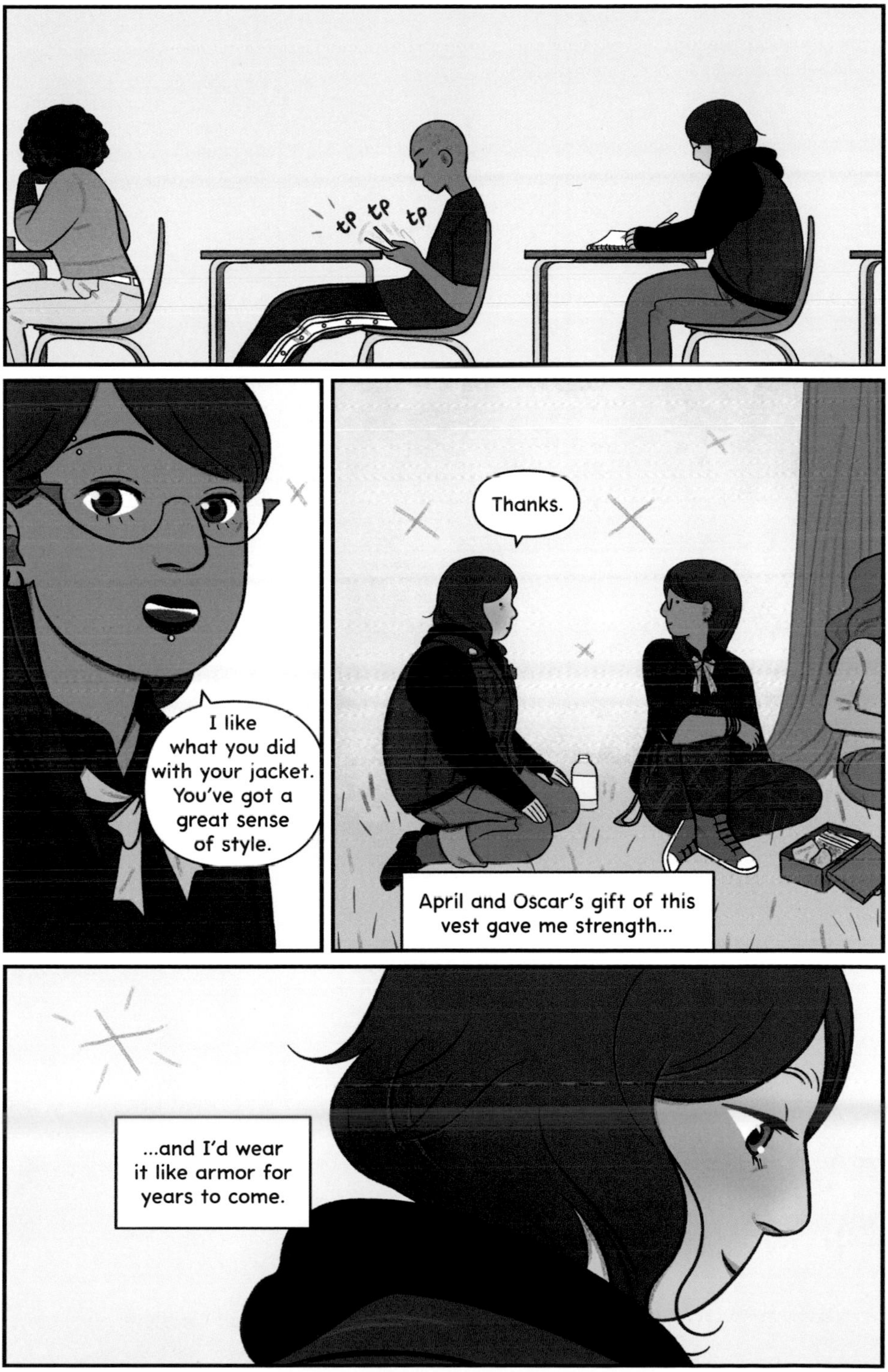
tp tp tp
I like what you did with your jacket. You've got a great sense of style.
Thanks.
April and Oscar's gift of this vest gave me strength...
...and I'd wear it like armor for years to come.

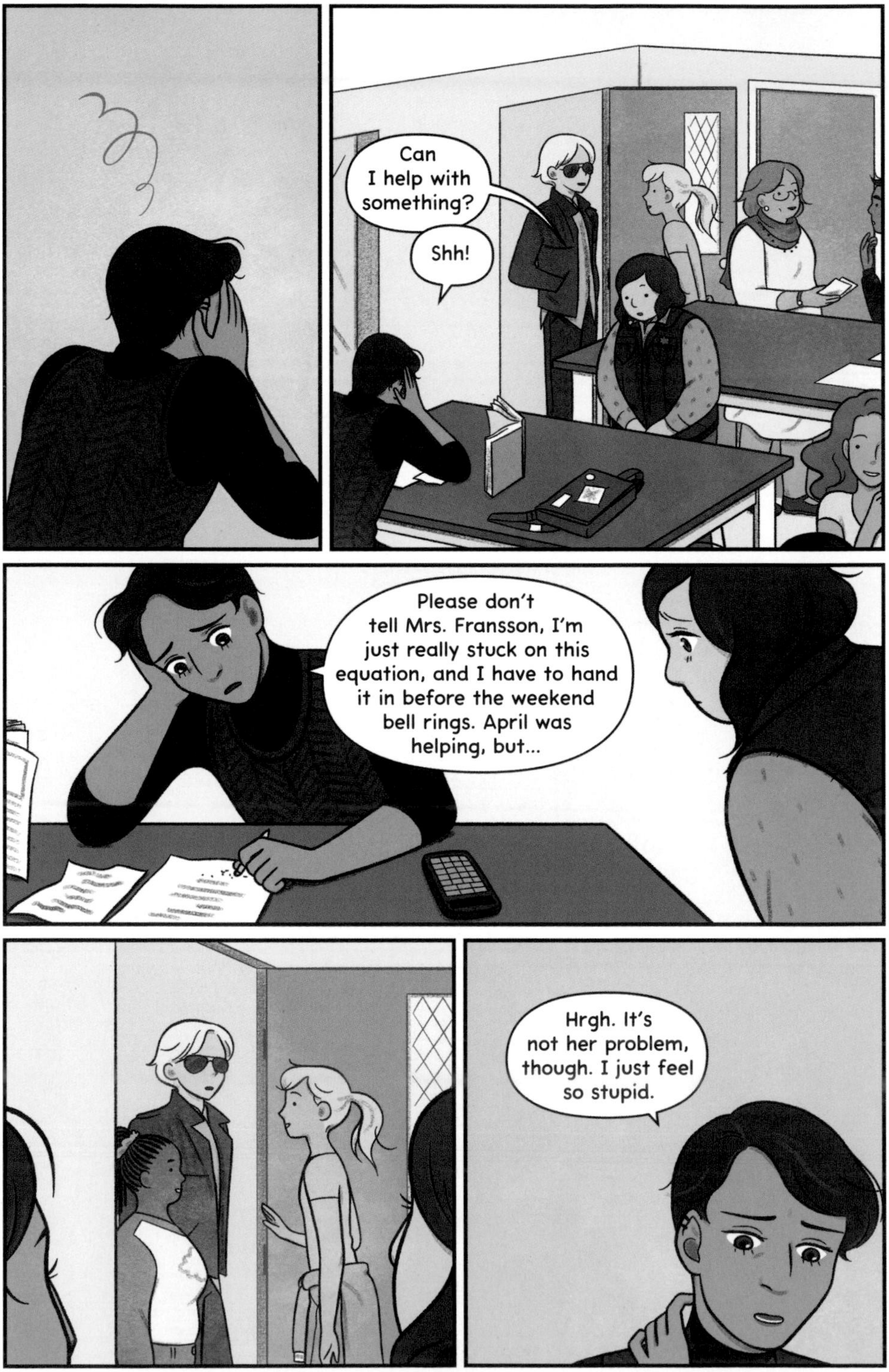
Can I help with something?
Shh!
Please don't tell Mrs. Fransson, I'm just really stuck on this equation, and I have to hand it in before the weekend bell rings. April was helping, but...
Hrgh. It's not her problem, though. I just feel so stupid.

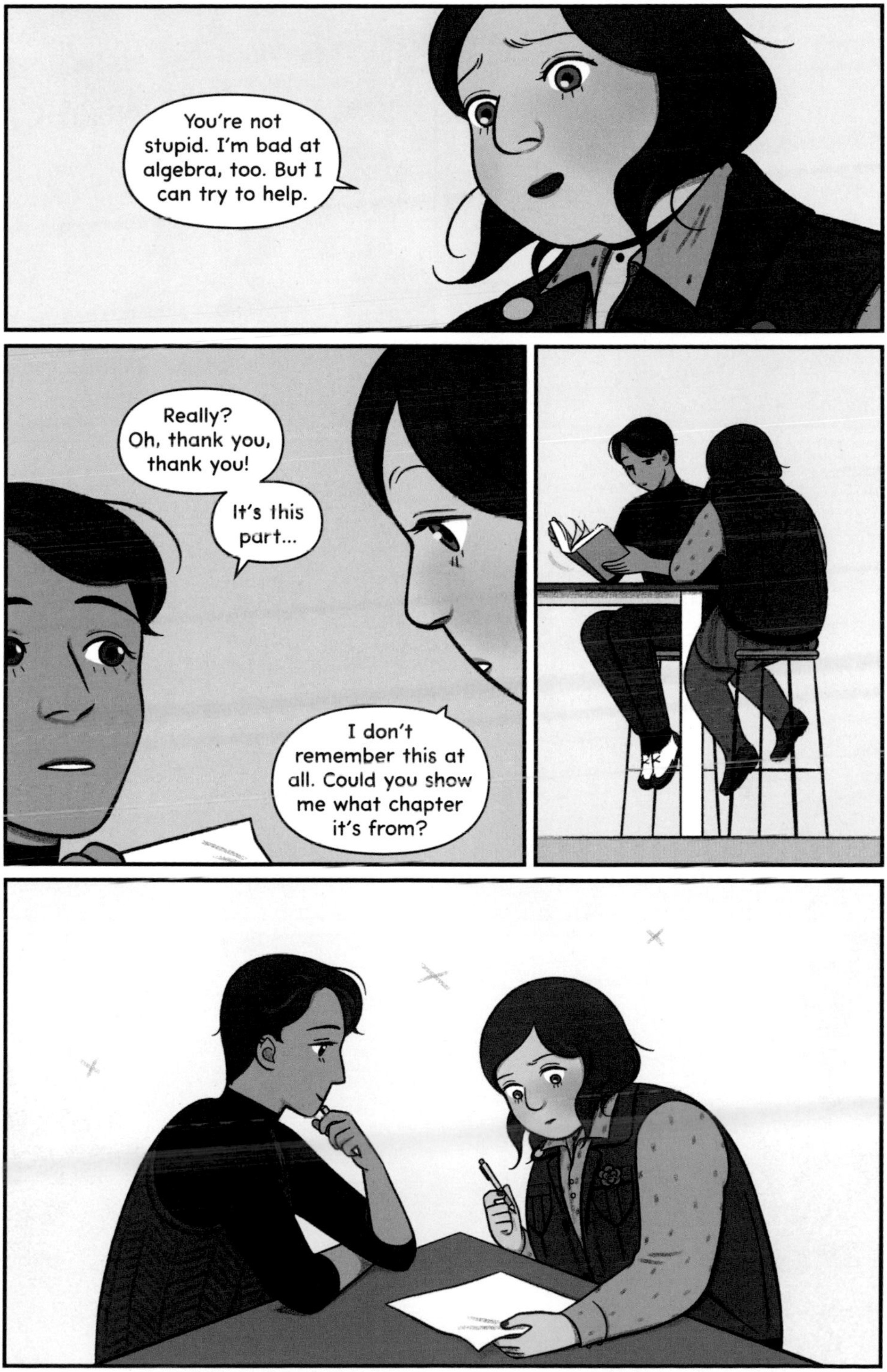
You're not stupid. I'm bad at algebra, too. But I can try to help.
Really? Oh, thank you, thank you!
It's this part...
I don't remember this at all. Could you show me what chapter it's from?

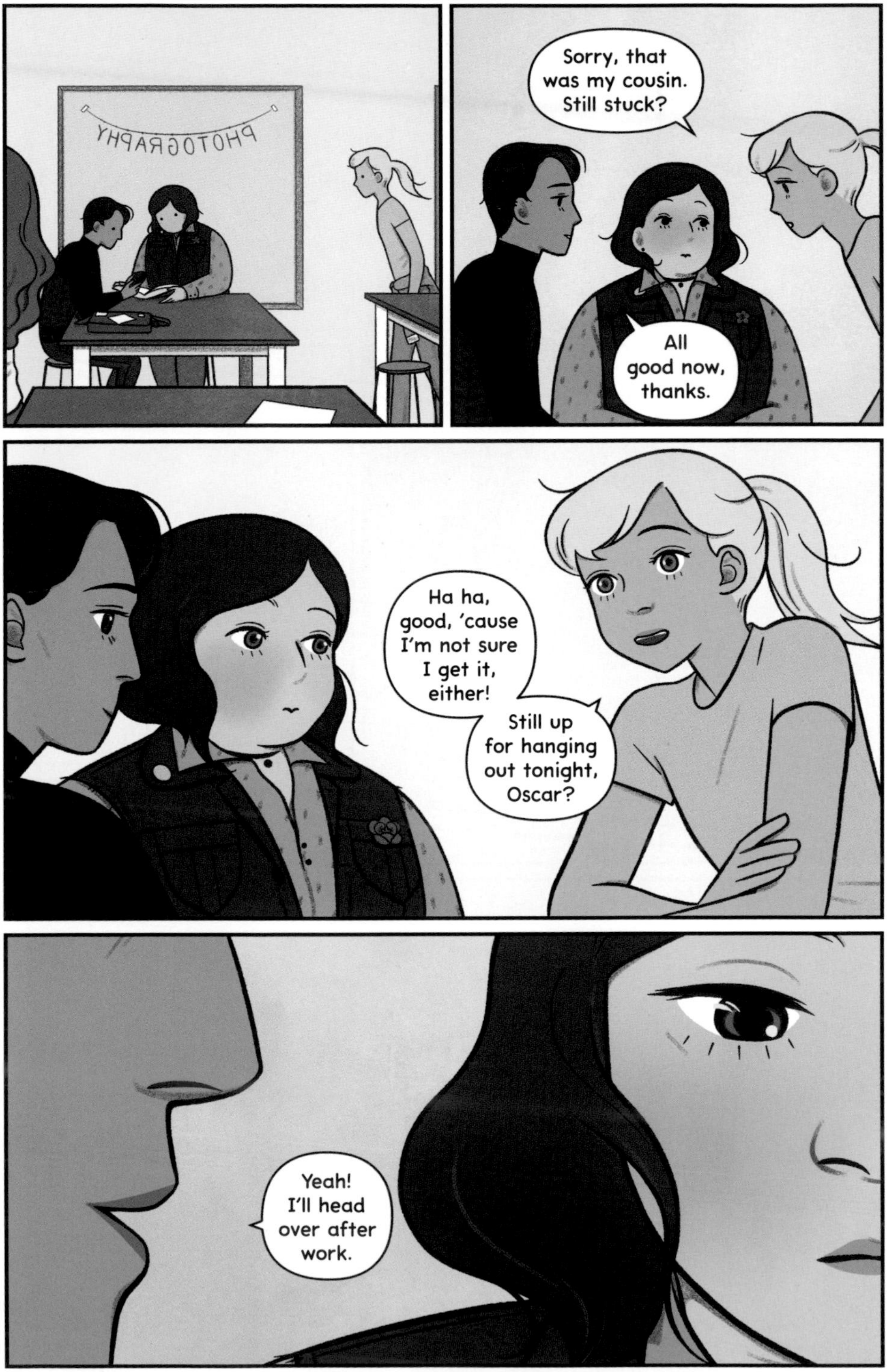
PHOTOGRAPHY
Sorry, that was my cousin. Still stuck?
All good now, thanks.
Ha ha, good, 'cause I'm not sure I get it, either!
Still up for hanging out tonight, Oscar?
Yeah! I'll head over after work.

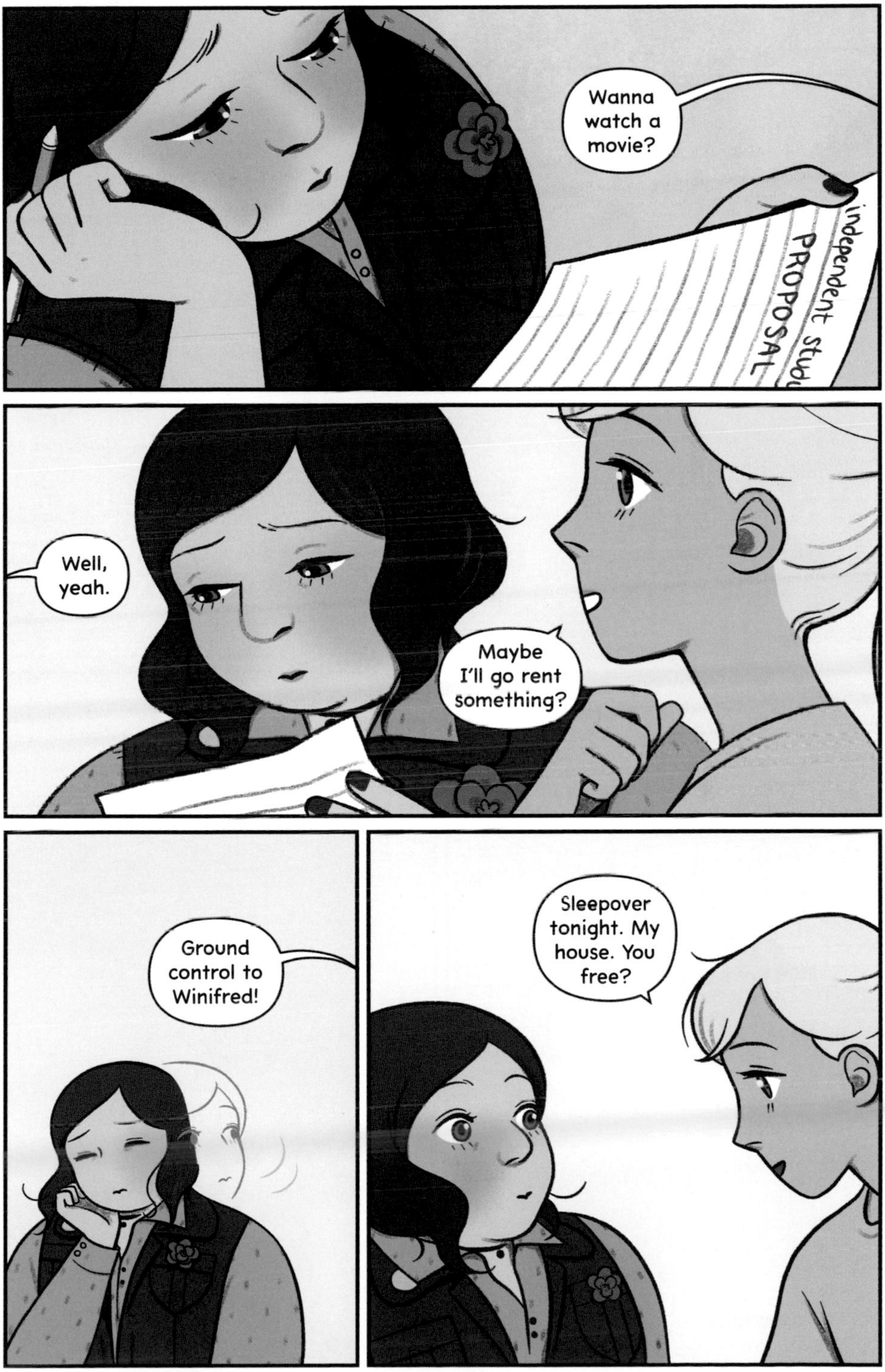
Wanna watch a movie?
independent study
PROPOSAL
Well, yeah.
Maybe I'll go rent something?
Ground control to Winifred!
Sleepover tonight. My house. You free?

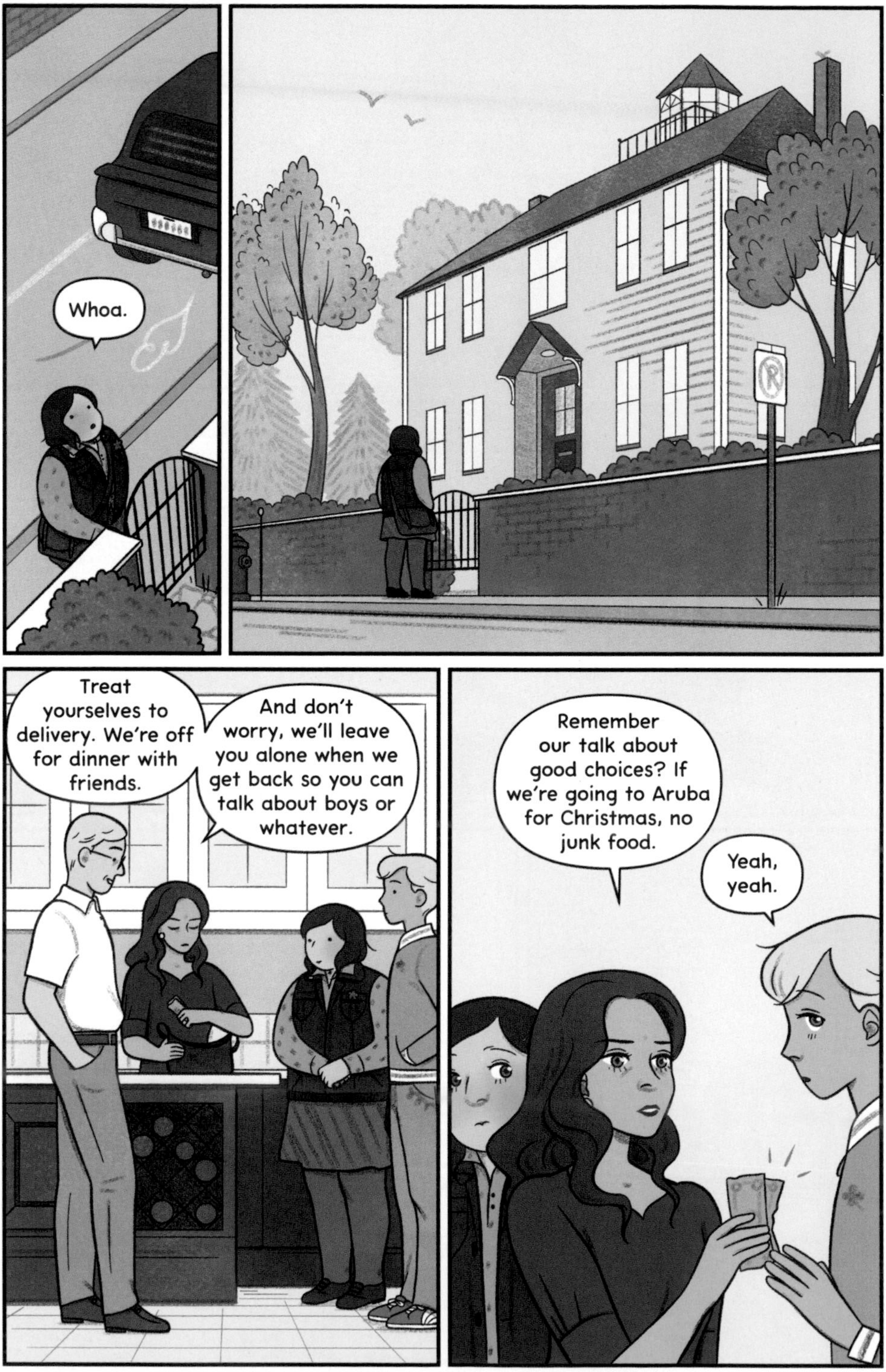

Whoa.
Treat yourselves to delivery. We're off for dinner with friends.
And don't worry, we'll leave you alone when we get back so you can talk about boys or whatever.
Remember our talk about good choices? If we're going to Aruba for Christmas, no junk food.
Yeah, yeah.

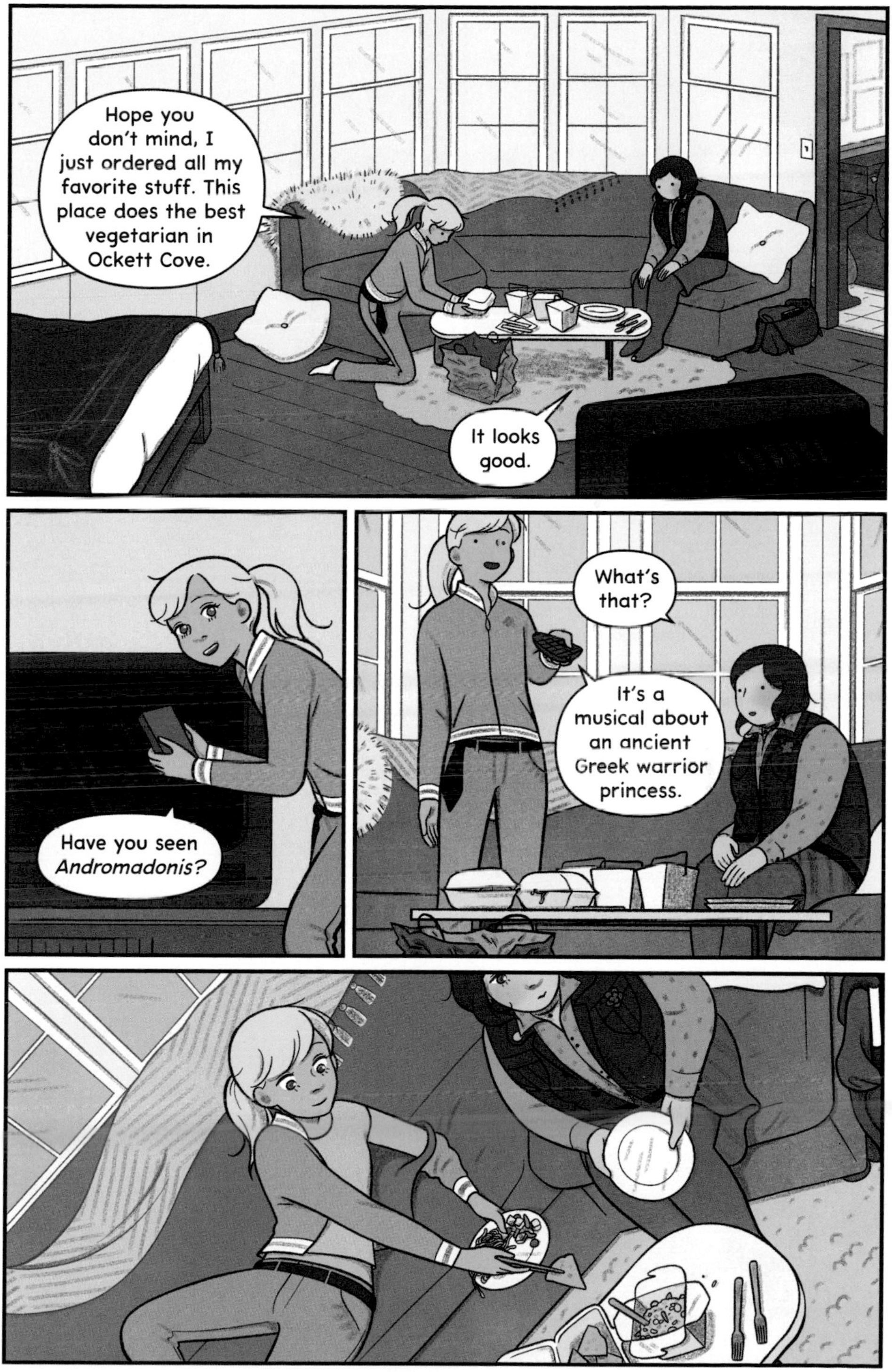
Hope you don't mind, I just ordered all my favorite stuff. This place does the best vegetarian in Ockett Cove.
It looks good.
Have you seen *Andromadonis?*
What's that?
It's a musical about an ancient Greek warrior princess.

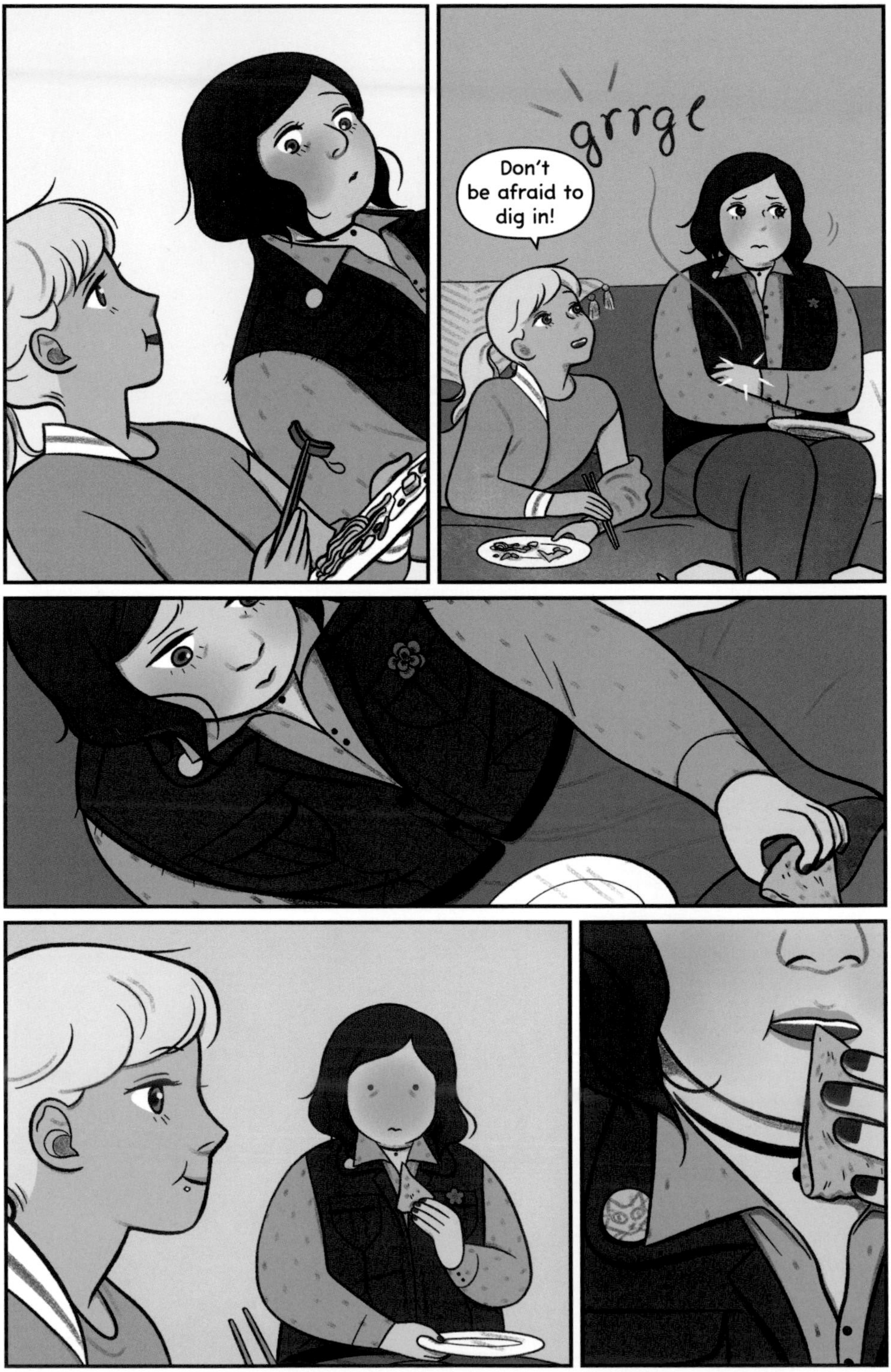
grrgl
Don't be afraid to dig in!

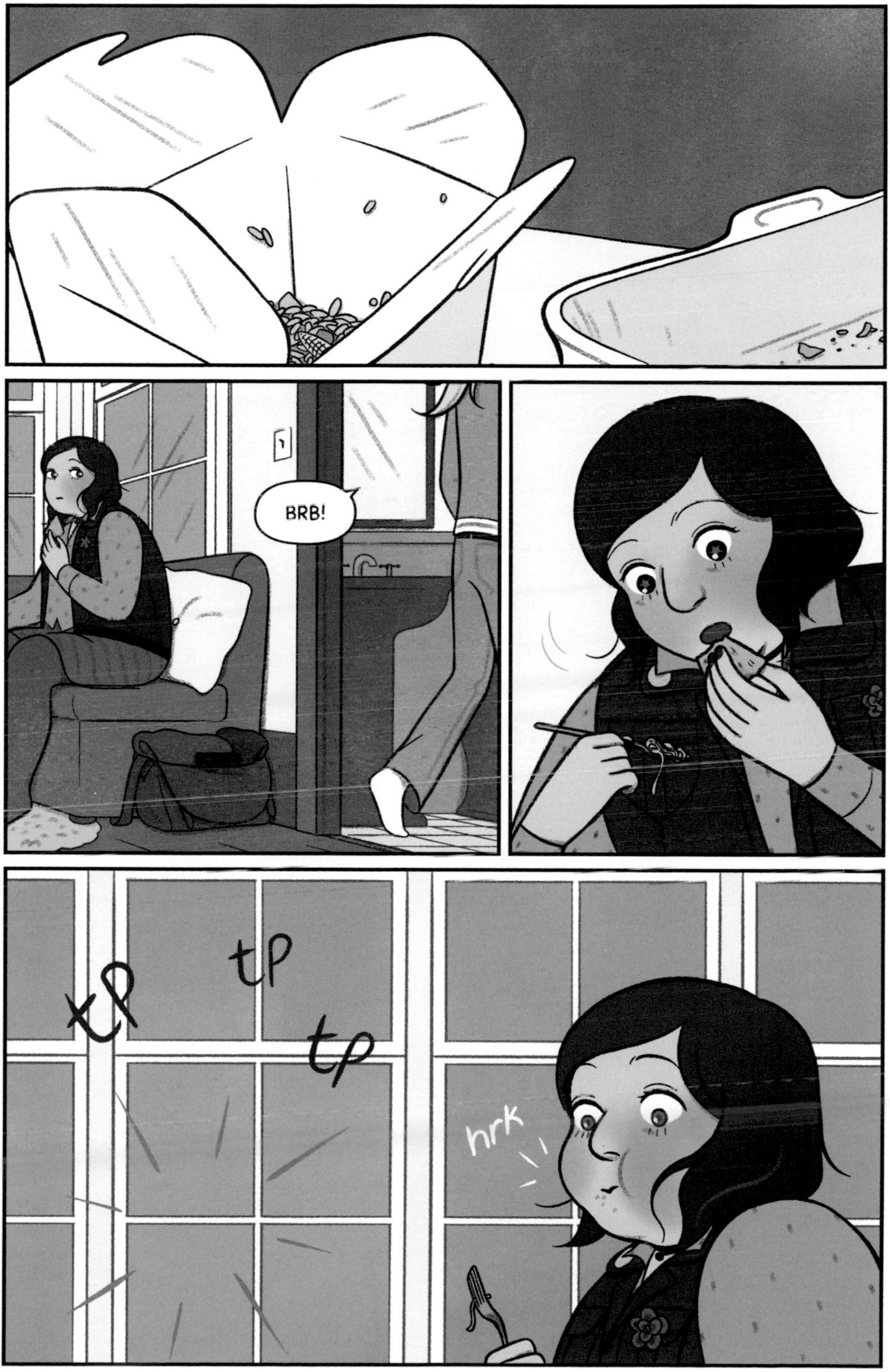
BRB!
tp
tp
tp
hrk

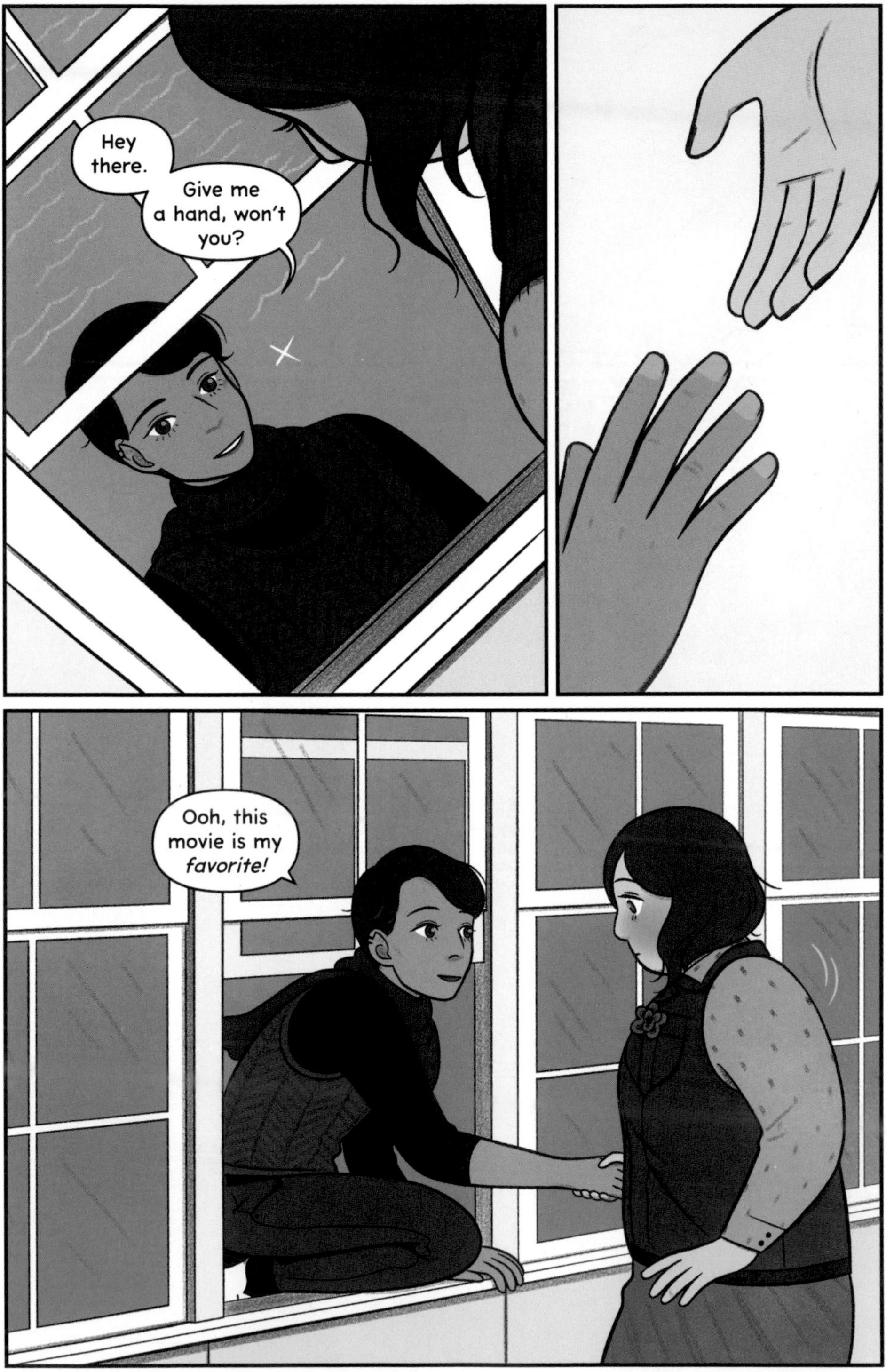
Hey there.
Give me a hand, won't you?
Ooh, this movie is my *favorite!*

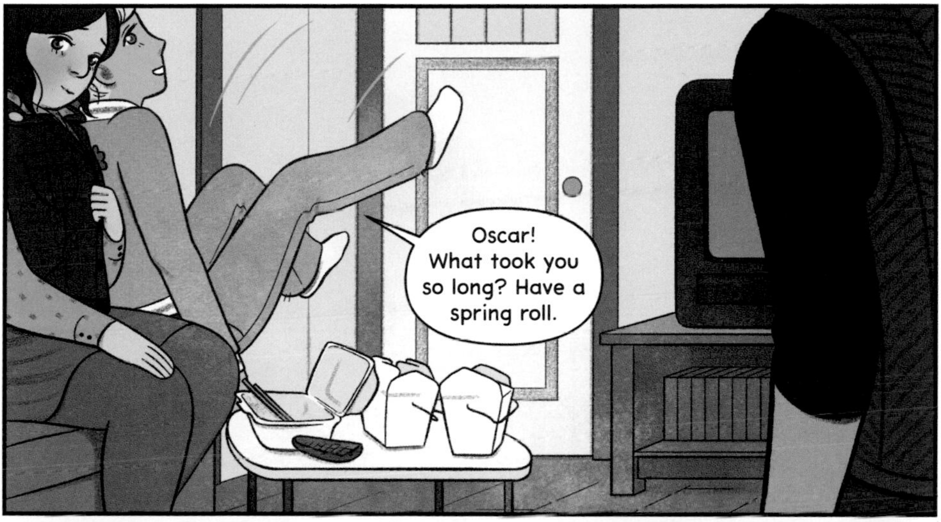

Oscar! What took you so long? Have a spring roll.

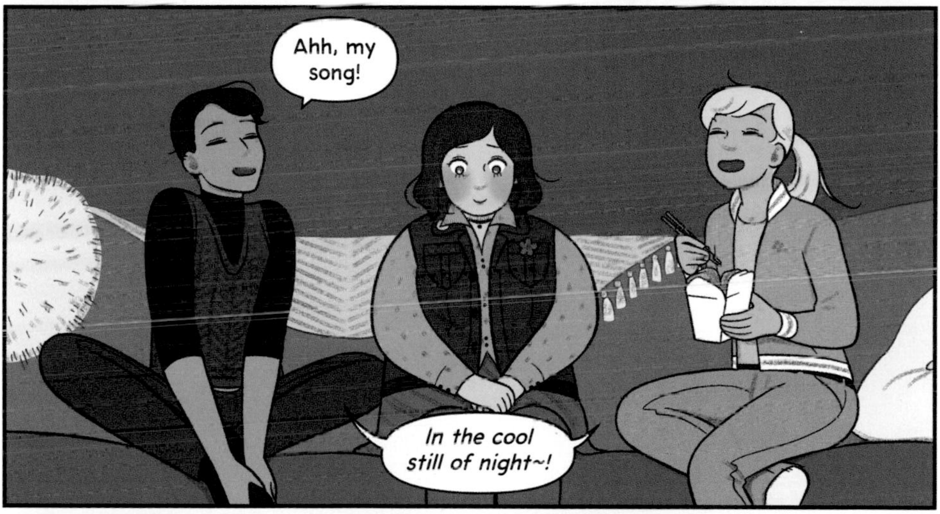

Ahh, my song!
In the cool still of night~!

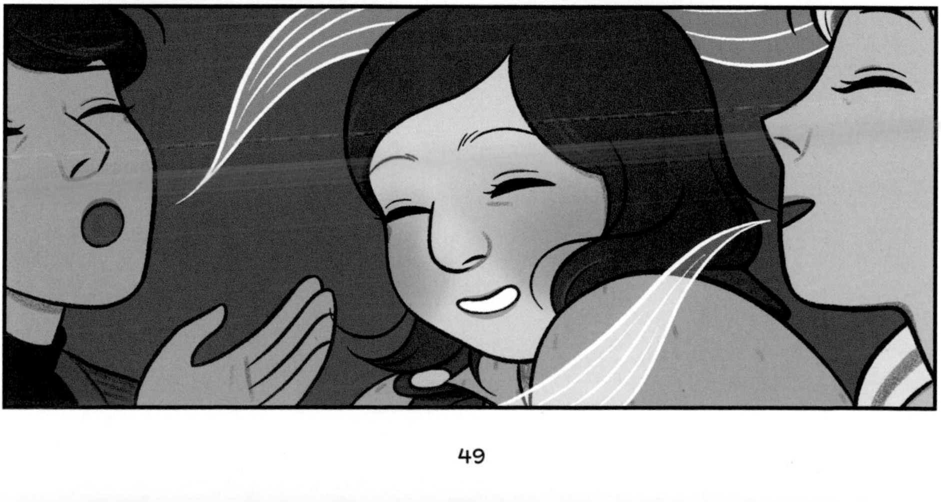

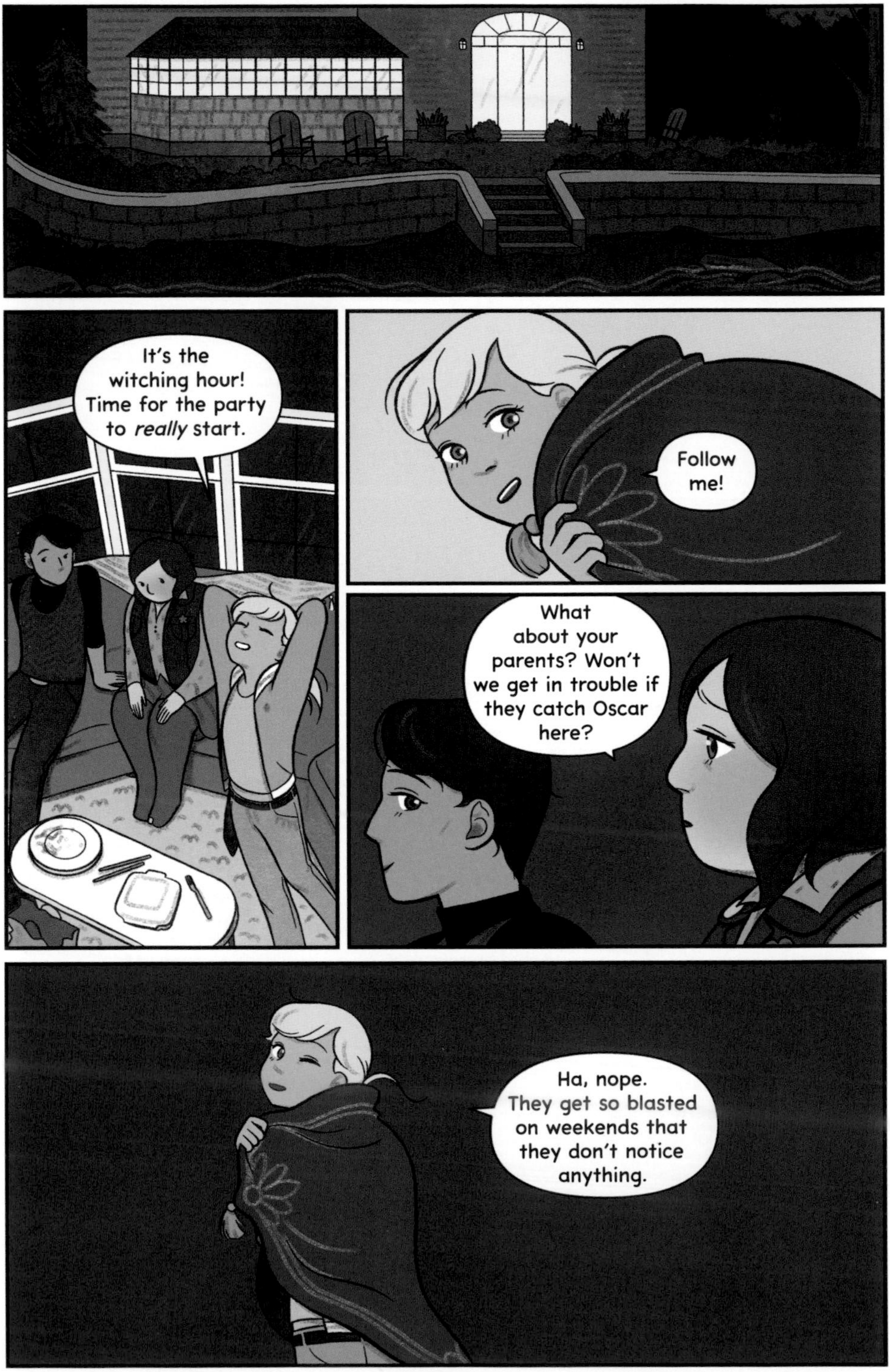
It's the witching hour! Time for the party to *really* start.
Follow me!
What about your parents? Won't we get in trouble if they catch Oscar here?
Ha, nope. They get so blasted on weekends that they don't notice anything.

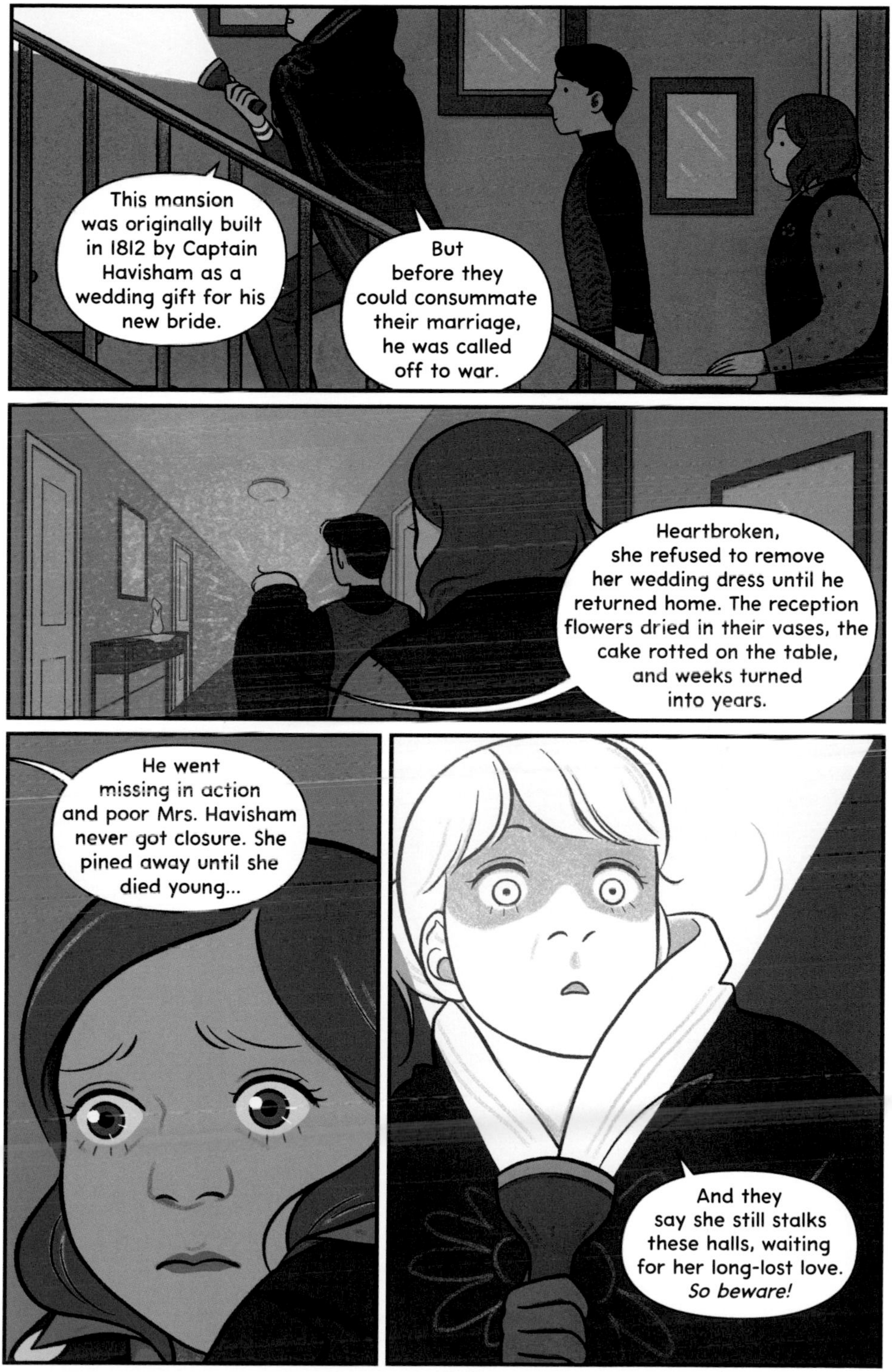
This mansion was originally built in 1812 by Captain Havisham as a wedding gift for his new bride.
But before they could consummate their marriage, he was called off to war.
Heartbroken, she refused to remove her wedding dress until he returned home. The reception flowers dried in their vases, the cake rotted on the table, and weeks turned into years.
He went missing in action and poor Mrs. Havisham never got closure. She pined away until she died young...
And they say she still stalks these halls, waiting for her long-lost love. *So beware!*

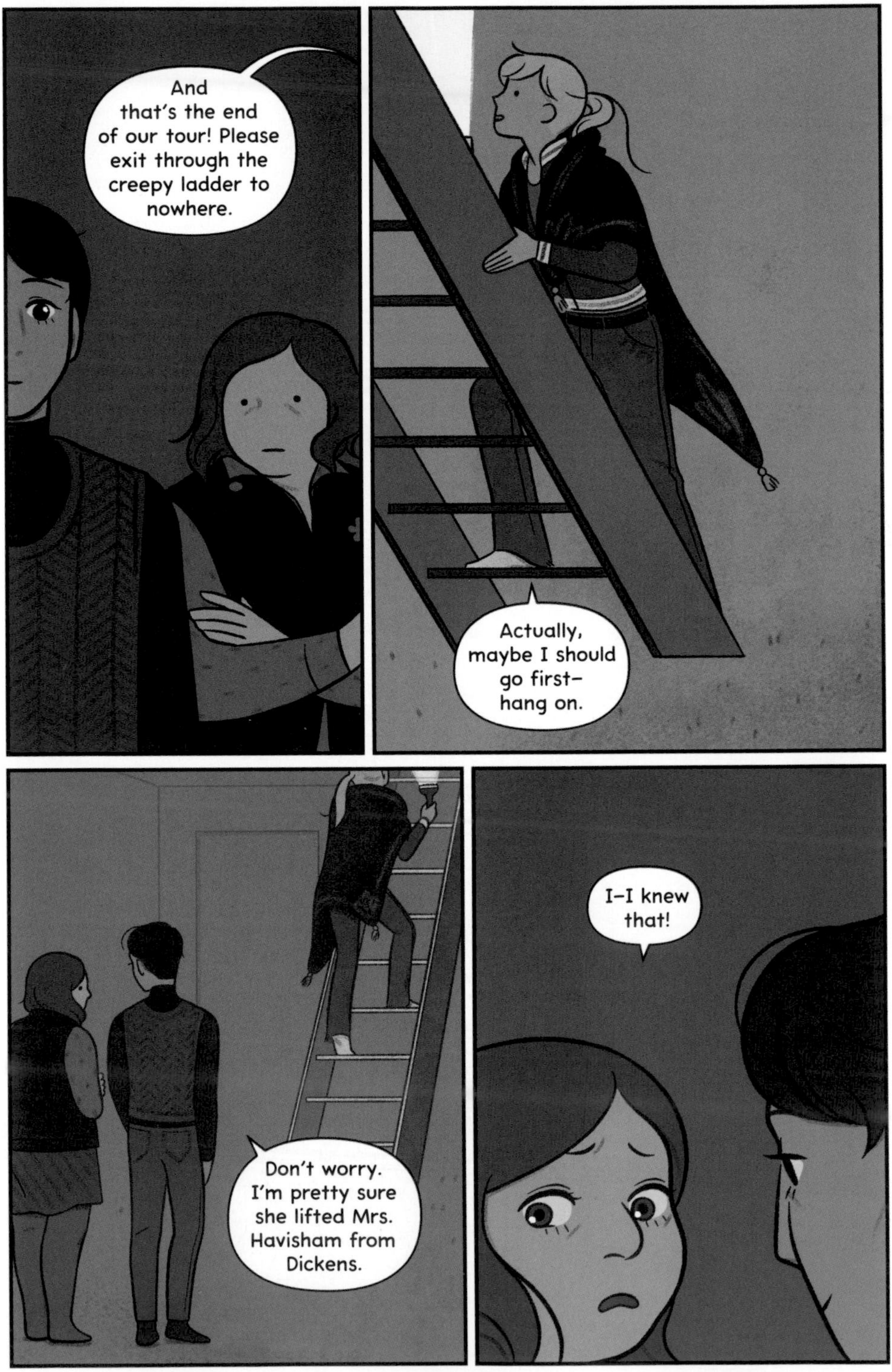
And that's the end of our tour! Please exit through the creepy ladder to nowhere.
Actually, maybe I should go first– hang on.
Don't worry. I'm pretty sure she lifted Mrs. Havisham from Dickens.
I–I knew that!

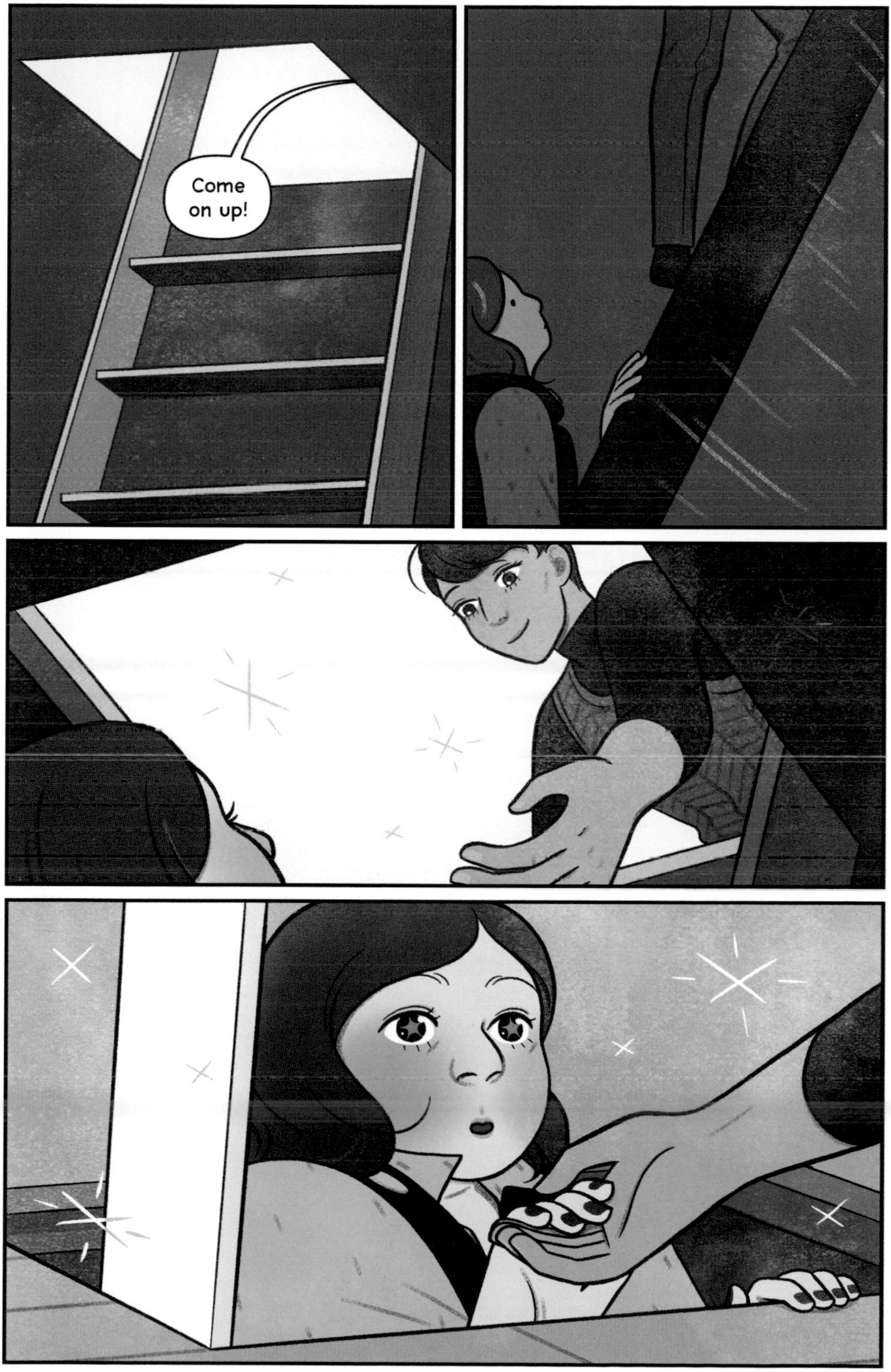
Come on up!

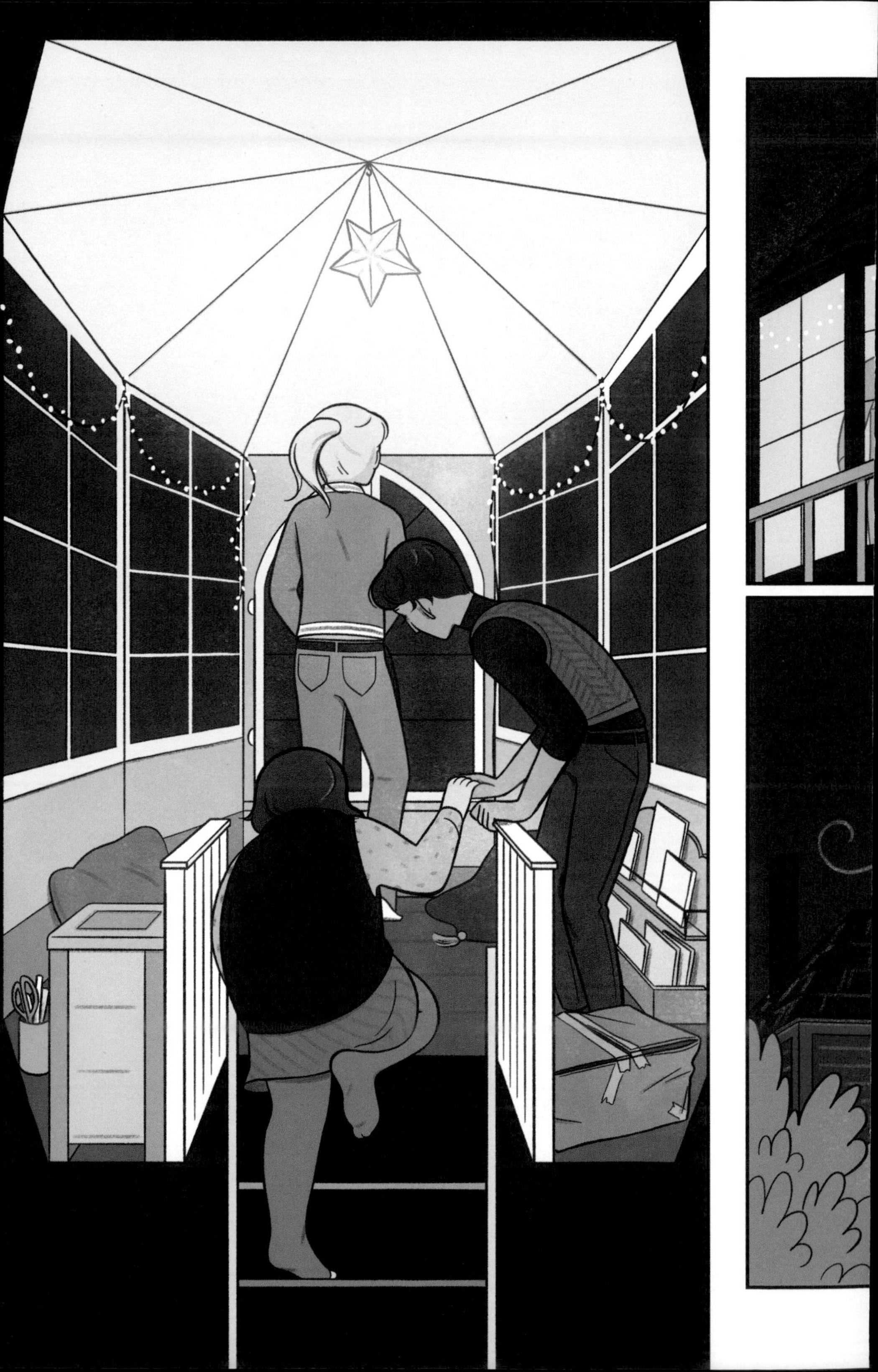

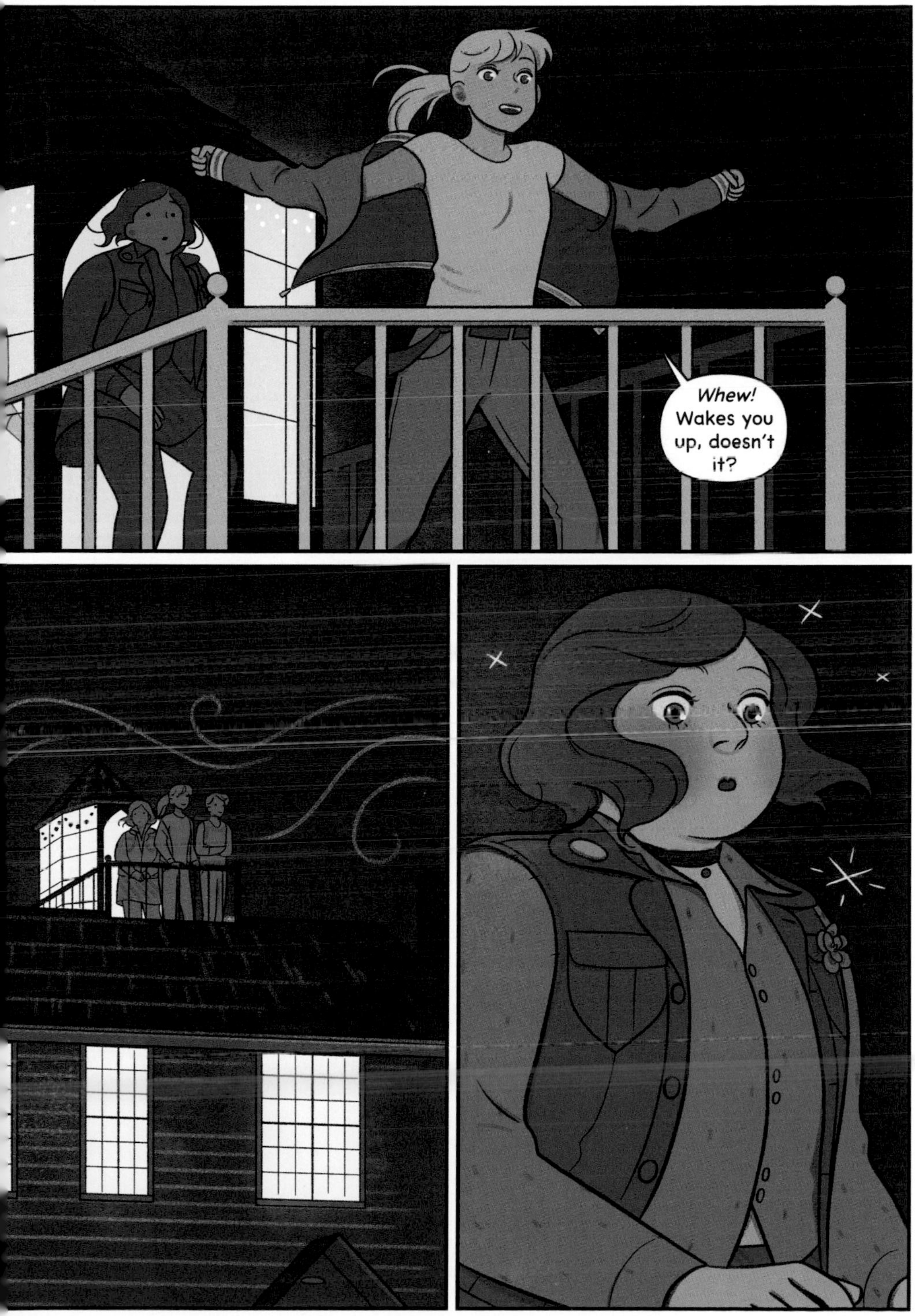
Whew! Wakes you up, doesn't it?

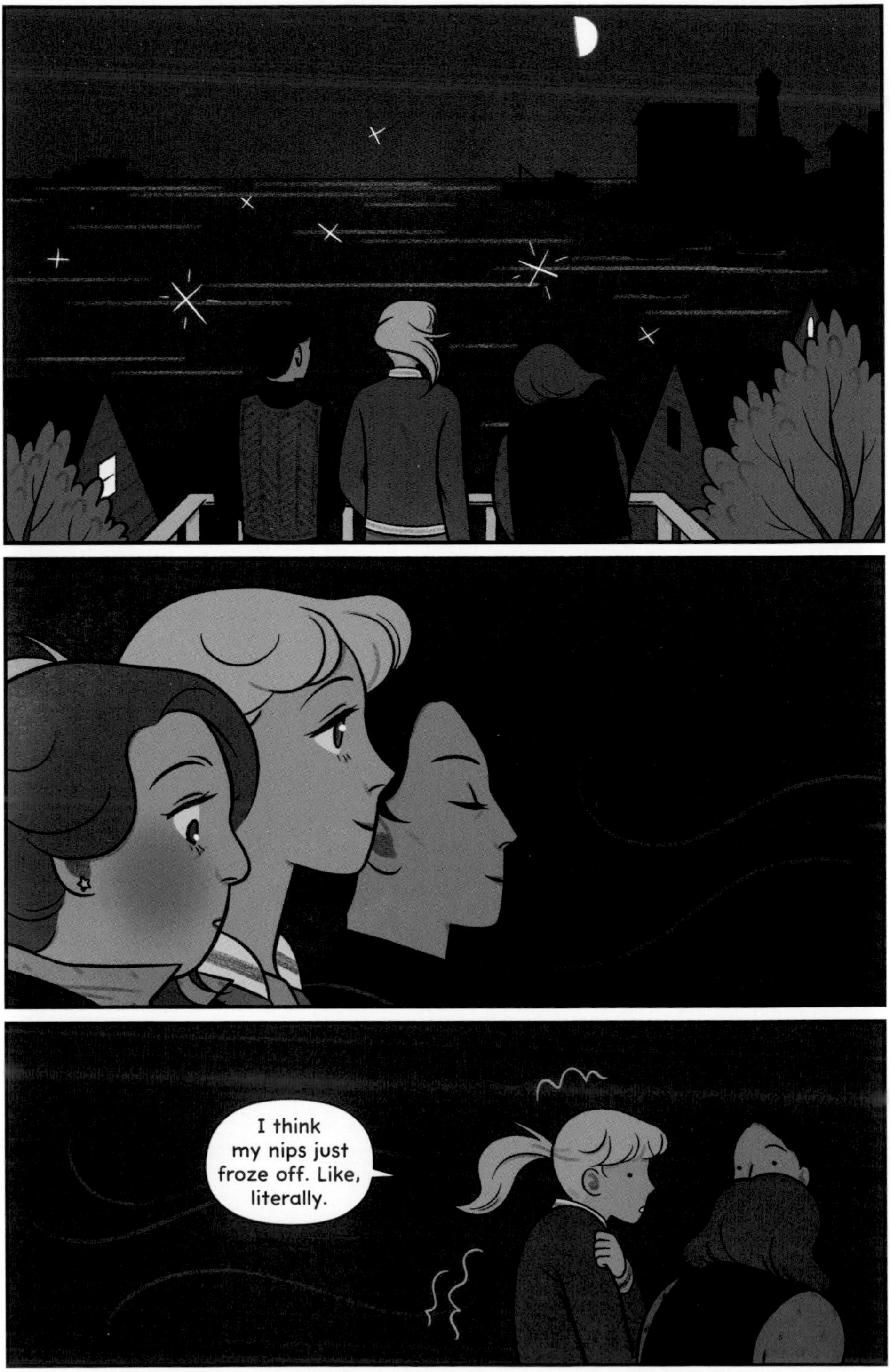
I think my nips just froze off. Like, literally.

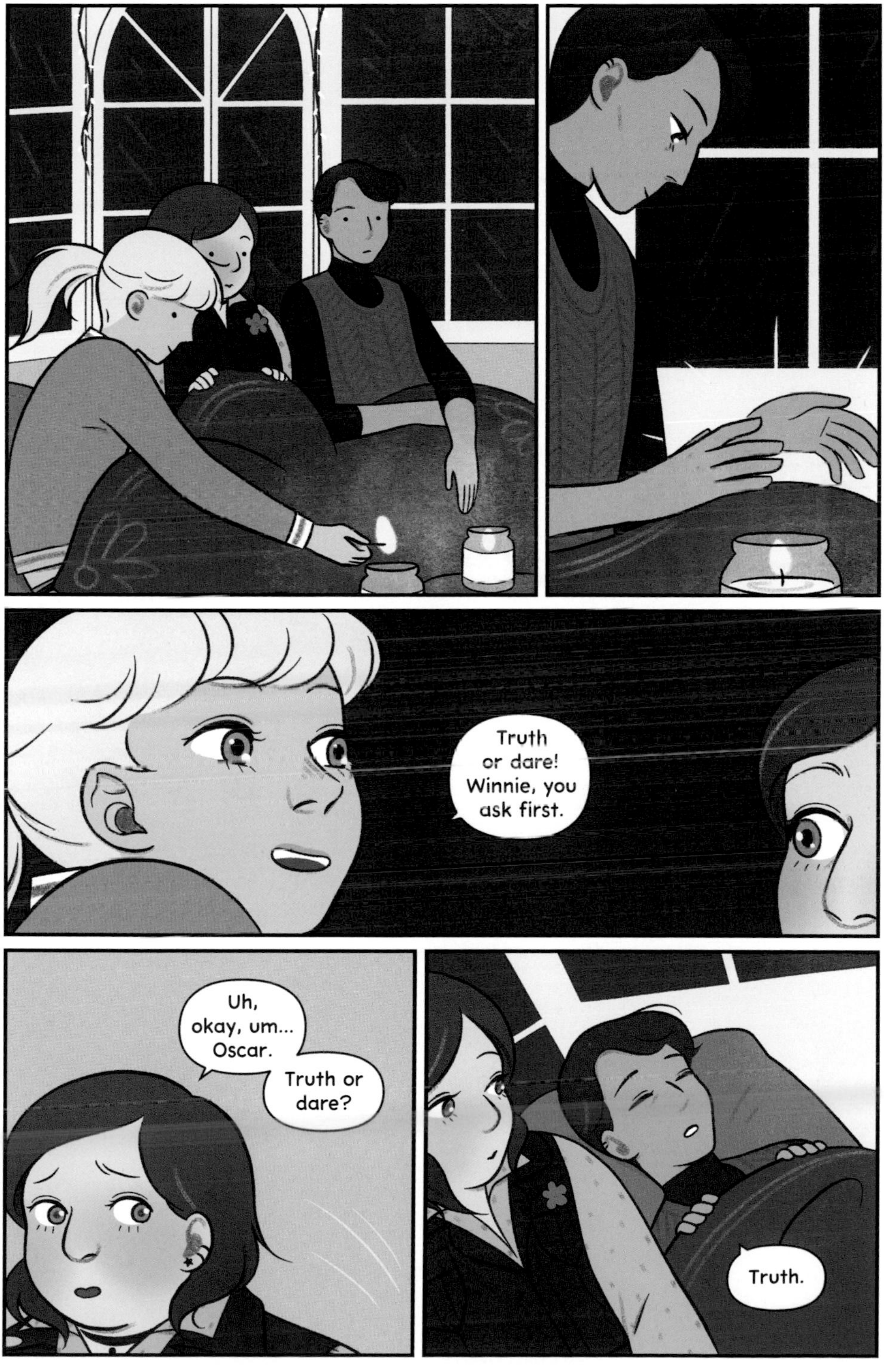
Truth or dare! Winnie, you ask first.
Uh, okay, um... Oscar.
Truth or dare?
Truth.

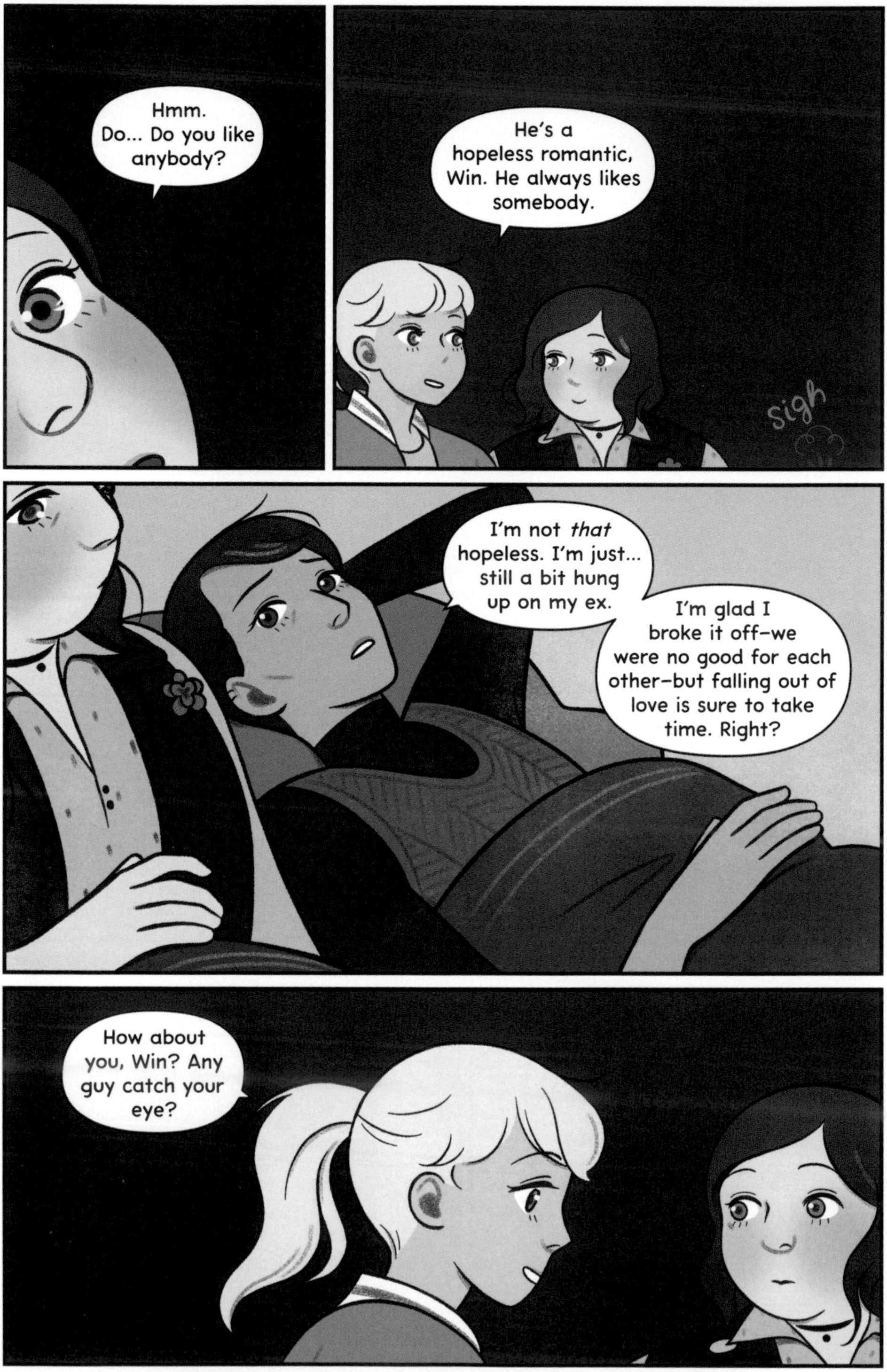
Hmm. Do... Do you like anybody?
He's a hopeless romantic, Win. He always likes somebody.
sigh
I'm not *that* hopeless. I'm just... still a bit hung up on my ex.
I'm glad I broke it off–we were no good for each other–but falling out of love is sure to take time. Right?
How about you, Win? Any guy catch your eye?

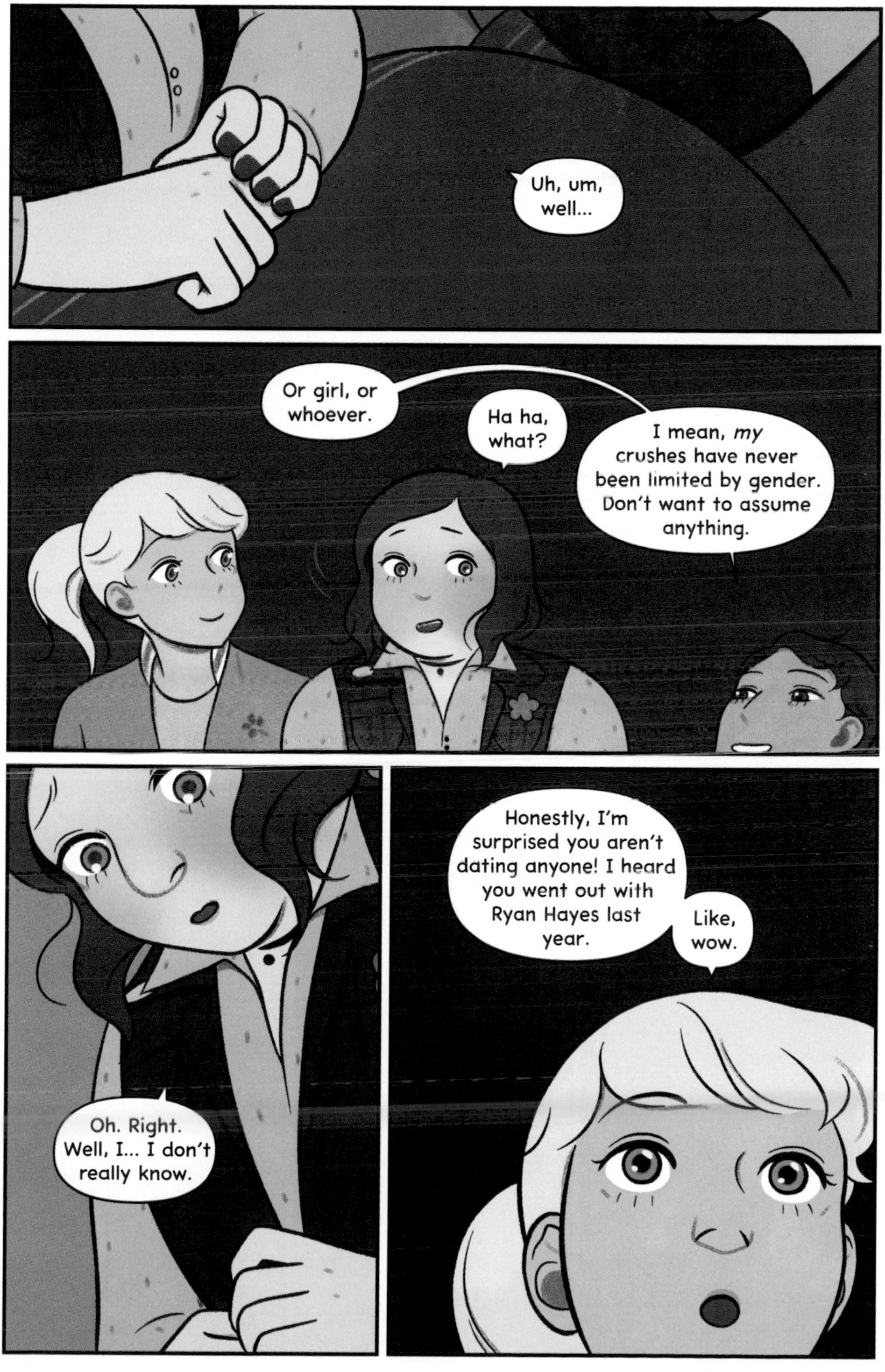

Uh, um, well...
Or girl, or whoever.
Ha ha, what?
I mean, *my* crushes have never been limited by gender. Don't want to assume anything.
Oh. Right. Well, I... I don't really know.
Honestly, I'm surprised you aren't dating anyone! I heard you went out with Ryan Hayes last year.
Like, wow.

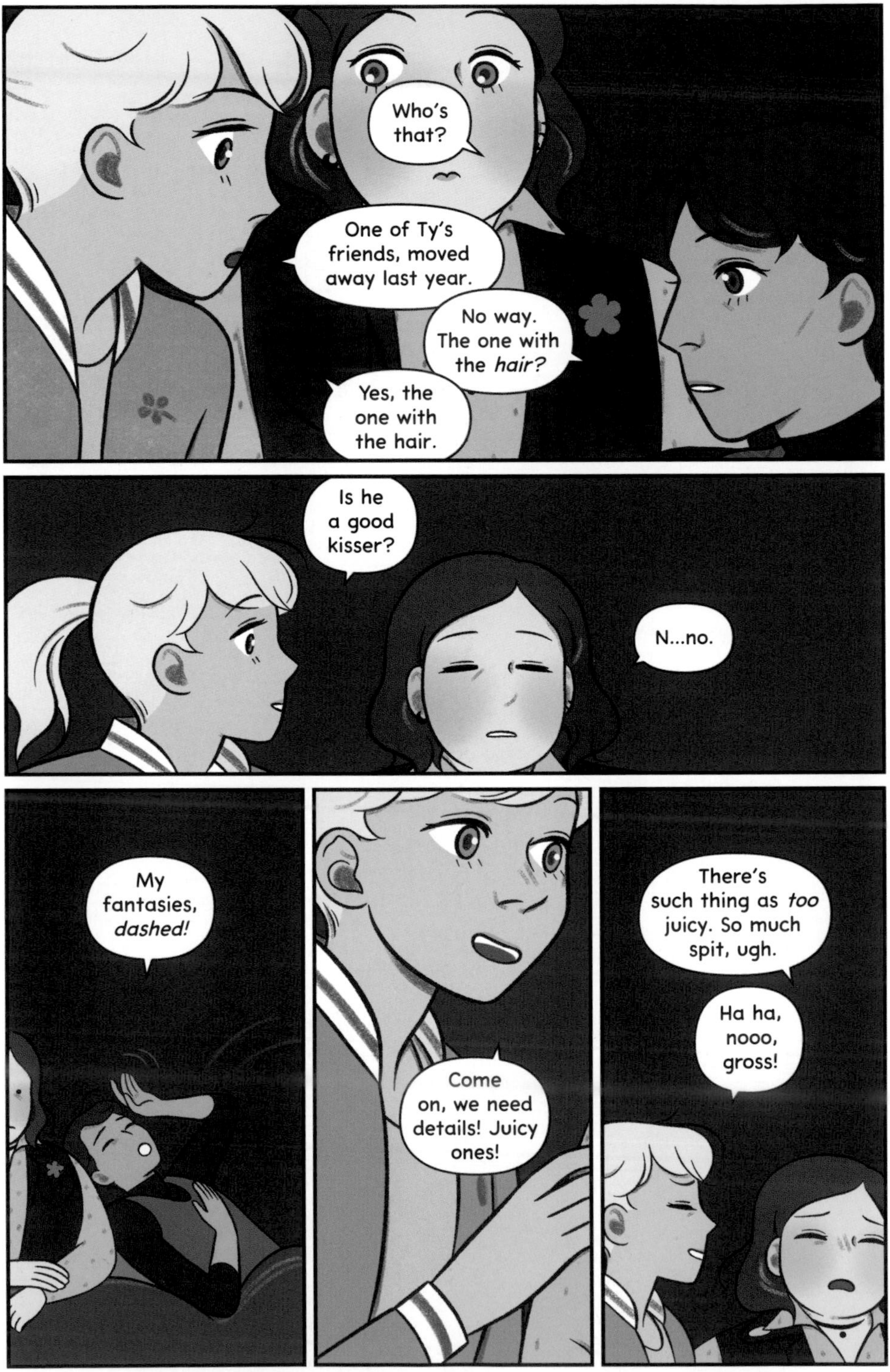

Who's that?
One of Ty's friends, moved away last year.
No way. The one with the *hair?*
Yes, the one with the hair.
Is he a good kisser?
N...no.
My fantasies, *dashed!*
Come on, we need details! Juicy ones!
There's such thing as *too* juicy. So much spit, ugh.
Ha ha, nooo, gross!

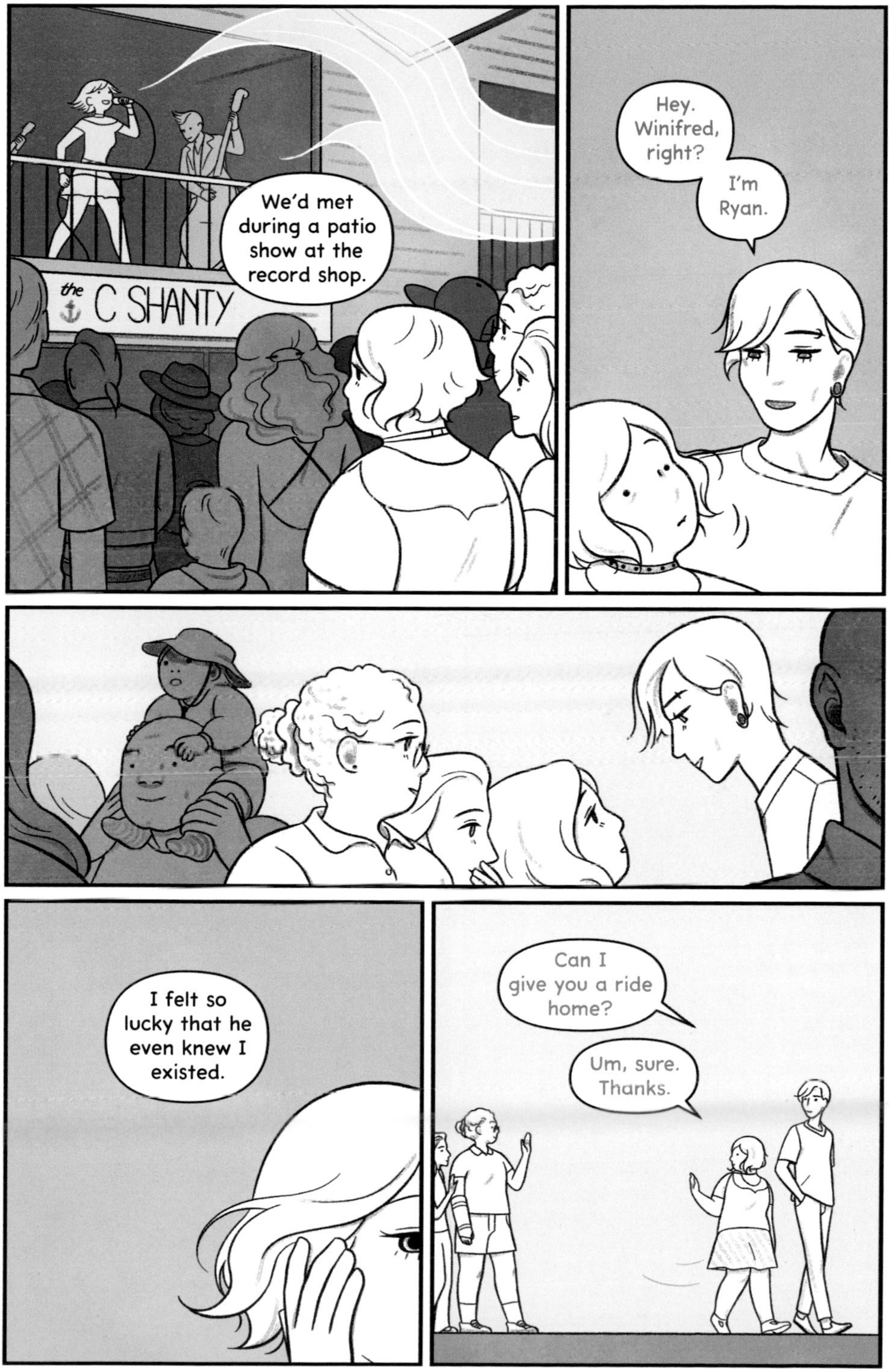
We'd met during a patio show at the record shop.
the C SHANTY
Hey. Winifred, right?
I'm Ryan.
I felt so lucky that he even knew I existed.
Can I give you a ride home?
Um, sure. Thanks.

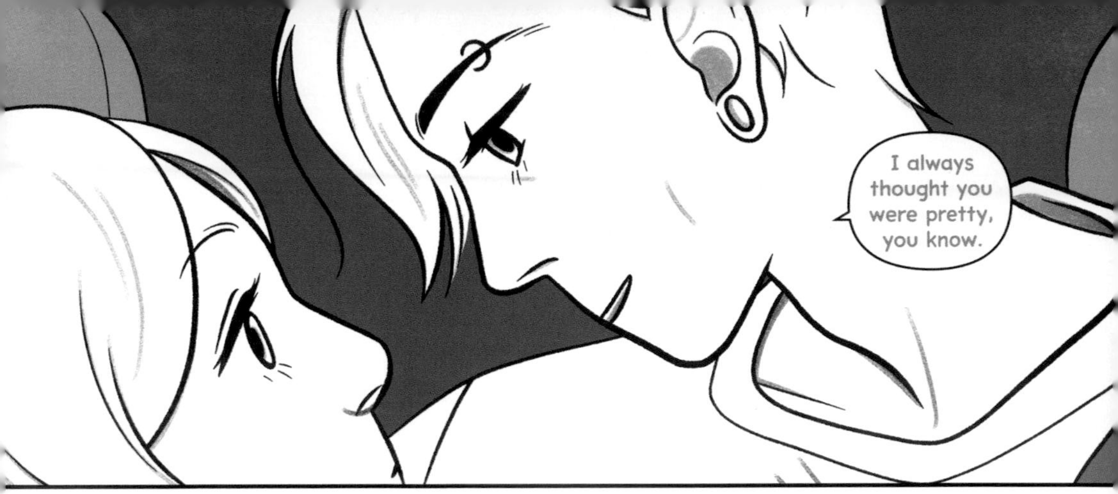
I always thought you were pretty, you know.

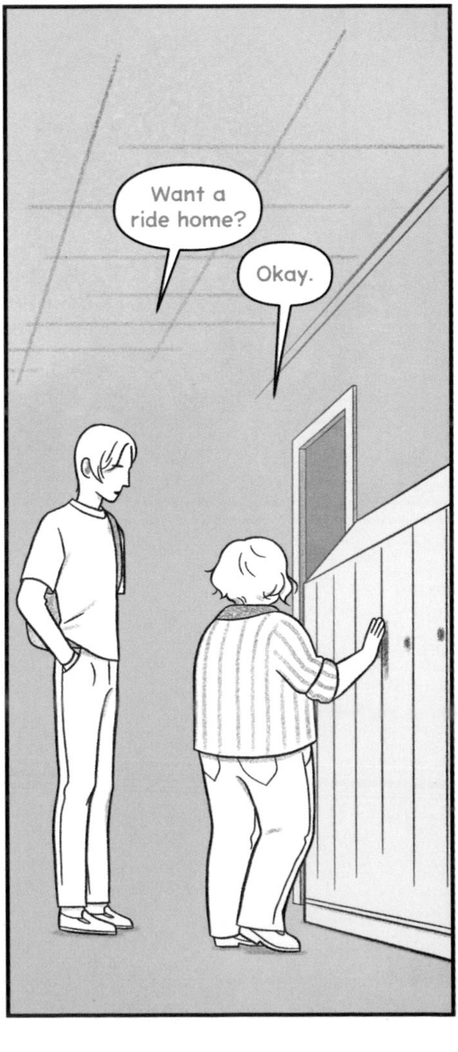
Want a ride home?
Okay.

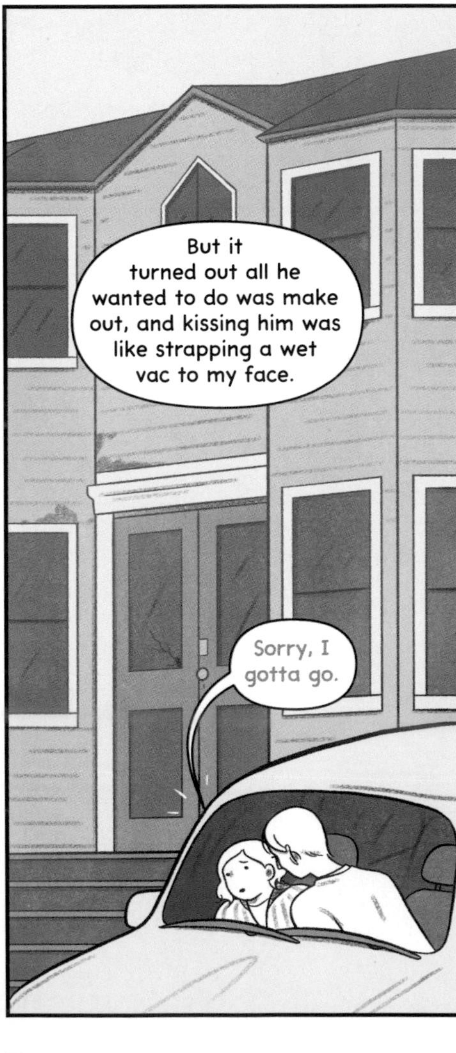
But it turned out all he wanted to do was make out, and kissing him was like strapping a wet vac to my face.
Sorry, I gotta go.

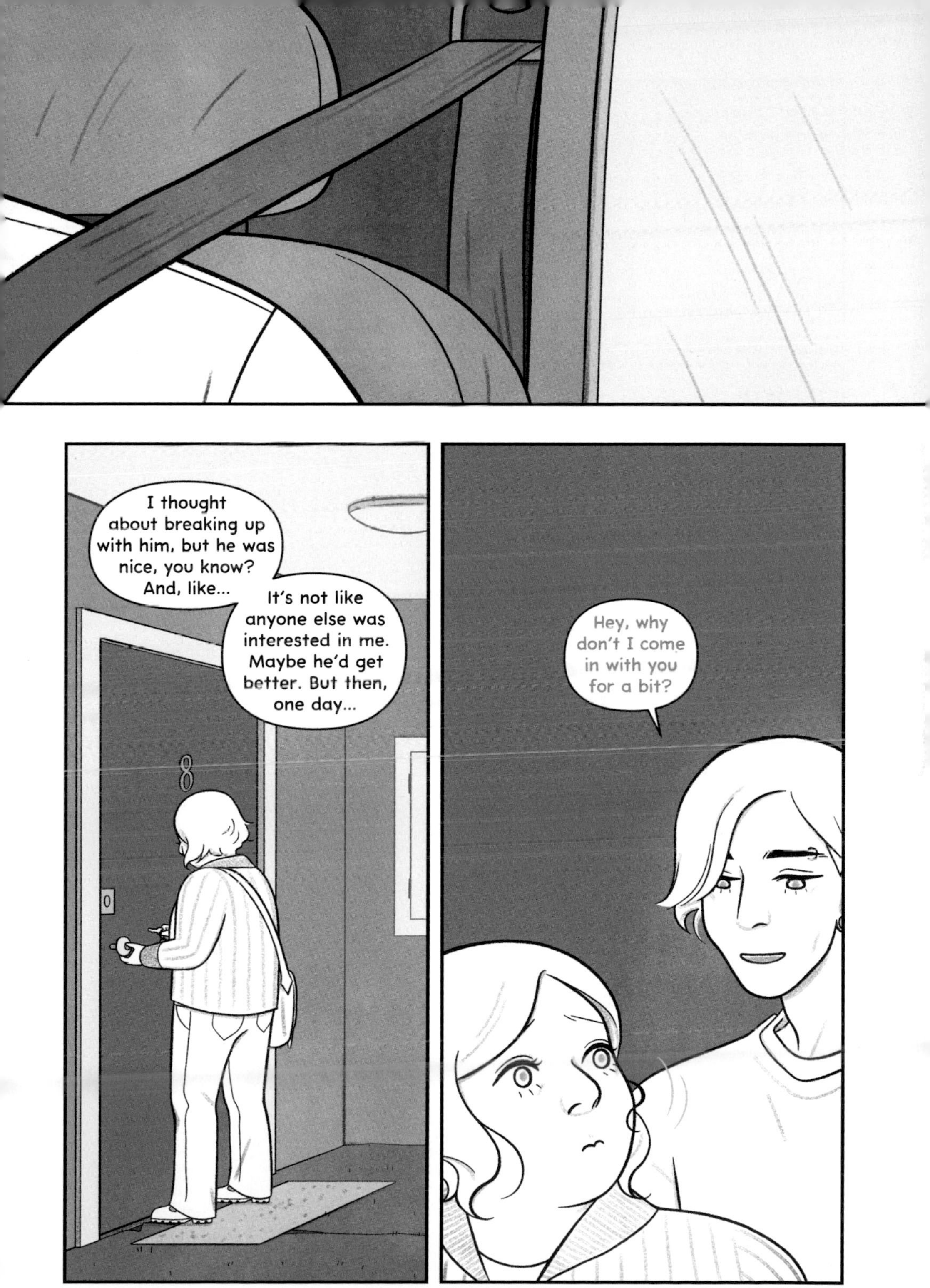
I thought about breaking up with him, but he was nice, you know? And, like...
It's not like anyone else was interested in me. Maybe he'd get better. But then, one day...
Hey, why don't I come in with you for a bit?

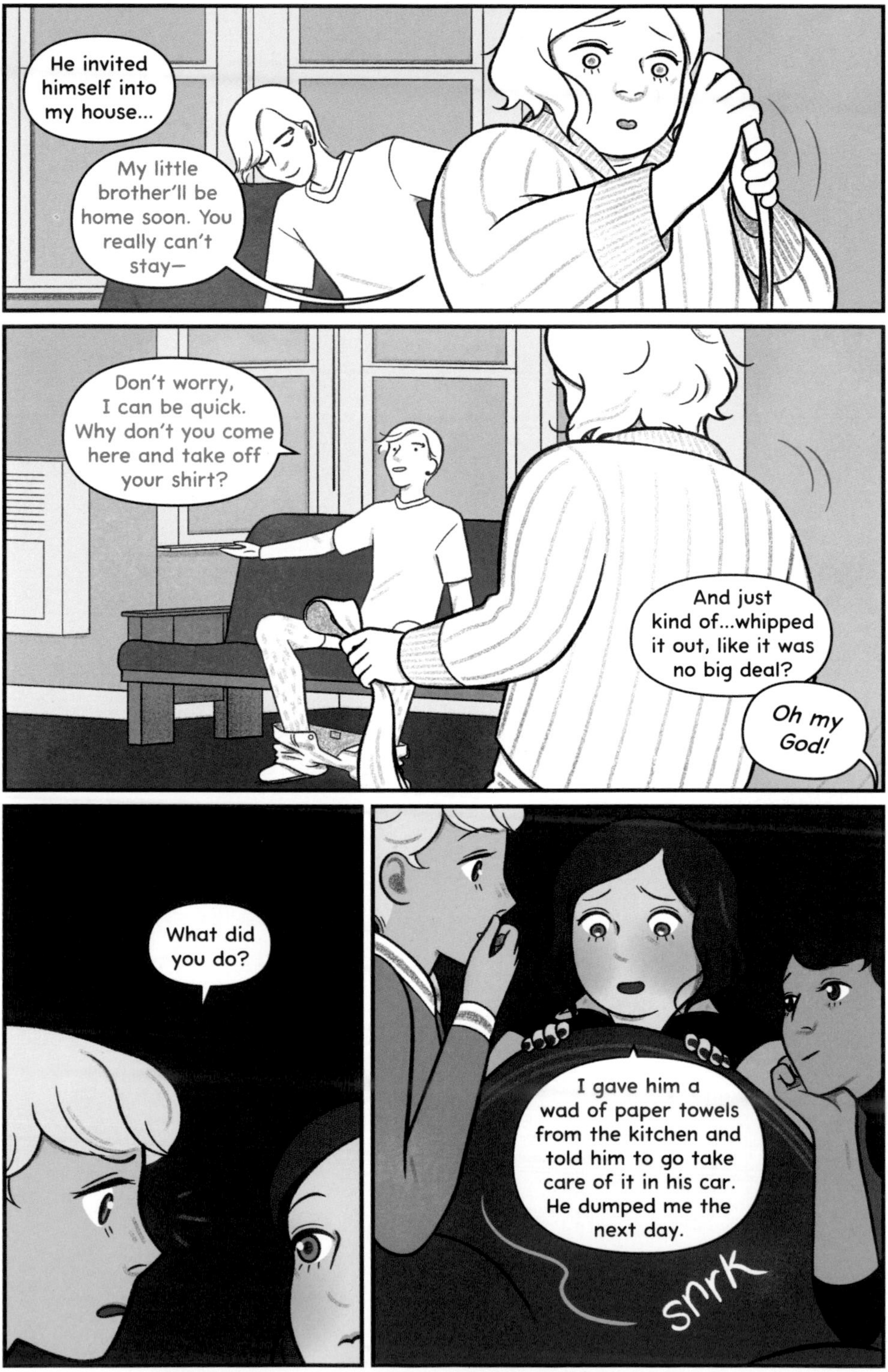
He invited himself into my house...
My little brother'll be home soon. You really can't stay—
Don't worry, I can be quick. Why don't you come here and take off your shirt?
And just kind of...whipped it out, like it was no big deal?
Oh my God!
What did you do?
I gave him a wad of paper towels from the kitchen and told him to go take care of it in his car. He dumped me the next day.
snrk

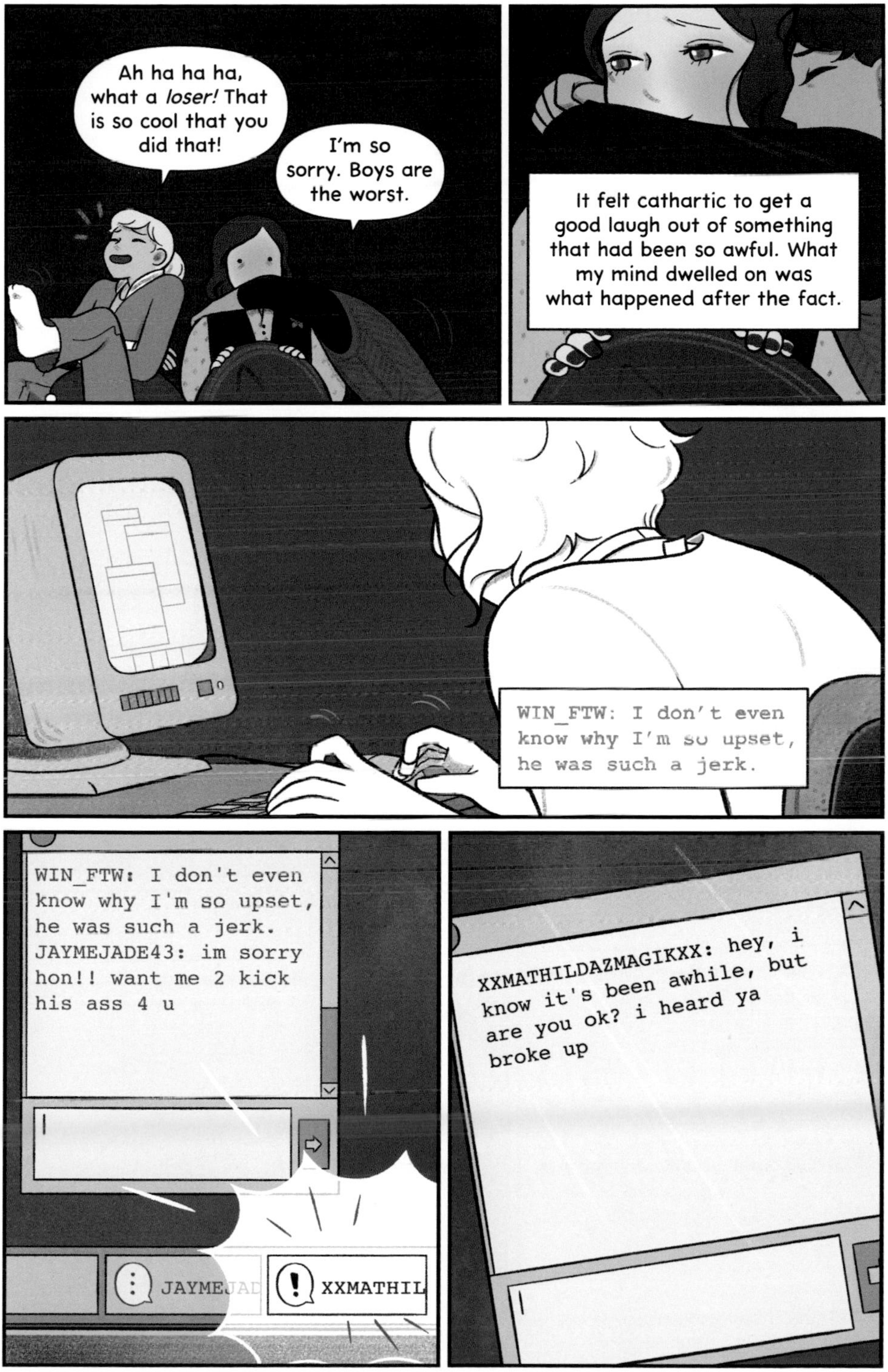

Ah ha ha ha, what a *loser!* That is so cool that you did that!
I'm so sorry. Boys are the worst.
It felt cathartic to get a good laugh out of something that had been so awful. What my mind dwelled on was what happened after the fact.
WIN_FTW: I don't even know why I'm so upset, he was such a jerk.
WIN_FTW: I don't even know why I'm so upset, he was such a jerk.
JAYMEJADE43: im sorry hon!! want me 2 kick his ass 4 u
JAYMEJAD
XXMATHIL
XXMATHILDAZMAGIKXX: hey, i know it's been awhile, but are you ok? i heard ya broke up

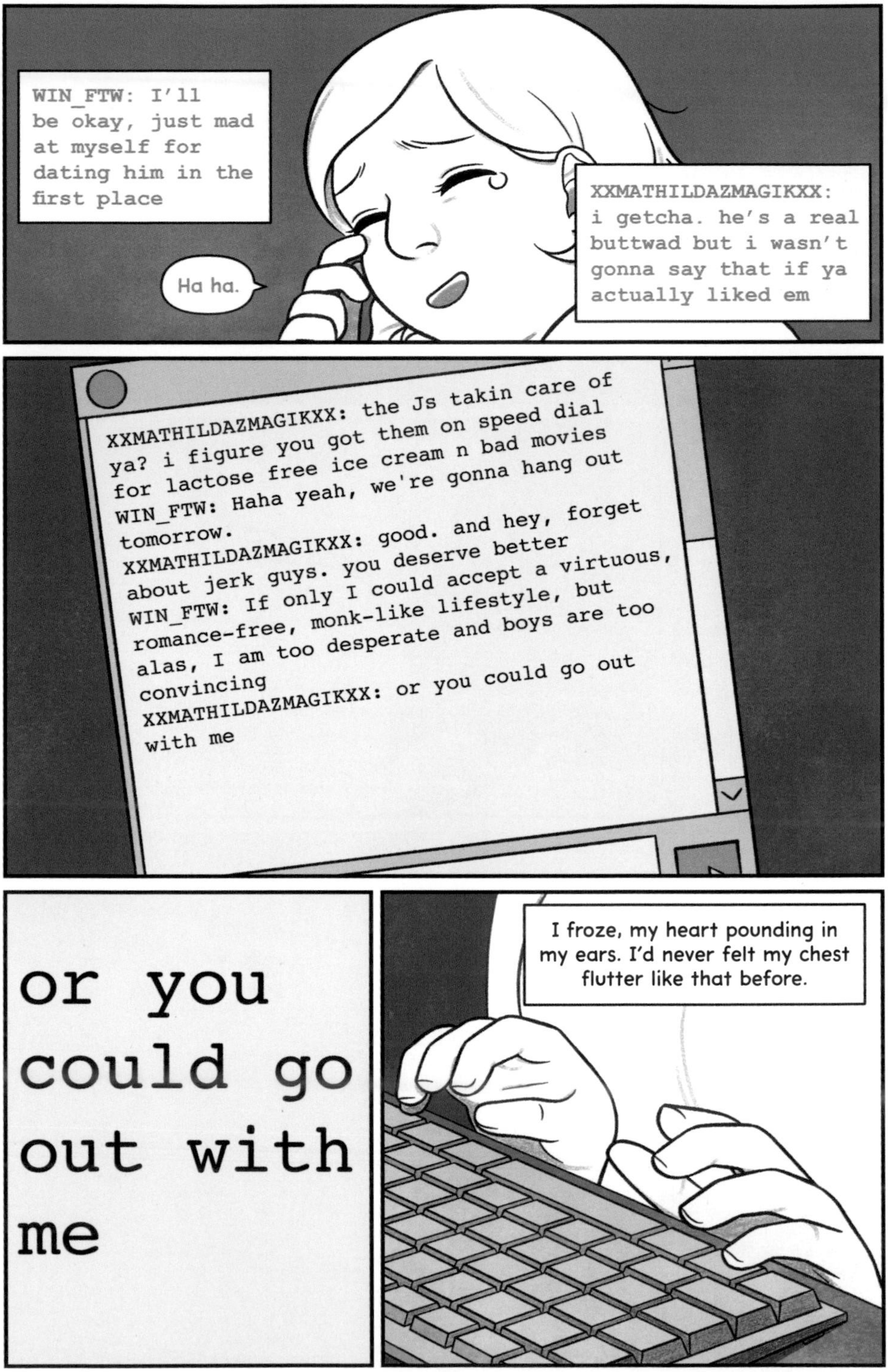
WIN_FTW: I'll be okay, just mad at myself for dating him in the first place
Ha ha.
XXMATHILDAZMAGIKXX: i getcha. he's a real buttwad but i wasn't gonna say that if ya actually liked em
XXMATHILDAZMAGIKXX: the Js takin care of ya? i figure you got them on speed dial for lactose free ice cream n bad movies
WIN_FTW: Haha yeah, we're gonna hang out tomorrow.
XXMATHILDAZMAGIKXX: good. and hey, forget about jerk guys. you deserve better
WIN_FTW: If only I could accept a virtuous, romance-free, monk-like lifestyle, but alas, I am too desperate and boys are too convincing
XXMATHILDAZMAGIKXX: or you could go out with me
or you could go out with me
I froze, my heart pounding in my ears. I'd never felt my chest flutter like that before.

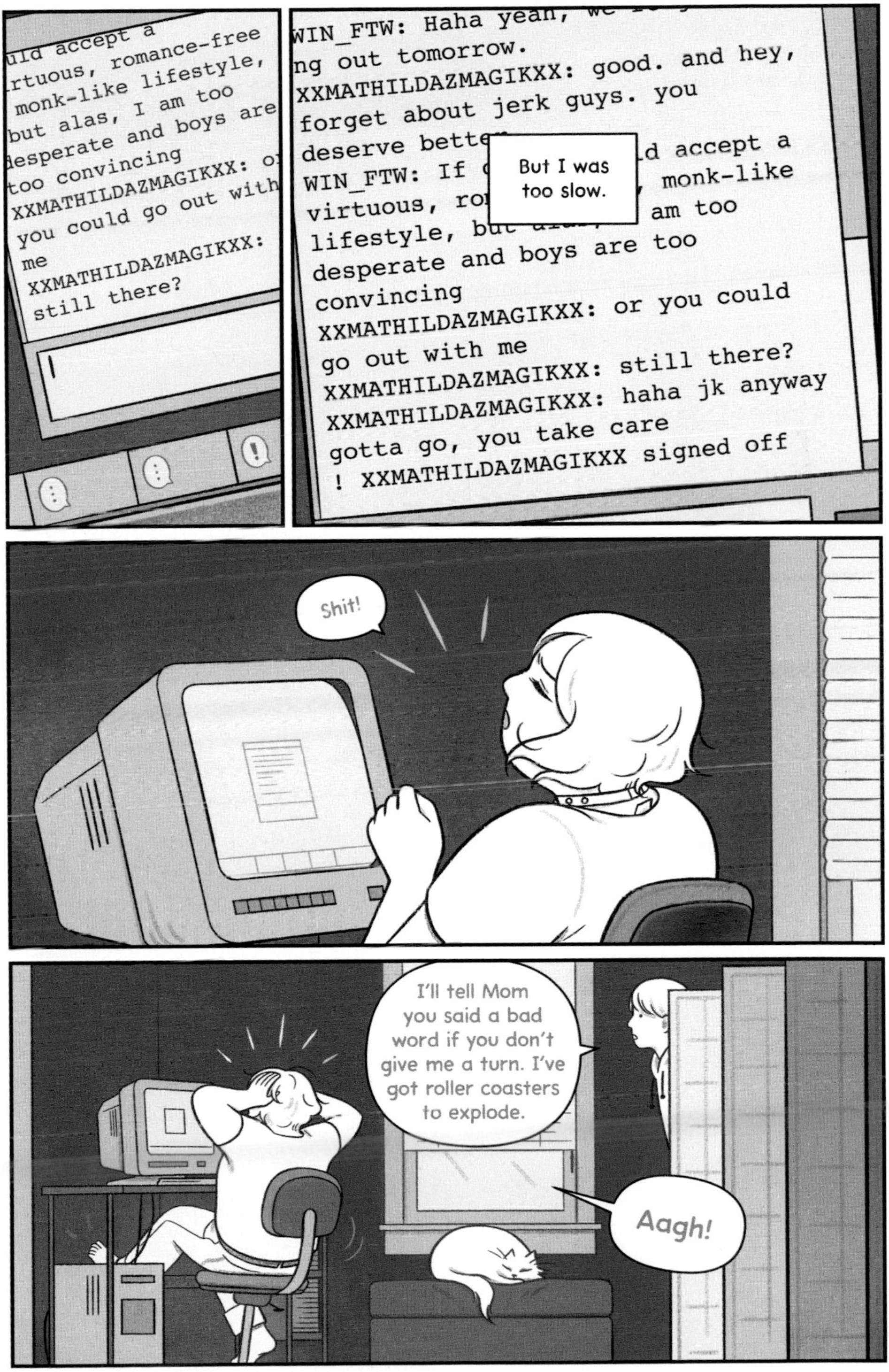

ng out tomorrow.
XXMATHILDAZMAGIKXX: good. and hey,
forget about jerk guys. you
desperate and boys are too
convincing
XXMATHILDAZMAGIKXX: or you could
go out with me
XXMATHILDAZMAGIKXX: still there?
XXMATHILDAZMAGIKXX: haha jk anyway
gotta go, you take care
! XXMATHILDAZMAGIKXX signed off
But I was too slow.
Shit!
I'll tell Mom you said a bad word if you don't give me a turn. I've got roller coasters to explode.
Aagh!

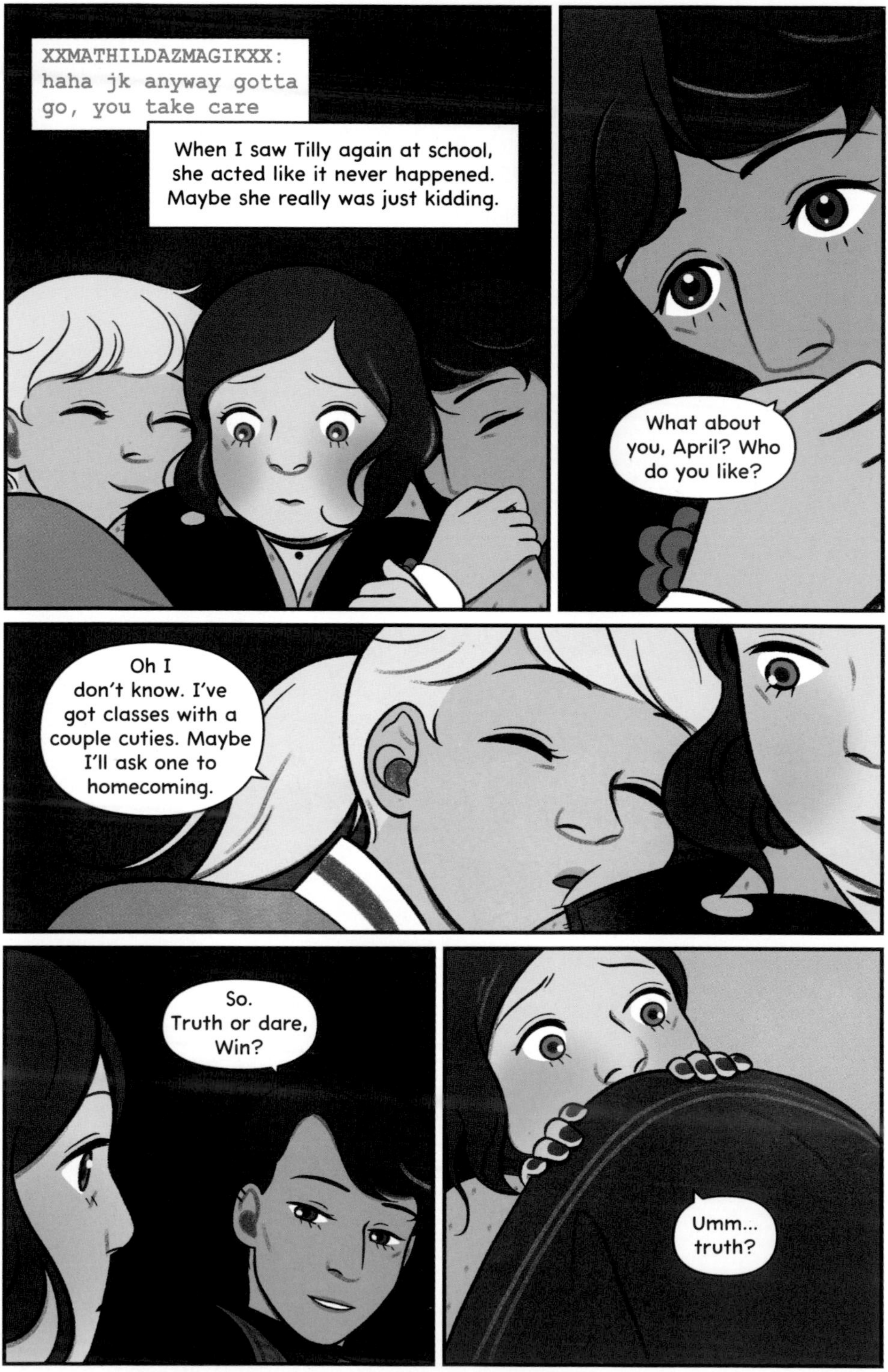
XXMATHILDAZMAGIKXX:
haha jk anyway gotta go, you take care
When I saw Tilly again at school, she acted like it never happened. Maybe she really was just kidding.
What about you, April? Who do you like?
Oh I don't know. I've got classes with a couple cuties. Maybe I'll ask one to homecoming.
So. Truth or dare, Win?
Umm... truth?

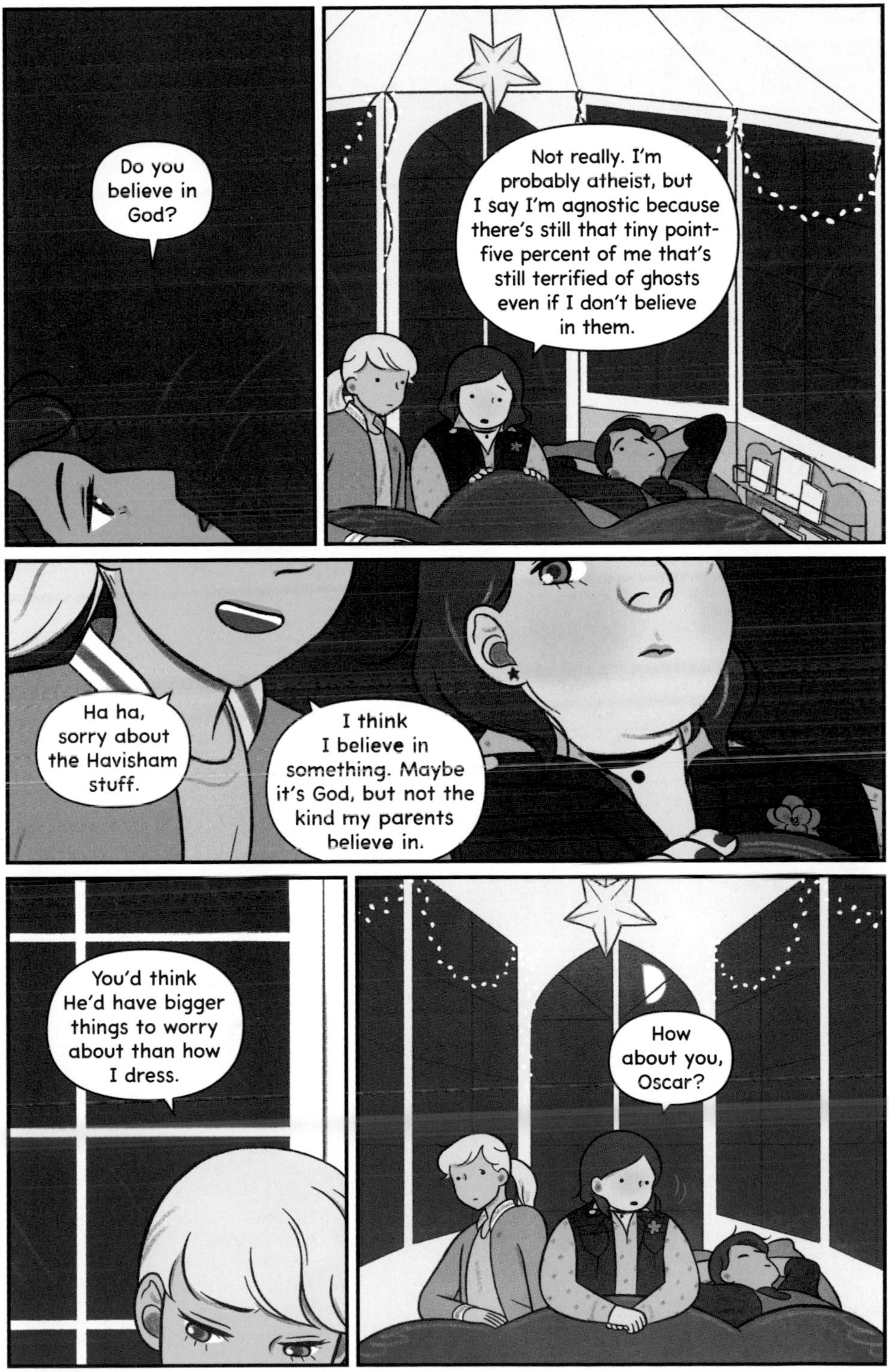
Do you believe in God?
Not really. I'm probably atheist, but I say I'm agnostic because there's still that tiny point-five percent of me that's still terrified of ghosts even if I don't believe in them.
Ha ha, sorry about the Havisham stuff.
I think I believe in something. Maybe it's God, but not the kind my parents believe in.
You'd think He'd have bigger things to worry about than how I dress.
How about you, Oscar?

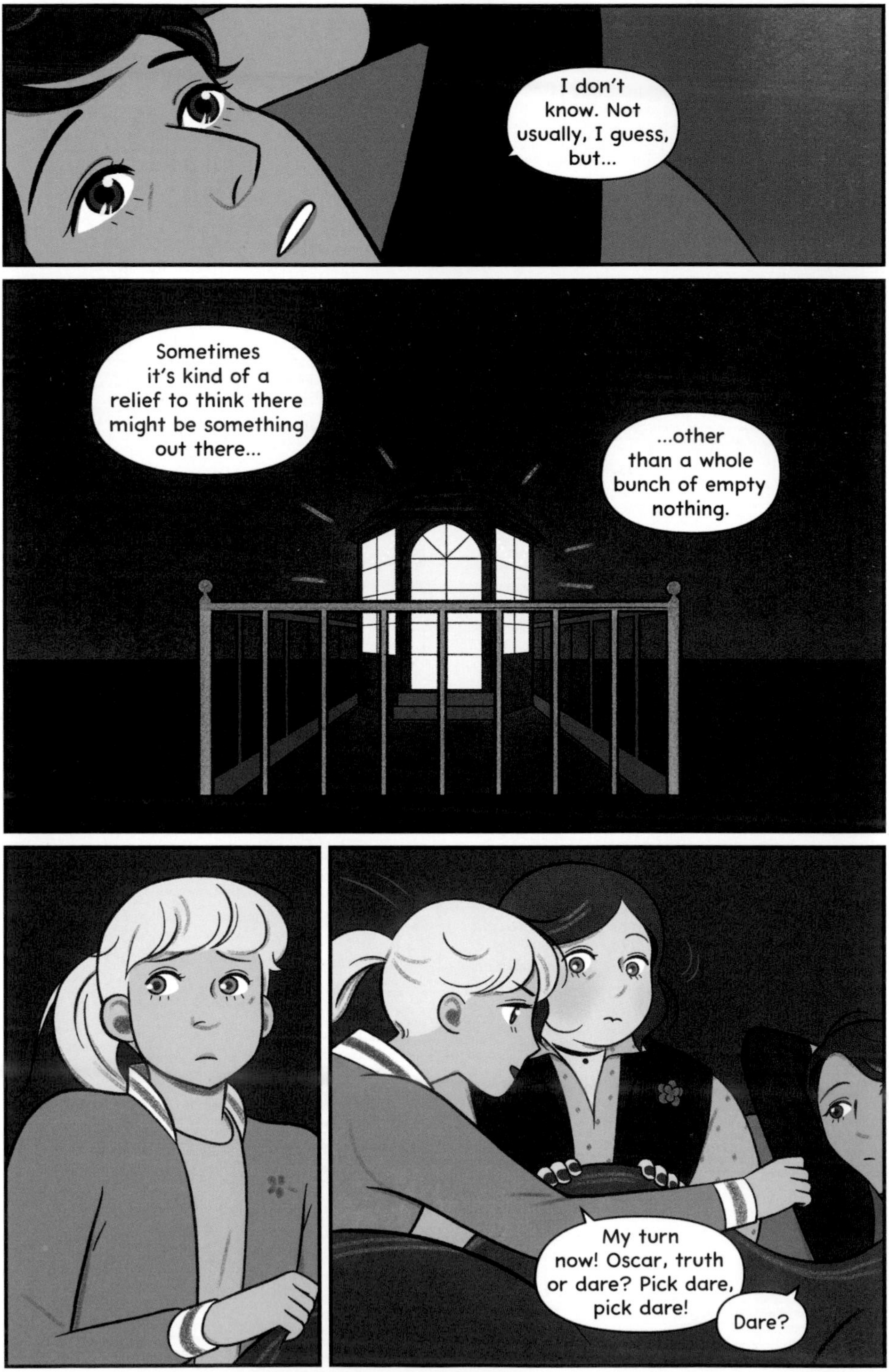

I don't know. Not usually, I guess, but...
Sometimes it's kind of a relief to think there might be something out there...
...other than a whole bunch of empty nothing.
My turn now! Oscar, truth or dare? Pick dare, pick dare!
Dare?

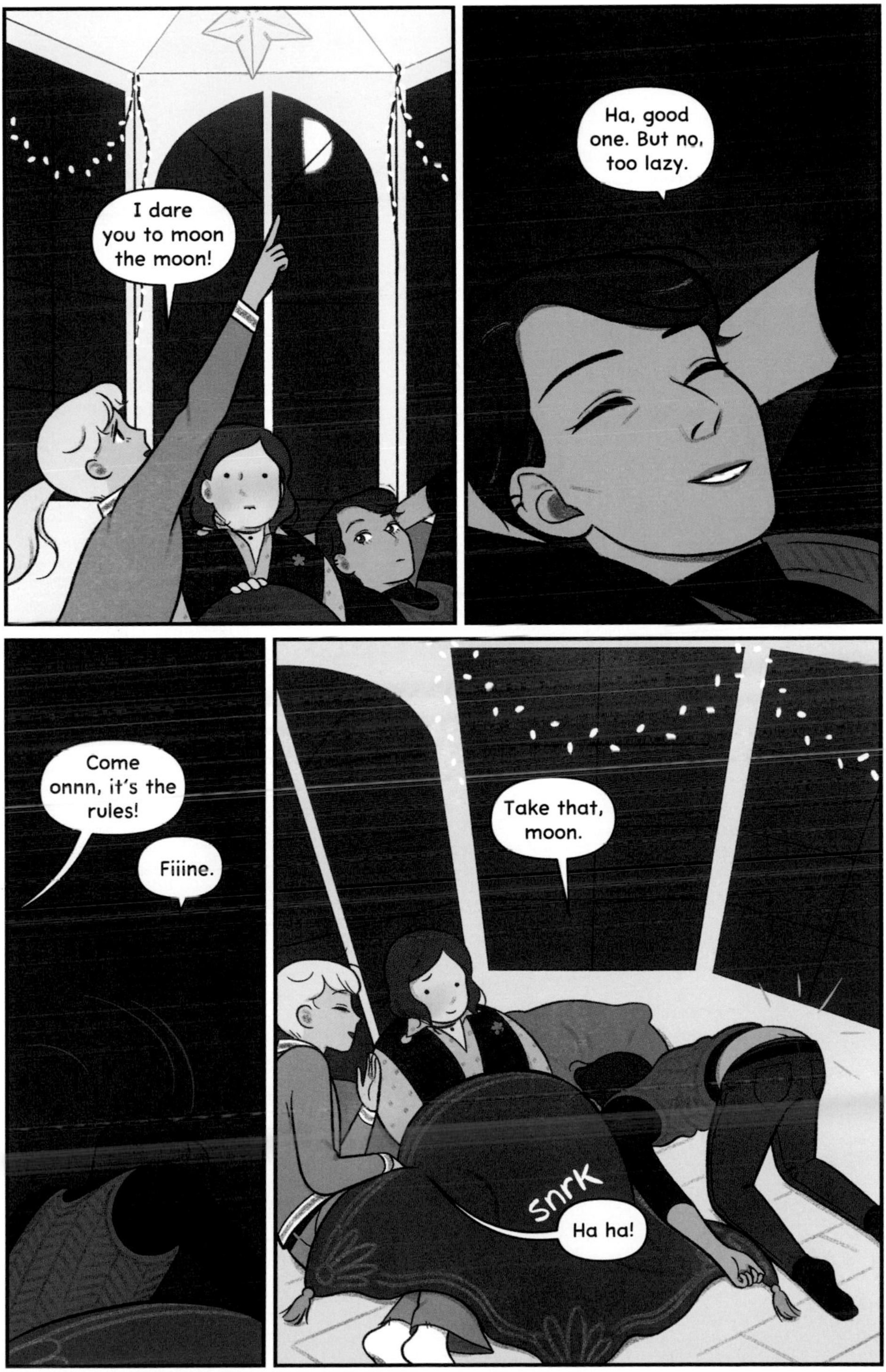
I dare you to moon the moon!
Ha, good one. But no, too lazy.
Come onnn, it's the rules!
Fiiine.
Take that, moon.
snrk
Ha ha!

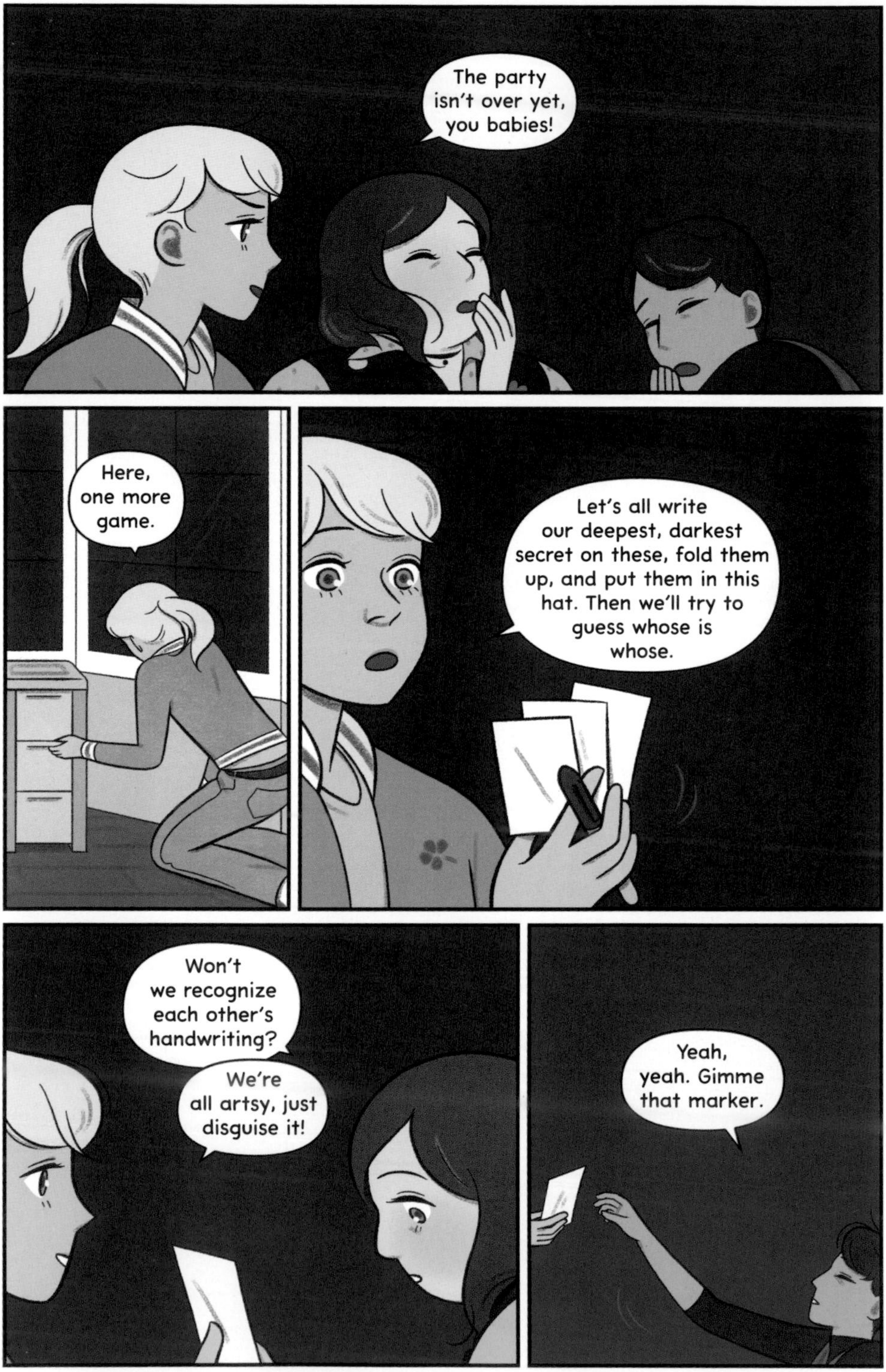
The party isn't over yet, you babies!
Here, one more game.
Let's all write our deepest, darkest secret on these, fold them up, and put them in this hat. Then we'll try to guess whose is whose.
Won't we recognize each other's handwriting?
We're all artsy, just disguise it!
Yeah, yeah. Gimme that marker.

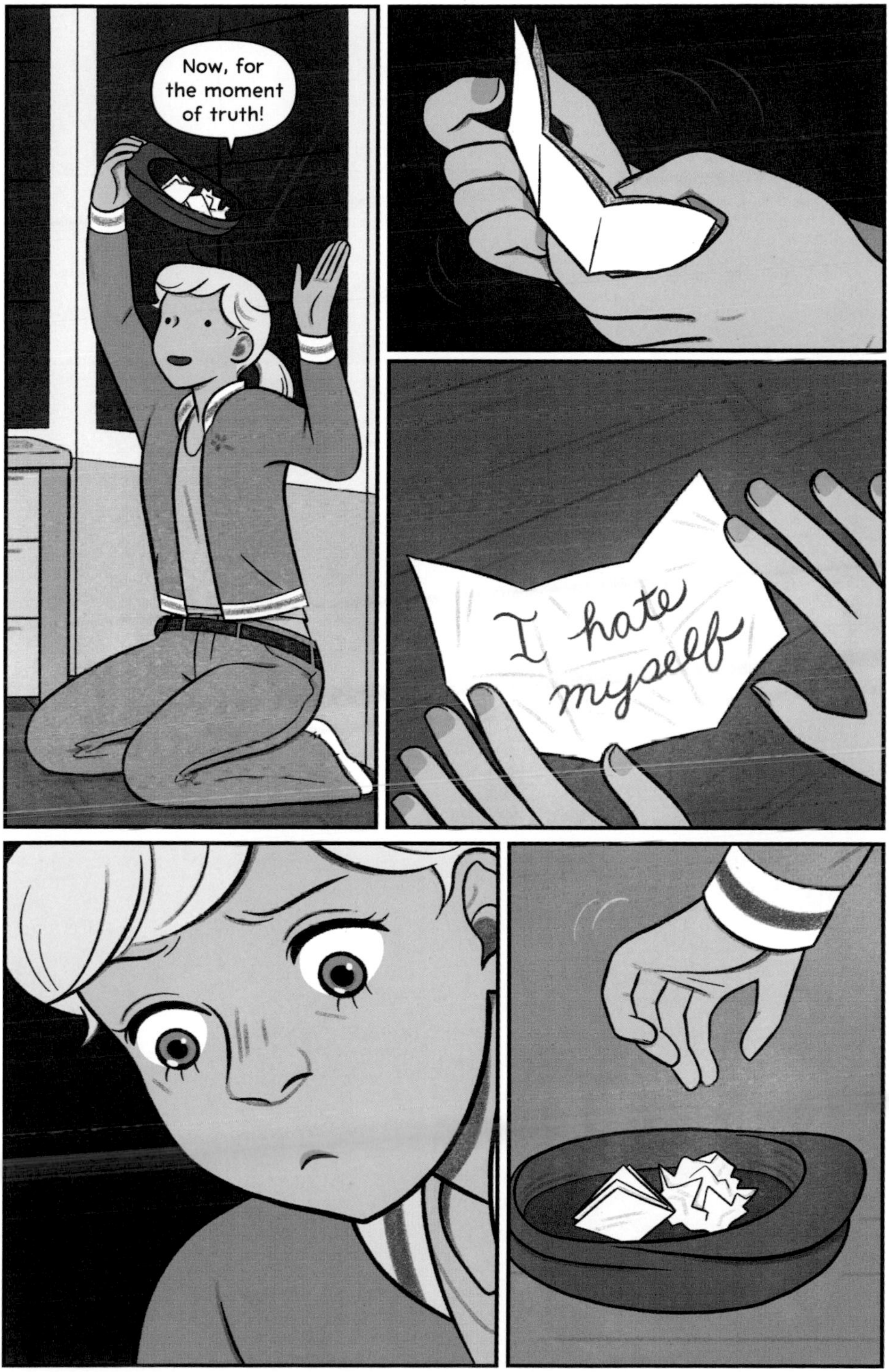
Now, for the moment of truth!
I hate myself

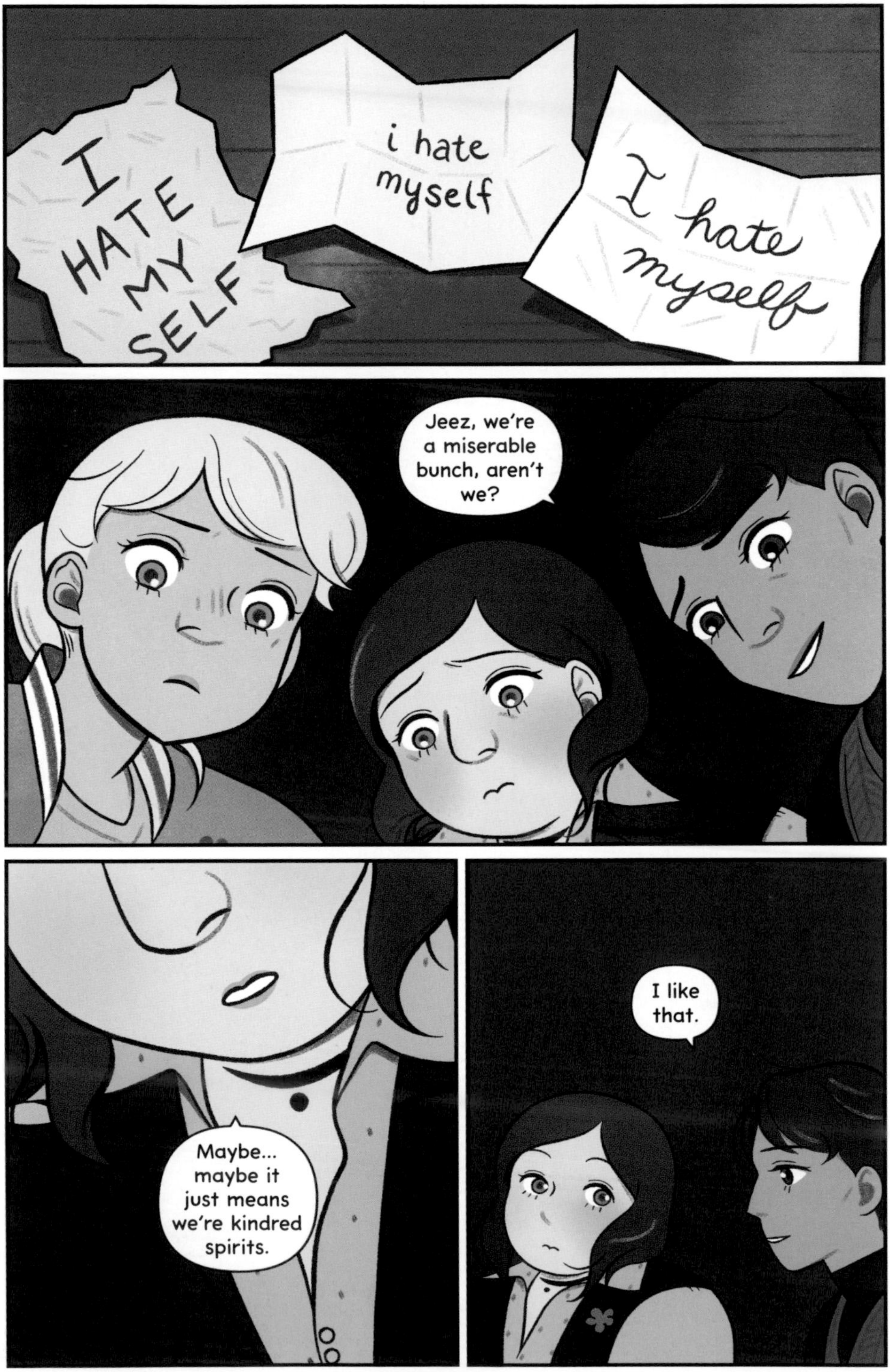
I HATE MY SELF
i hate myself
I hate myself
Jeez, we're a miserable bunch, aren't we?
Maybe... maybe it just means we're kindred spirits.
I like that.

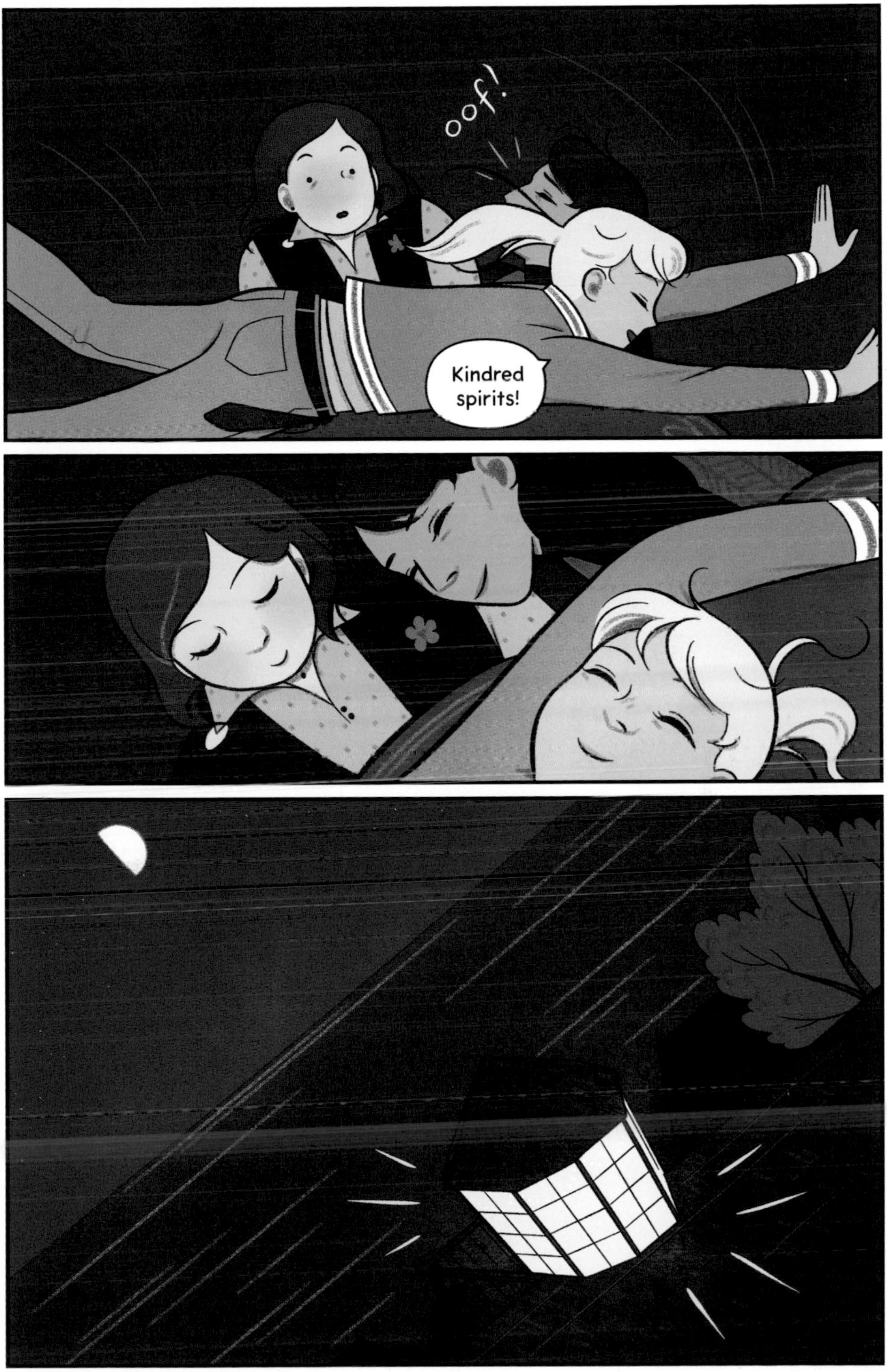
oof!
Kindred spirits!

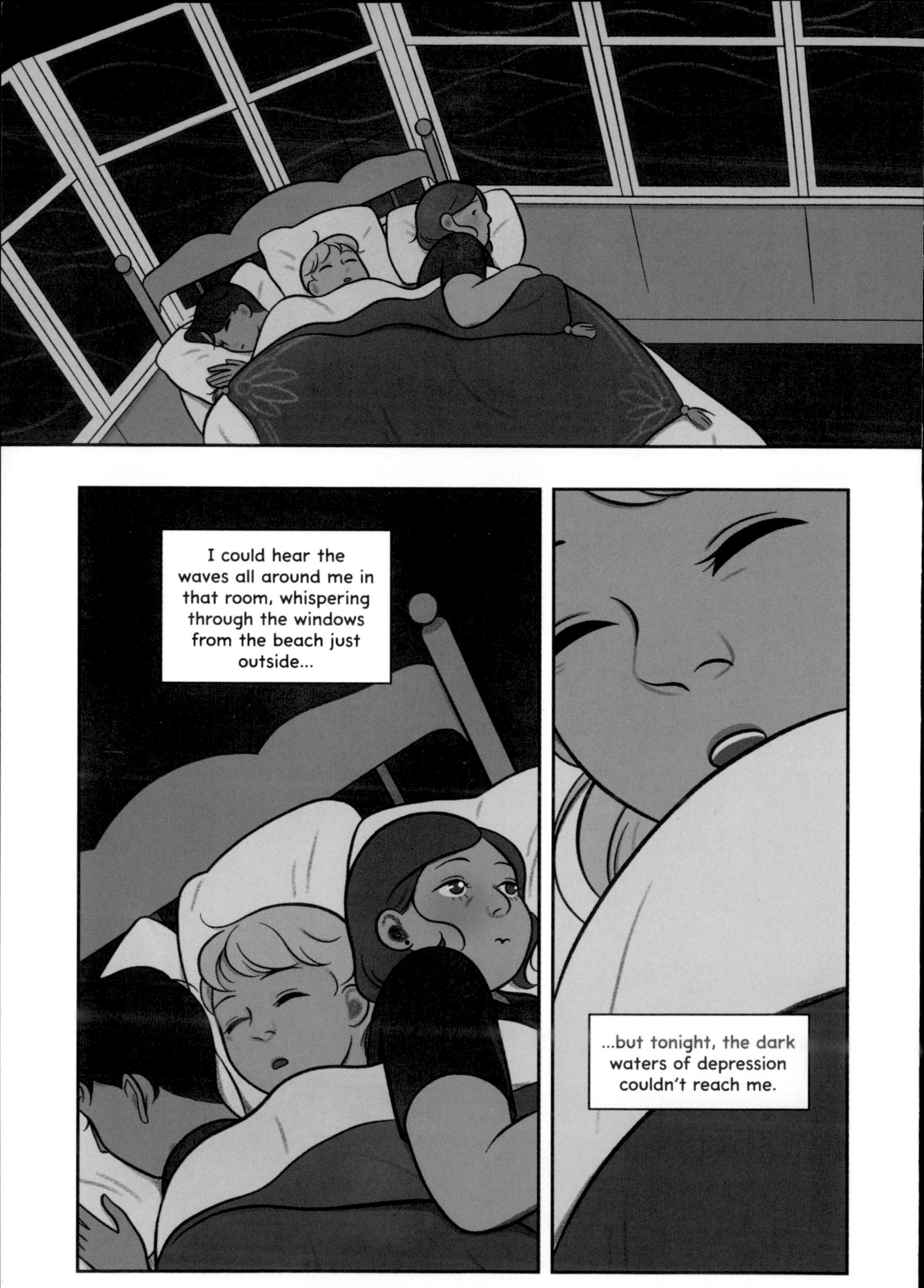
I could hear the waves all around me in that room, whispering through the windows from the beach just outside...
...but tonight, the dark waters of depression couldn't reach me.

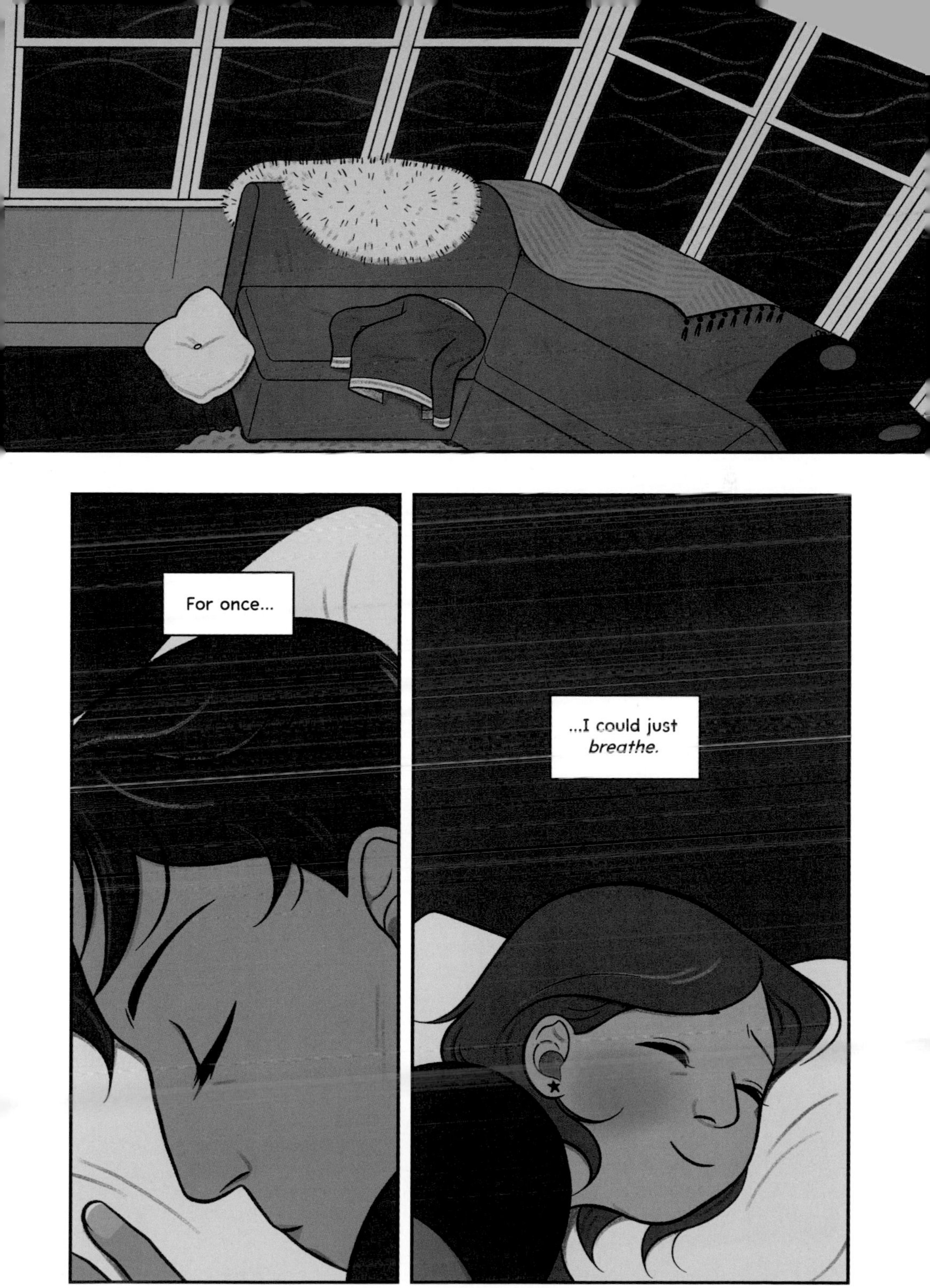
For once...
...I could just *breathe.*

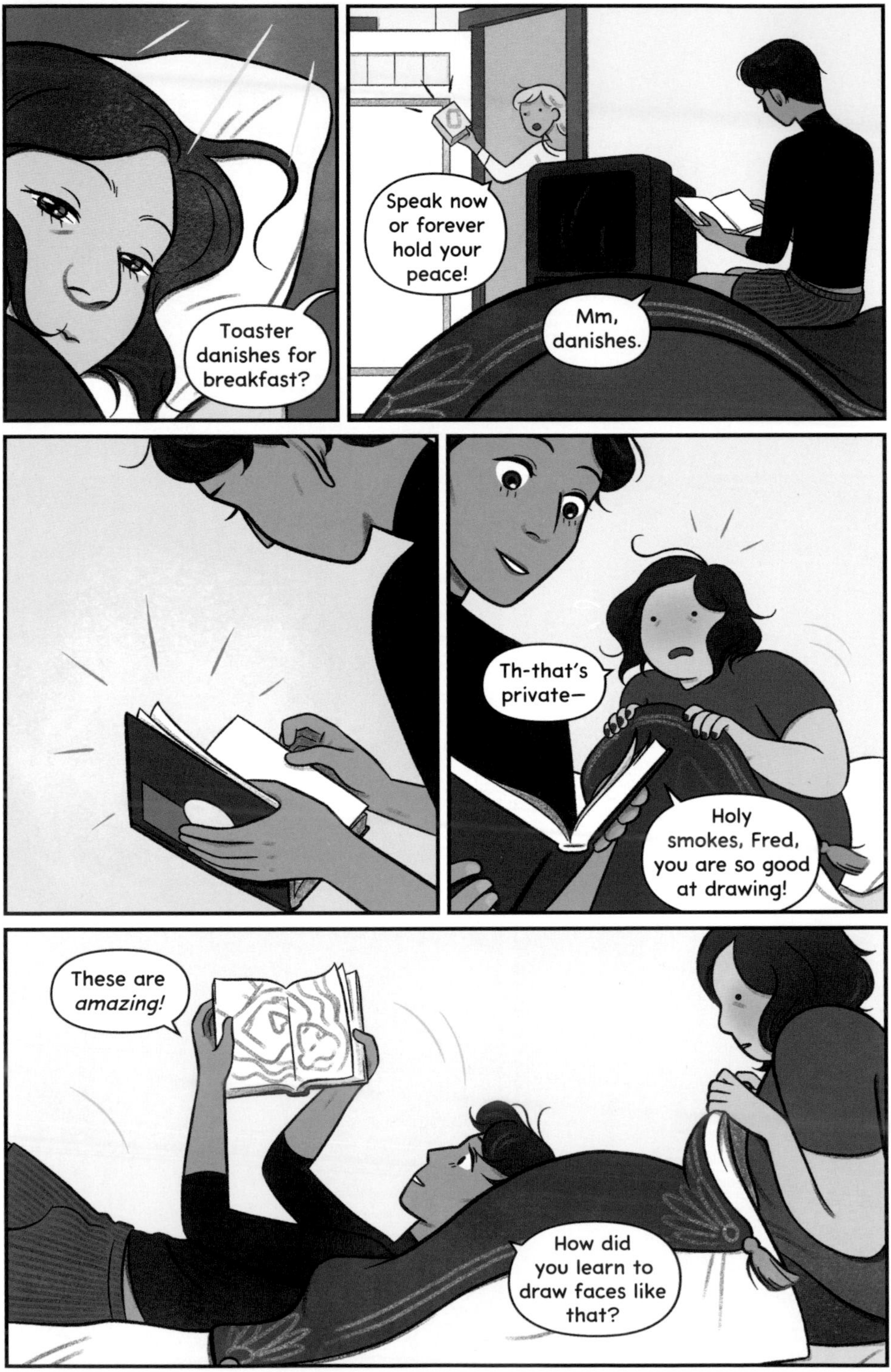
Toaster danishes for breakfast?
Speak now or forever hold your peace!
Mm, danishes.
Th-that's private—
Holy smokes, Fred, you are so good at drawing!
These are *amazing!*
How did you learn to draw faces like that?

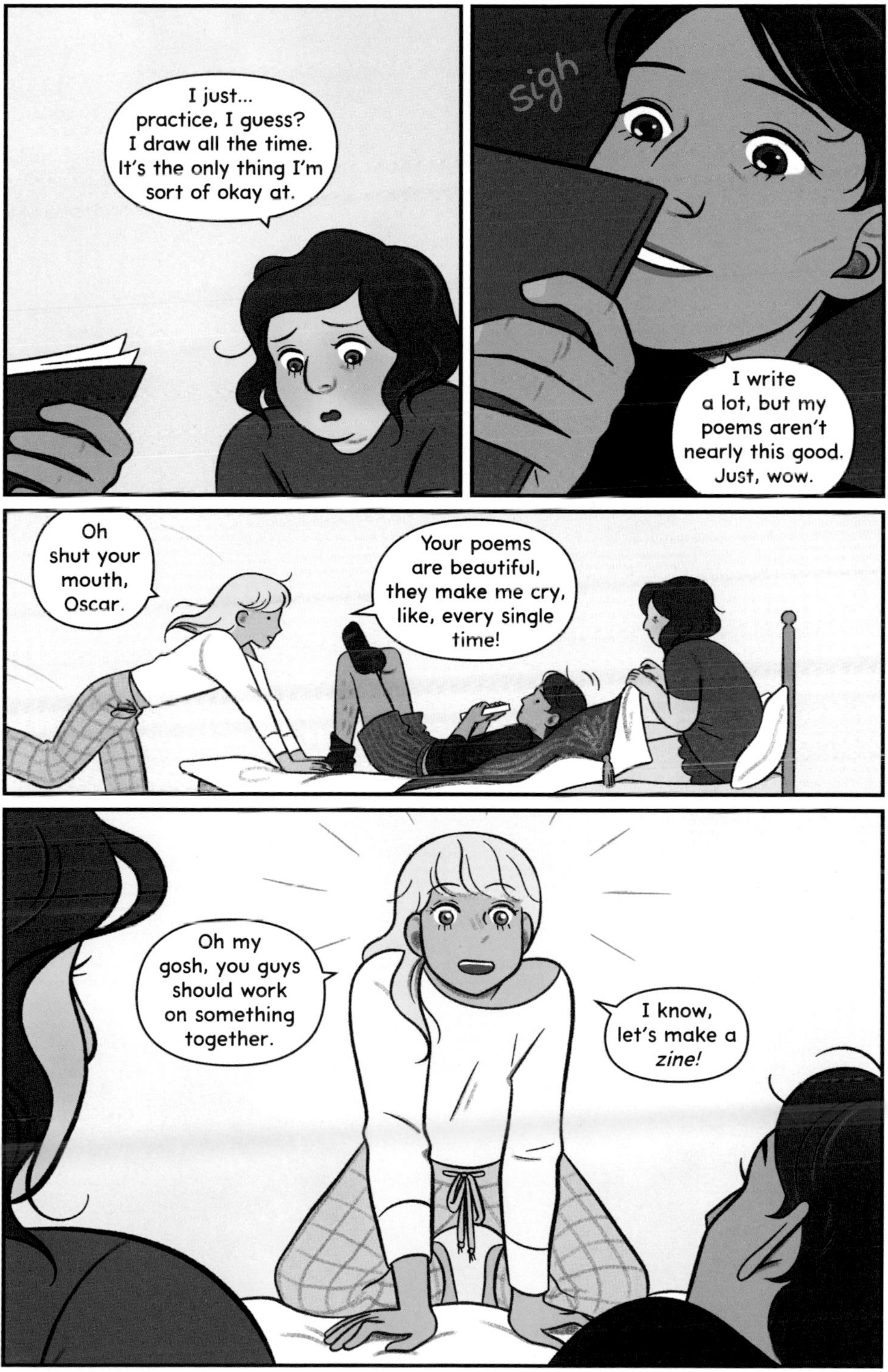
I just... practice, I guess? I draw all the time. It's the only thing I'm sort of okay at.
sigh
I write a lot, but my poems aren't nearly this good. Just, wow.
Oh shut your mouth, Oscar.
Your poems are beautiful, they make me cry, like, every single time!
Oh my gosh, you guys should work on something together.
I know, let's make a *zine!*

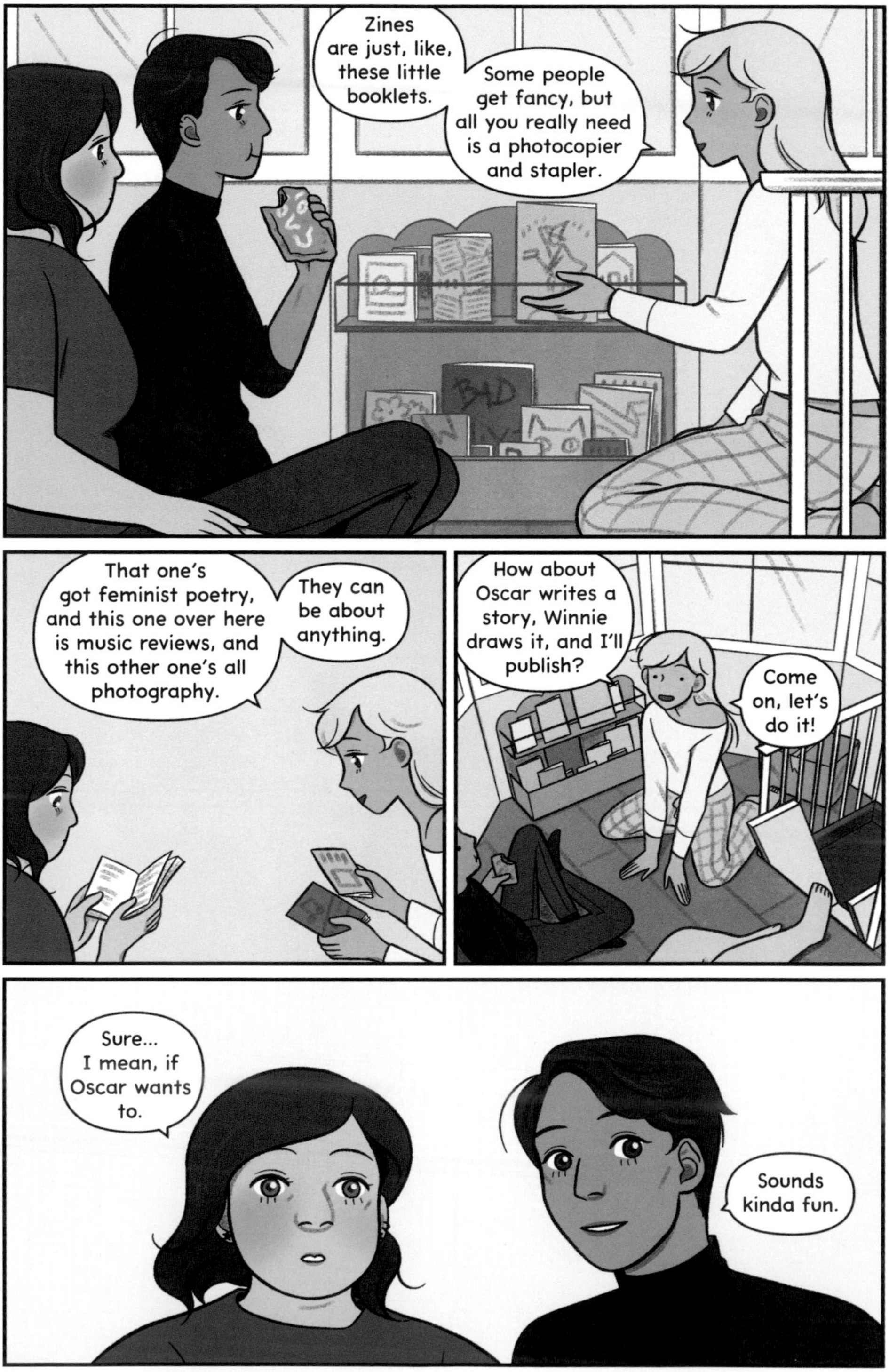
Zines are just, like, these little booklets.
Some people get fancy, but all you really need is a photocopier and stapler.
BAD
That one's got feminist poetry, and this one over here is music reviews, and this other one's all photography.
They can be about anything.
How about Oscar writes a story, Winnie draws it, and I'll publish?
Come on, let's do it!
Sure... I mean, if Oscar wants to.
Sounds kinda fun.

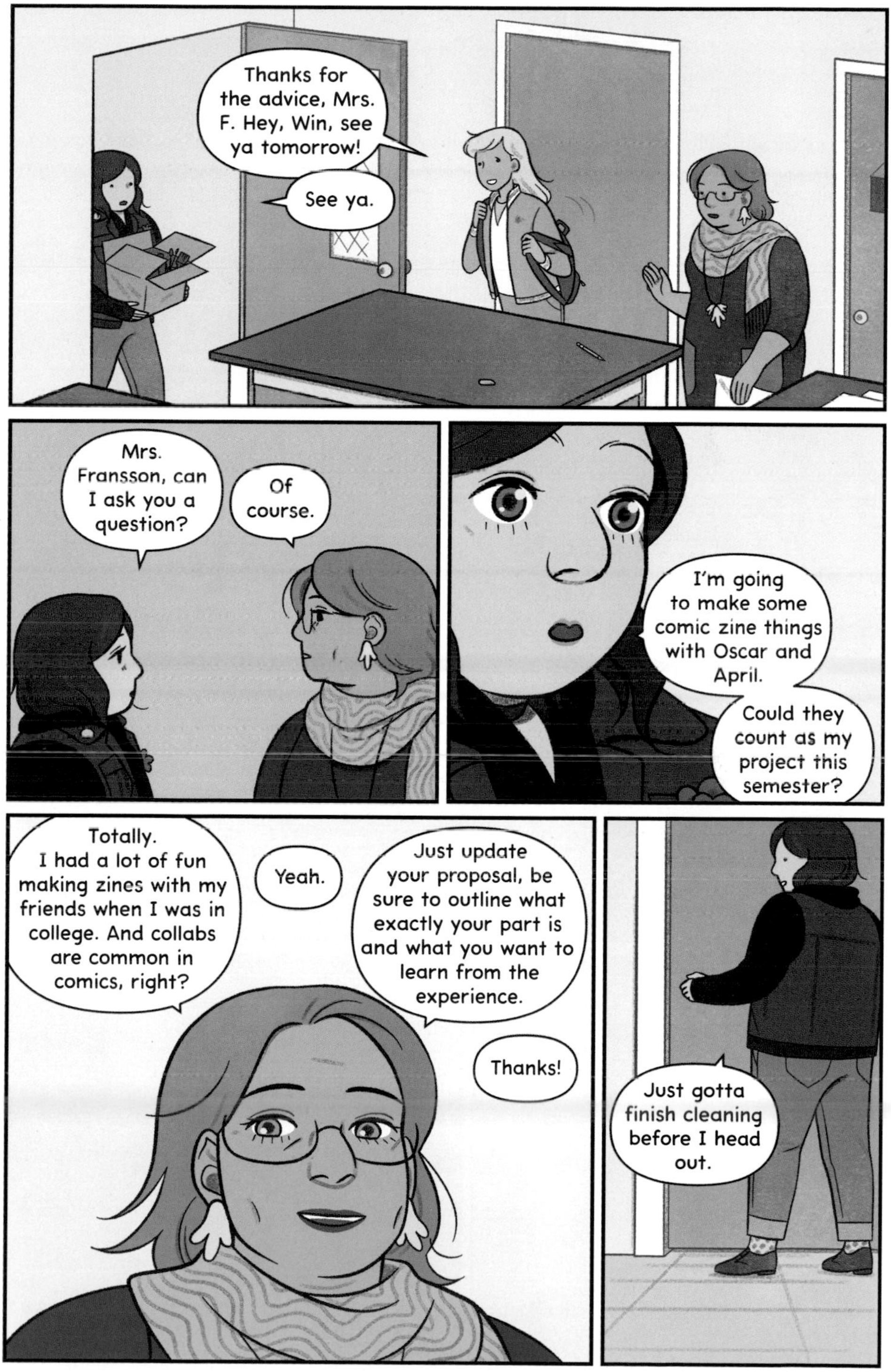
Thanks for the advice, Mrs. F. Hey, Win, see ya tomorrow!
See ya.
Mrs. Fransson, can I ask you a question?
Of course.
I'm going to make some comic zine things with Oscar and April.
Could they count as my project this semester?
Totally. I had a lot of fun making zines with my friends when I was in college. And collabs are common in comics, right?
Yeah.
Just update your proposal, be sure to outline what exactly your part is and what you want to learn from the experience.
Thanks!
Just gotta finish cleaning before I head out.

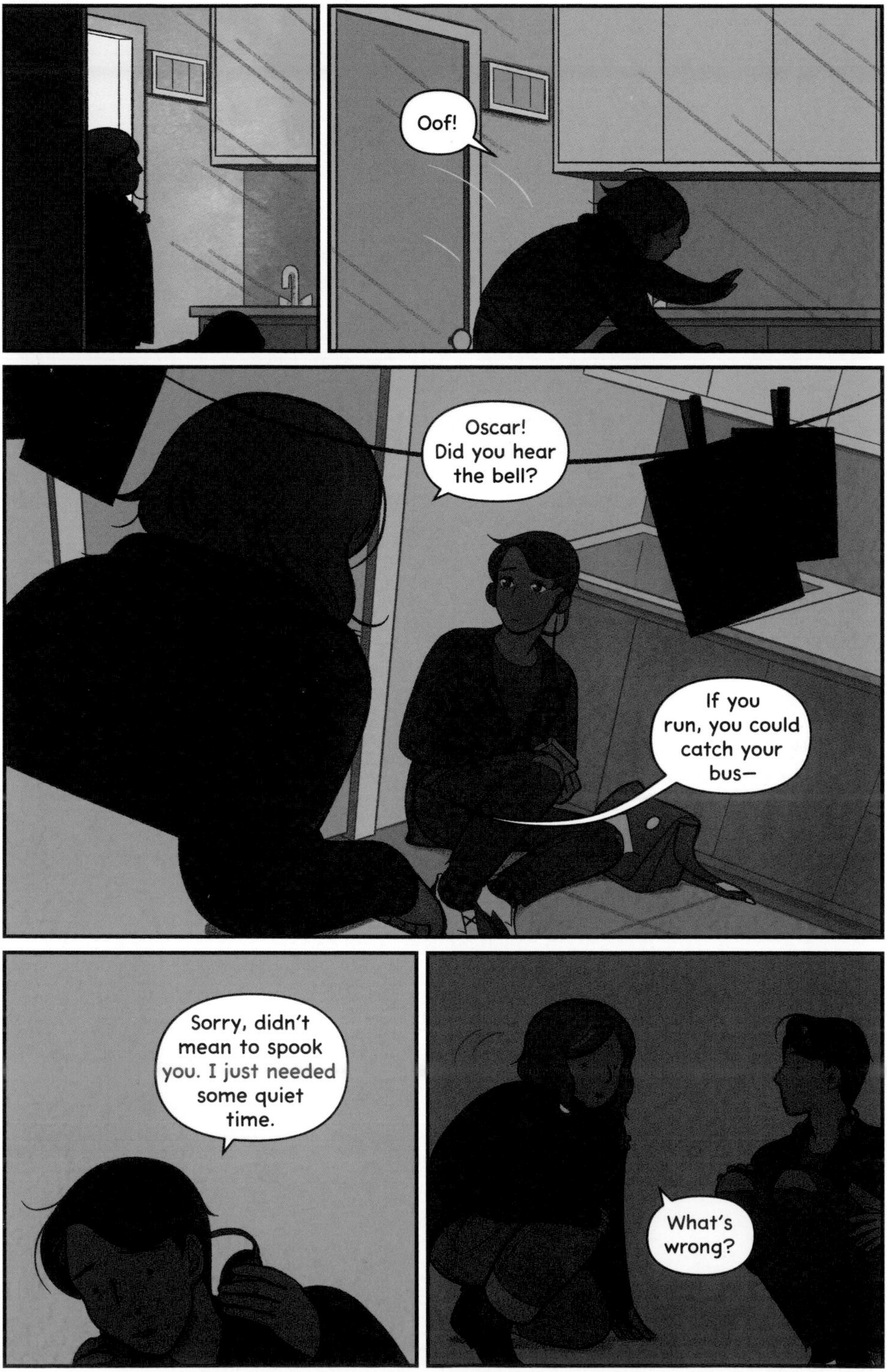
Oof!
Oscar! Did you hear the bell?
If you run, you could catch your bus—
Sorry, didn't mean to spook you. I just needed some quiet time.
What's wrong?

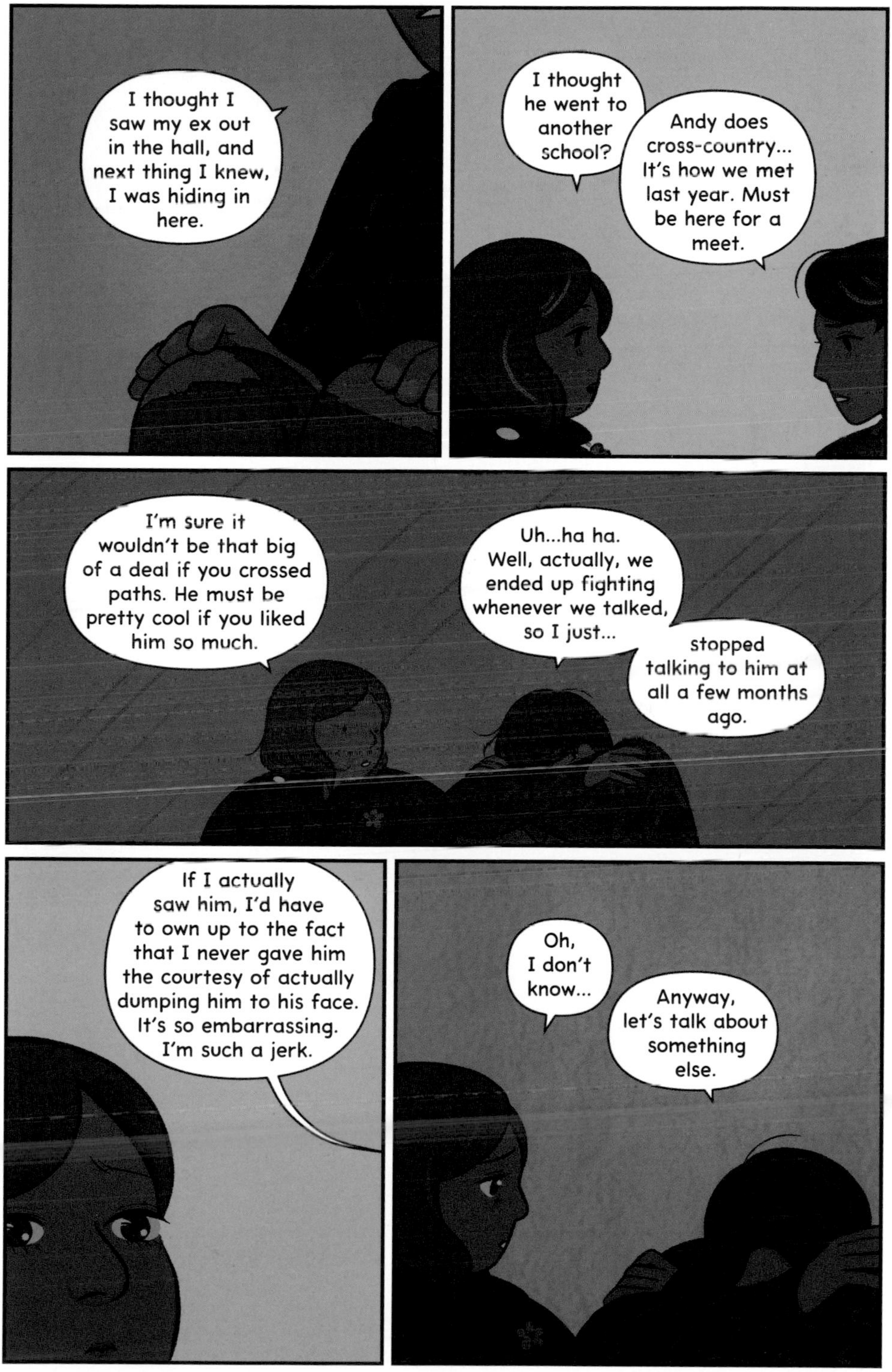

I thought I saw my ex out in the hall, and next thing I knew, I was hiding in here.
I thought he went to another school?
Andy does cross-country... It's how we met last year. Must be here for a meet.
I'm sure it wouldn't be that big of a deal if you crossed paths. He must be pretty cool if you liked him so much.
Uh...ha ha. Well, actually, we ended up fighting whenever we talked, so I just...
stopped talking to him at all a few months ago.
If I actually saw him, I'd have to own up to the fact that I never gave him the courtesy of actually dumping him to his face. It's so embarrassing. I'm such a jerk.
Oh, I don't know...
Anyway, let's talk about something else.

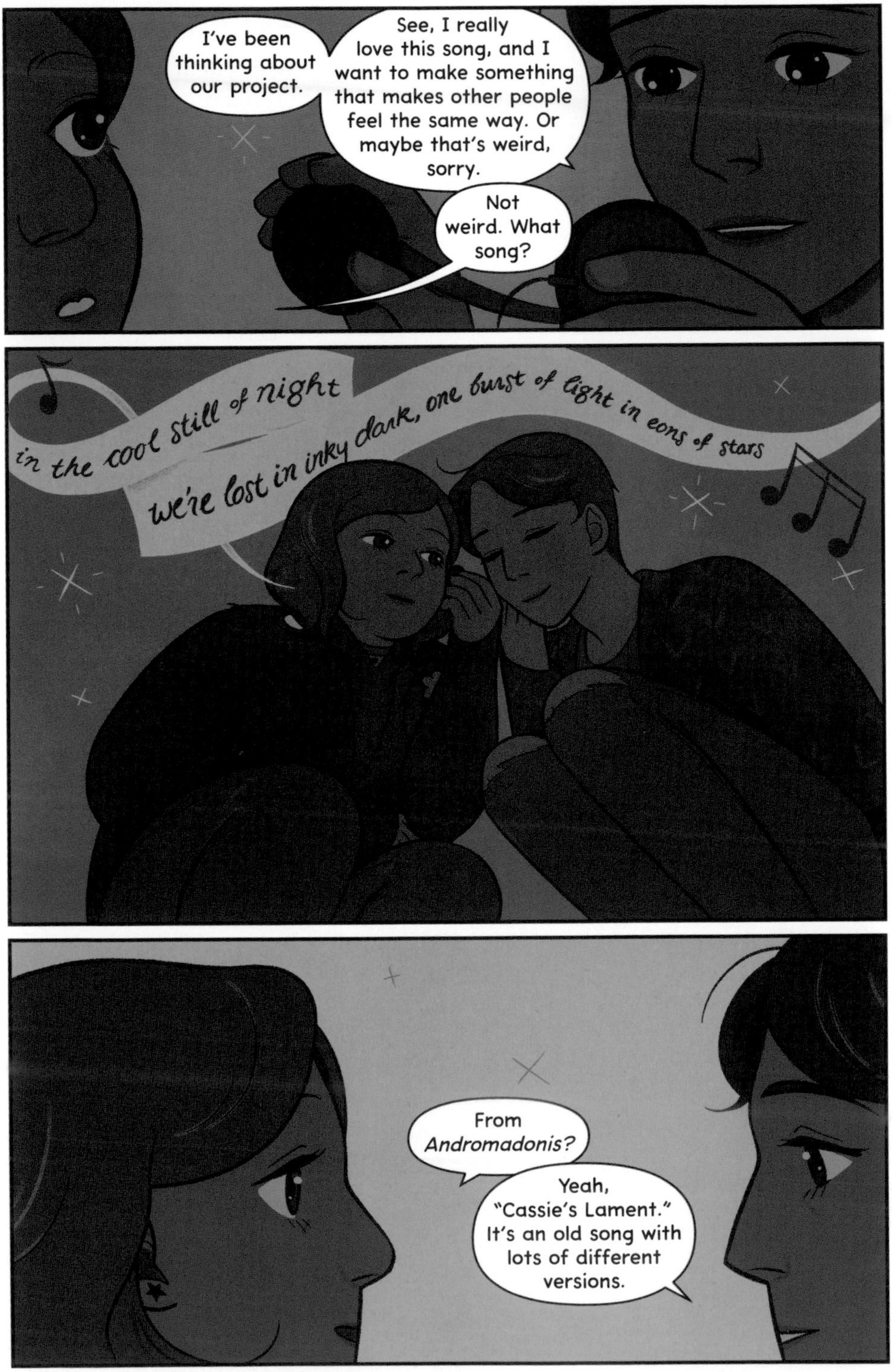
I've been thinking about our project.
See, I really love this song, and I want to make something that makes other people feel the same way. Or maybe that's weird, sorry.
Not weird. What song?
in the cool still of night
we're lost in inky dark, one burst of light in eons of stars
From *Andromadonis?*
Yeah, "Cassie's Lament." It's an old song with lots of different versions.

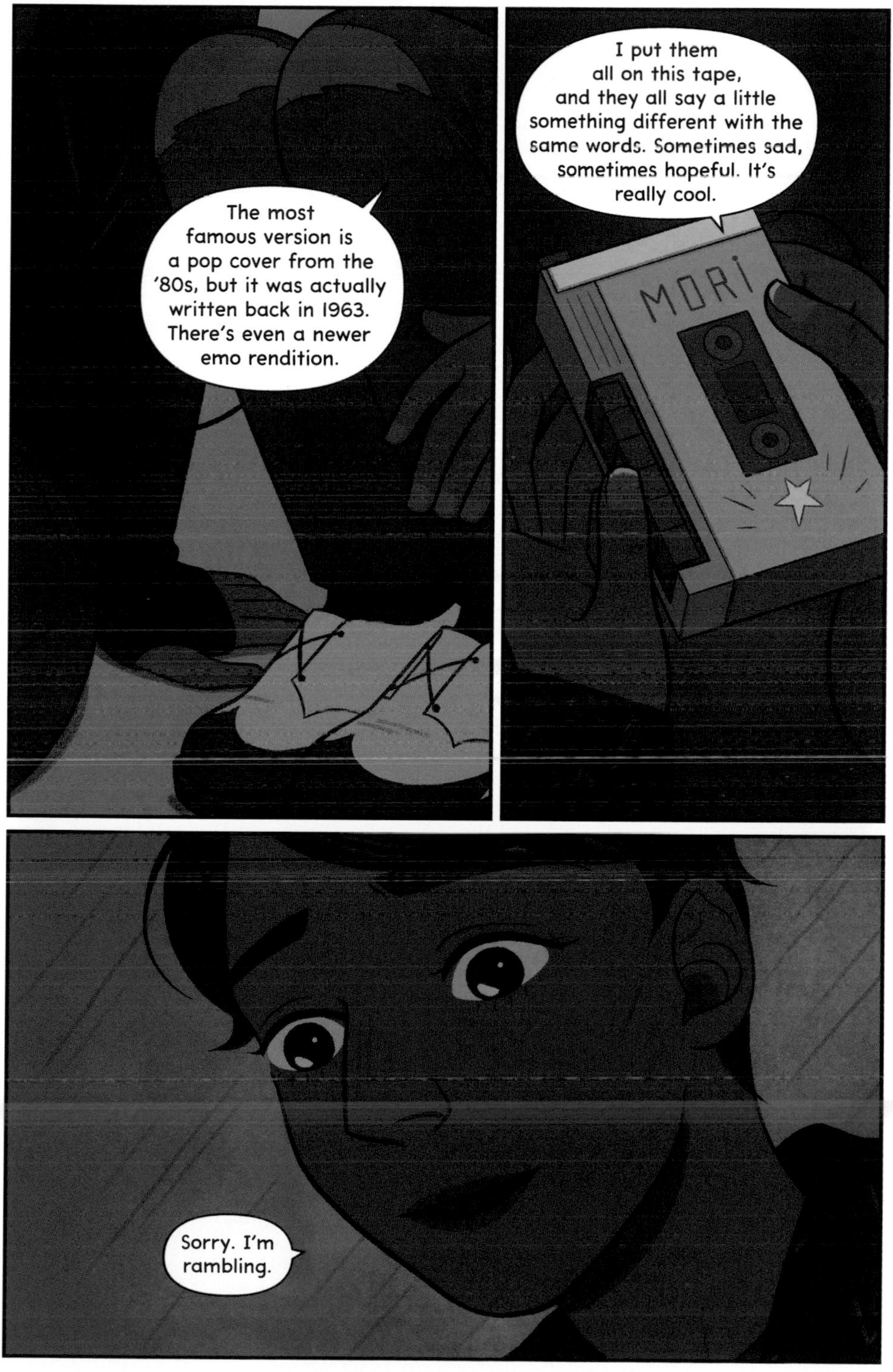
The most famous version is a pop cover from the '80s, but it was actually written back in 1963. There's even a newer emo rendition.
I put them all on this tape, and they all say a little something different with the same words. Sometimes sad, sometimes hopeful. It's really cool.
MORI
Sorry. I'm rambling.

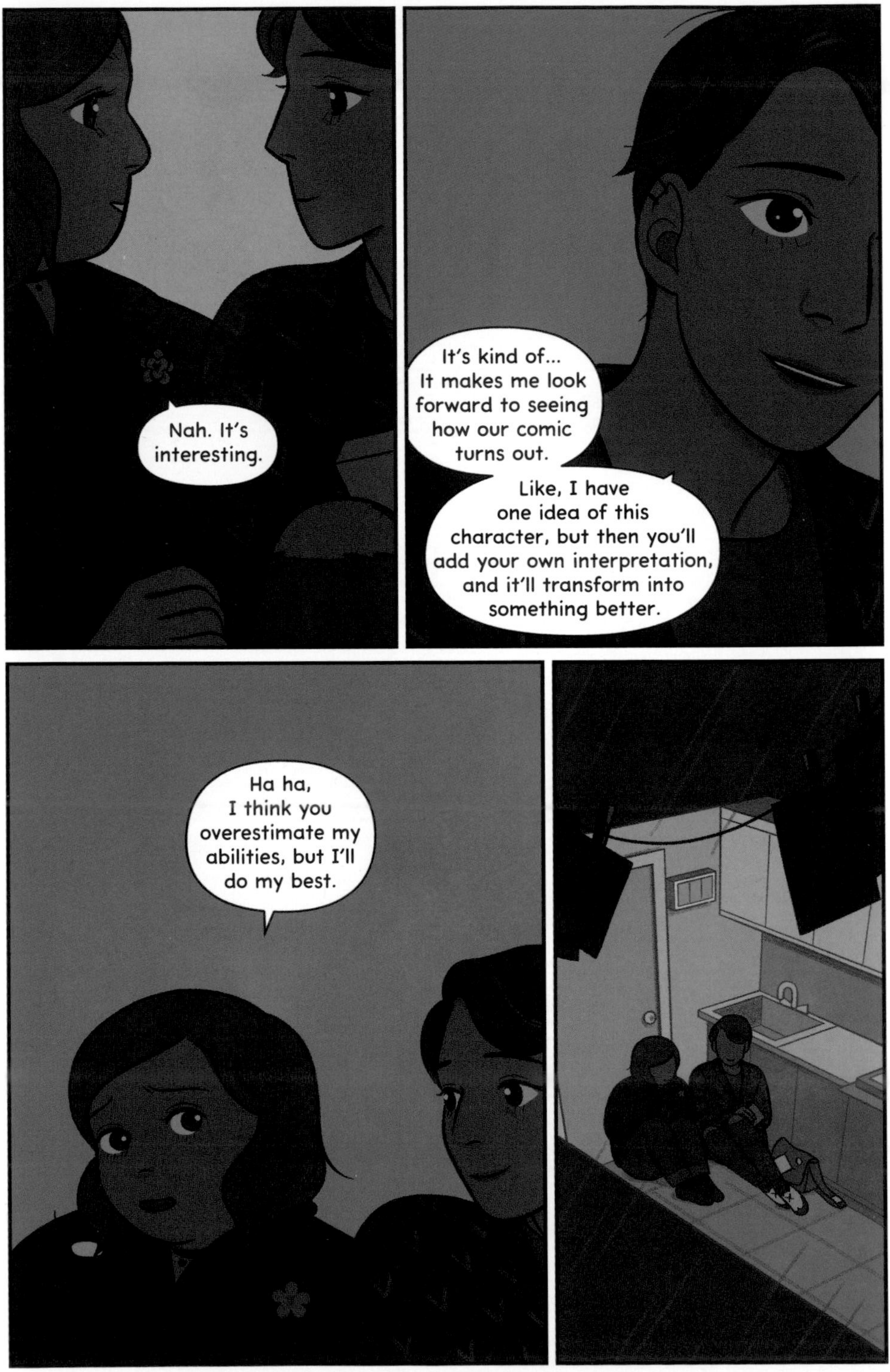
Nah. It's interesting.
It's kind of... It makes me look forward to seeing how our comic turns out.
Like, I have one idea of this character, but then you'll add your own interpretation, and it'll transform into something better.
Ha ha, I think you overestimate my abilities, but I'll do my best.

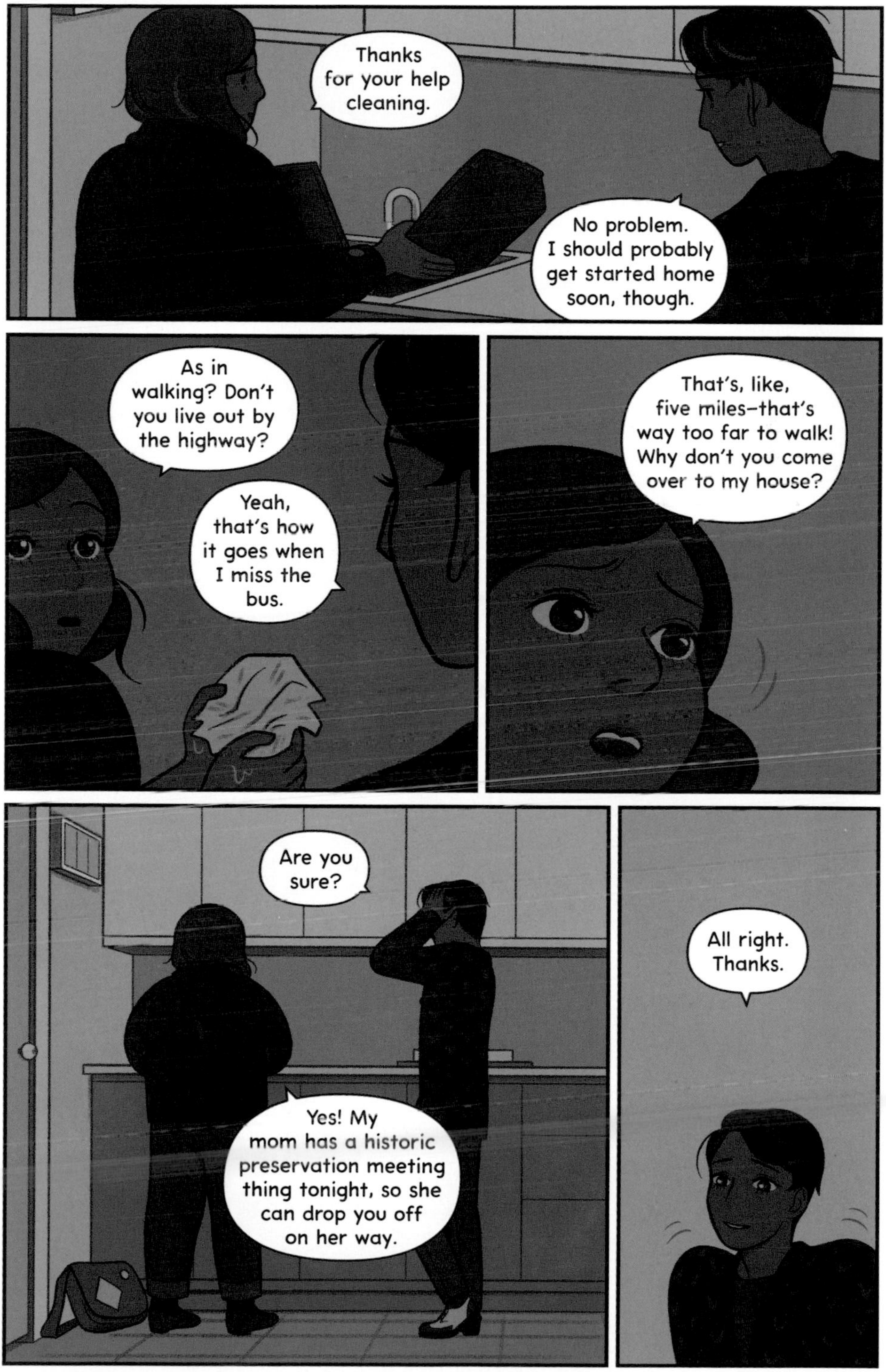

Thanks for your help cleaning.
No problem. I should probably get started home soon, though.
As in walking? Don't you live out by the highway?
Yeah, that's how it goes when I miss the bus.
That's, like, five miles—that's way too far to walk! Why don't you come over to my house?
Are you sure?
Yes! My mom has a historic preservation meeting thing tonight, so she can drop you off on her way.
All right. Thanks.

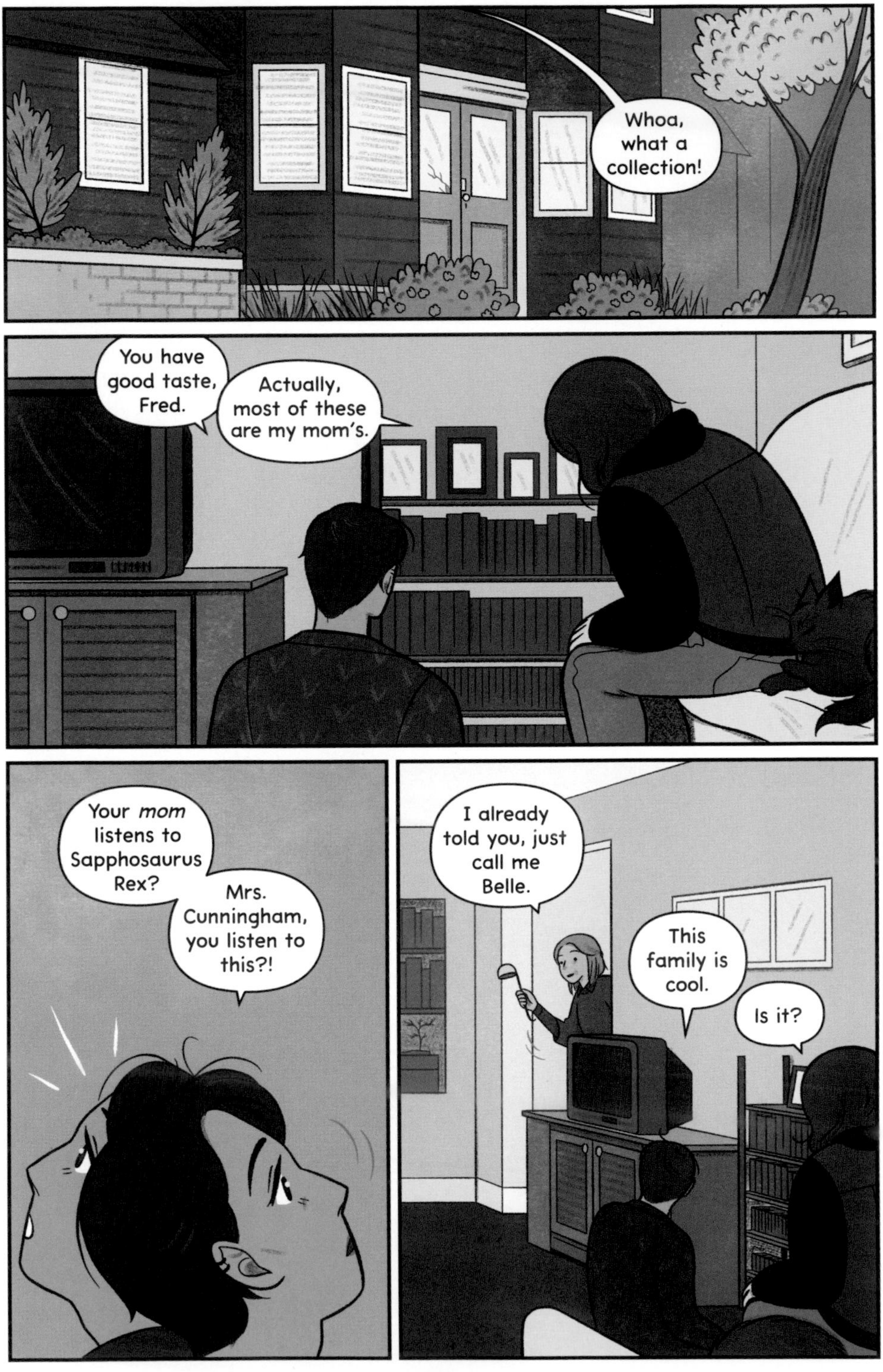
Whoa, what a collection!
You have good taste, Fred.
Actually, most of these are my mom's.
Your *mom* listens to Sapphosaurus Rex?
Mrs. Cunningham, you listen to this?!
I already told you, just call me Belle.
This family is cool.
Is it?

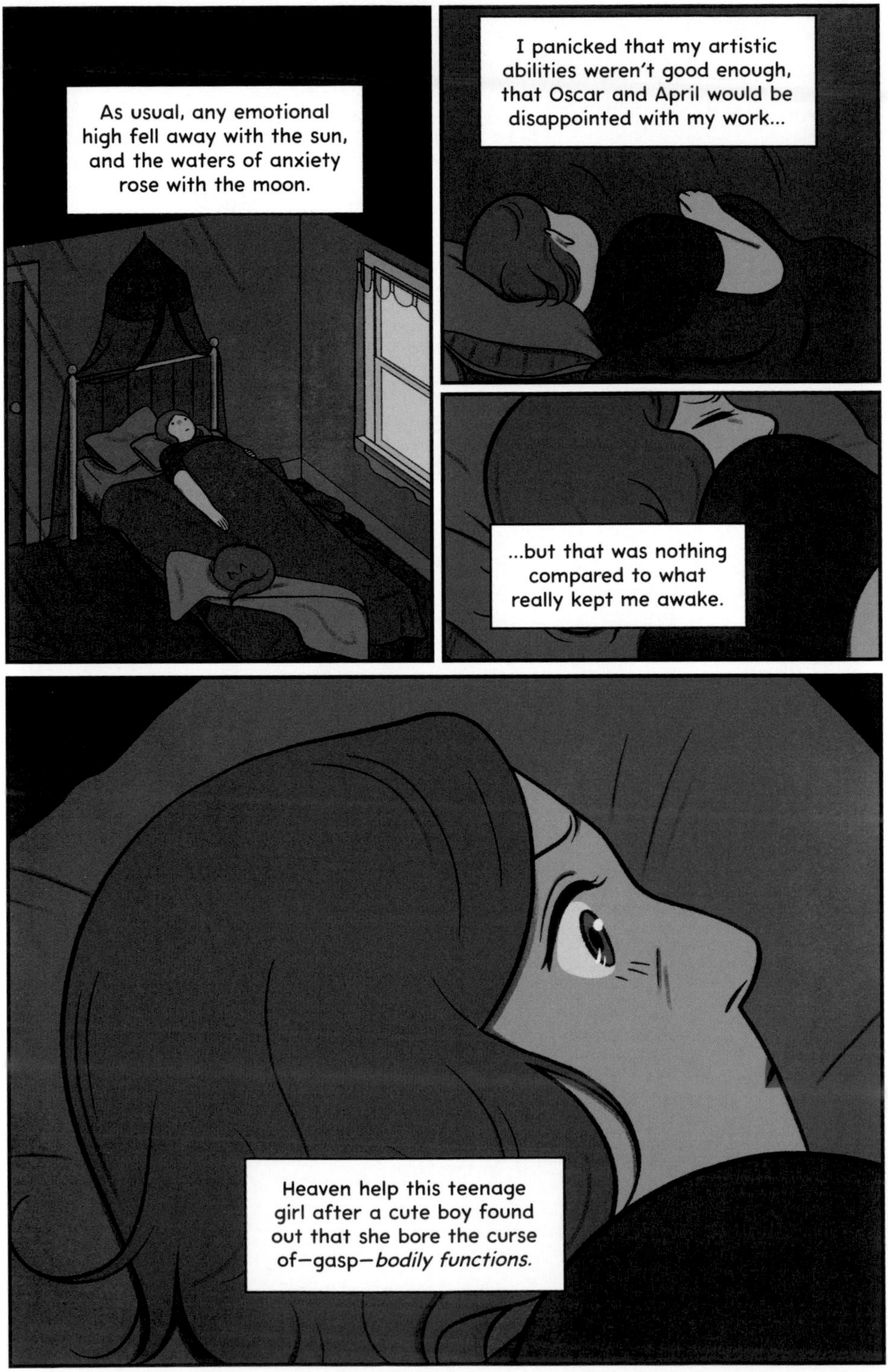
As usual, any emotional high fell away with the sun, and the waters of anxiety rose with the moon.
I panicked that my artistic abilities weren't good enough, that Oscar and April would be disappointed with my work...
...but that was nothing compared to what really kept me awake.
Heaven help this teenage girl after a cute boy found out that she bore the curse of—gasp—*bodily functions.*

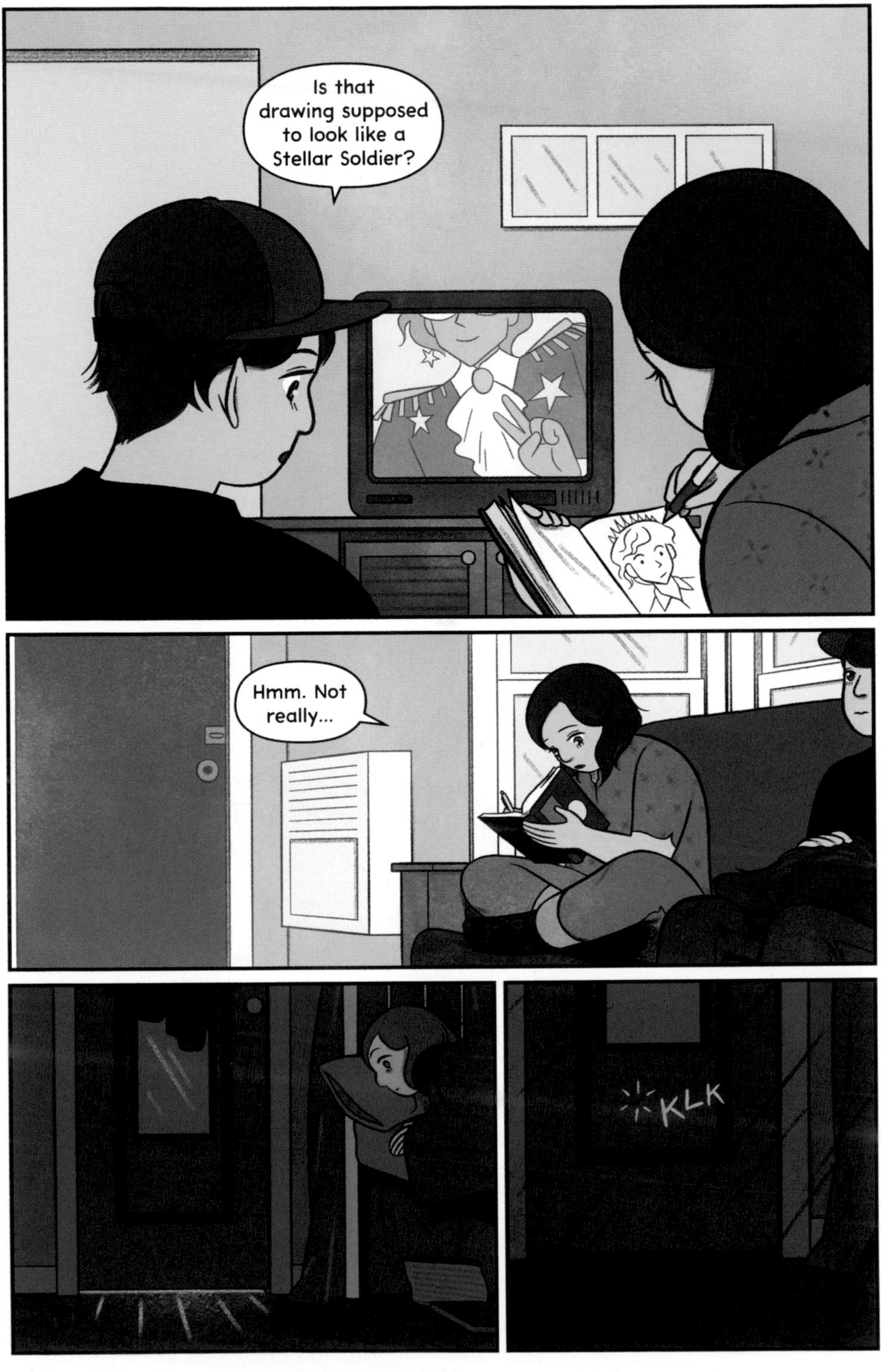

Is that drawing supposed to look like a Stellar Soldier?
Hmm. Not really...
KLK

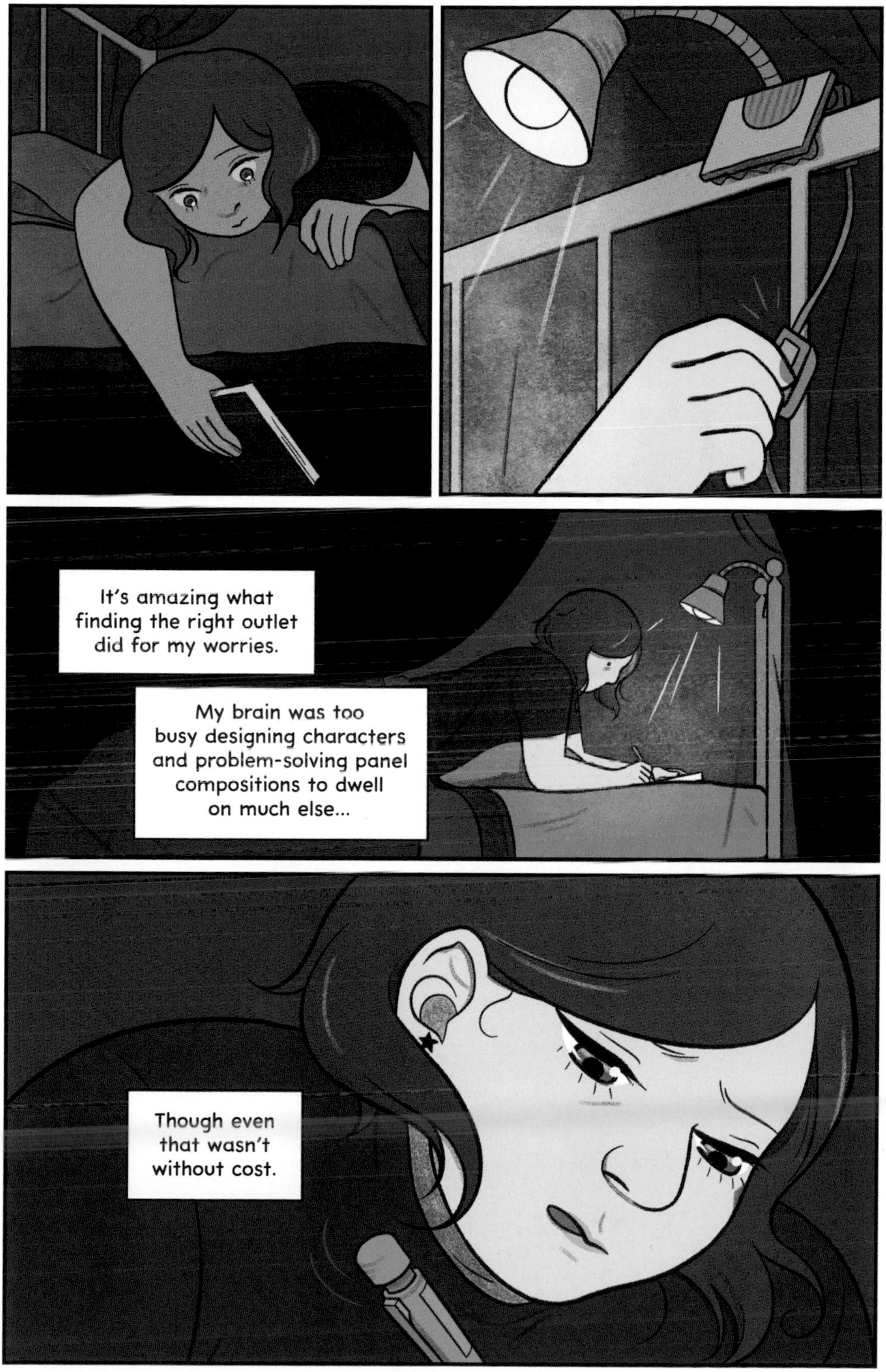
It's amazing what finding the right outlet did for my worries.
My brain was too busy designing characters and problem-solving panel compositions to dwell on much else...
Though even that wasn't without cost.

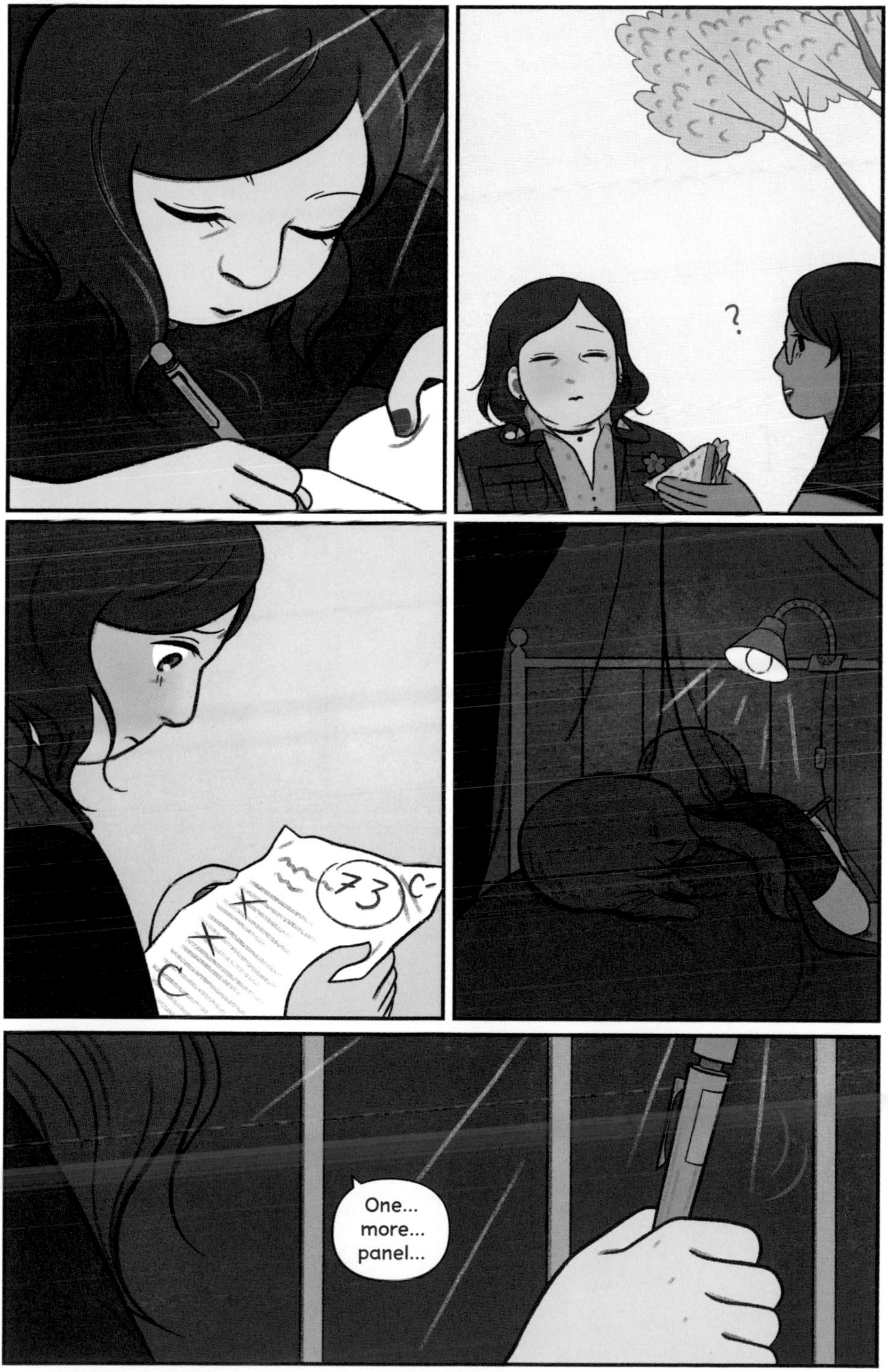
?
73
C-
One... more... panel...

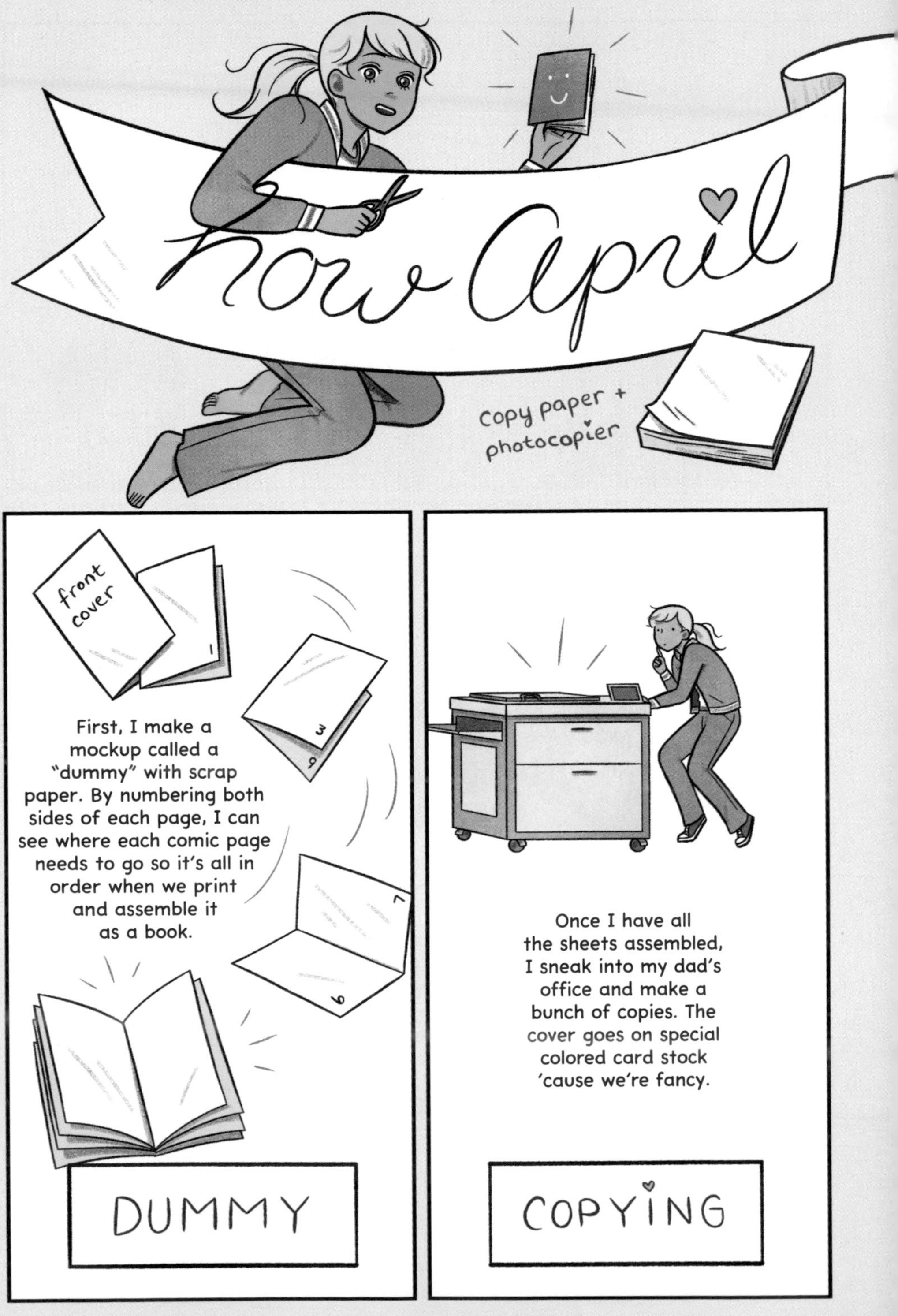
how April
copy paper + photocopier
front cover
First, I make a mockup called a "dummy" with scrap paper. By numbering both sides of each page, I can see where each comic page needs to go so it's all in order when we print and assemble it as a book.
DUMMY
Once I have all the sheets assembled, I sneak into my dad's office and make a bunch of copies. The cover goes on special colored card stock 'cause we're fancy.
COPYING

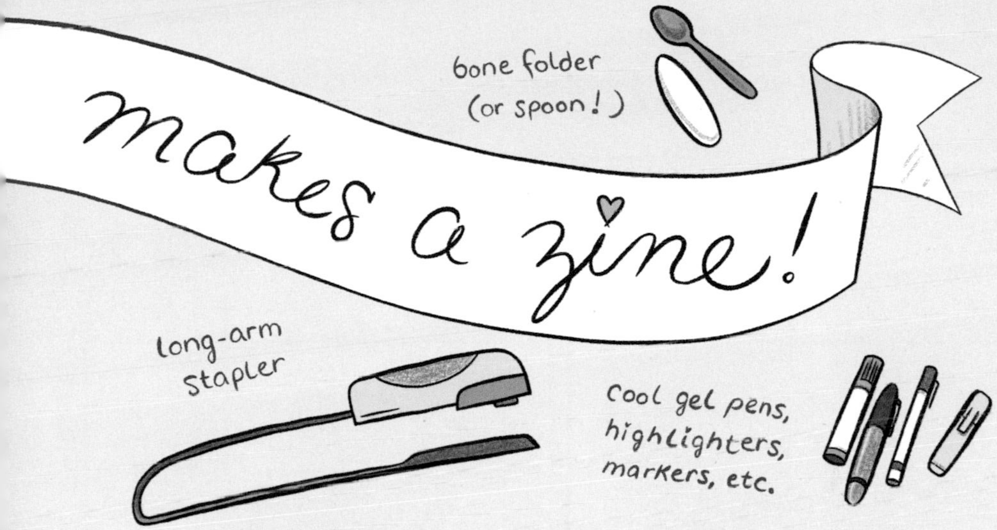
makes a zine!
bone folder
(or spoon!)
long-arm
stapler
cool gel pens,
highlighters,
markers, etc.

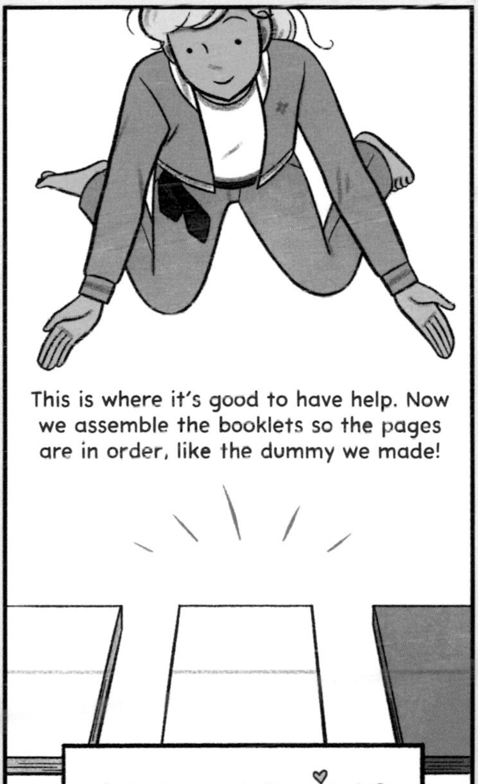
This is where it's good to have help. Now we assemble the booklets so the pages are in order, like the dummy we made!
ASSEMBLING

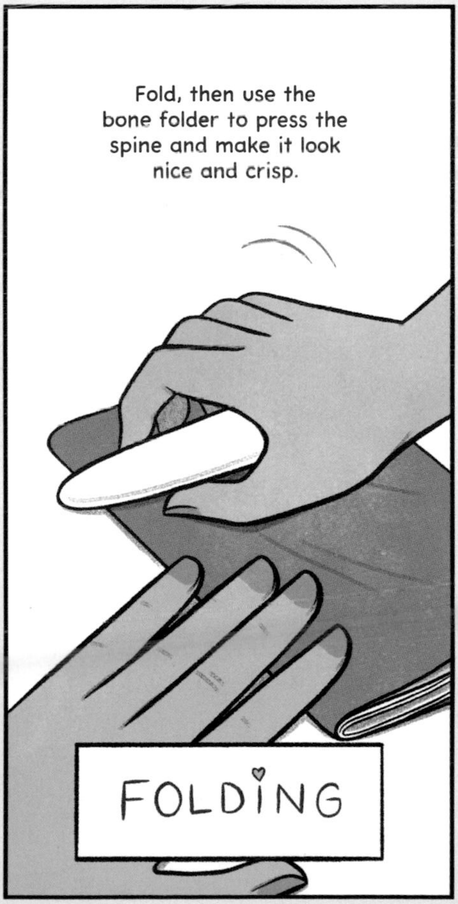
Fold, then use the bone folder to press the spine and make it look nice and crisp.
FOLDING

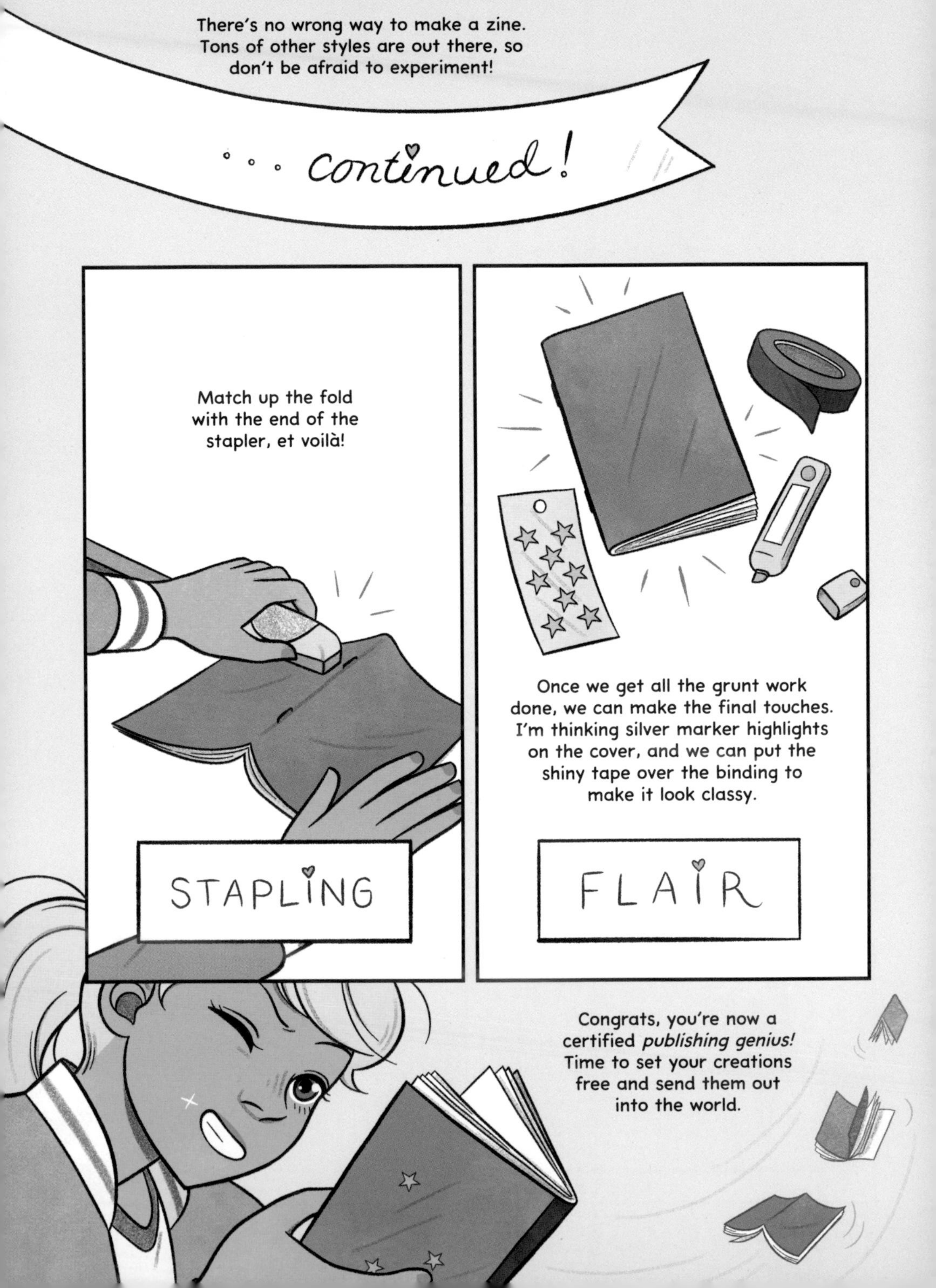
There's no wrong way to make a zine. Tons of other styles are out there, so don't be afraid to experiment!
... continued!
Match up the fold with the end of the stapler, et voilà!
STAPLING
Once we get all the grunt work done, we can make the final touches. I'm thinking silver marker highlights on the cover, and we can put the shiny tape over the binding to make it look classy.
FLAIR
Congrats, you're now a certified *publishing genius!* Time to set your creations free and send them out into the world.

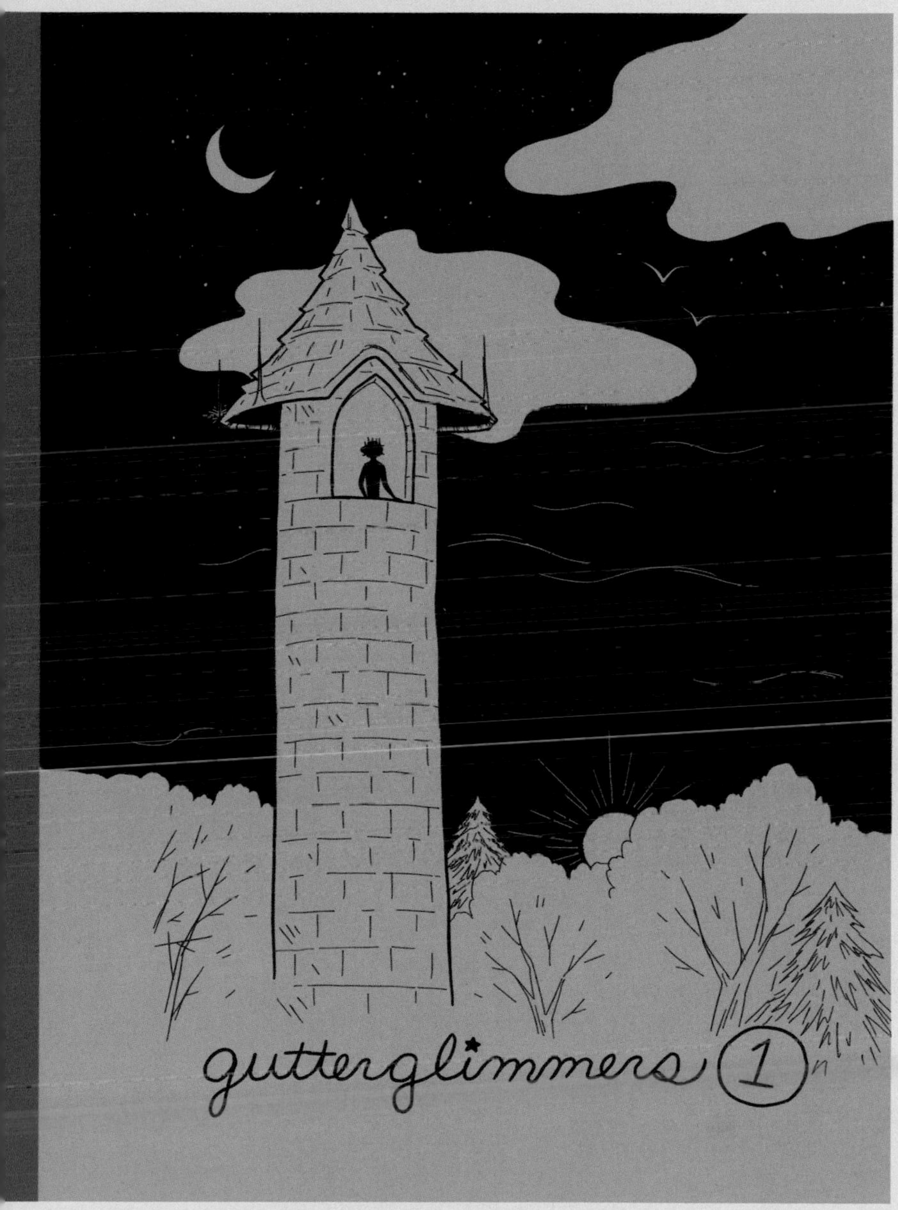
gutterglimmers 1

Once upon a time,
in a land far away,

Somewhere cradled
between the Haunted Wood
and Silver Mountains,

There stood a
tall stone tower,

Inside of which lived
a prince. At least he
thought he was a
prince, or maybe it
was just that he used
to be one; they exiled
him here so long ago,
it was hard to recall
through the cobwebs.

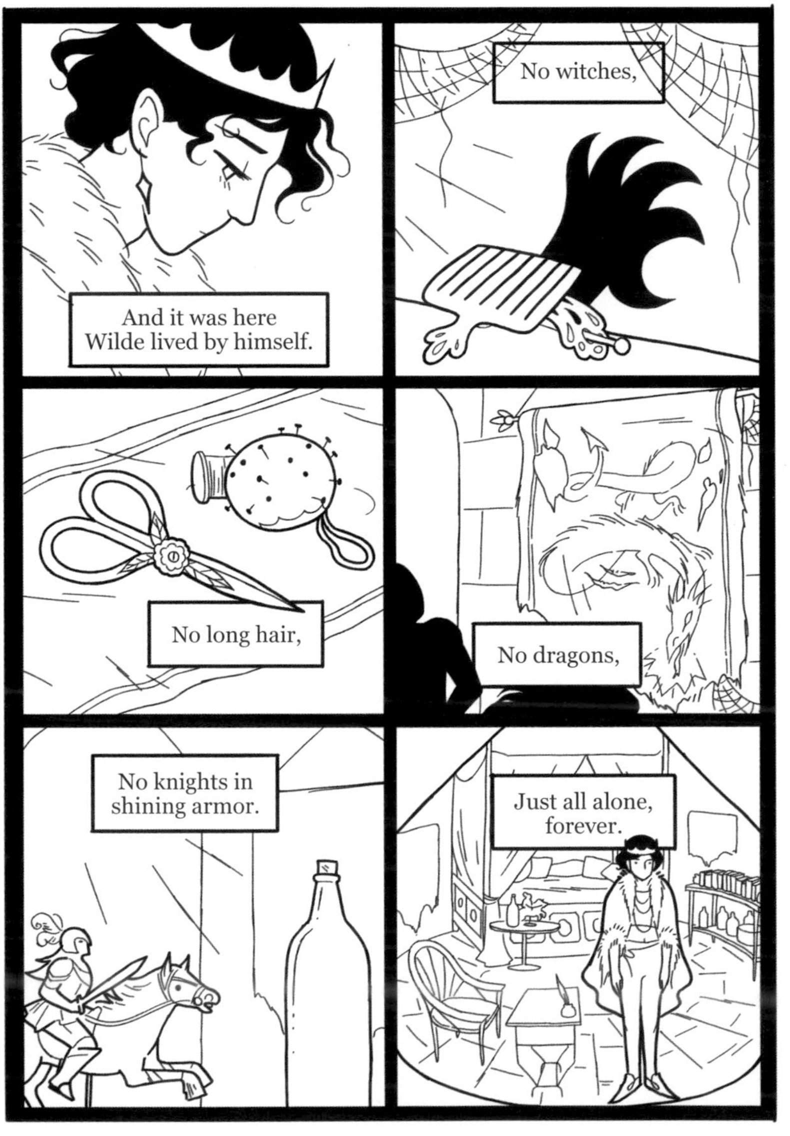
And it was here Wilde lived by himself.
No witches,
No long hair,
No dragons,
No knights in shining armor.
Just all alone, forever.

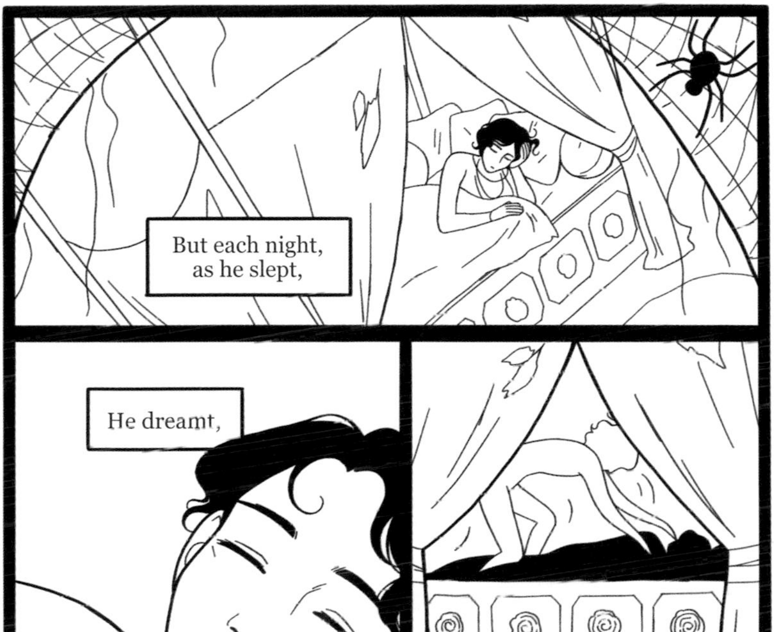
But each night, as he slept,
He dreamt,
And in his dreams, his soul was free...
To explore the world outside.

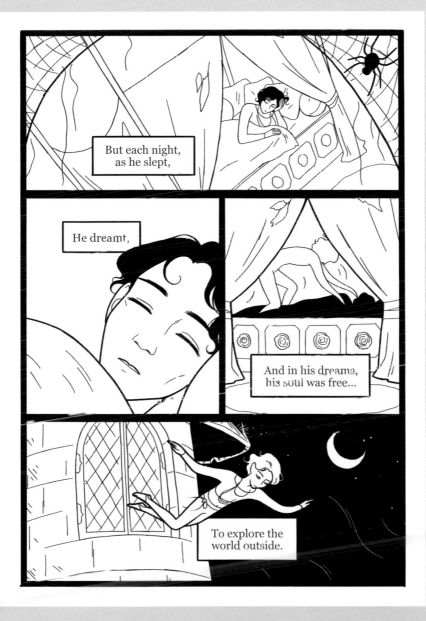

It was then he could
finally feel the soft
moss underfoot,

The bristle of wiry fur between his fingers,

And he could run until the salt of the sea filled his lungs and his legs gave out from underneath him.

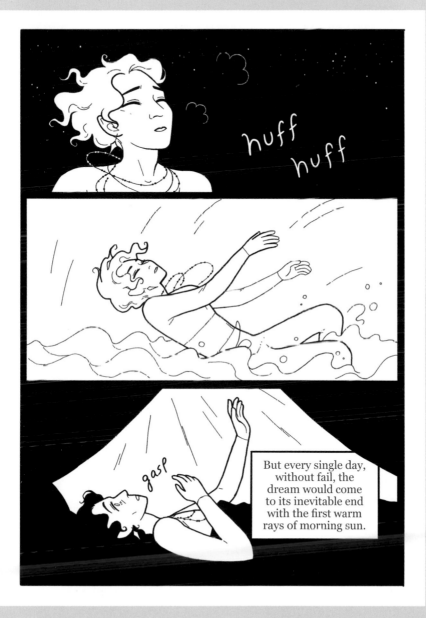

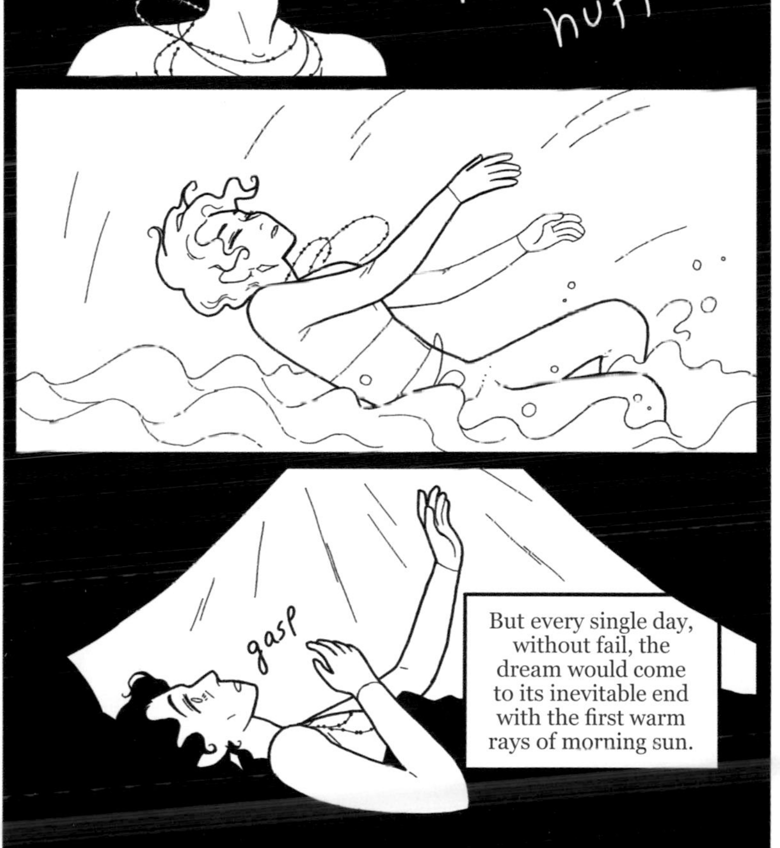
huff
huff
gasp
But every single day, without fail, the dream would come to its inevitable end with the first warm rays of morning sun.

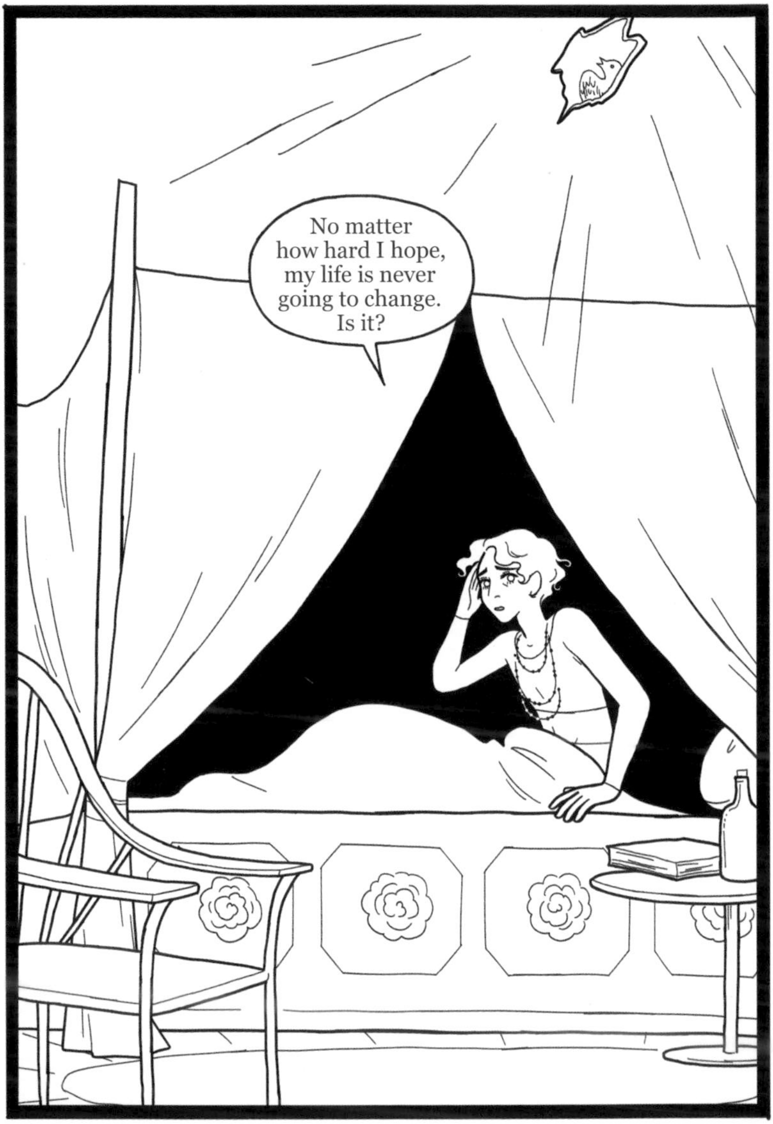
No matter how hard I hope, my life is never going to change. Is it?

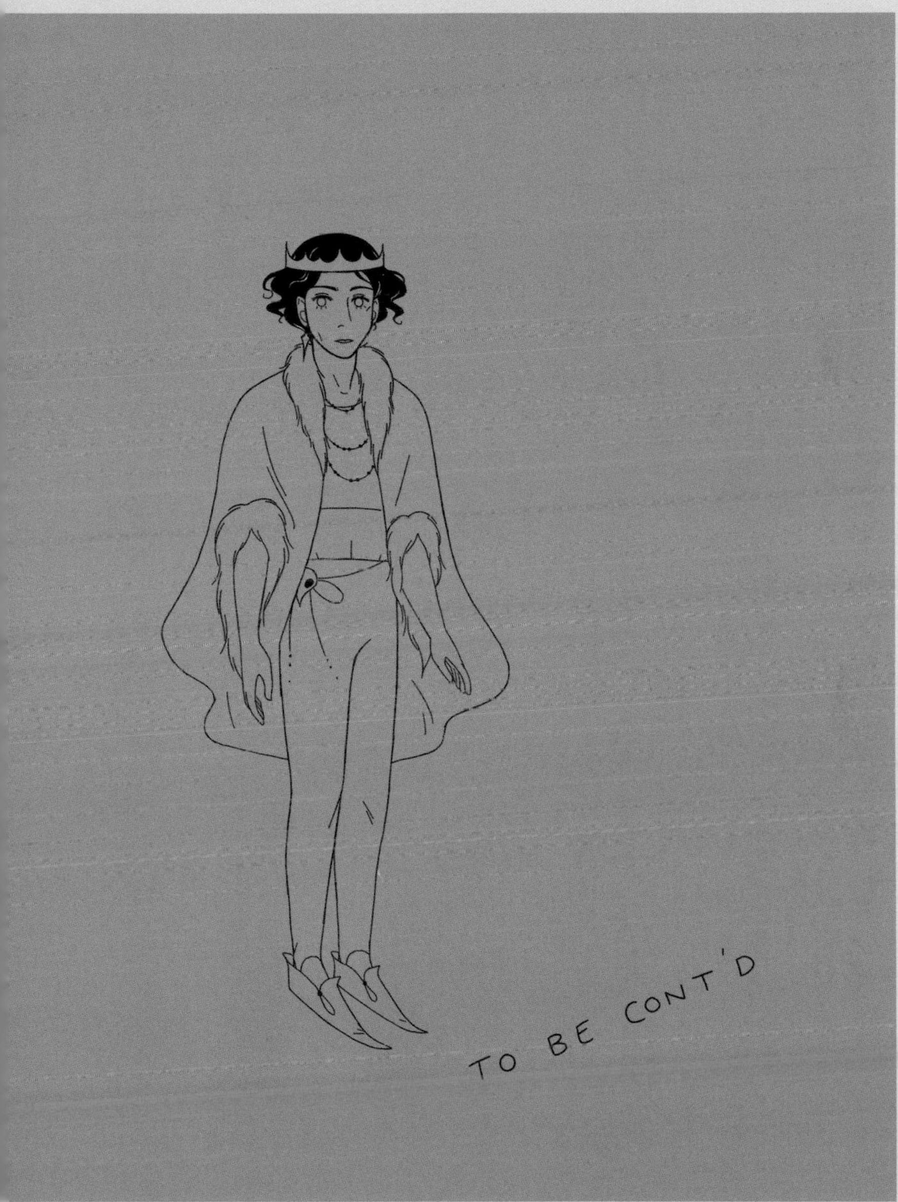
TO BE CONT'D

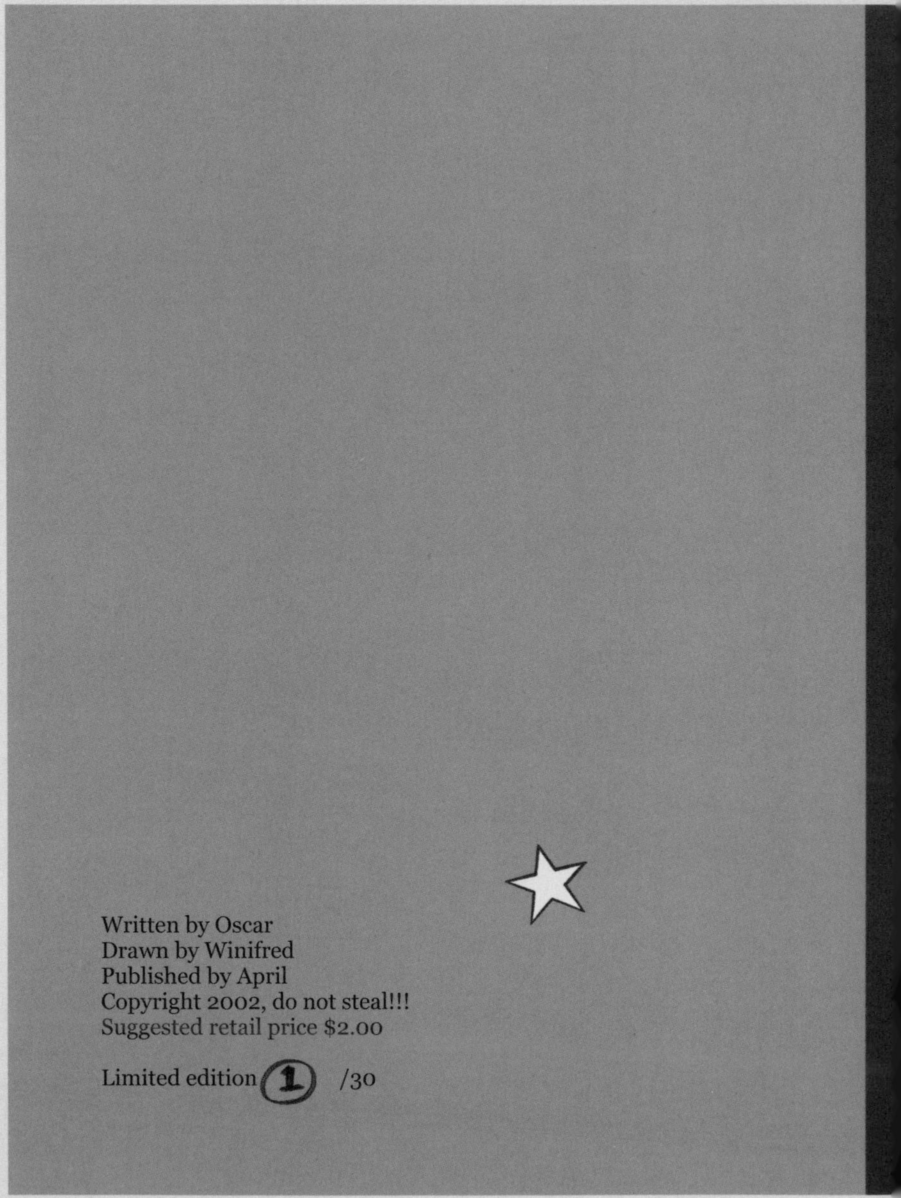
Written by Oscar
Drawn by Winifred
Published by April
Copyright 2002, do not steal!!!
Suggested retail price $2.00
Limited edition 1 /30

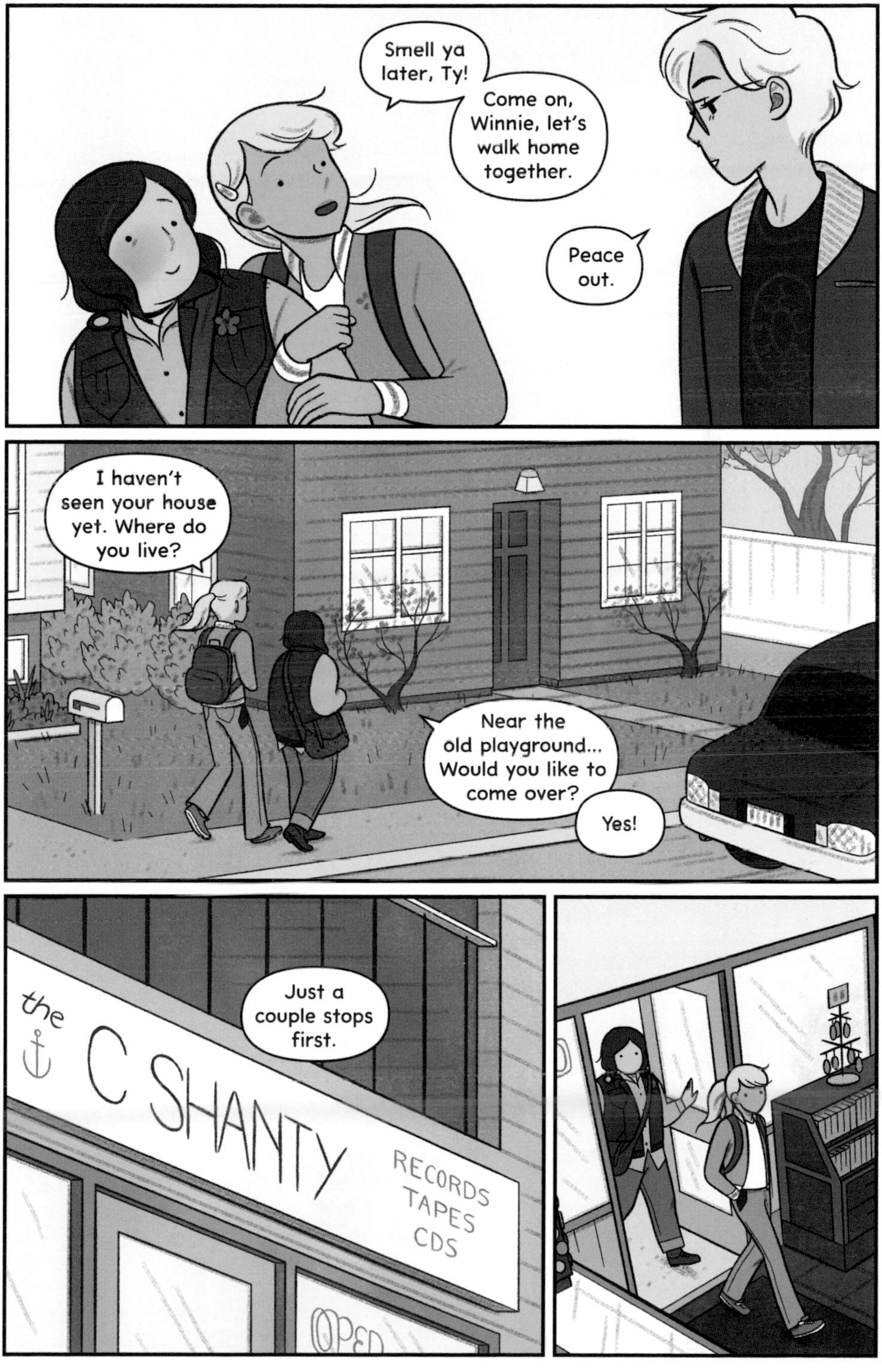
Smell ya later, Ty!
Come on, Winnie, let's walk home together.
Peace out.
I haven't seen your house yet. Where do you live?
Near the old playground... Would you like to come over?
Yes!
the C SHANTY
RECORDS TAPES CDS
Just a couple stops first.
OPEN

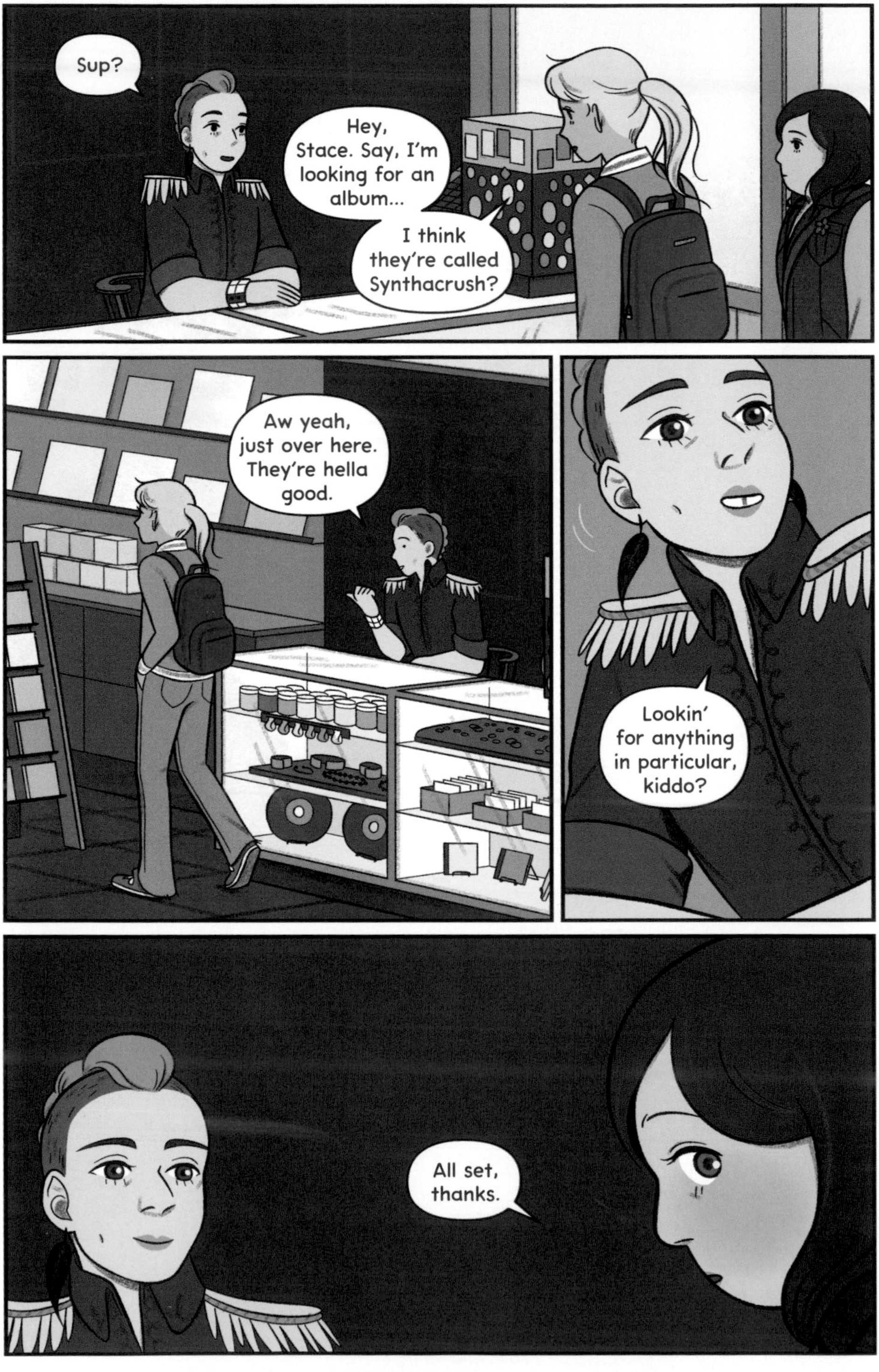
Sup?
Hey, Stace. Say, I'm looking for an album...
I think they're called Synthacrush?
Aw yeah, just over here. They're hella good.
Lookin' for anything in particular, kiddo?
All set, thanks.

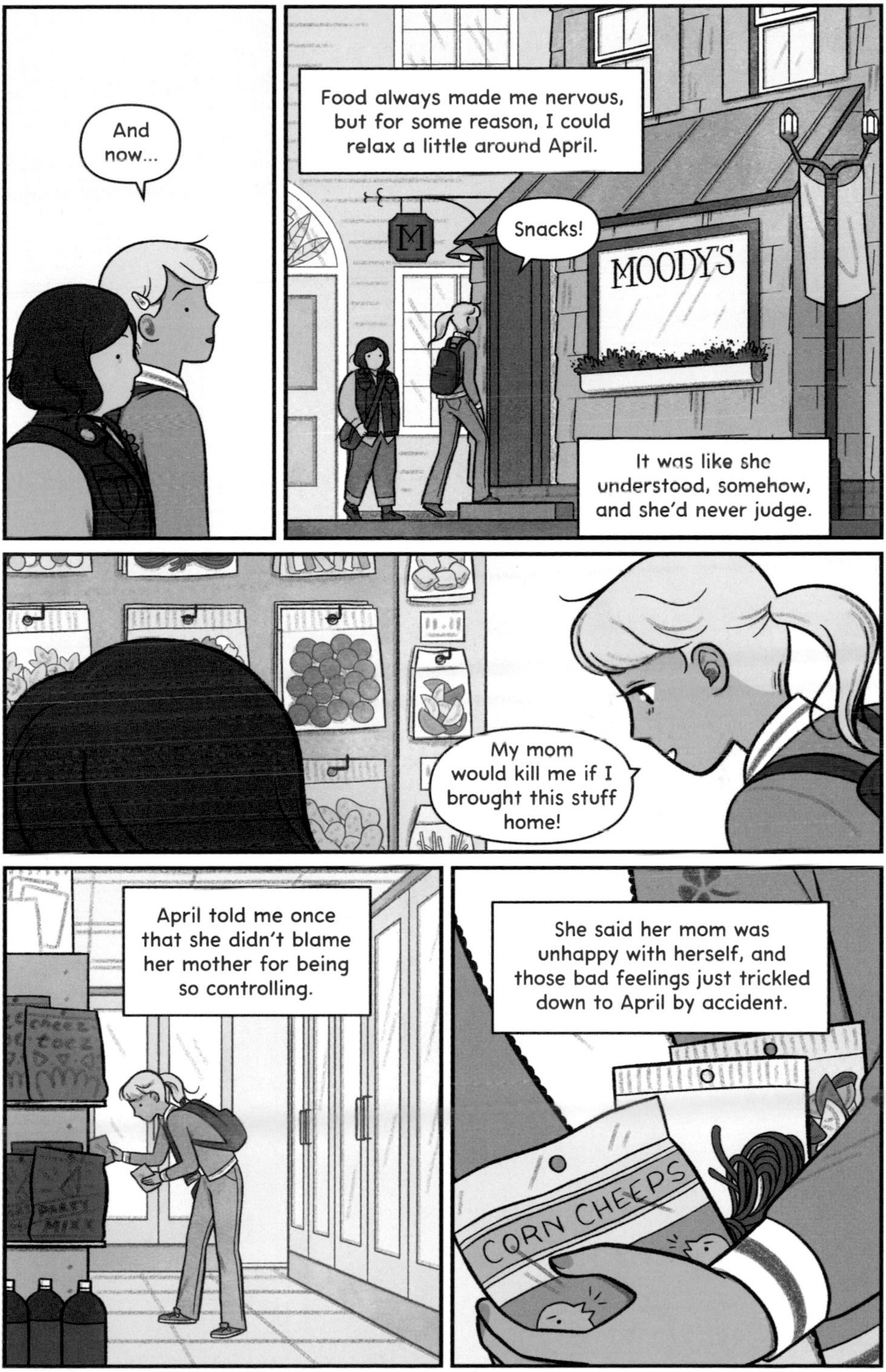
And now...
Food always made me nervous, but for some reason, I could relax a little around April.
Snacks!
MOODY'S
It was like she understood, somehow, and she'd never judge.
My mom would kill me if I brought this stuff home!
April told me once that she didn't blame her mother for being so controlling.
PARTY MIX
She said her mom was unhappy with herself, and those bad feelings just trickled down to April by accident.
CORN CHEEPS

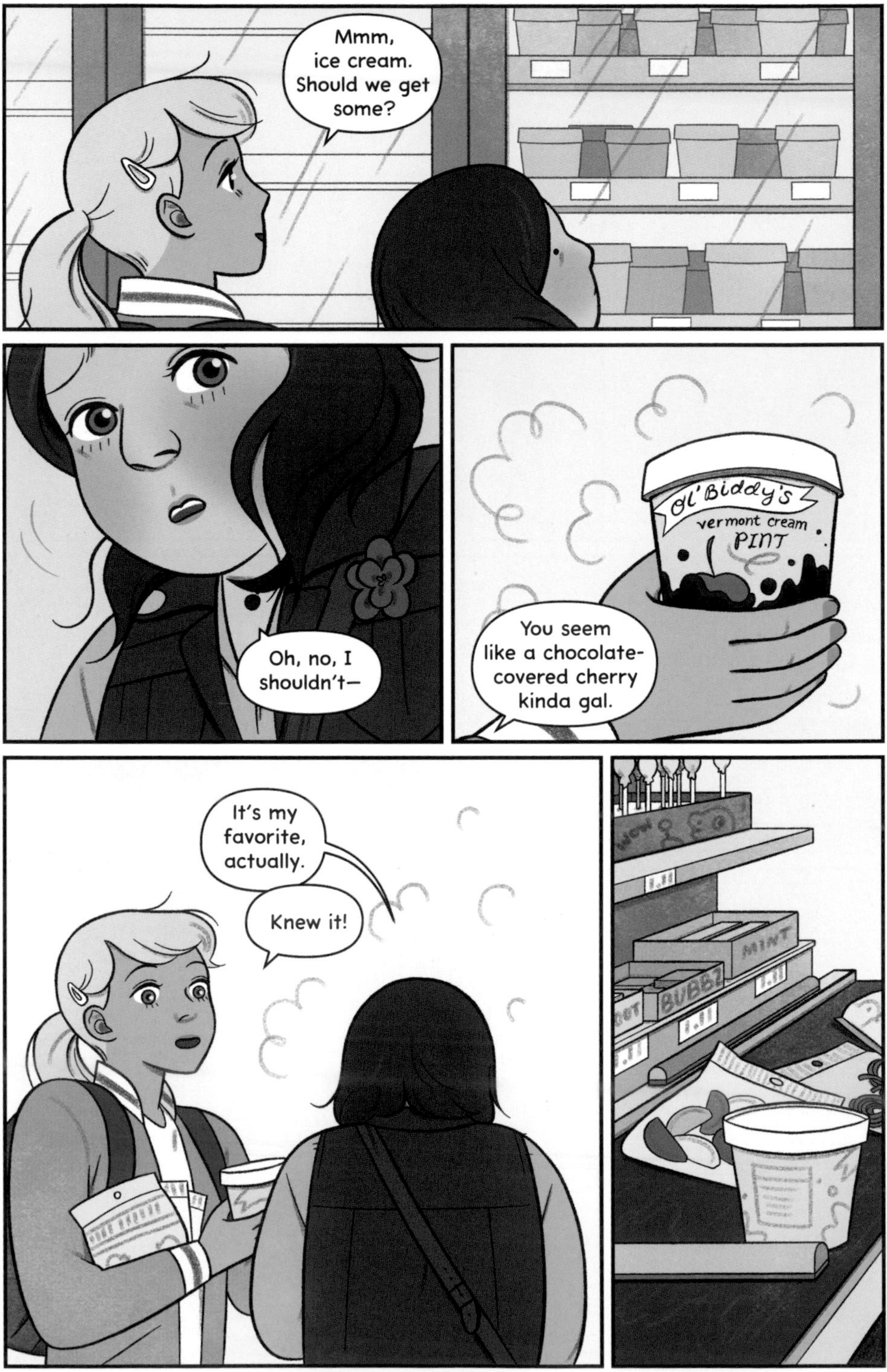
Mmm, ice cream. Should we get some?
Oh, no, I shouldn't—
Ol' Biddy's
vermont cream
PINT
You seem like a chocolate-covered cherry kinda gal.
It's my favorite, actually.
Knew it!
MINT

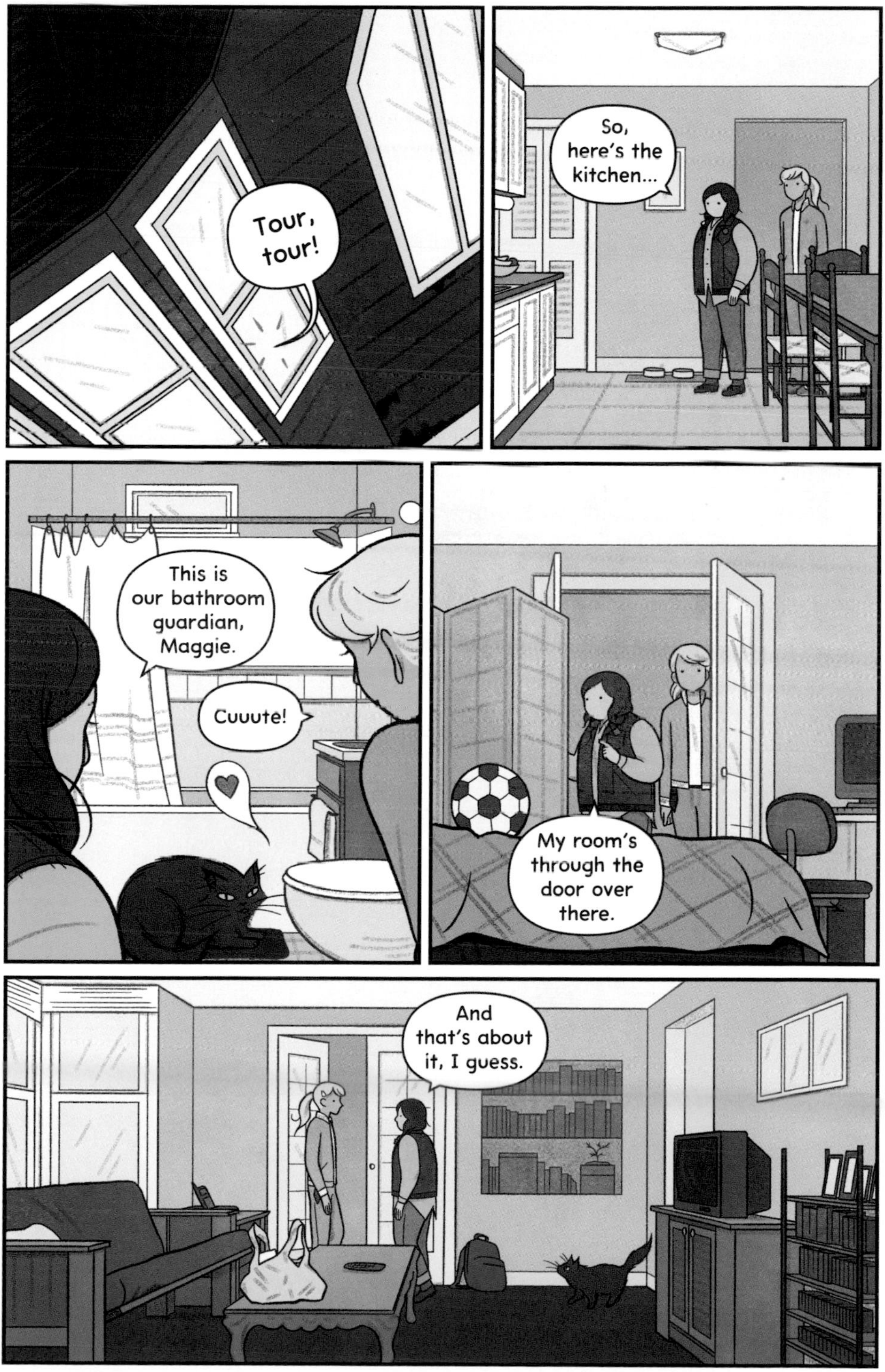
Tour, tour!
So, here's the kitchen...
This is our bathroom guardian, Maggie.
Cuuute!
My room's through the door over there.
And that's about it, I guess.

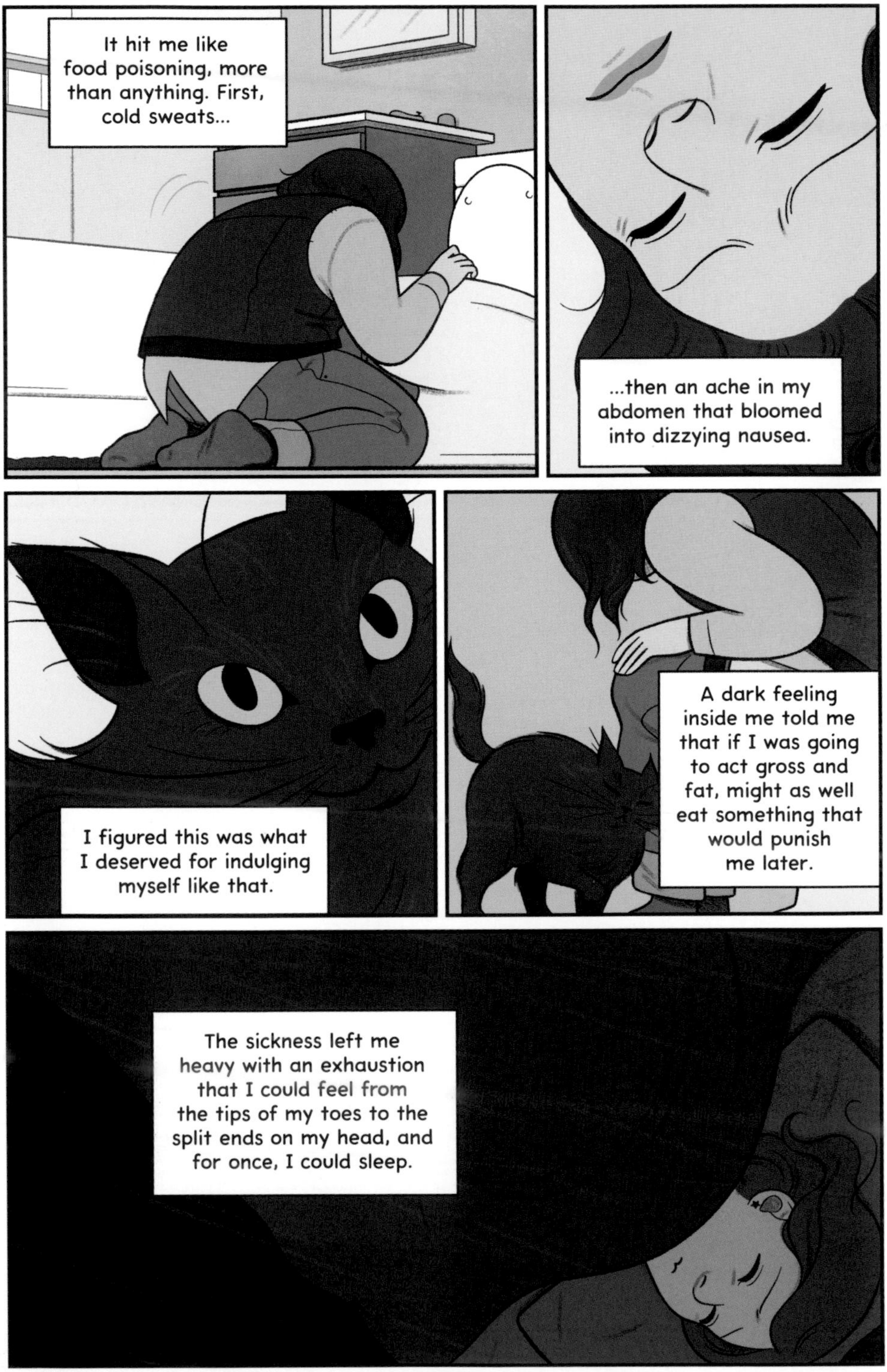
It hit me like food poisoning, more than anything. First, cold sweats...
...then an ache in my abdomen that bloomed into dizzying nausea.
I figured this was what I deserved for indulging myself like that.
A dark feeling inside me told me that if I was going to act gross and fat, might as well eat something that would punish me later.
The sickness left me heavy with an exhaustion that I could feel from the tips of my toes to the split ends on my head, and for once, I could sleep.

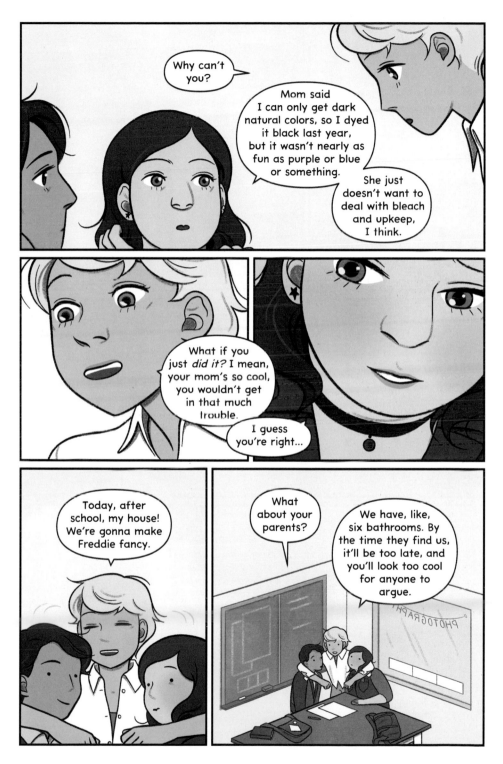

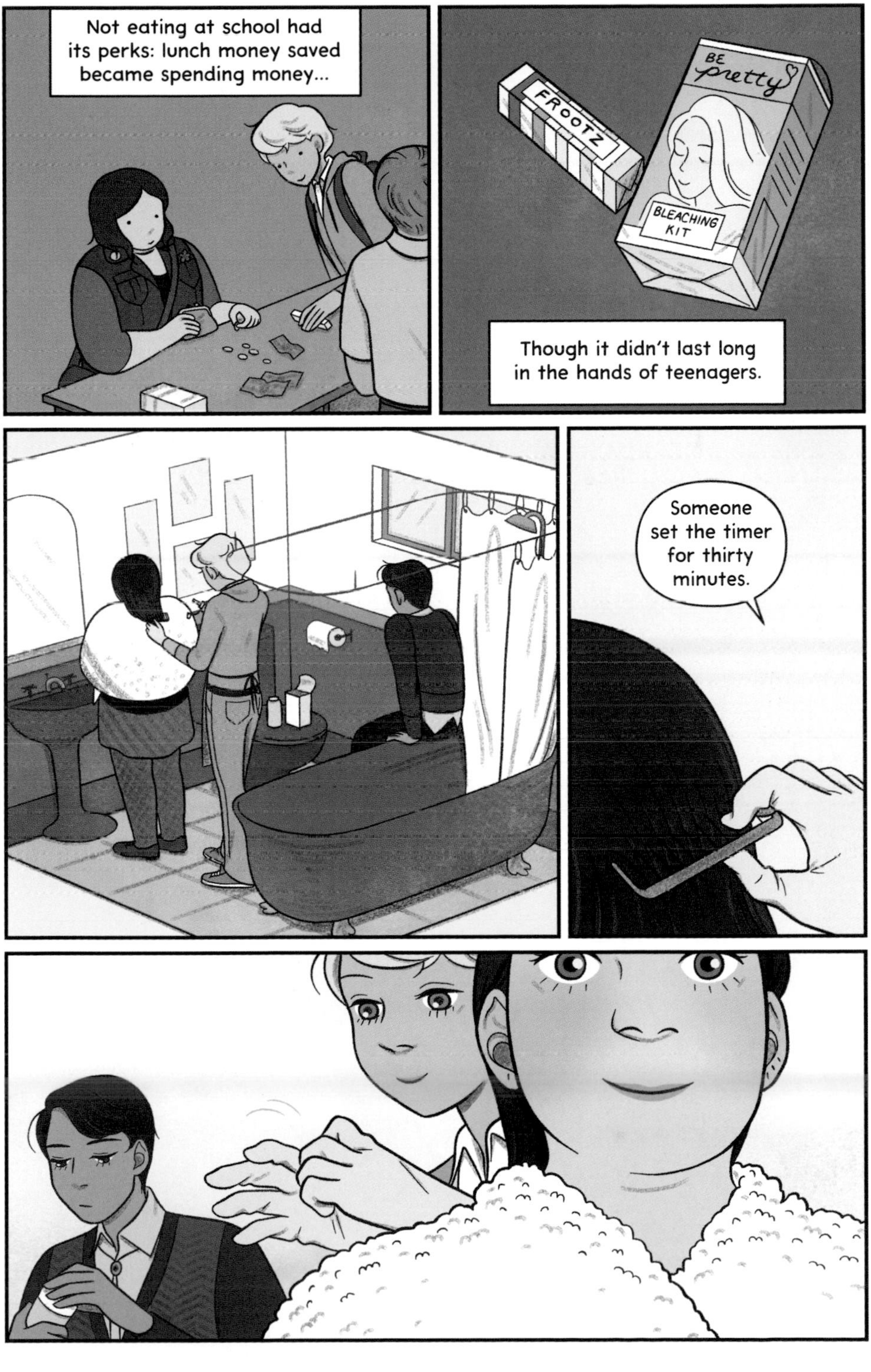
Not eating at school had its perks: lunch money saved became spending money...
FROOTZ
BE pretty
BLEACHING KIT
Though it didn't last long in the hands of teenagers.
Someone set the timer for thirty minutes.

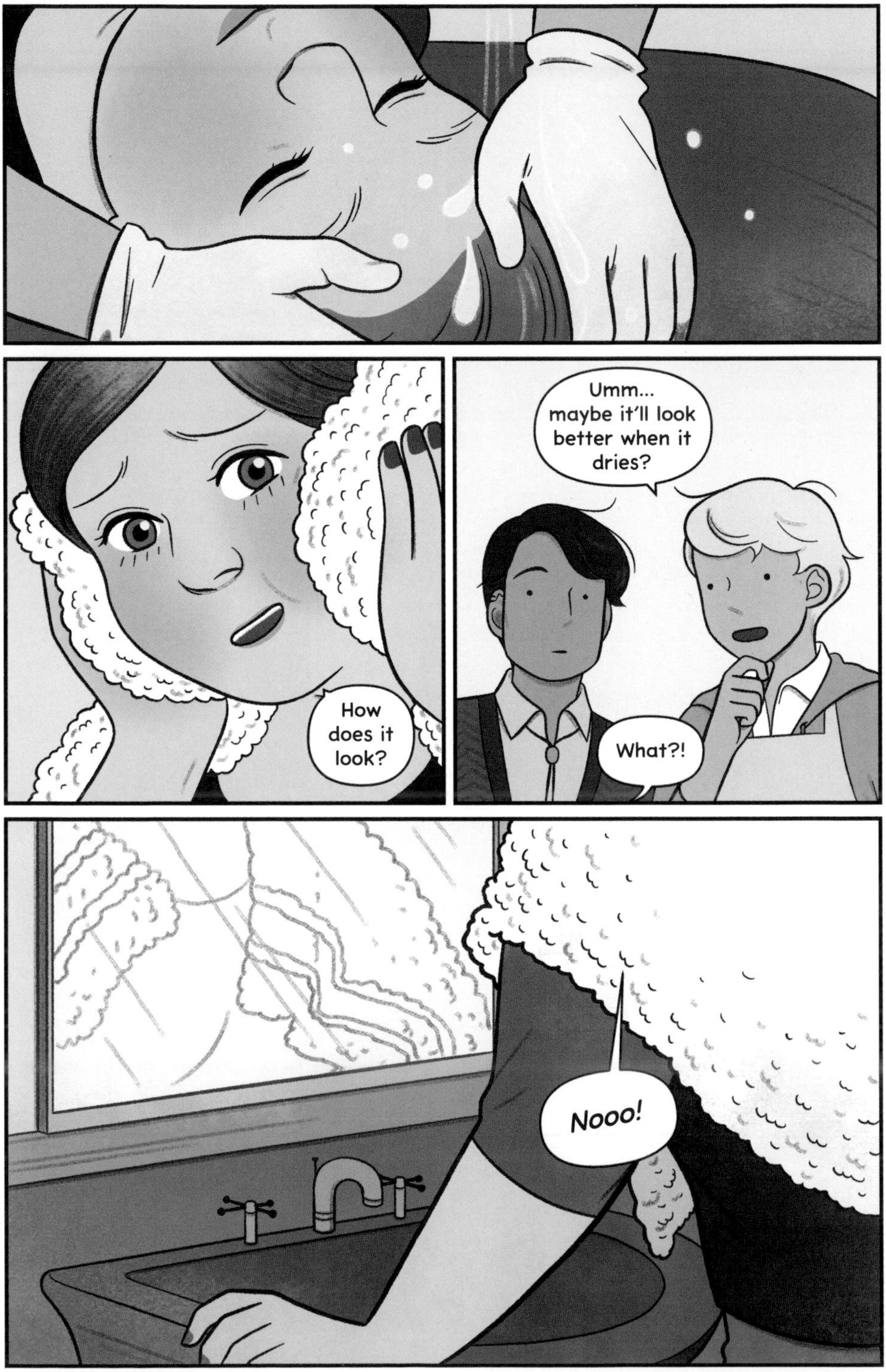
How does it look?
Umm... maybe it'll look better when it dries?
What?!
Nooo!

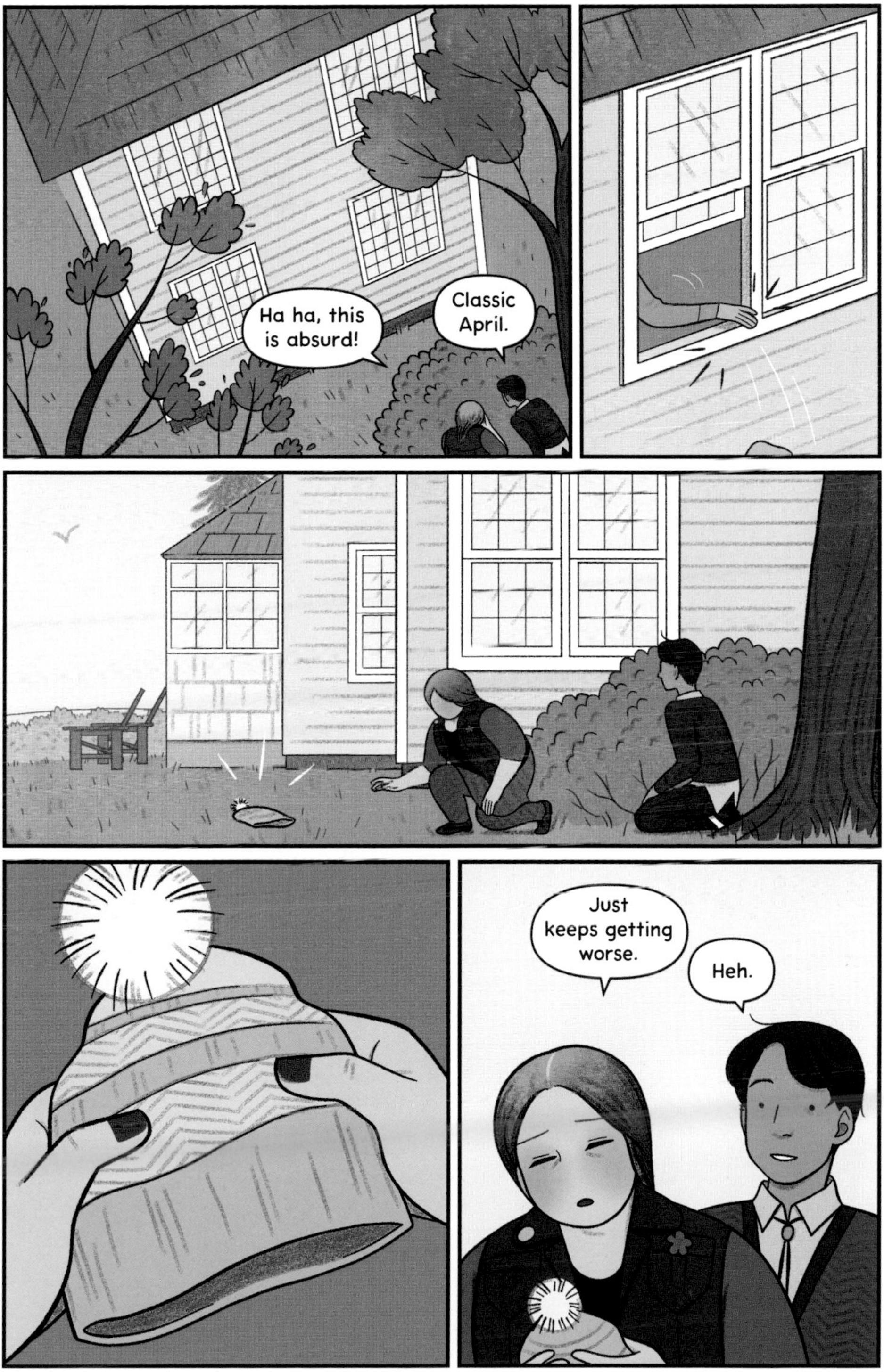
Ha ha, this is absurd!
Classic April.
Just keeps getting worse.
Heh.

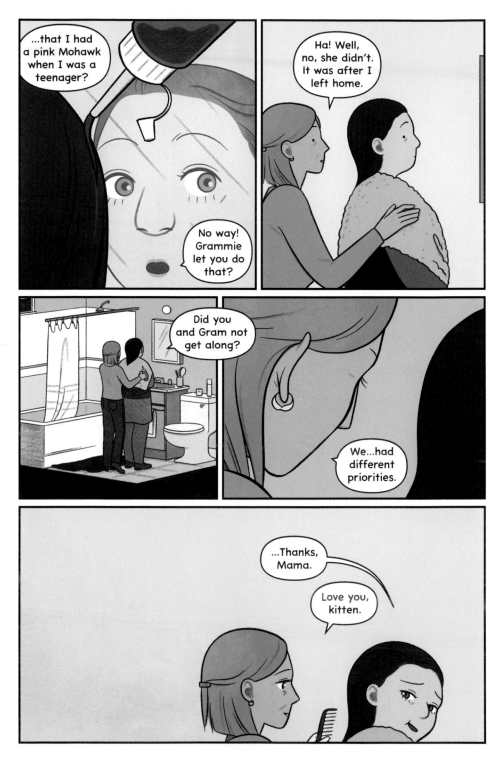

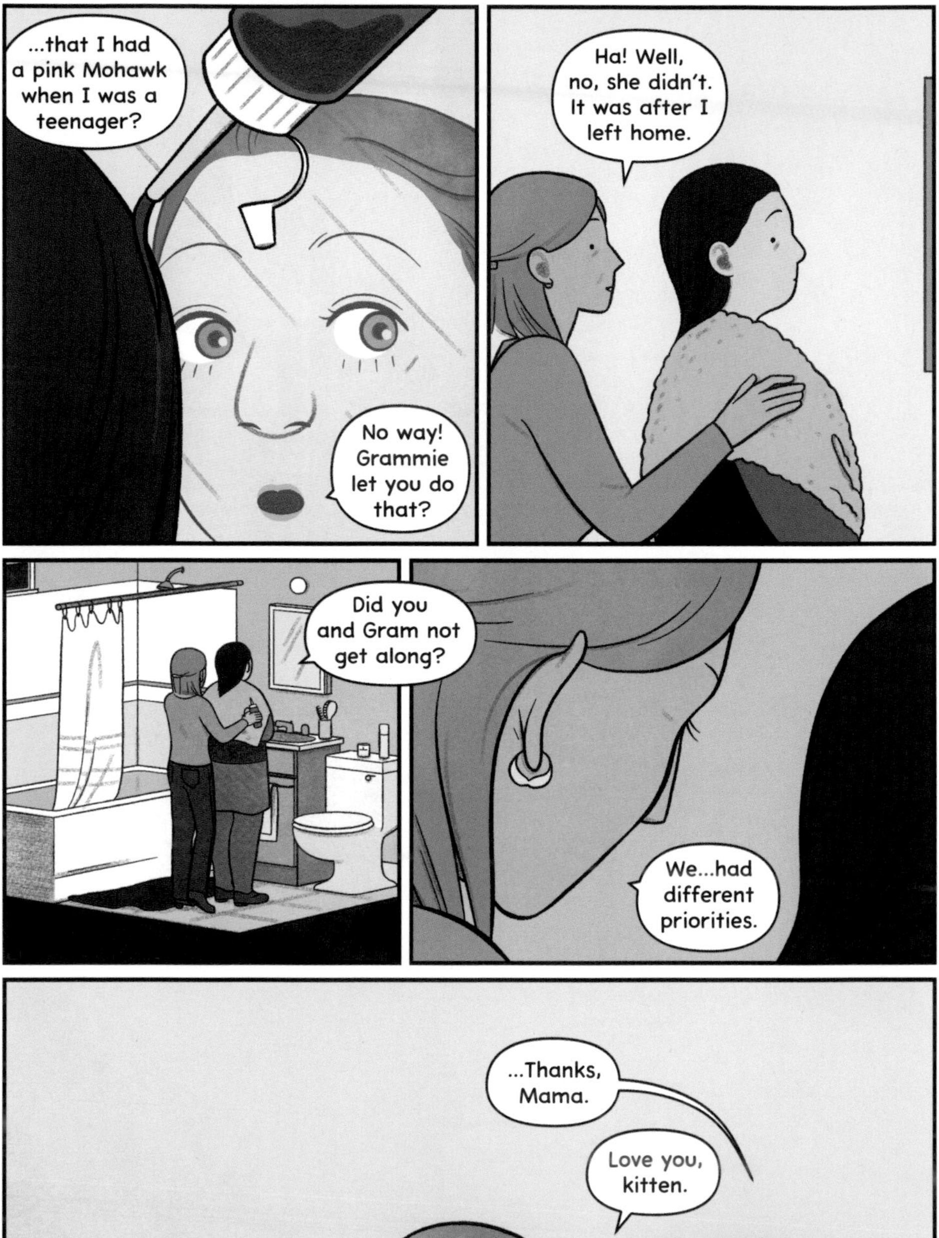
...that I had a pink Mohawk when I was a teenager?
No way! Grammie let you do that?
Ha! Well, no, she didn't. It was after I left home.
Did you and Gram not get along?
We...had different priorities.
...Thanks, Mama.
Love you, kitten.

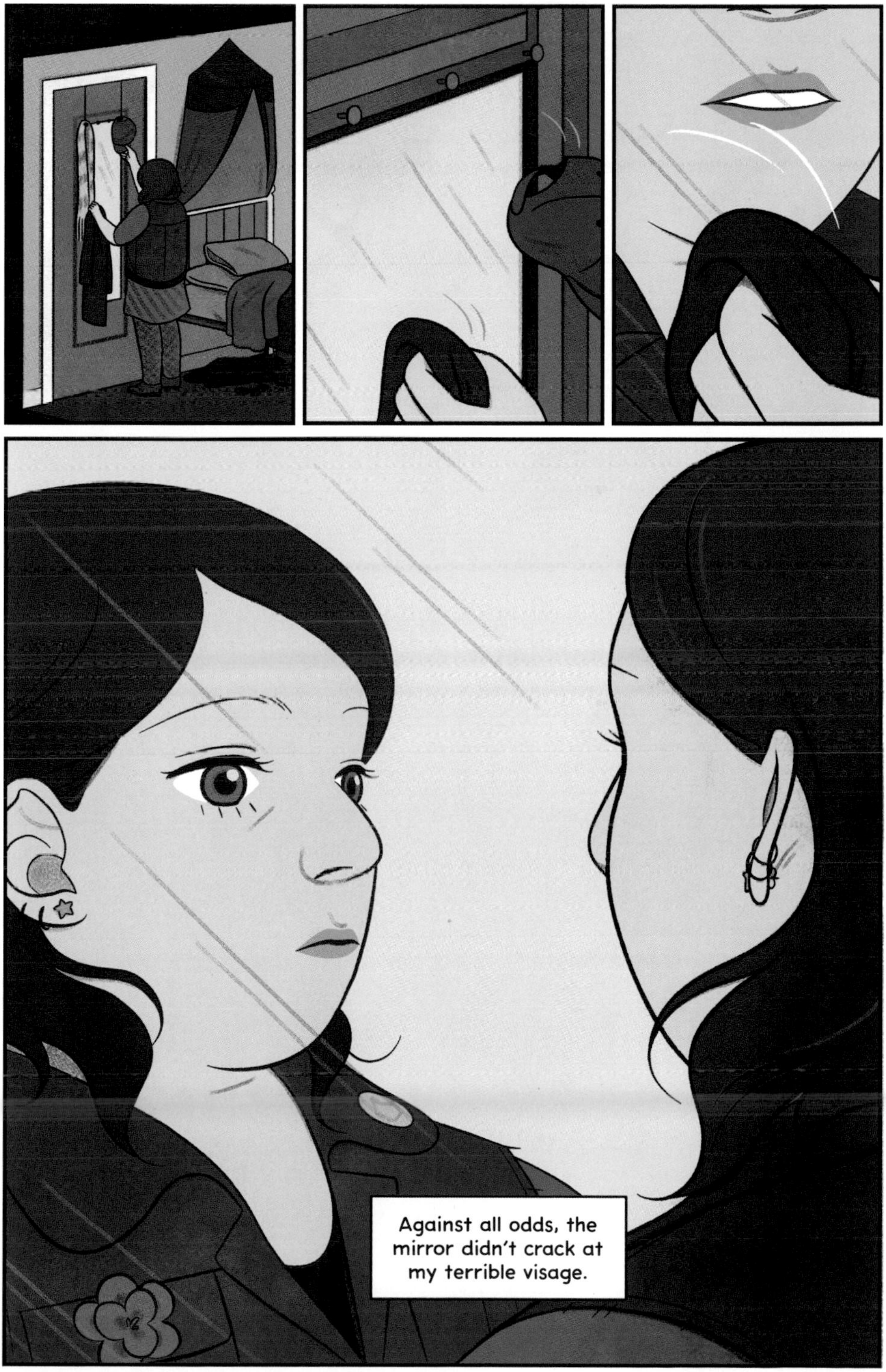
Against all odds, the mirror didn't crack at my terrible visage.

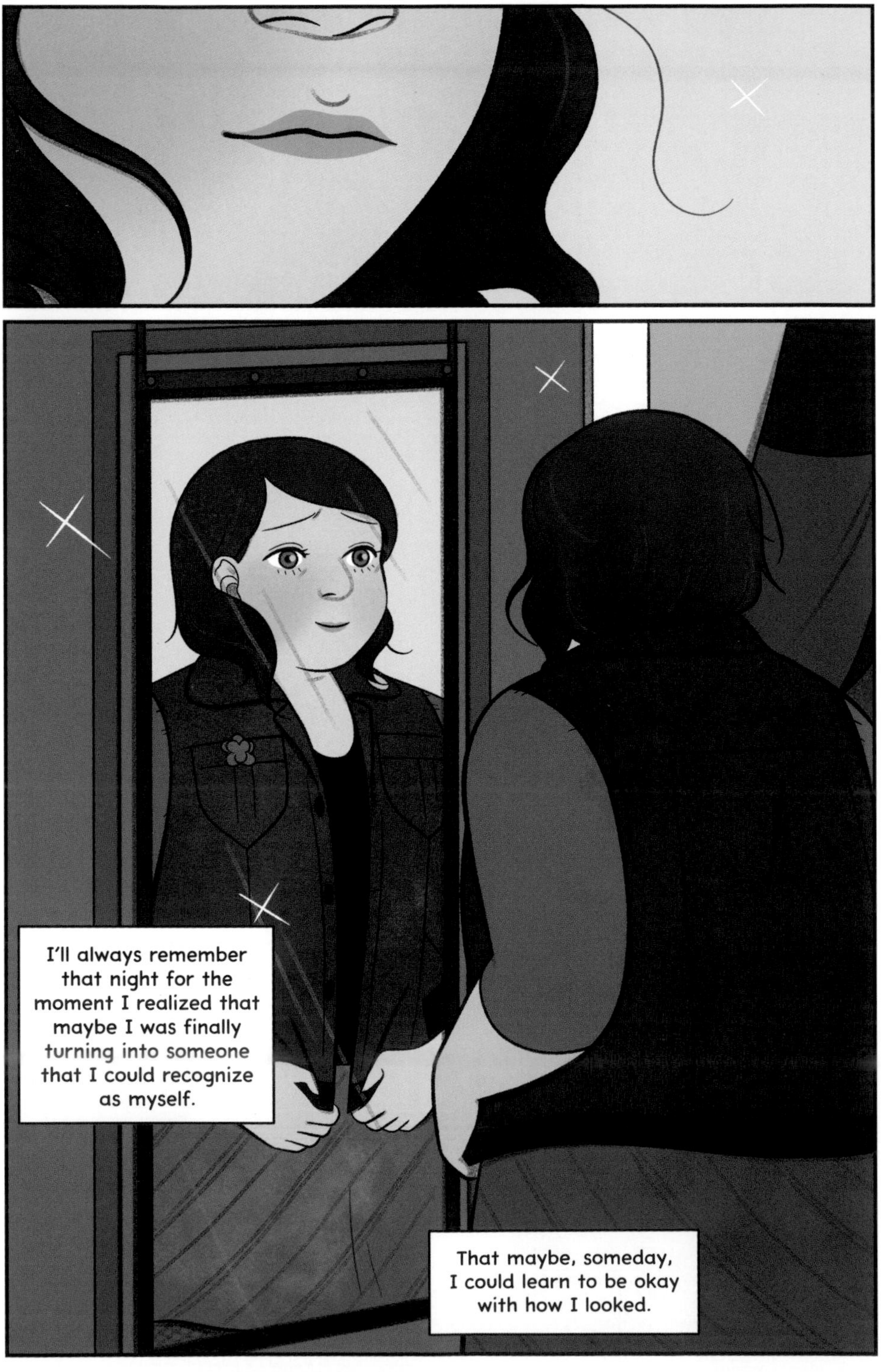
I'll always remember that night for the moment I realized that maybe I was finally turning into someone that I could recognize as myself.
That maybe, someday, I could learn to be okay with how I looked.

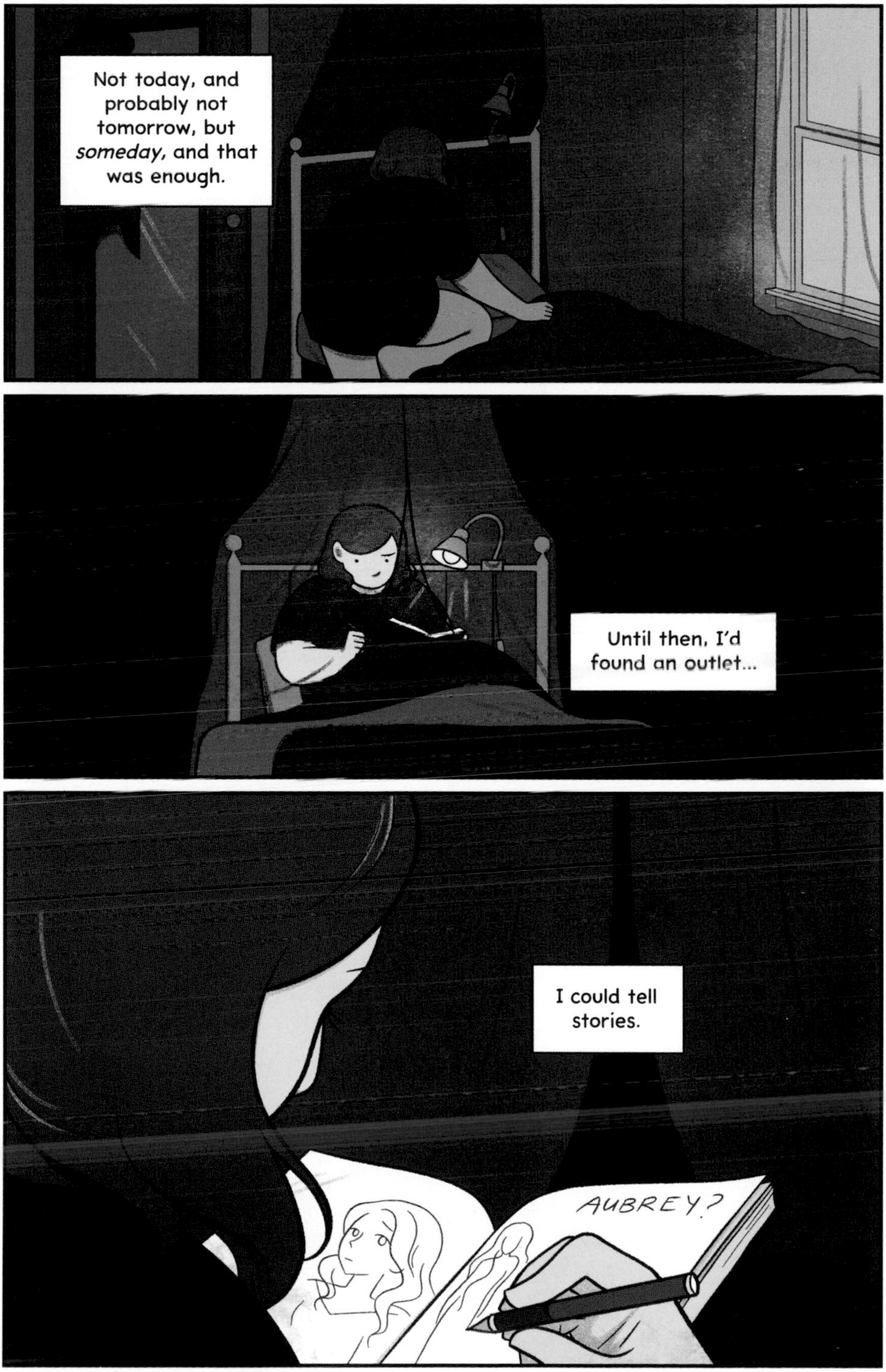
Not today, and probably not tomorrow, but *someday,* and that was enough.
Until then, I'd found an outlet...
I could tell stories.
AUBREY?

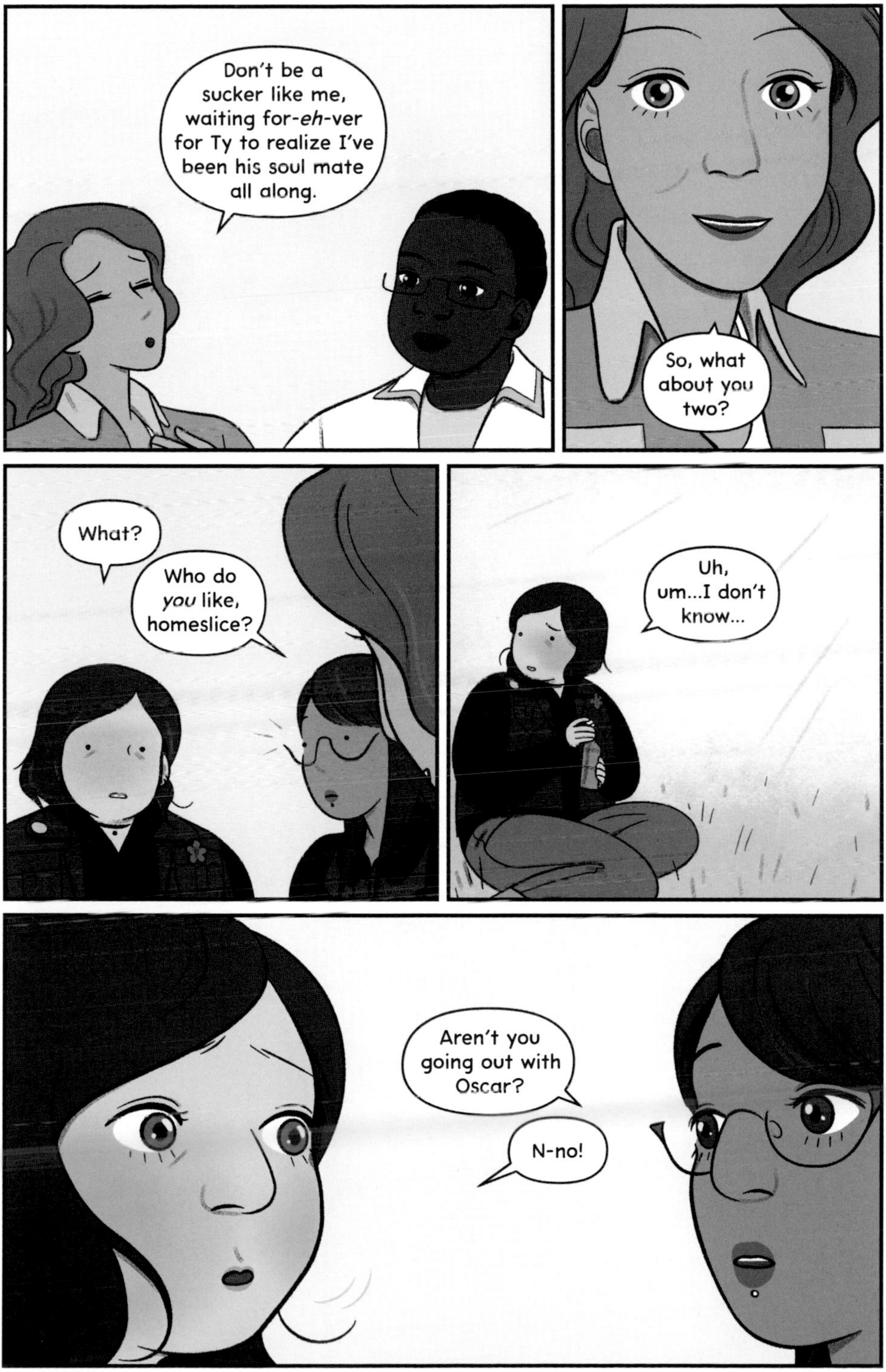
Don't be a sucker like me, waiting for-*eh*-ver for Ty to realize I've been his soul mate all along.
So, what about you two?
What?
Who do *you* like, homeslice?
Uh, um...I don't know...
Aren't you going out with Oscar?
N-no!

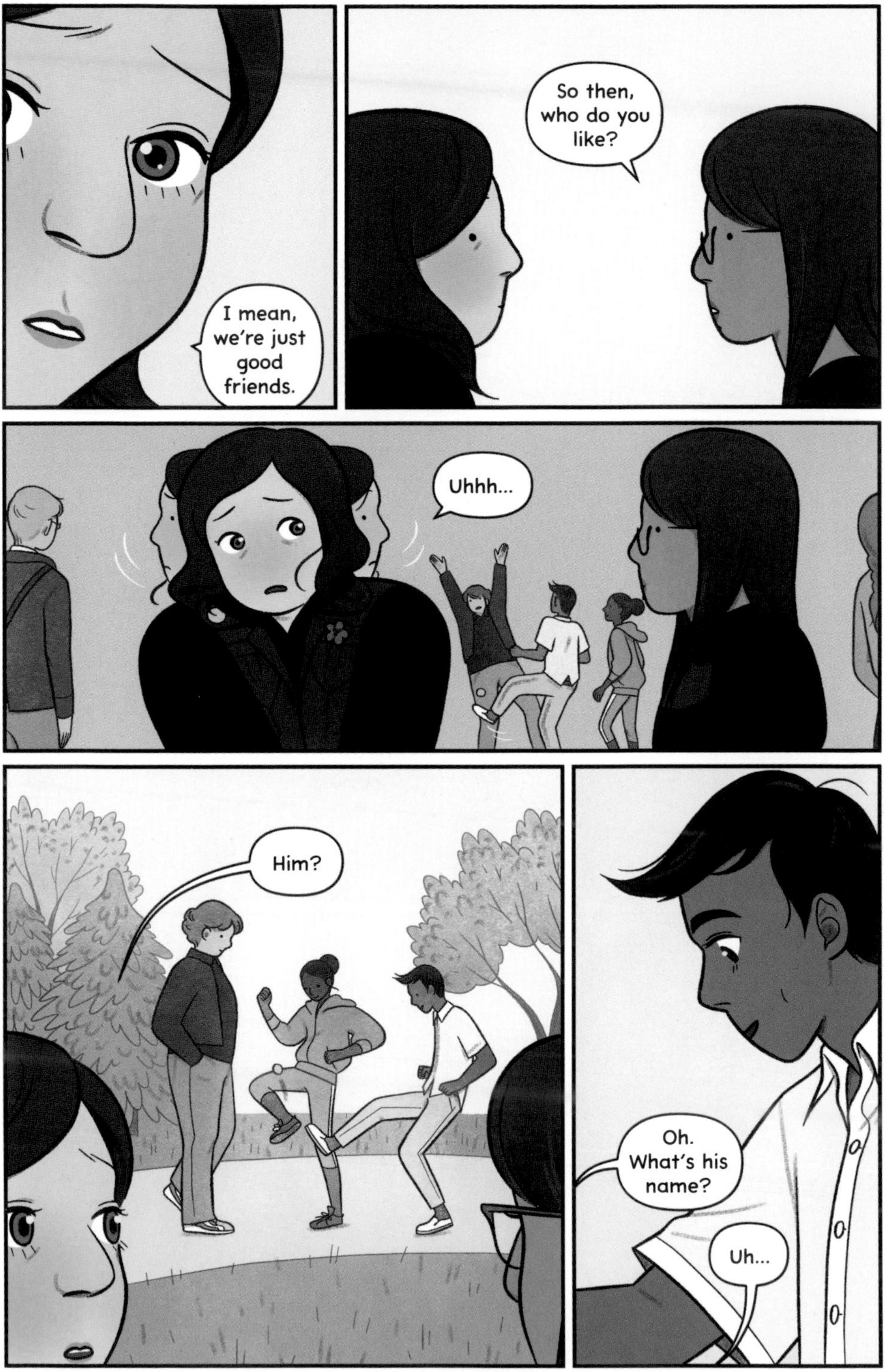
I mean, we're just good friends.
So then, who do you like?
Uhhh...
Him?
Oh. What's his name?
Uh...

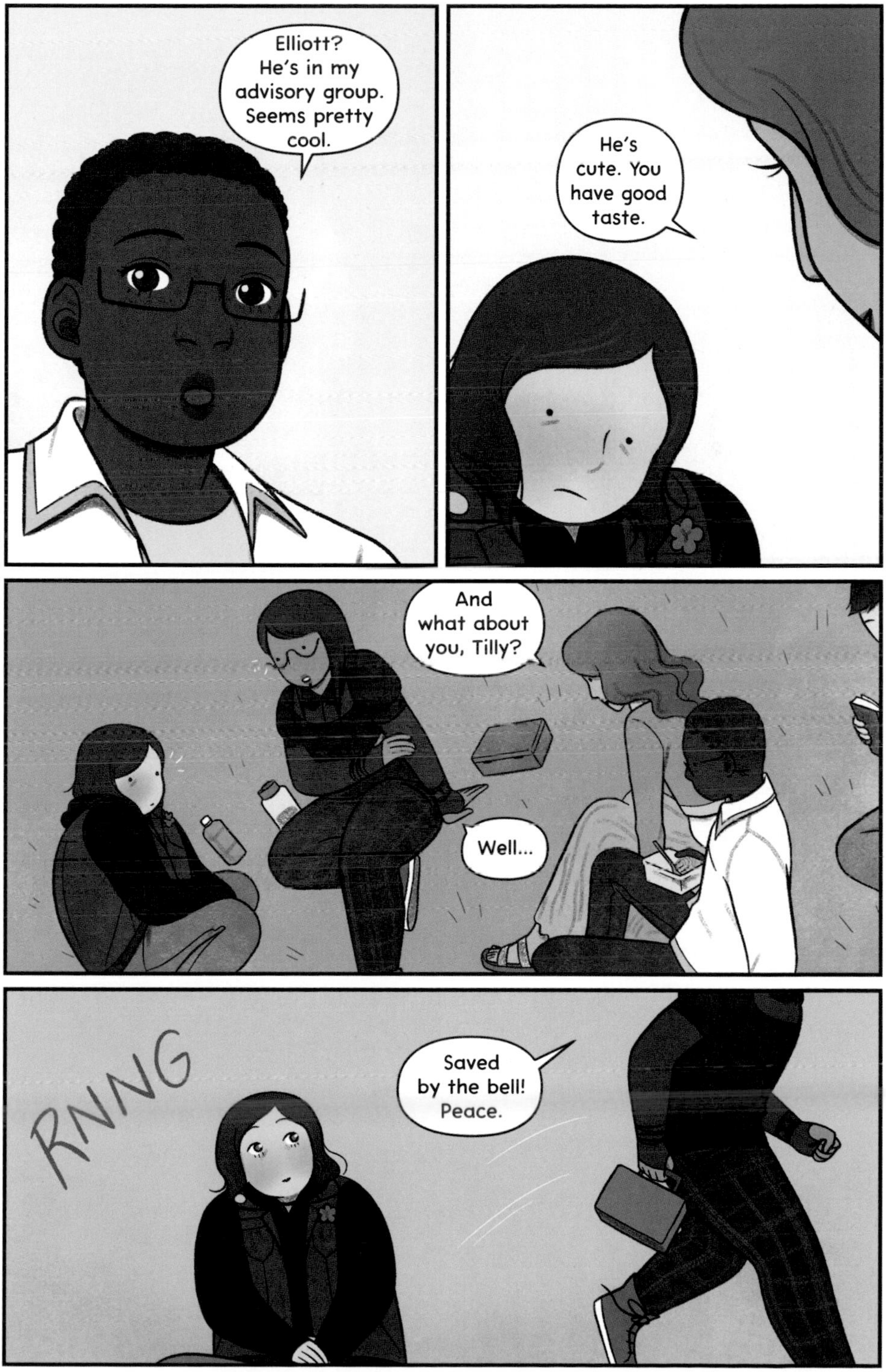
Elliott? He's in my advisory group. Seems pretty cool.
He's cute. You have good taste.
And what about you, Tilly?
Well...
RNNG
Saved by the bell! Peace.

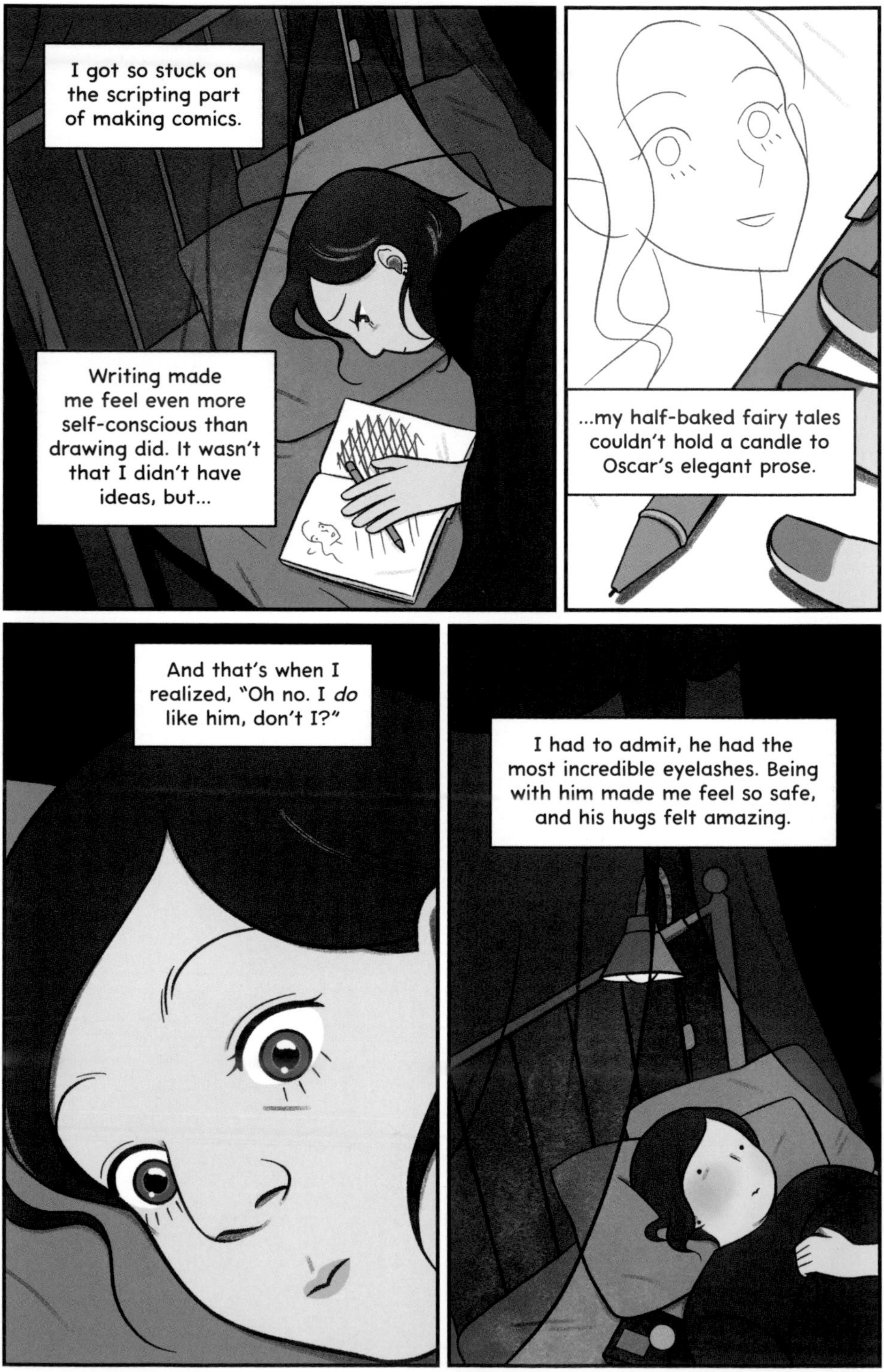
I got so stuck on the scripting part of making comics.
Writing made me feel even more self-conscious than drawing did. It wasn't that I didn't have ideas, but...
...my half-baked fairy tales couldn't hold a candle to Oscar's elegant prose.
And that's when I realized, "Oh no. I *do* like him, don't I?"
I had to admit, he had the most incredible eyelashes. Being with him made me feel so safe, and his hugs felt amazing.

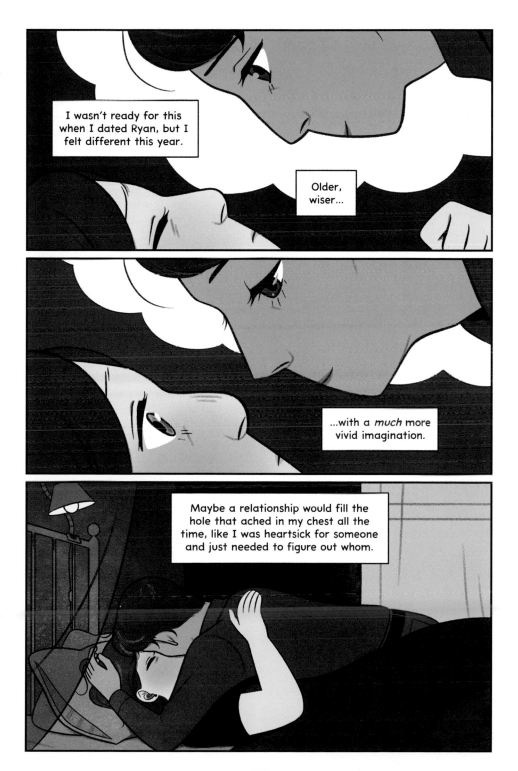

I wasn't ready for this when I dated Ryan, but I felt different this year.

Older, wiser...

...with a *much* more vivid imagination.

Maybe a relationship would fill the hole that ached in my chest all the time, like I was heartsick for someone and just needed to figure out whom.

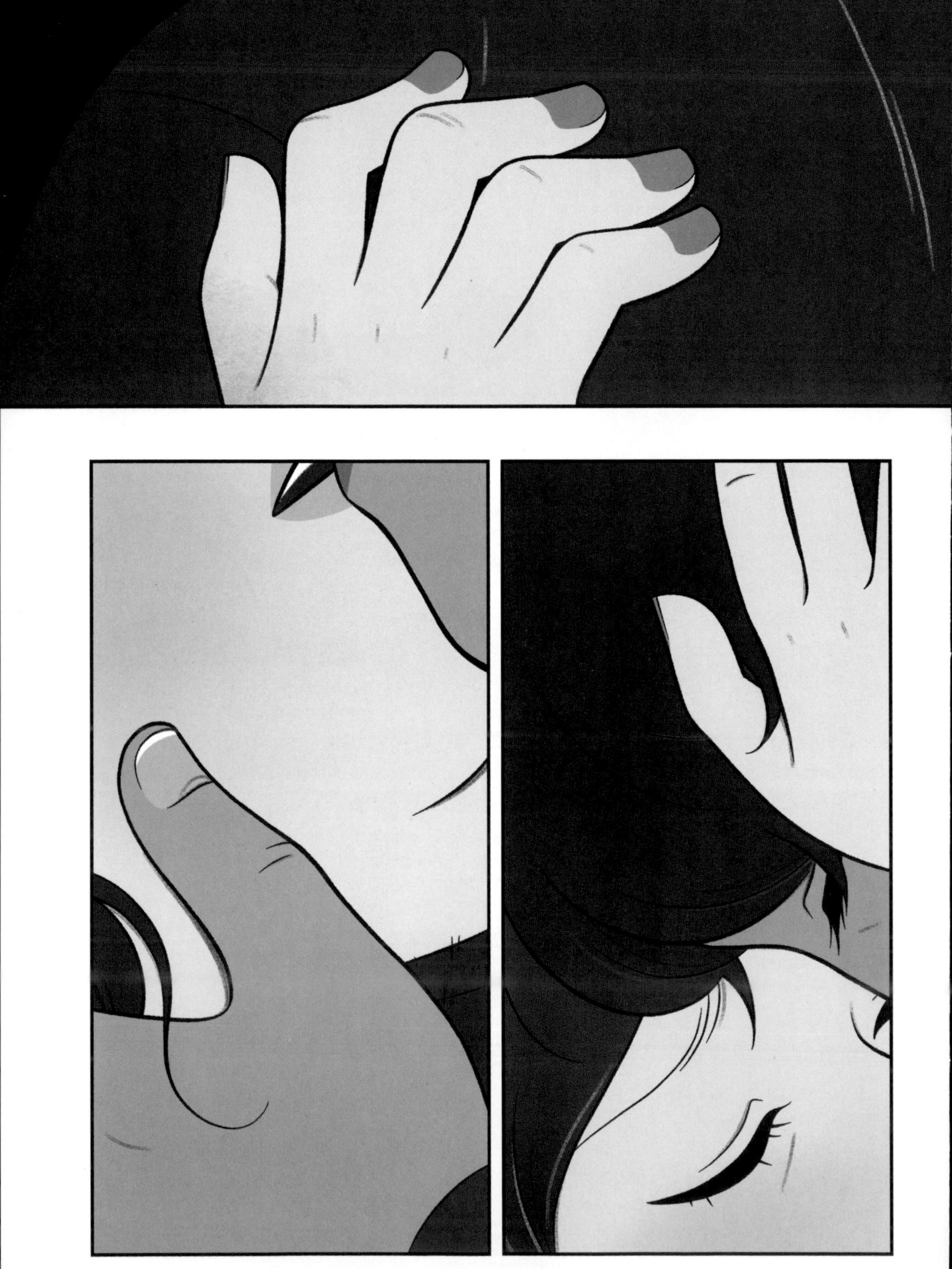

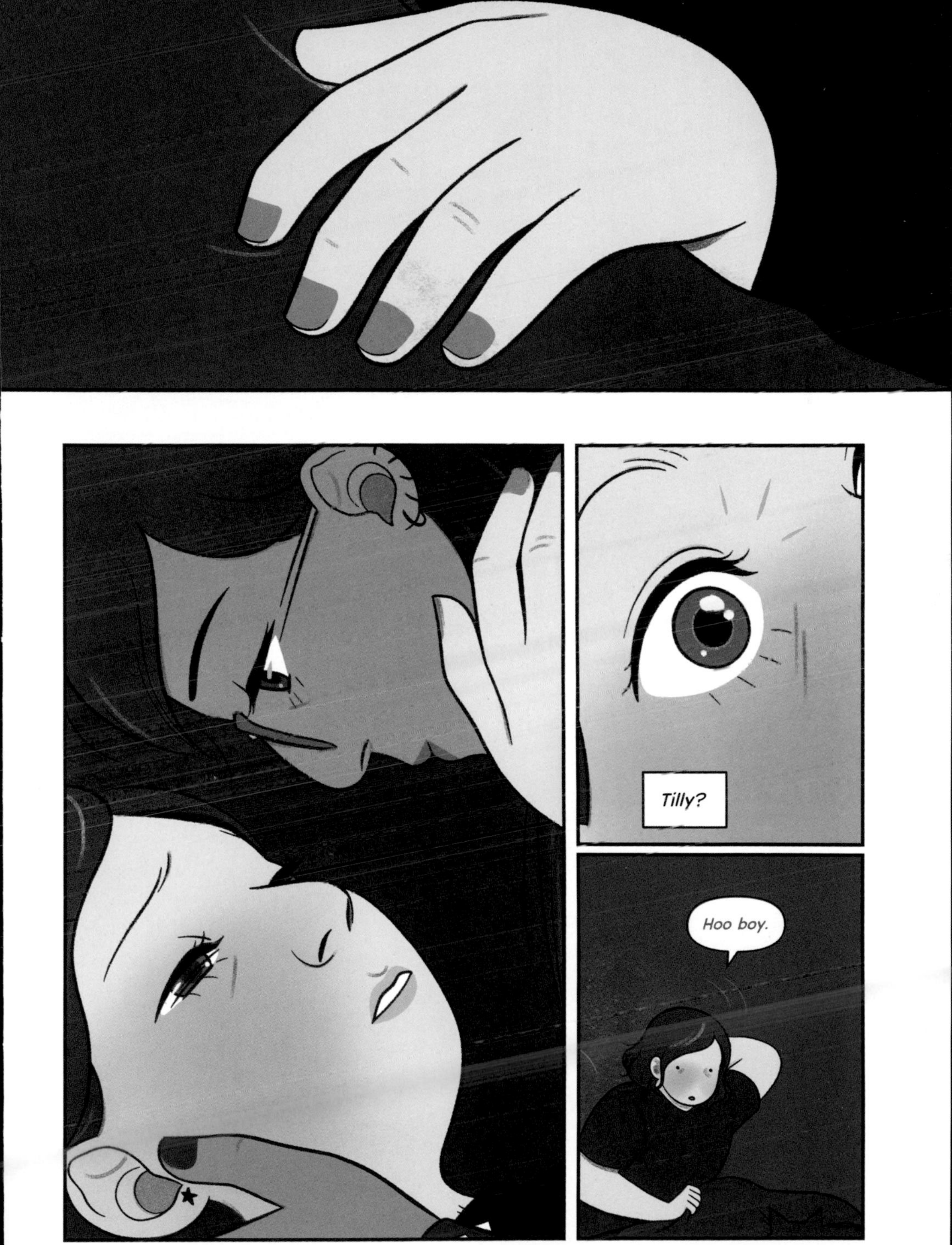
Tilly?
Hoo boy.

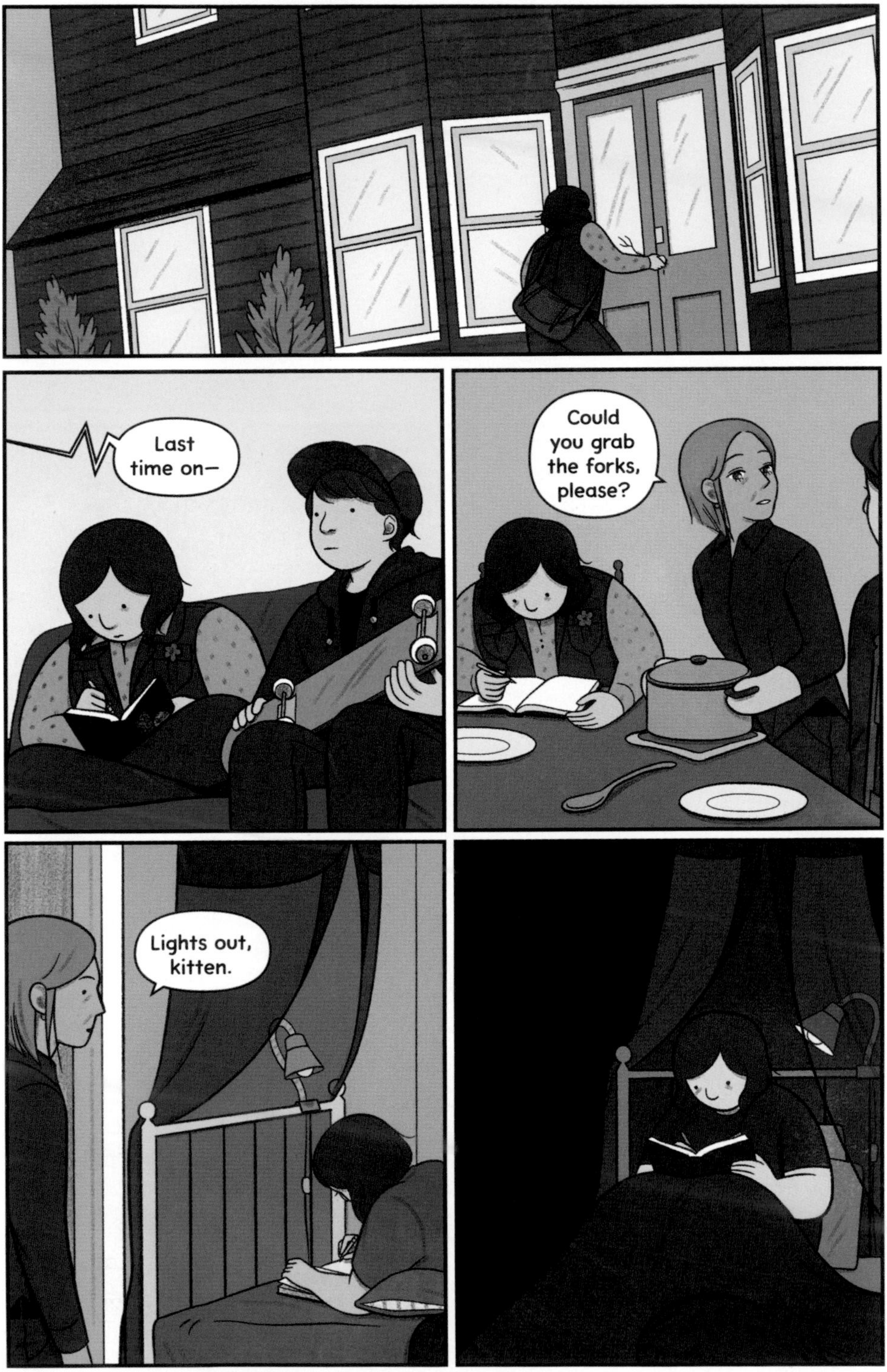
Last time on—
Could you grab the forks, please?
Lights out, kitten.

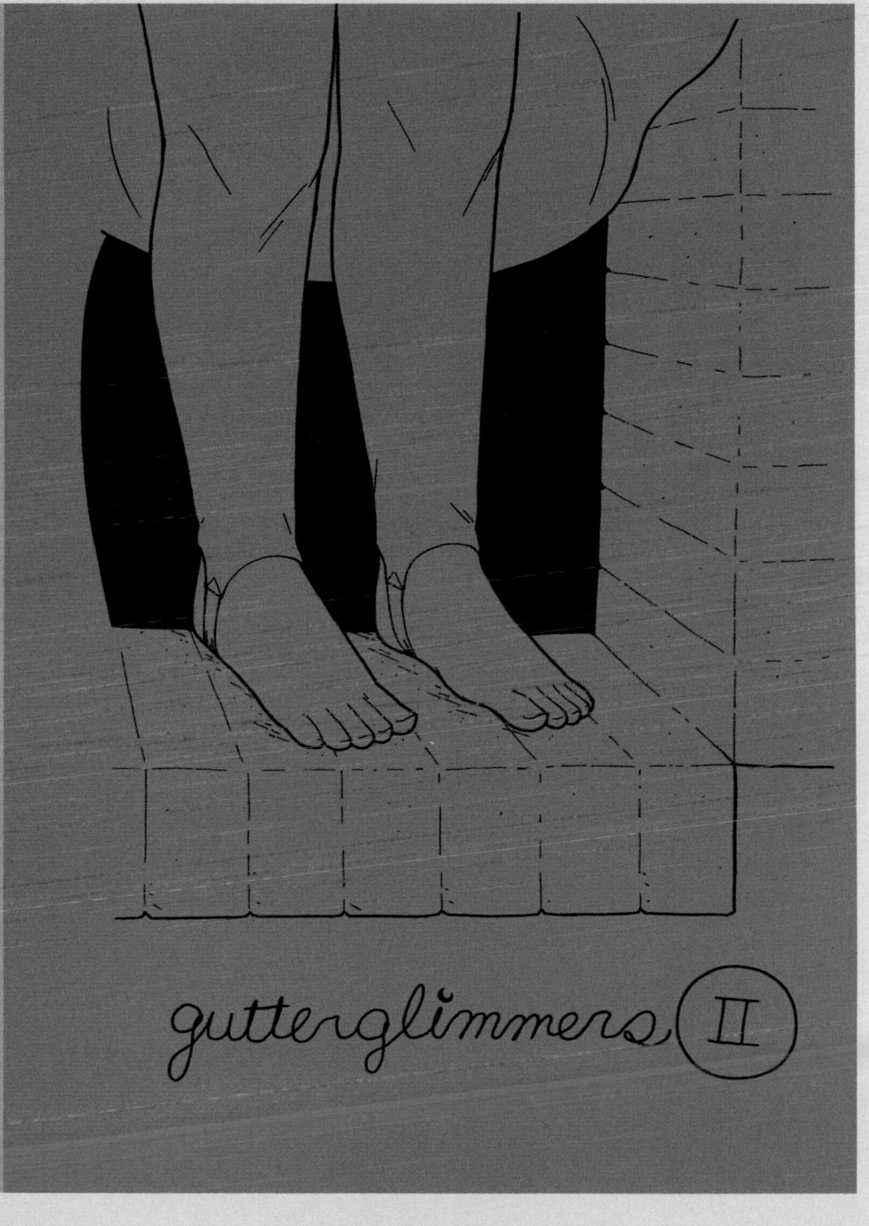
gutterglimmers II

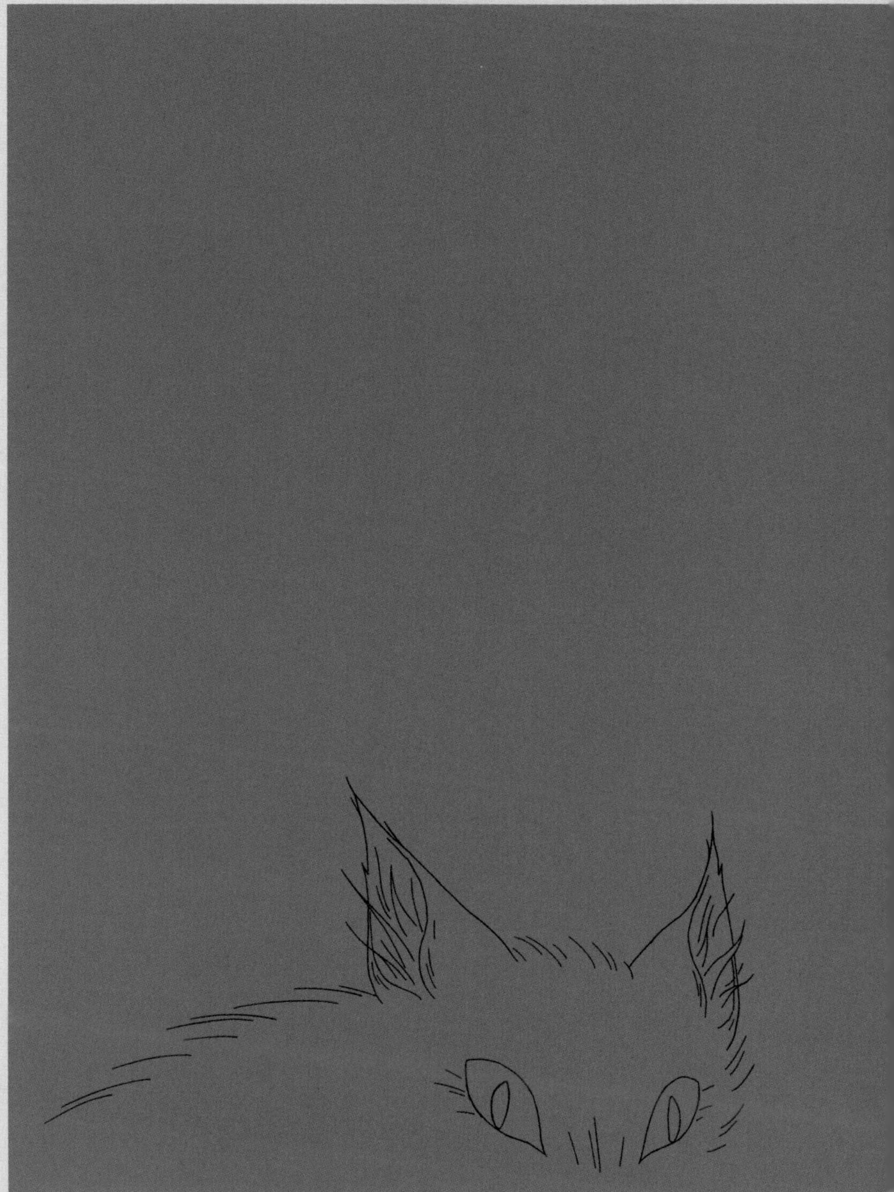

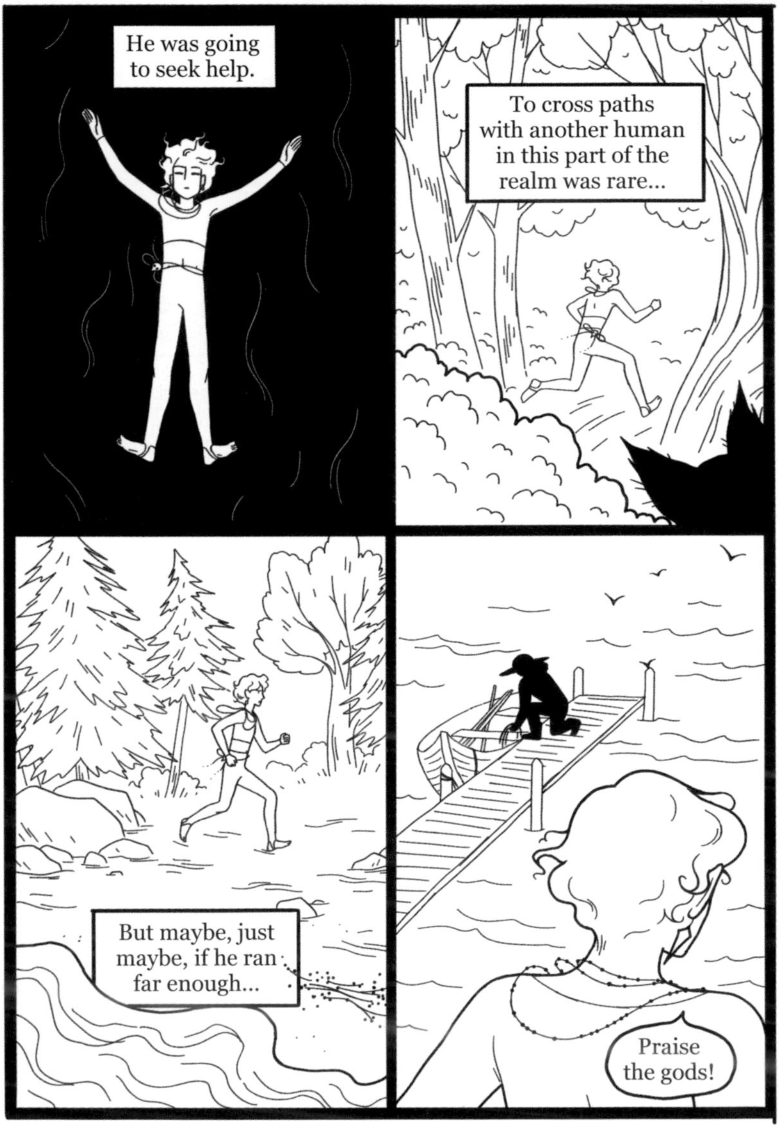
He was going to seek help.
To cross paths with another human in this part of the realm was rare...
But maybe, just maybe, if he ran far enough...
Praise the gods!

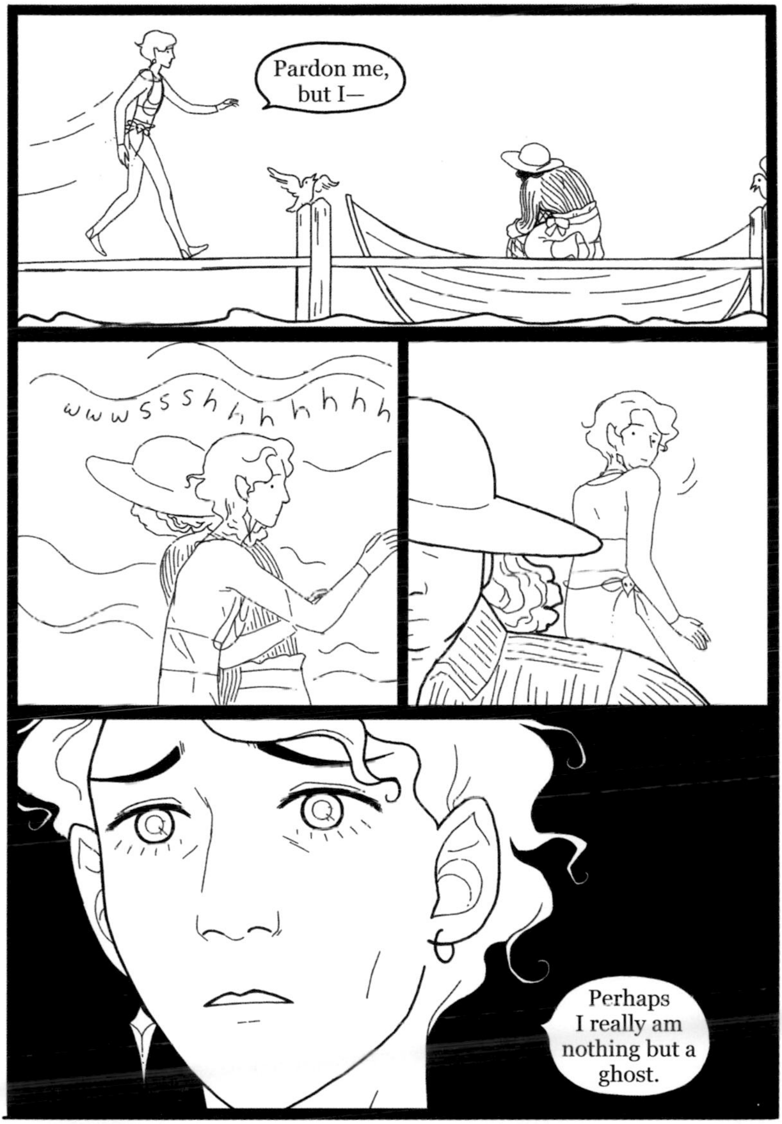
Pardon me, but I—
wwwssshhhhhhhh
Perhaps I really am nothing but a ghost.

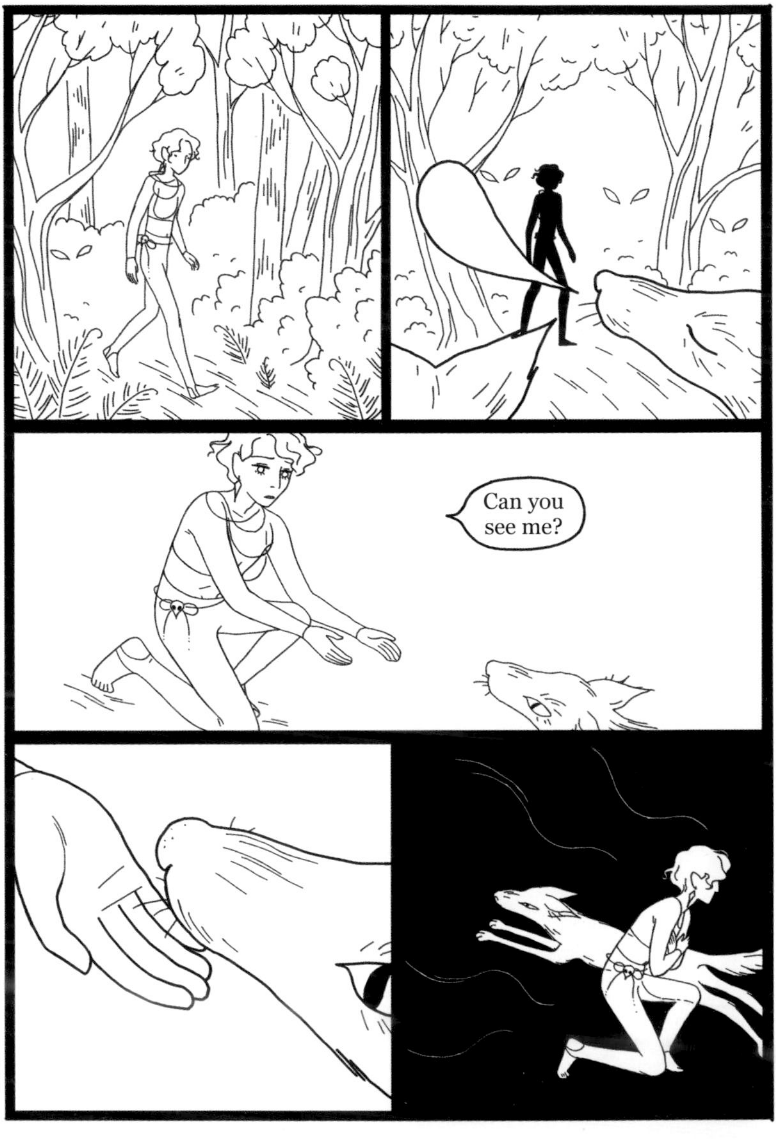
Can you see me?

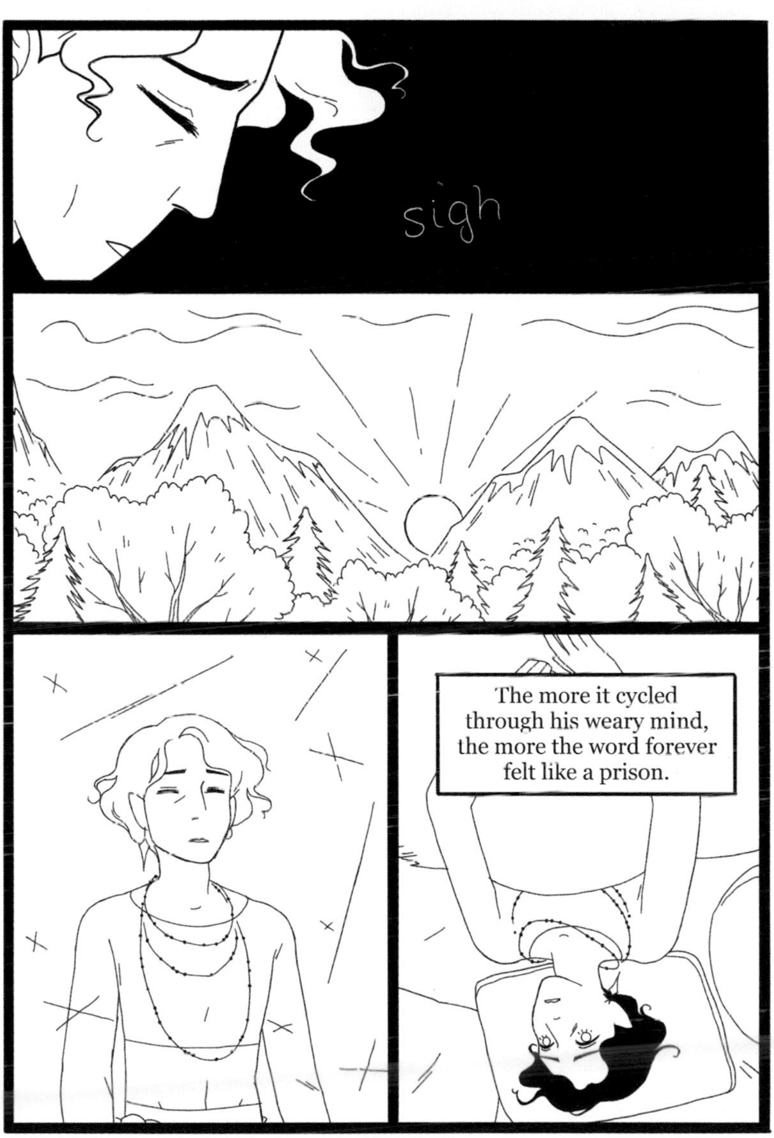
sigh
The more it cycled through his weary mind, the more the word forever felt like a prison.

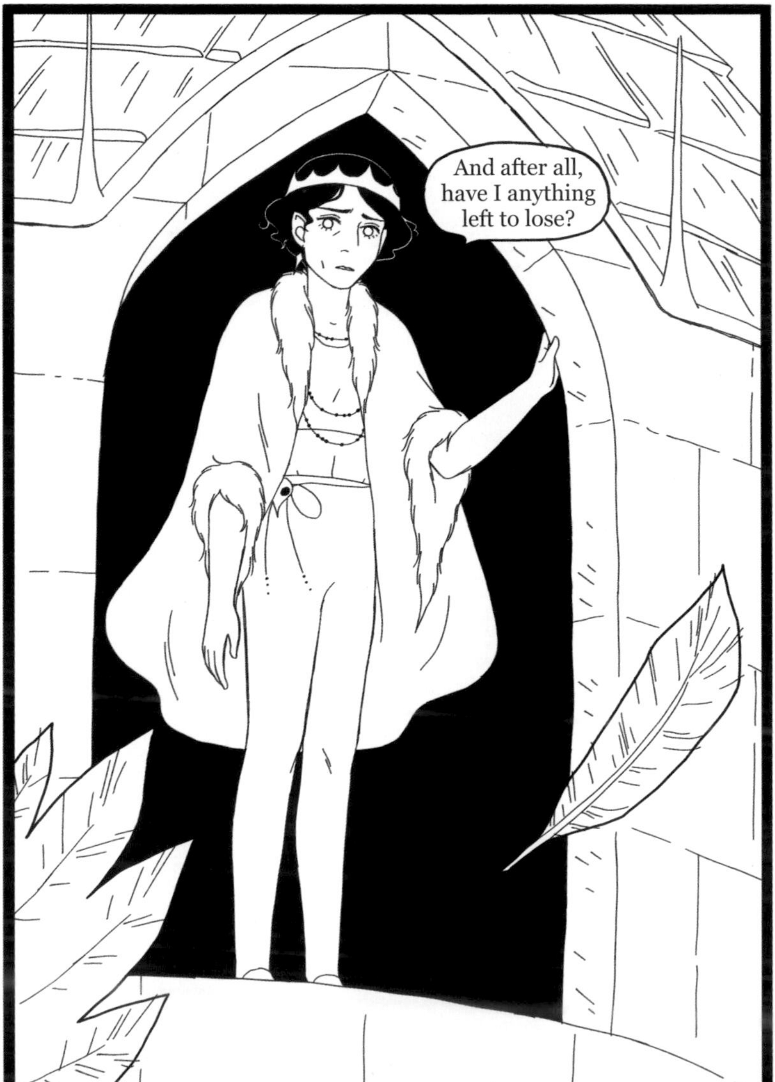
And after all, have I anything left to lose?

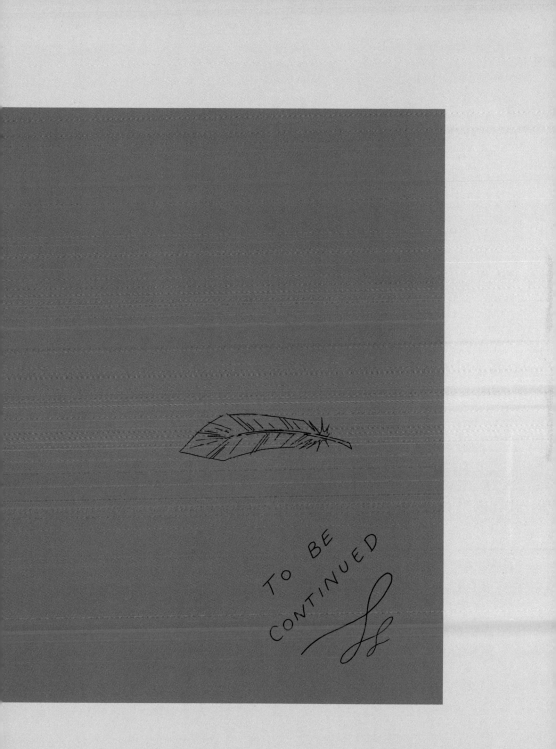

TO BE
CONTINUED

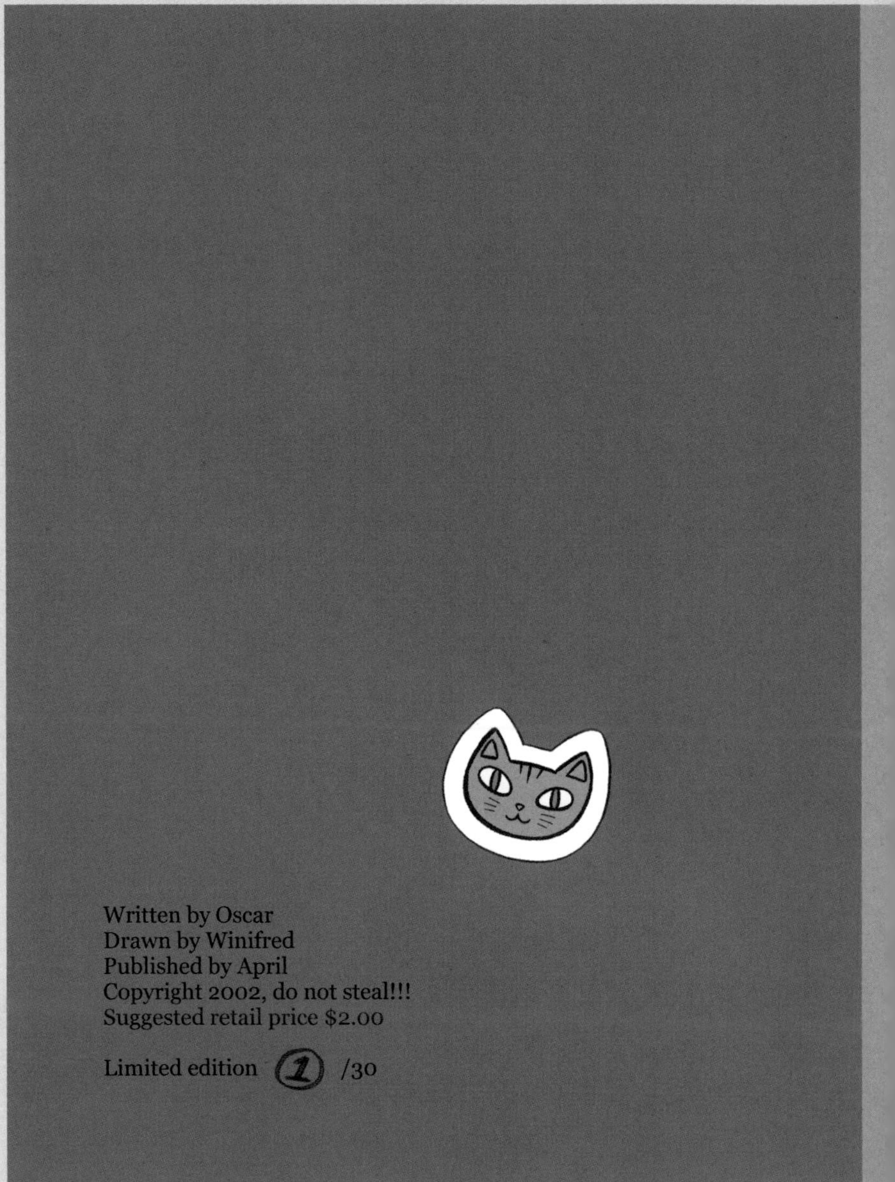
Written by Oscar
Drawn by Winifred
Published by April
Copyright 2002, do not steal!!!
Suggested retail price $2.00
Limited edition 1 /30

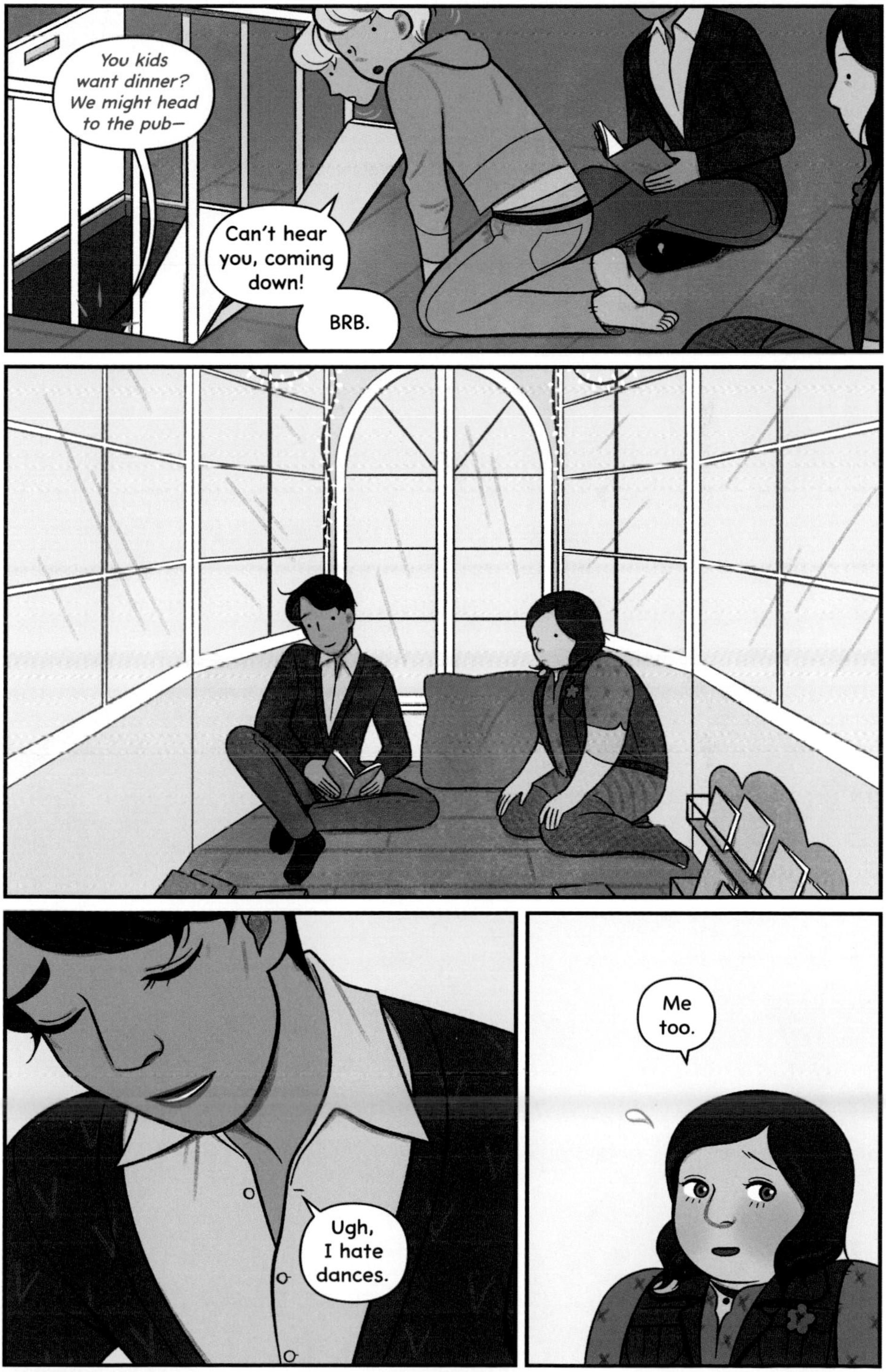
You kids want dinner? We might head to the pub—
Can't hear you, coming down!
BRB.
Ugh, I hate dances.
Me too.

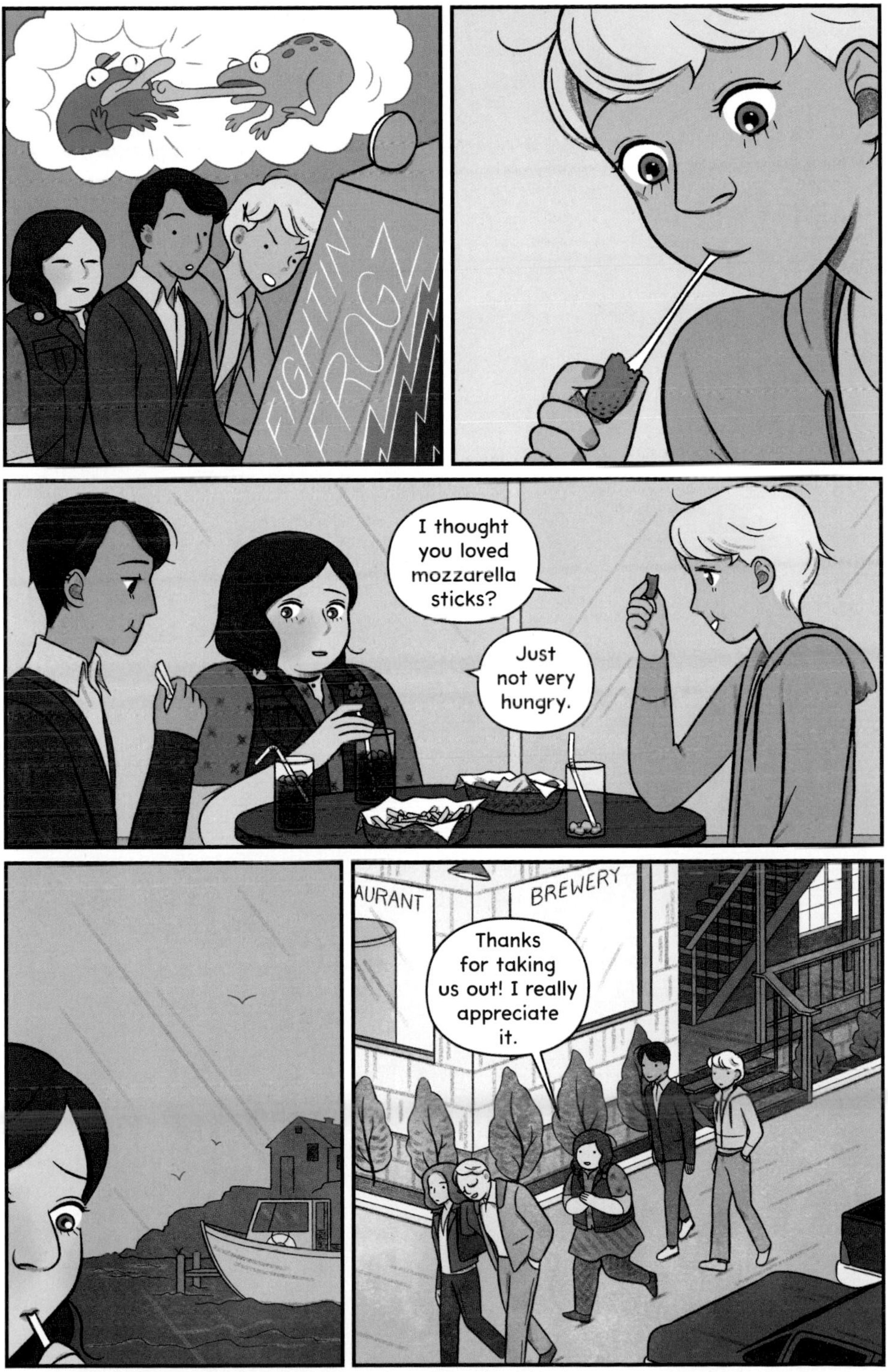
FIGHTIN' FROGZ
I thought you loved mozzarella sticks?
Just not very hungry.
AURANT
BREWERY
Thanks for taking us out! I really appreciate it.

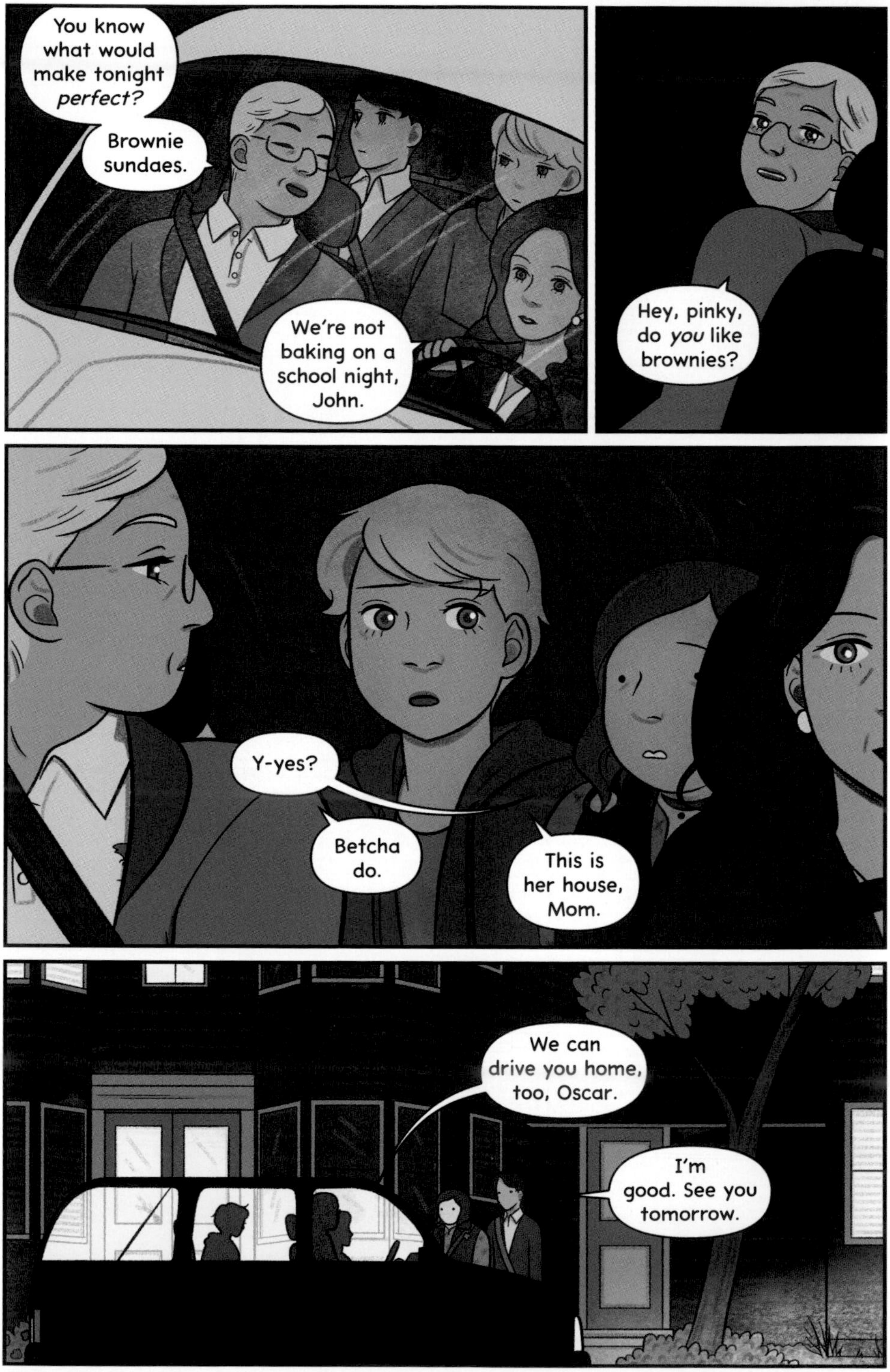
You know what would make tonight *perfect?*
Brownie sundaes.
We're not baking on a school night, John.
Hey, pinky, do *you* like brownies?
Y-yes?
Betcha do.
This is her house, Mom.
We can drive you home, too, Oscar.
I'm good. See you tomorrow.

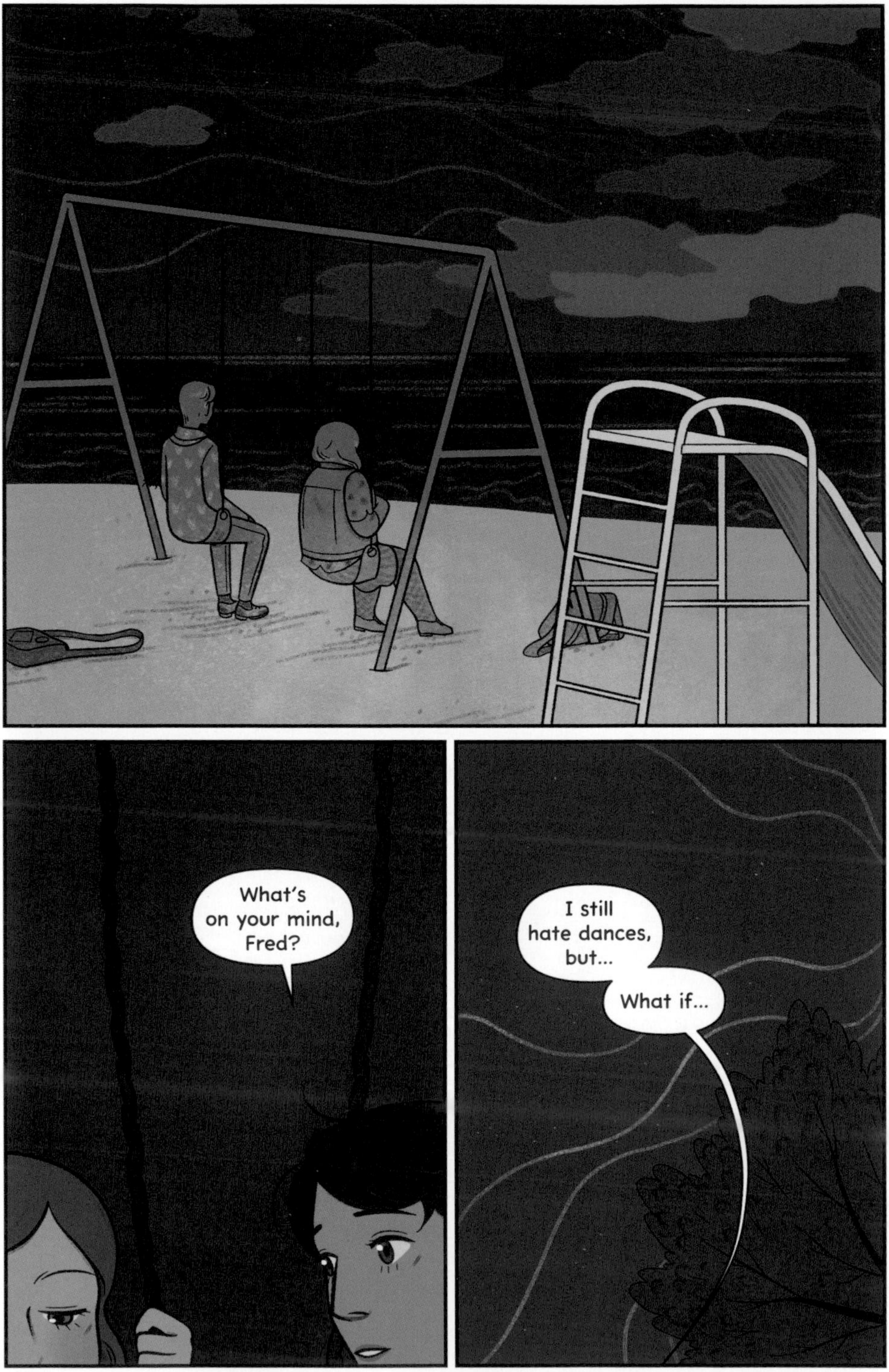
What's on your mind, Fred?
I still hate dances, but...
What if...

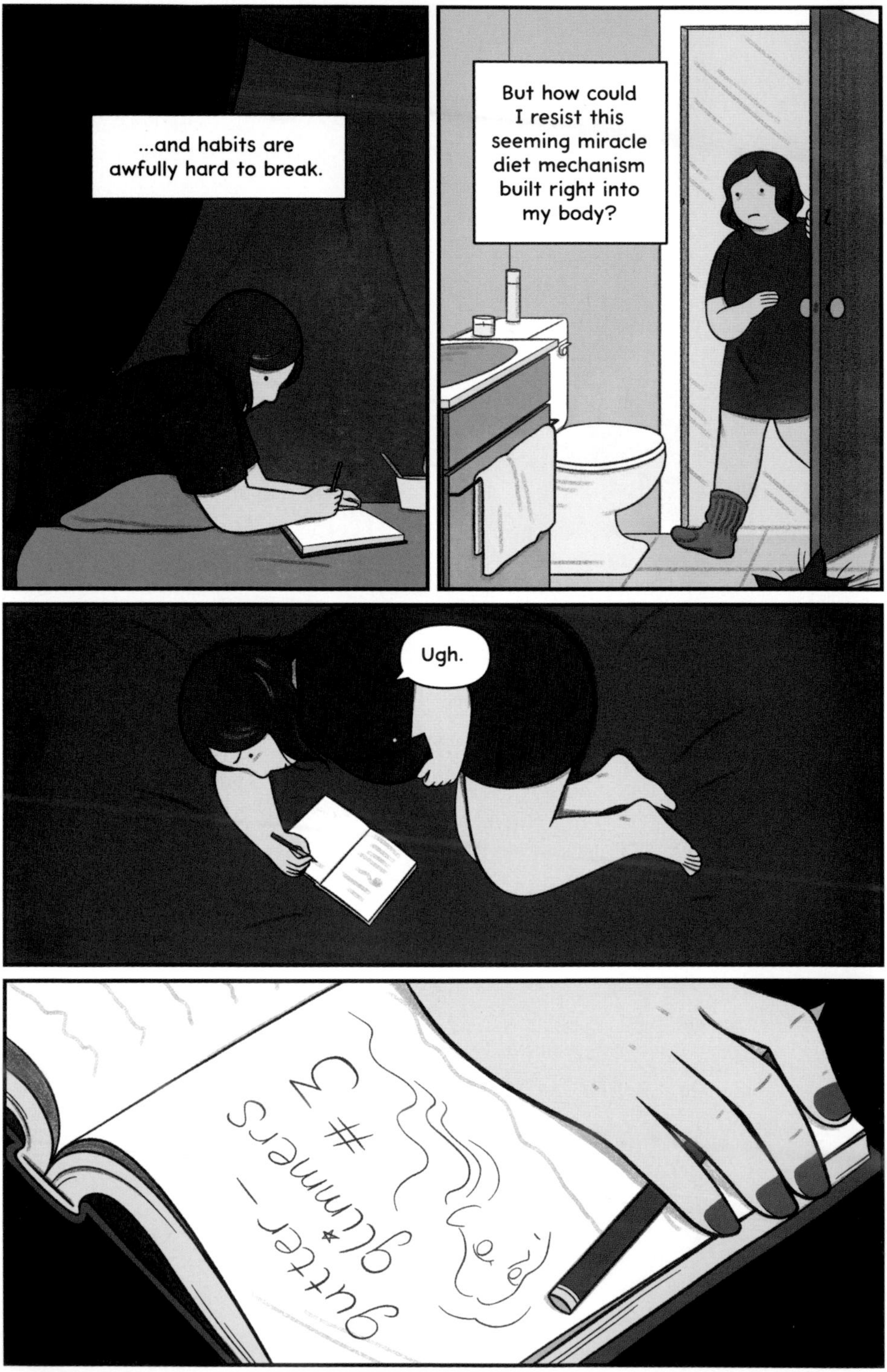
...and habits are awfully hard to break.
But how could I resist this seeming miracle diet mechanism built right into my body?
Ugh.
gutter glimmers #3

185

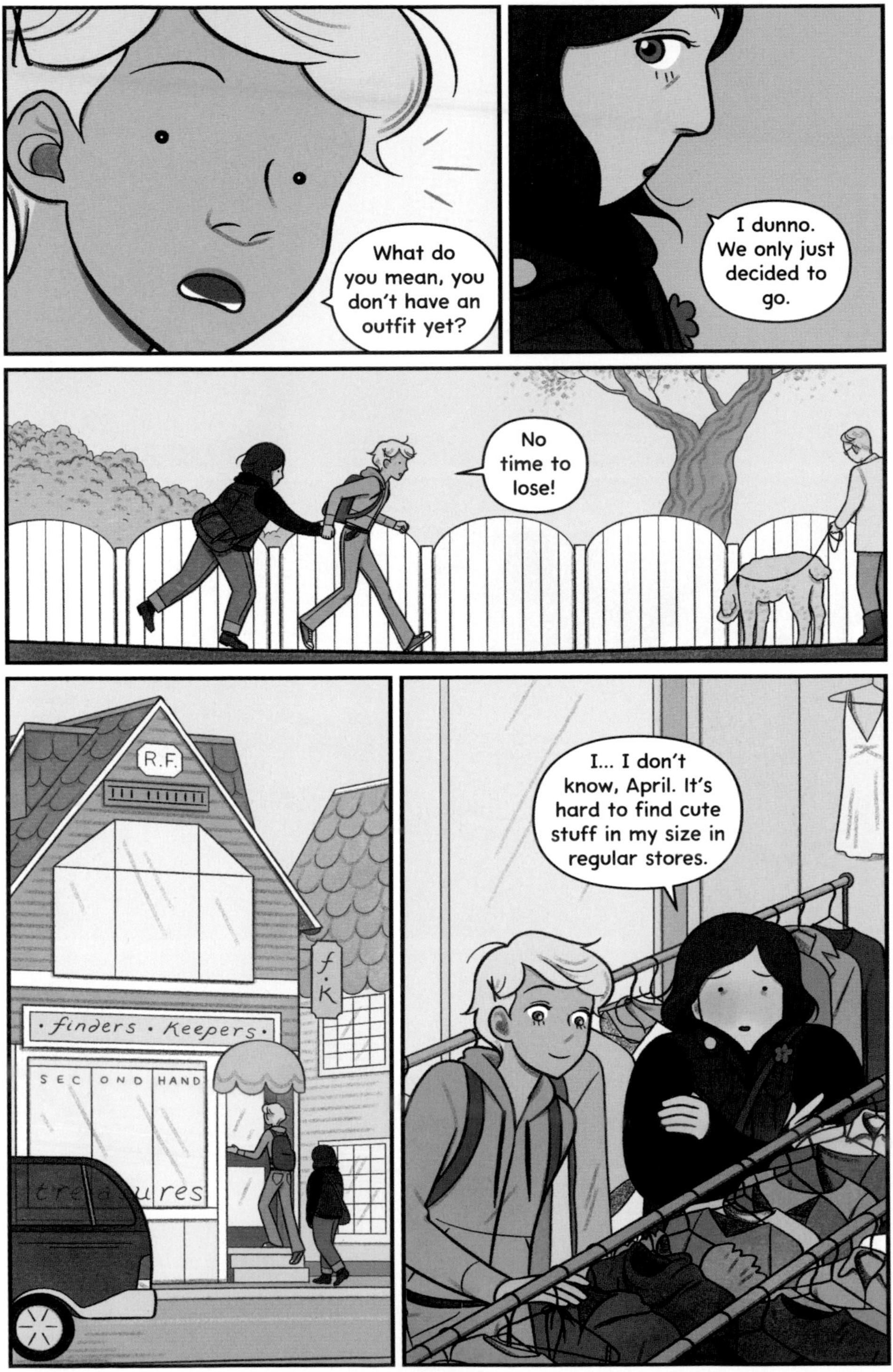
What do you mean, you don't have an outfit yet?
I dunno. We only just decided to go.
No time to lose!
R.F.
f.K
·finders · Keepers·
SEC OND HAND
I... I don't know, April. It's hard to find cute stuff in my size in regular stores.

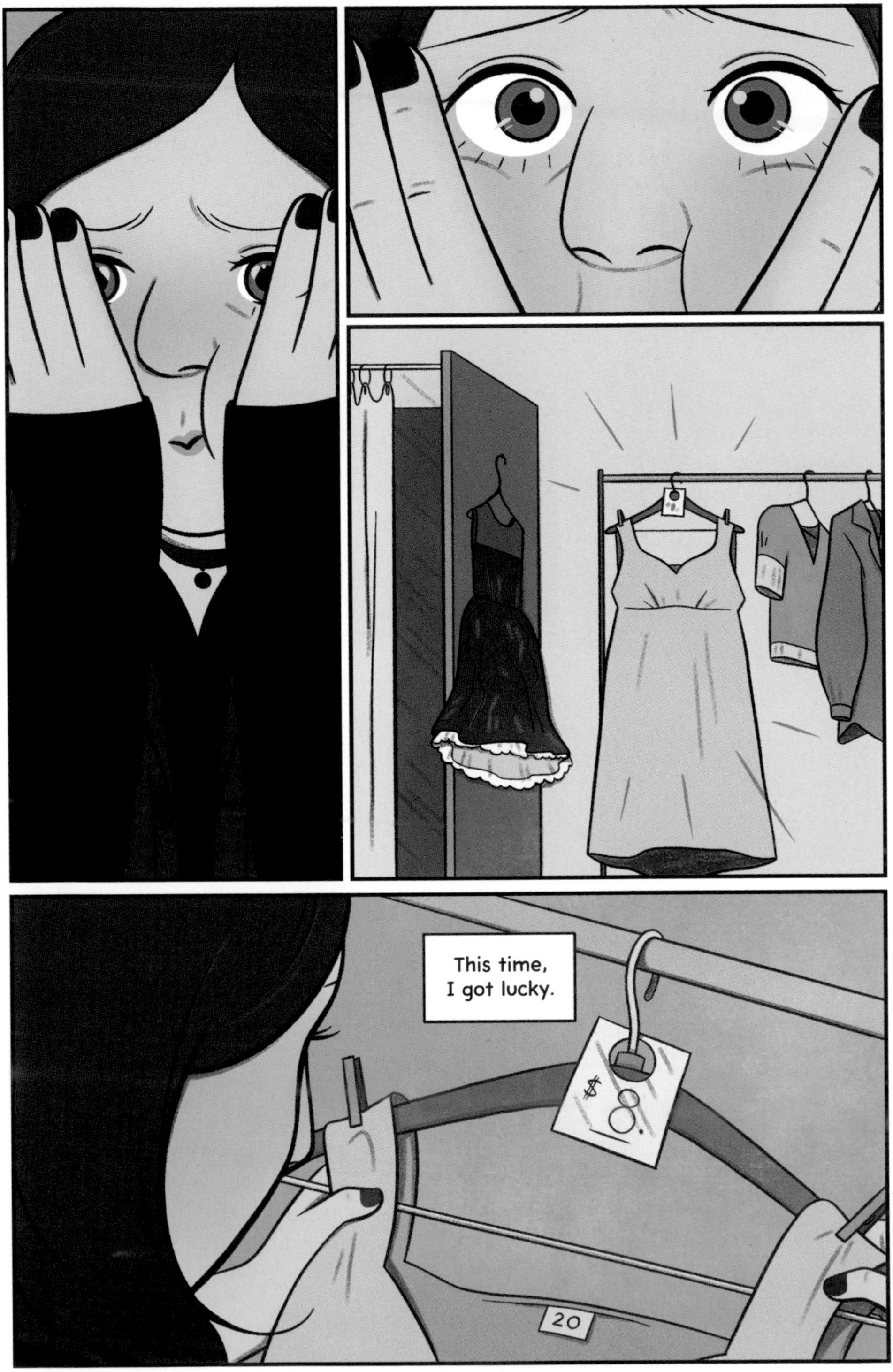
This time, I got lucky.
$8.
20

189

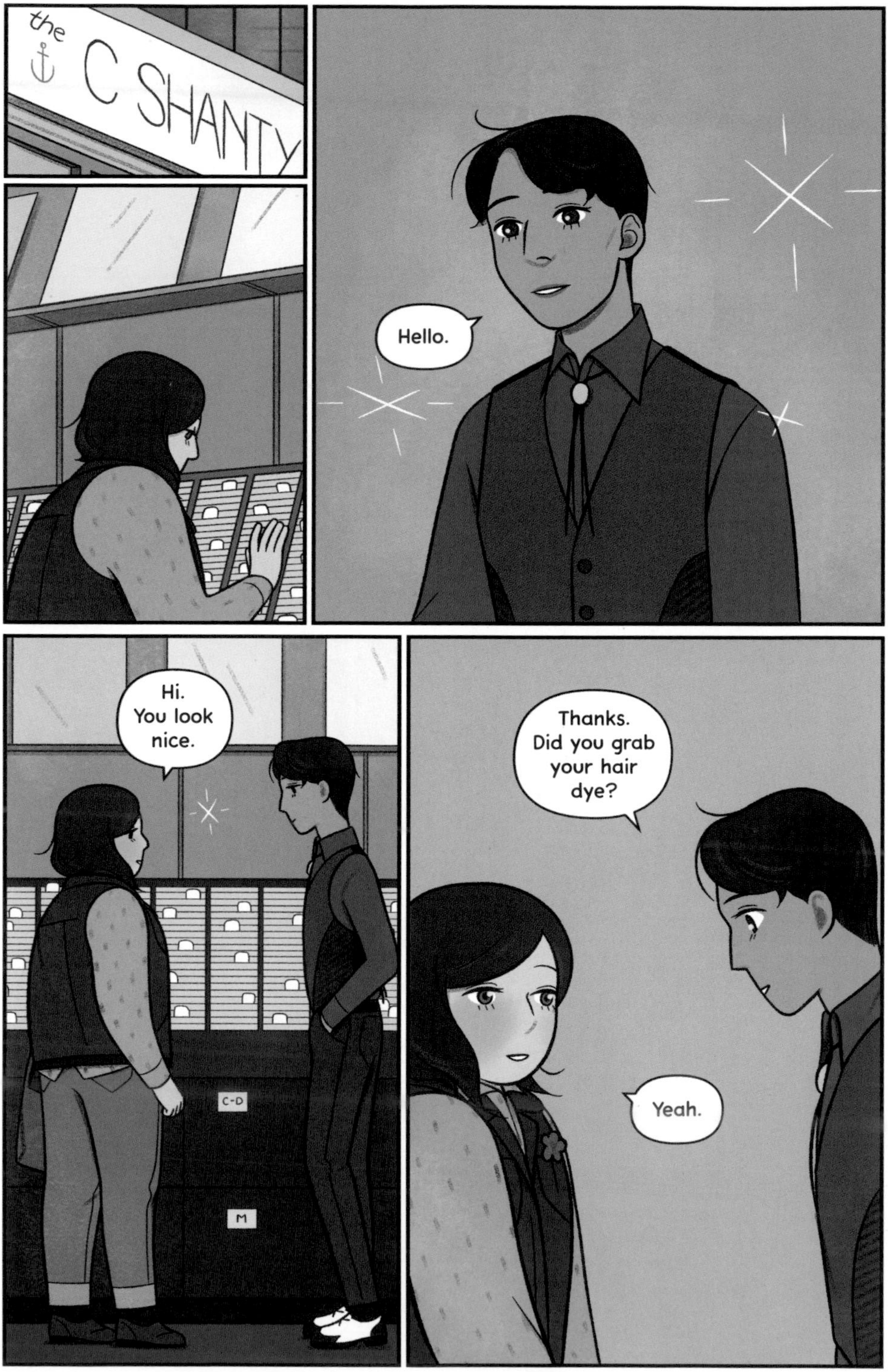
the C SHANTY
Hello.
Hi. You look nice.
C-D
M
Thanks. Did you grab your hair dye?
Yeah.

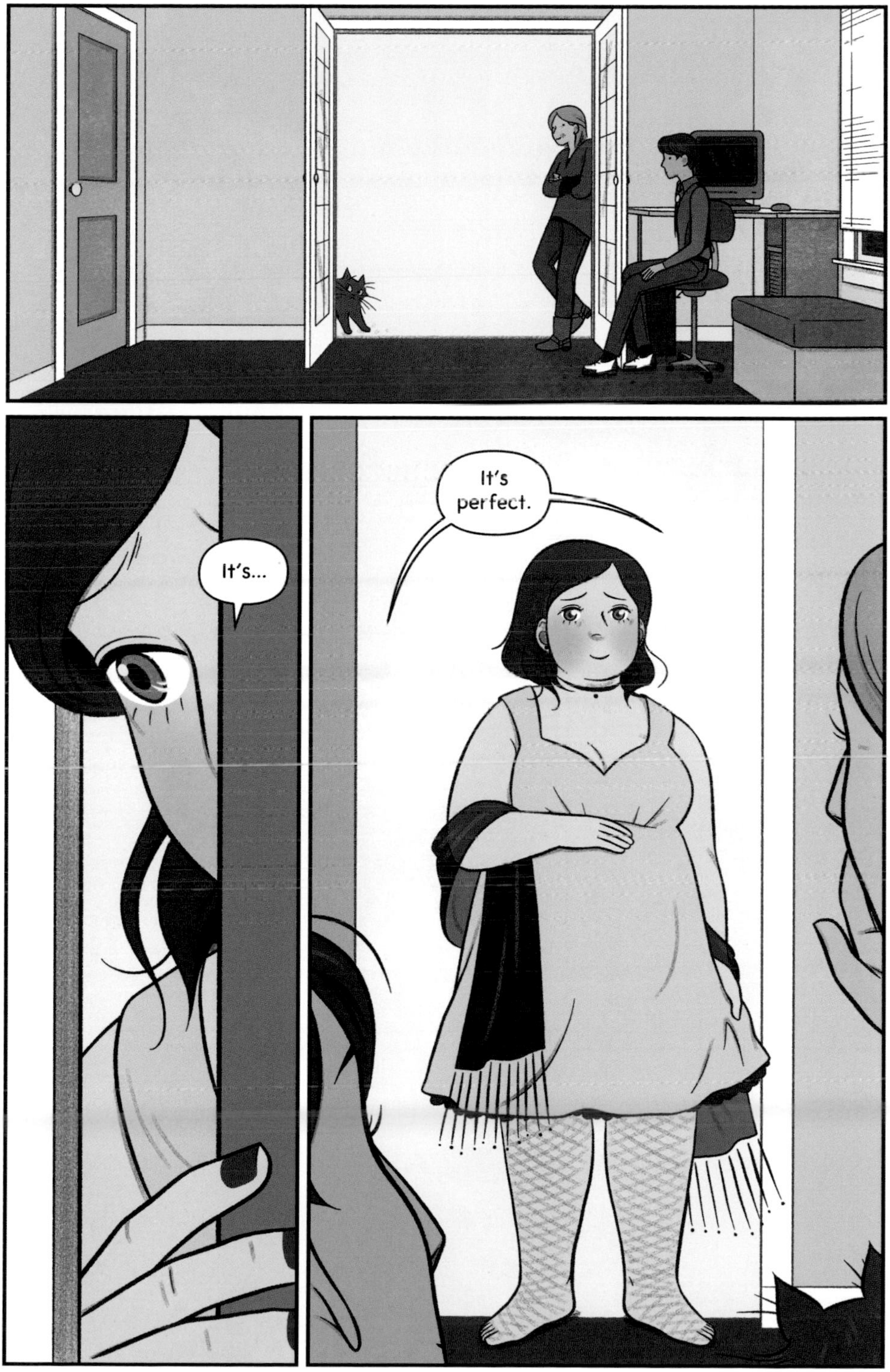
It's...
It's perfect.

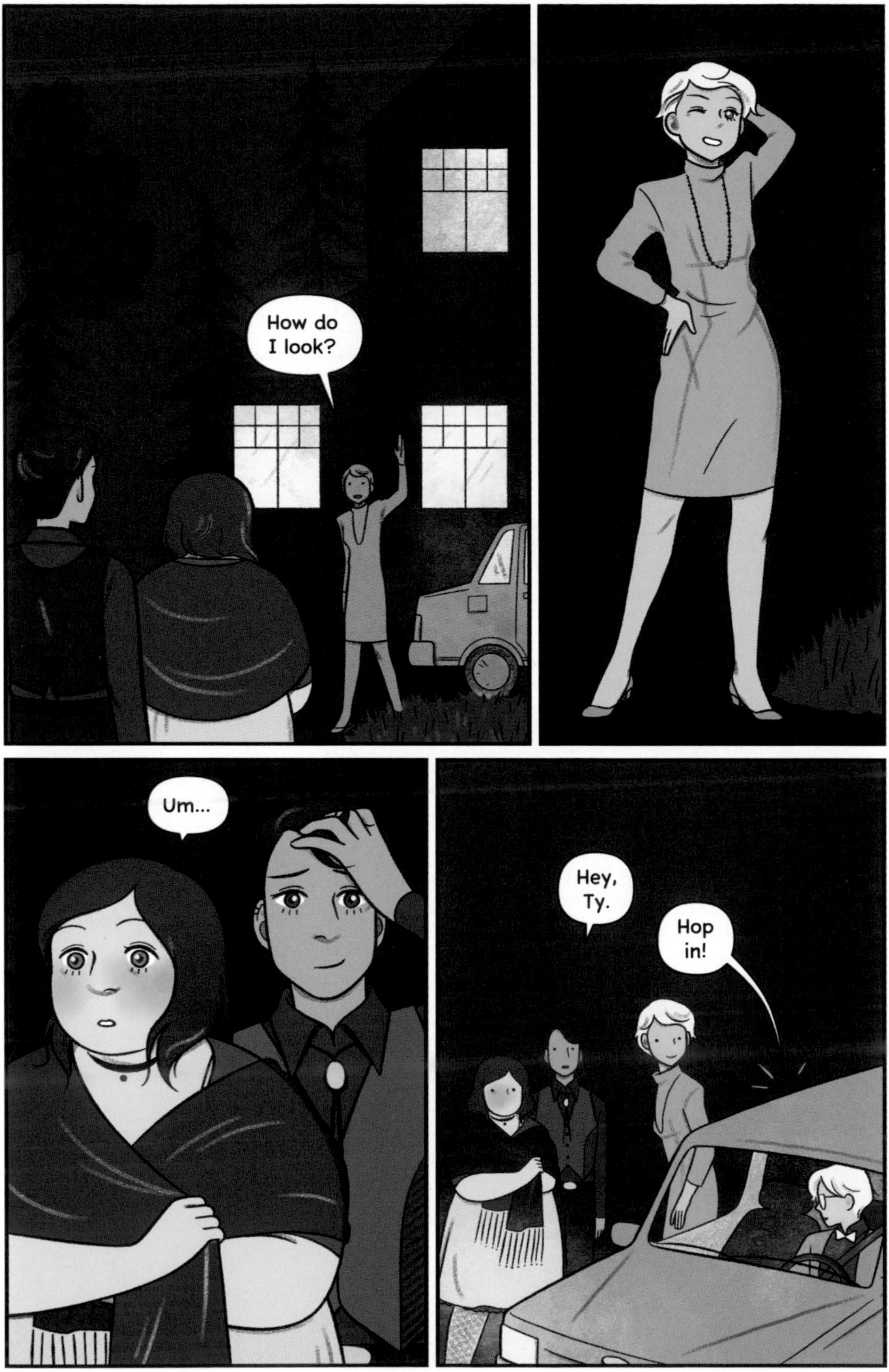
How do I look?
Um...
Hey, Ty.
Hop in!

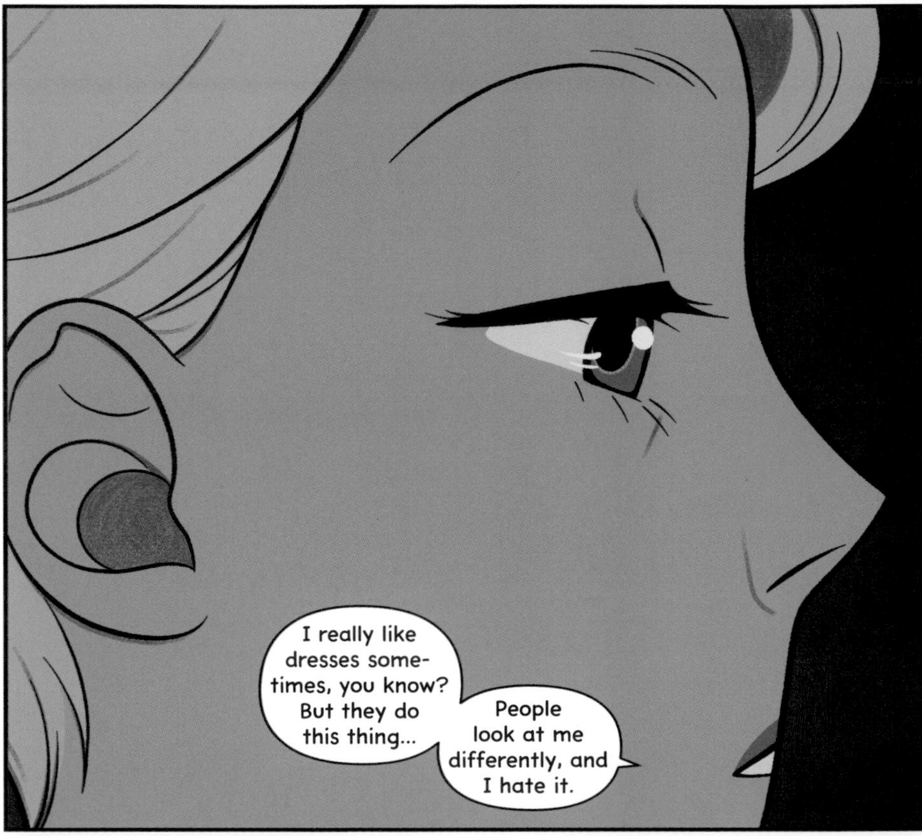

I really like dresses some-times, you know? But they do this thing...
People look at me differently, and I hate it.

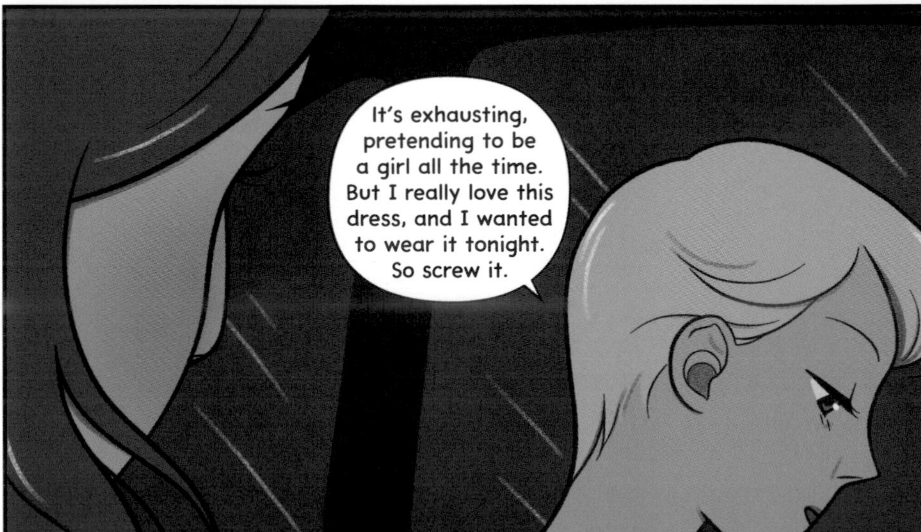

It's exhausting, pretending to be a girl all the time. But I really love this dress, and I wanted to wear it tonight. So screw it.

199

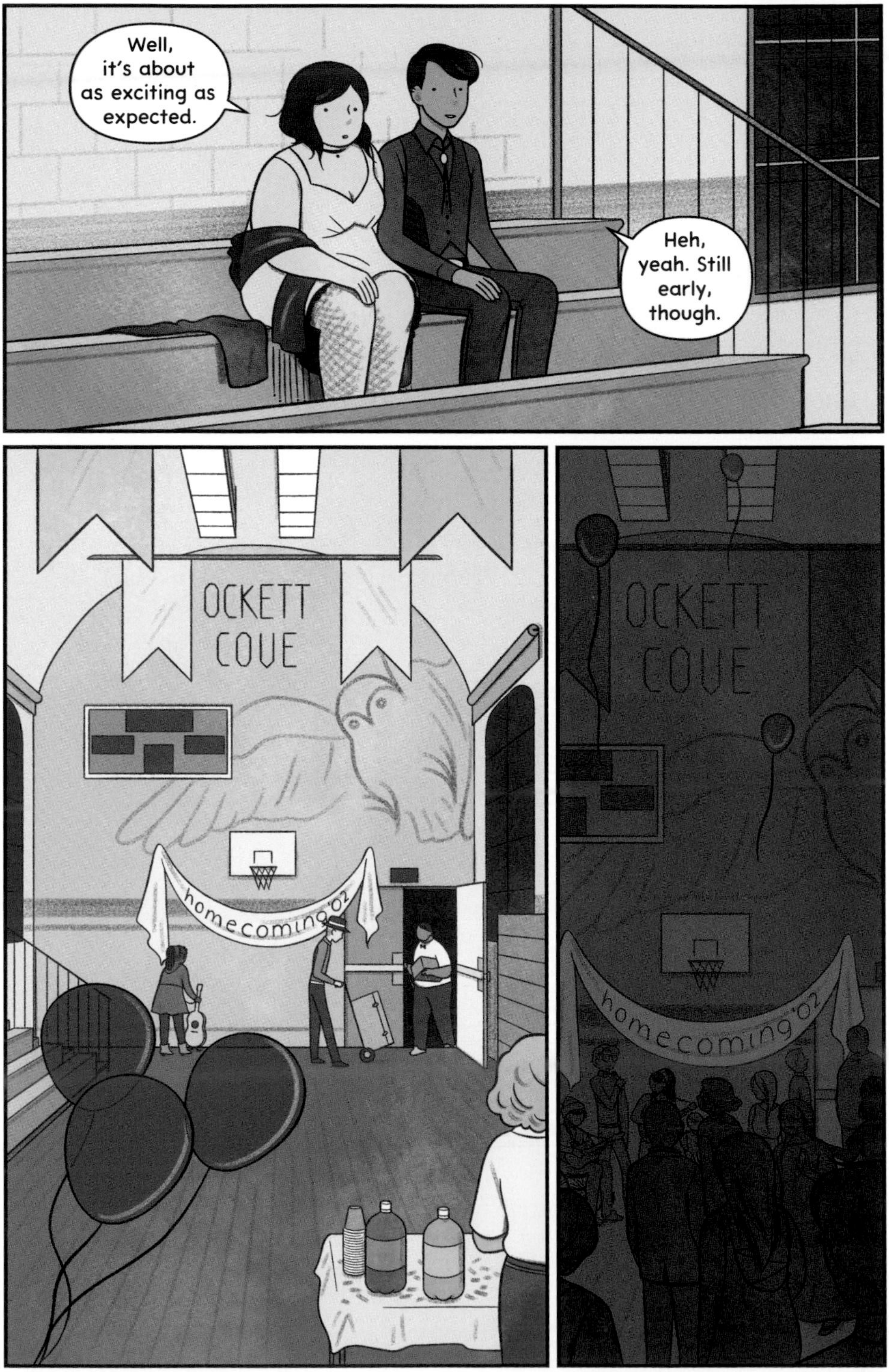
Well, it's about as exciting as expected.
Heh, yeah. Still early, though.
OCKETT COVE
homecoming '02
OCKETT COVE
homecoming '02

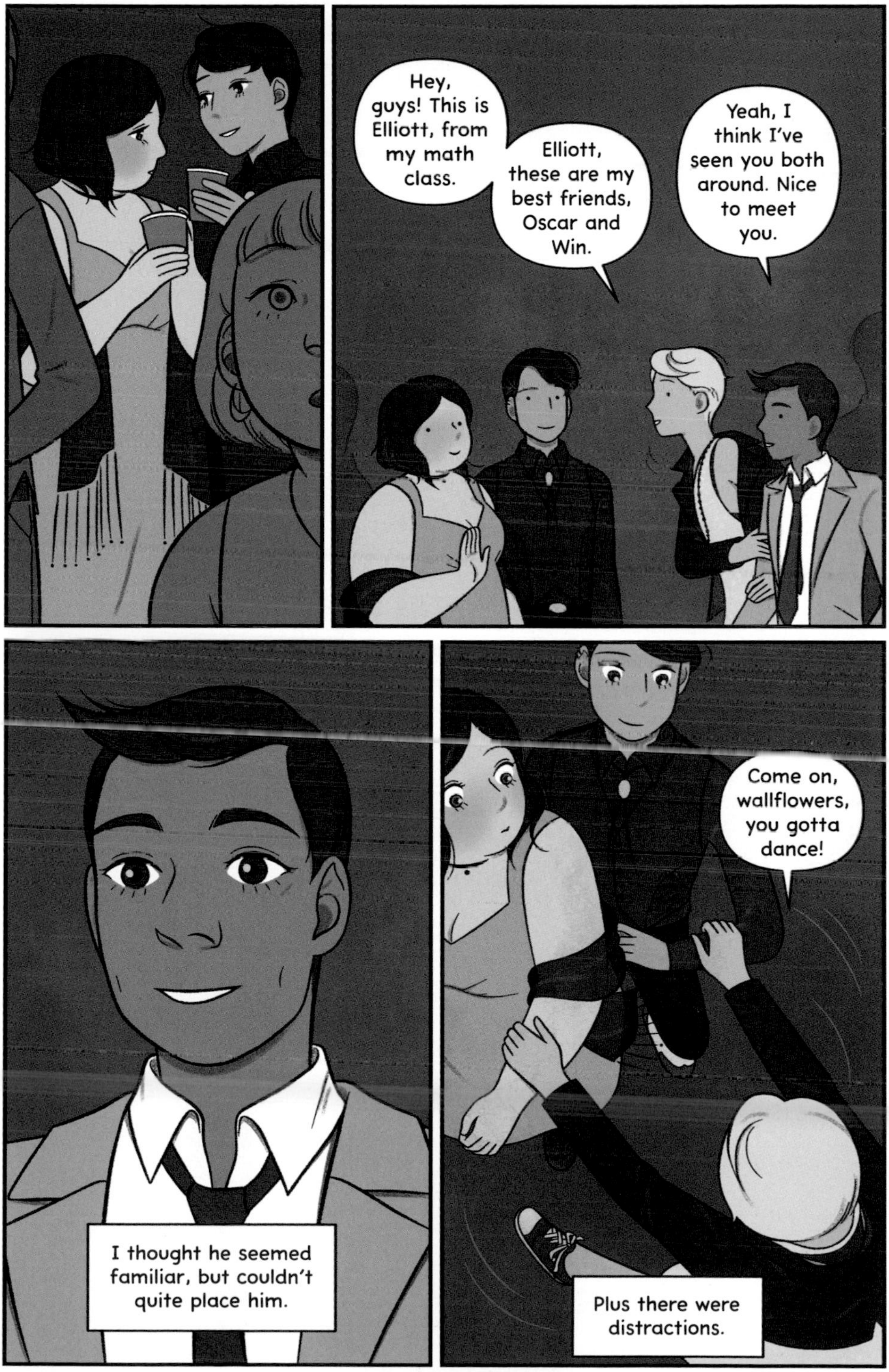
Hey, guys! This is Elliott, from my math class.
Elliott, these are my best friends, Oscar and Win.
Yeah, I think I've seen you both around. Nice to meet you.
I thought he seemed familiar, but couldn't quite place him.
Come on, wallflowers, you gotta dance!
Plus there were distractions.

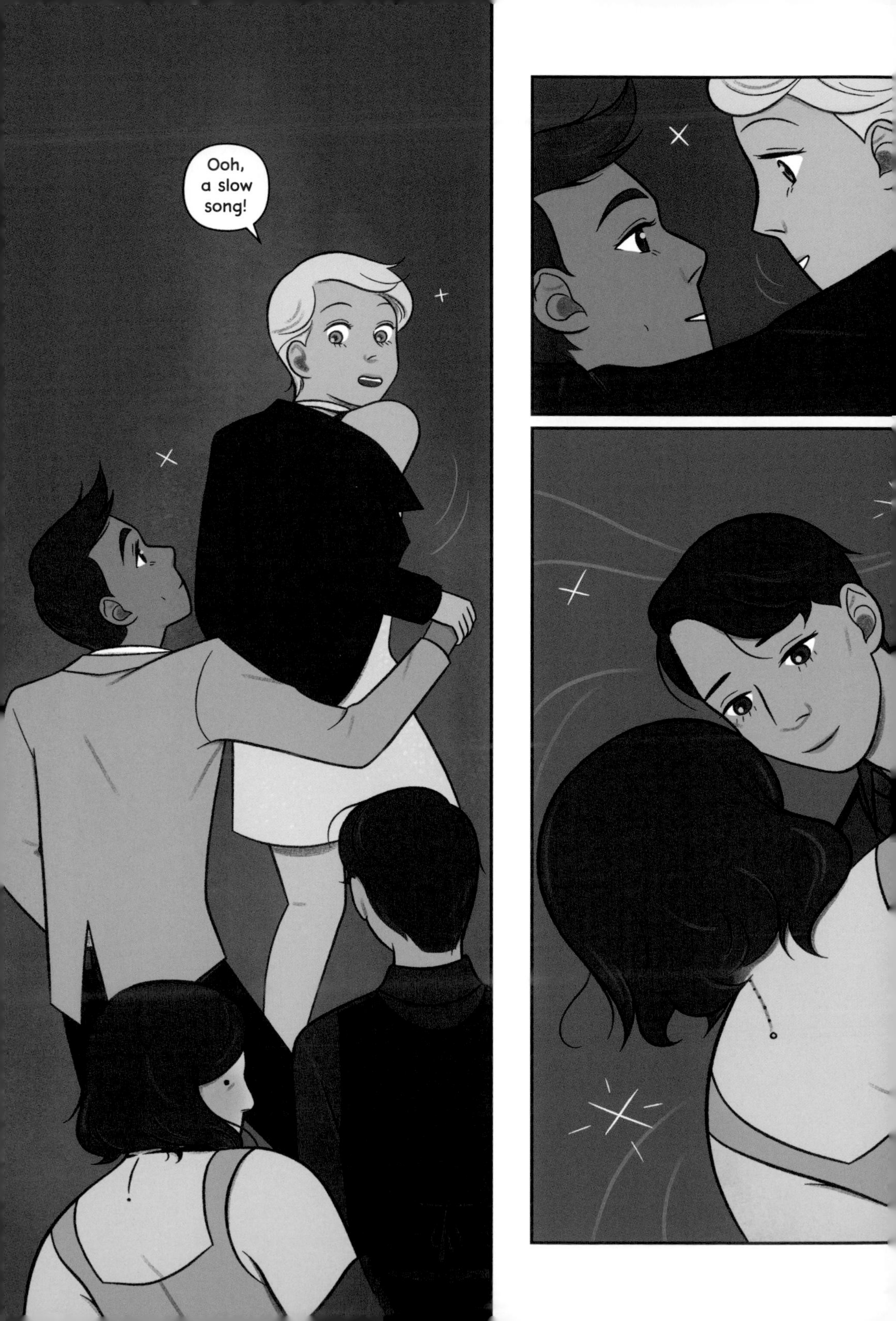
Ooh, a slow song!

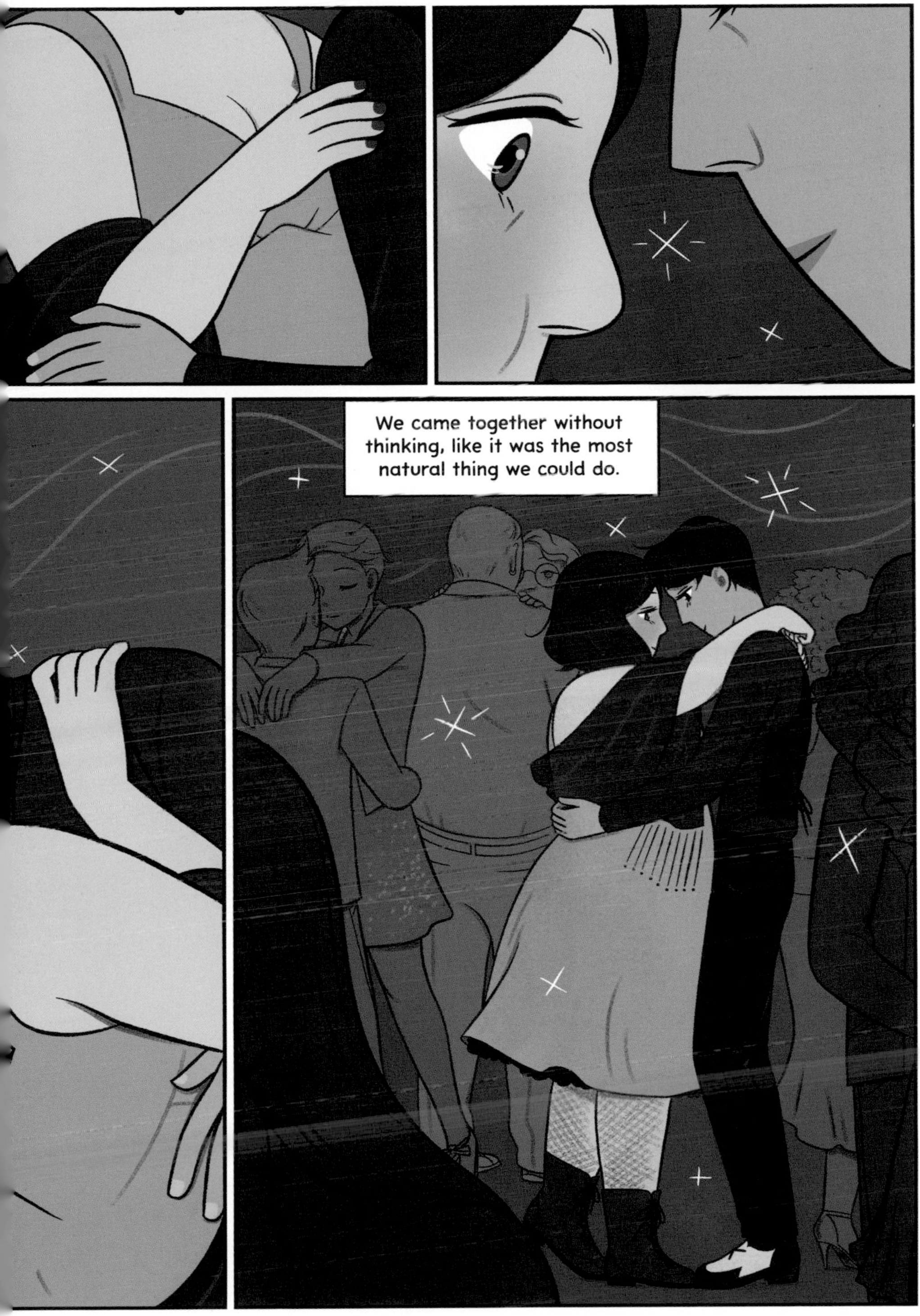
We came together without thinking, like it was the most natural thing we could do.

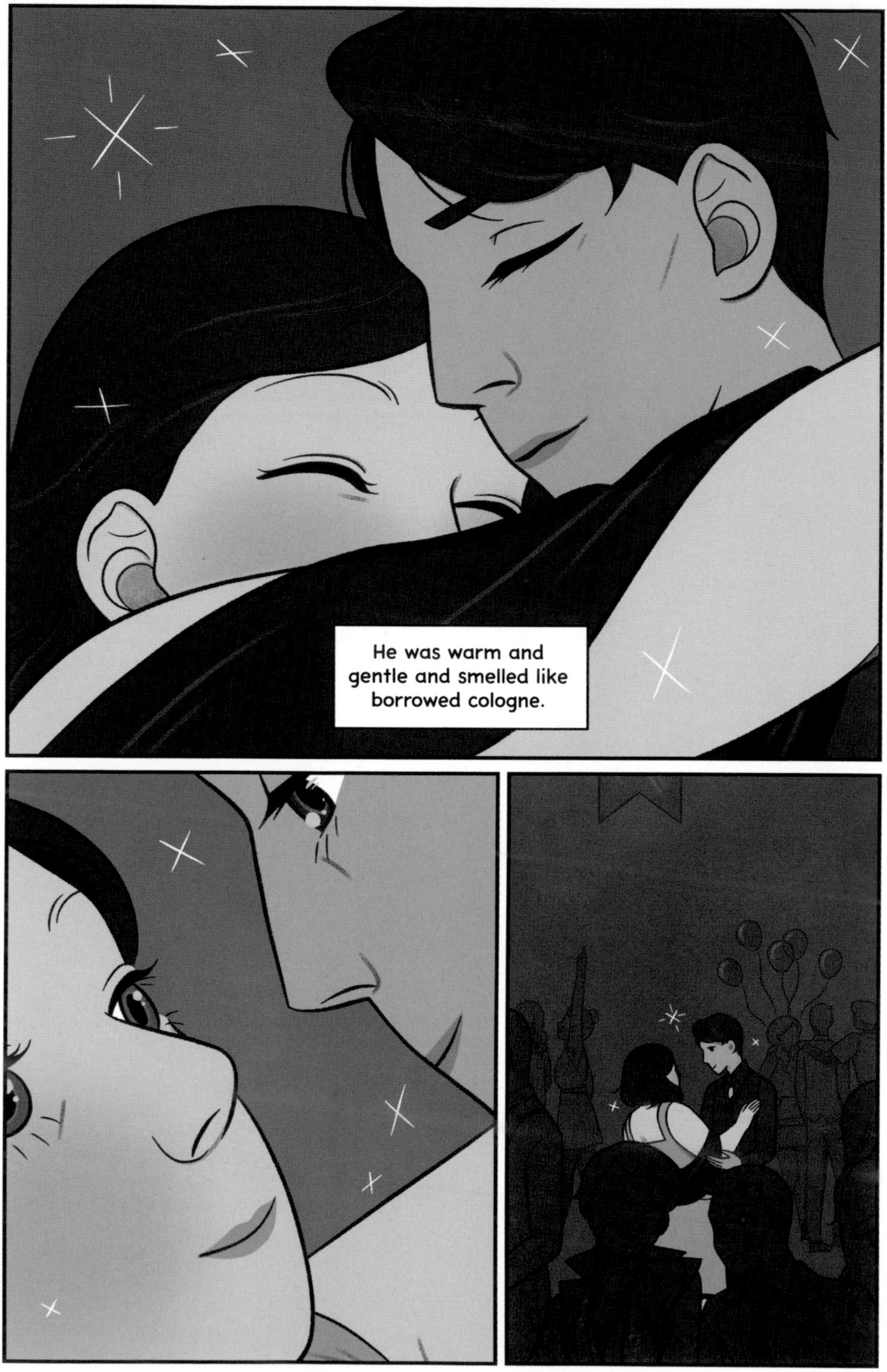
He was warm and
gentle and smelled like
borrowed cologne.

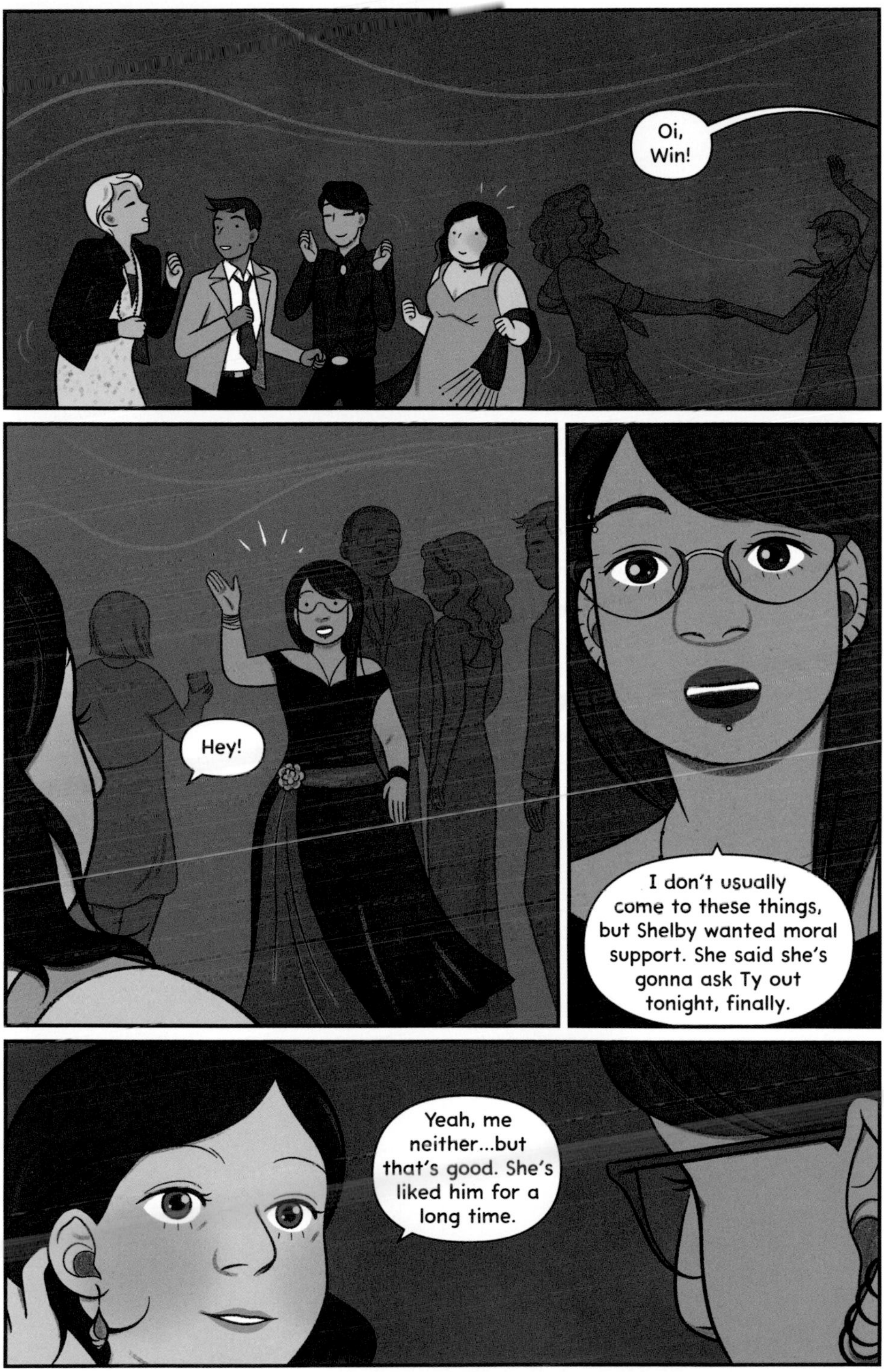
Oi, Win!
Hey!
I don't usually come to these things, but Shelby wanted moral support. She said she's gonna ask Ty out tonight, finally.
Yeah, me neither...but that's good. She's liked him for a long time.

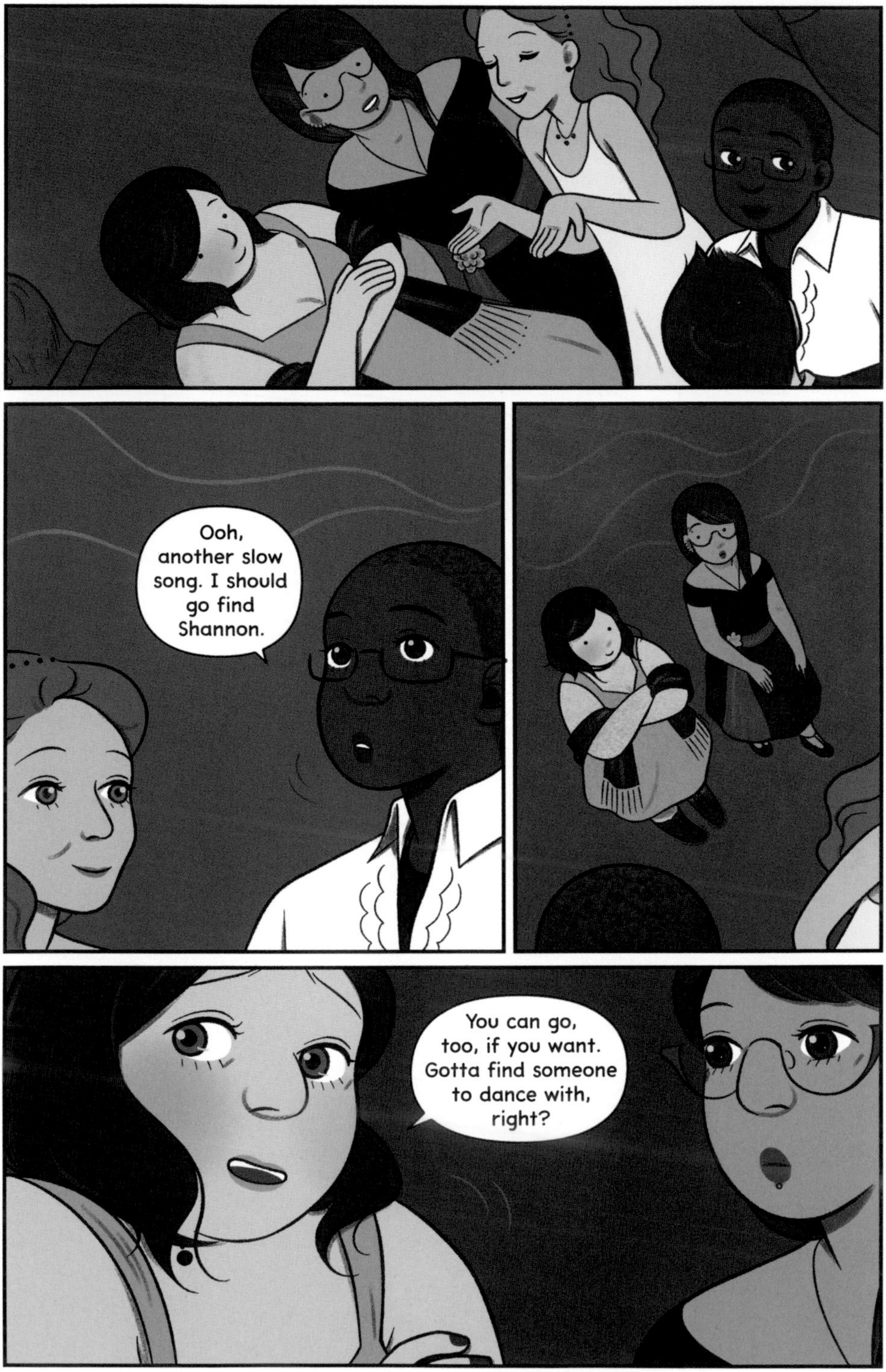
Ooh, another slow song. I should go find Shannon.
You can go, too, if you want. Gotta find someone to dance with, right?

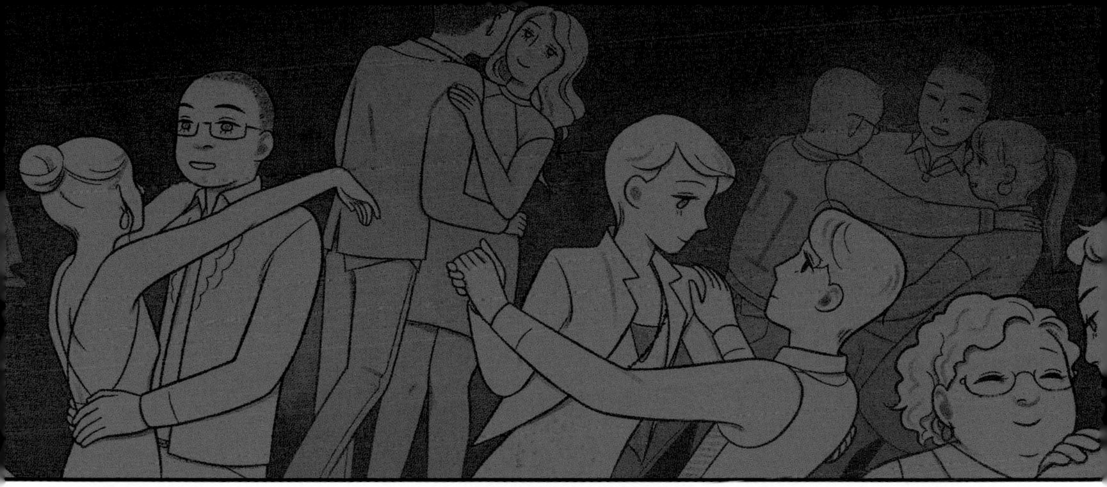

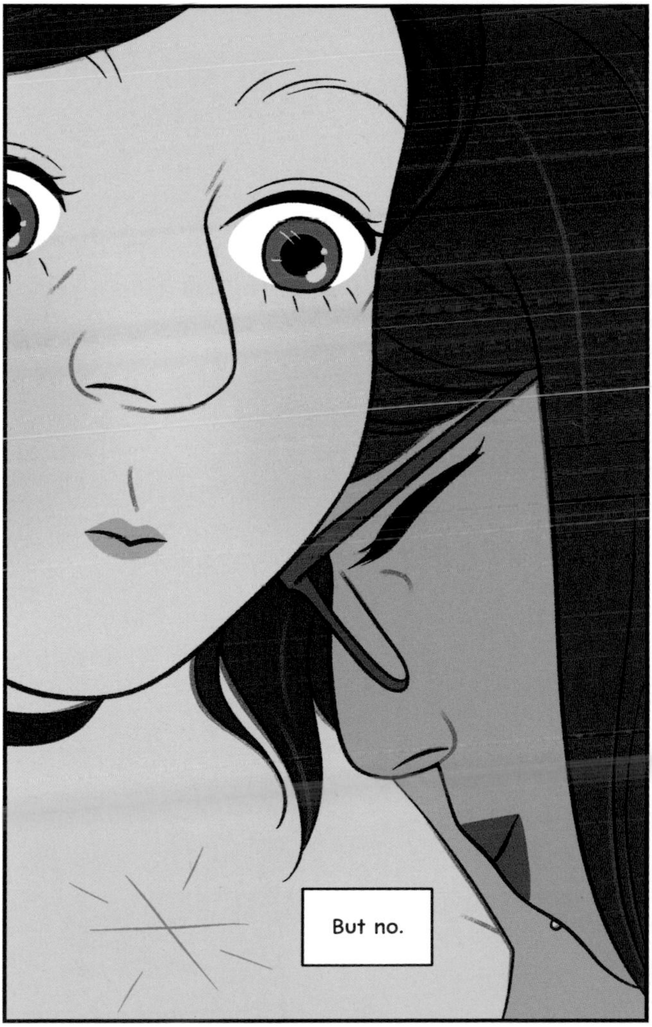
But no.

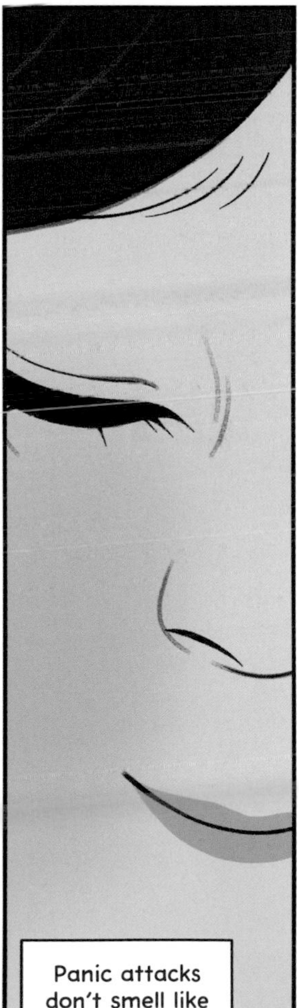
Panic attacks don't smell like lilacs.

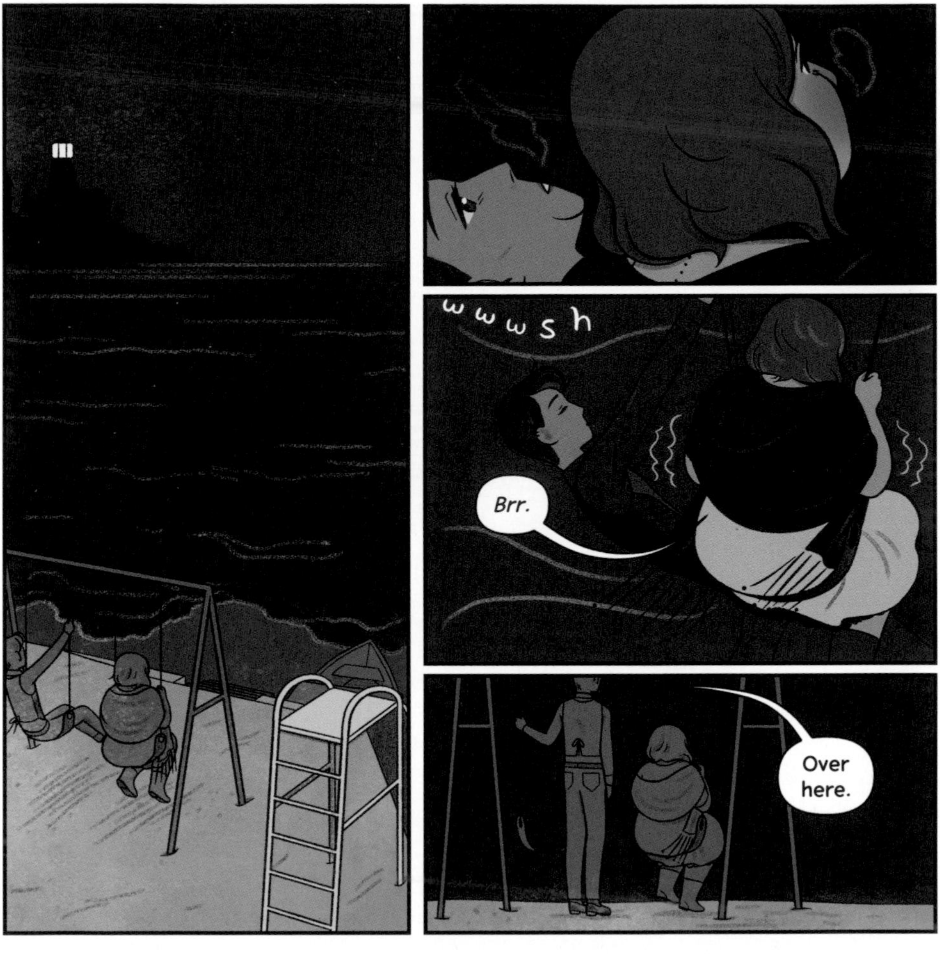
wwwsh
Brr.
Over here.

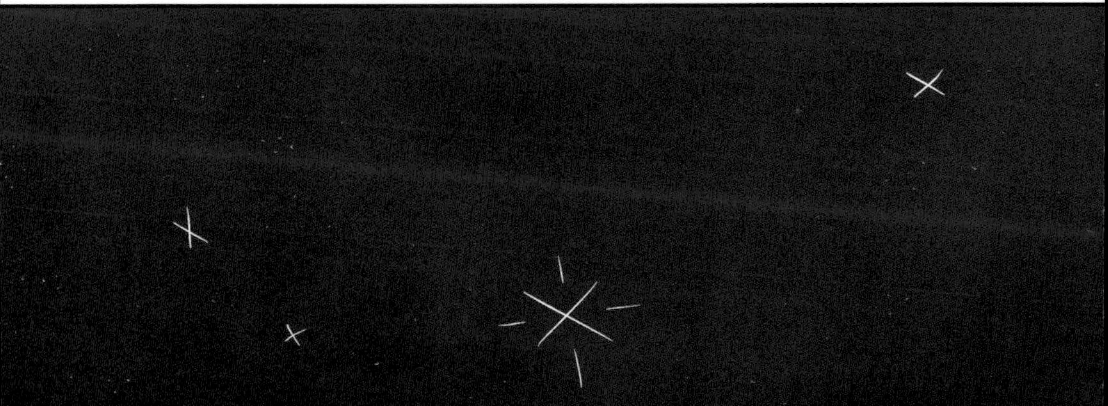

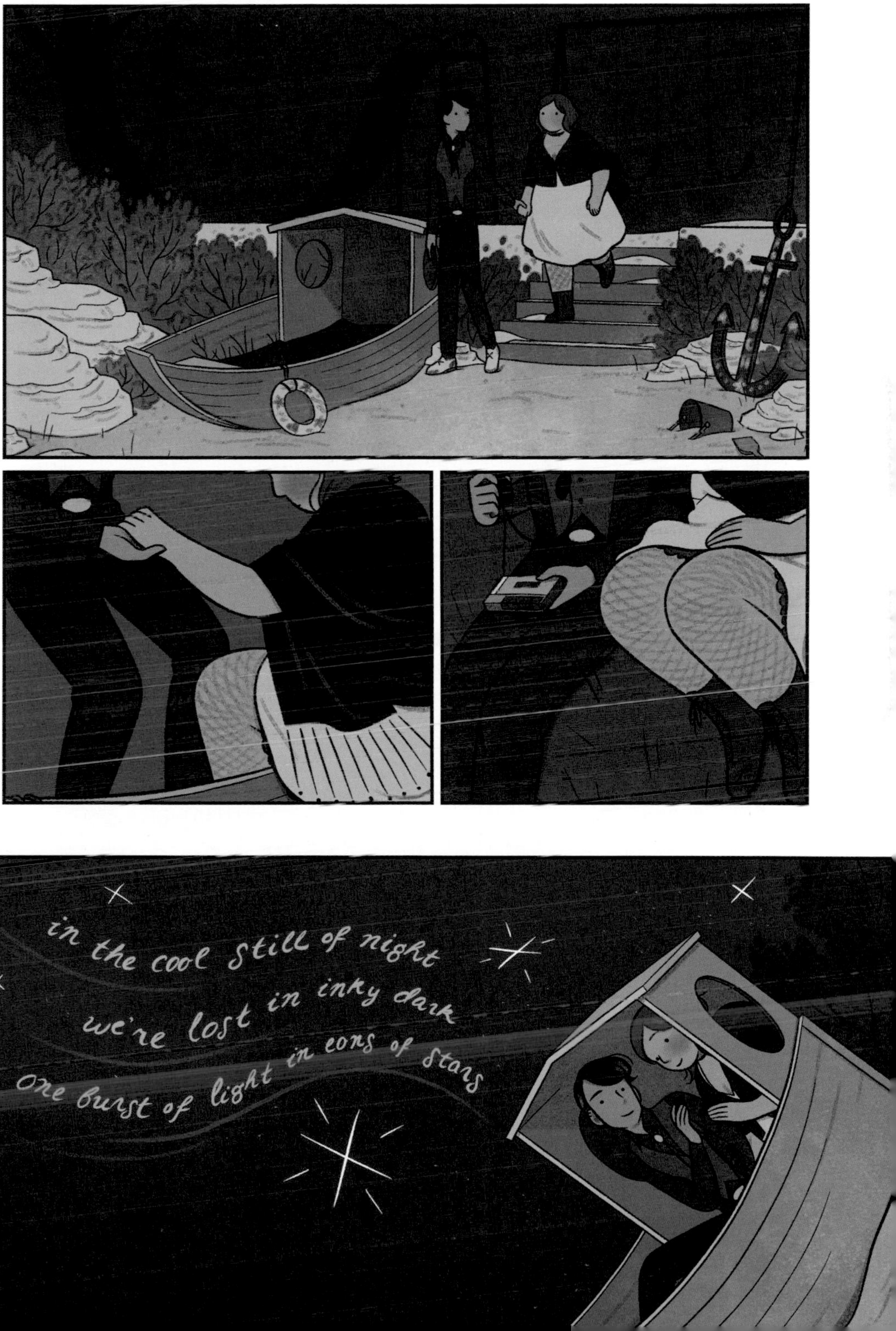
in the cool still of night
we're lost in inky dark
One burst of light in eons of stars

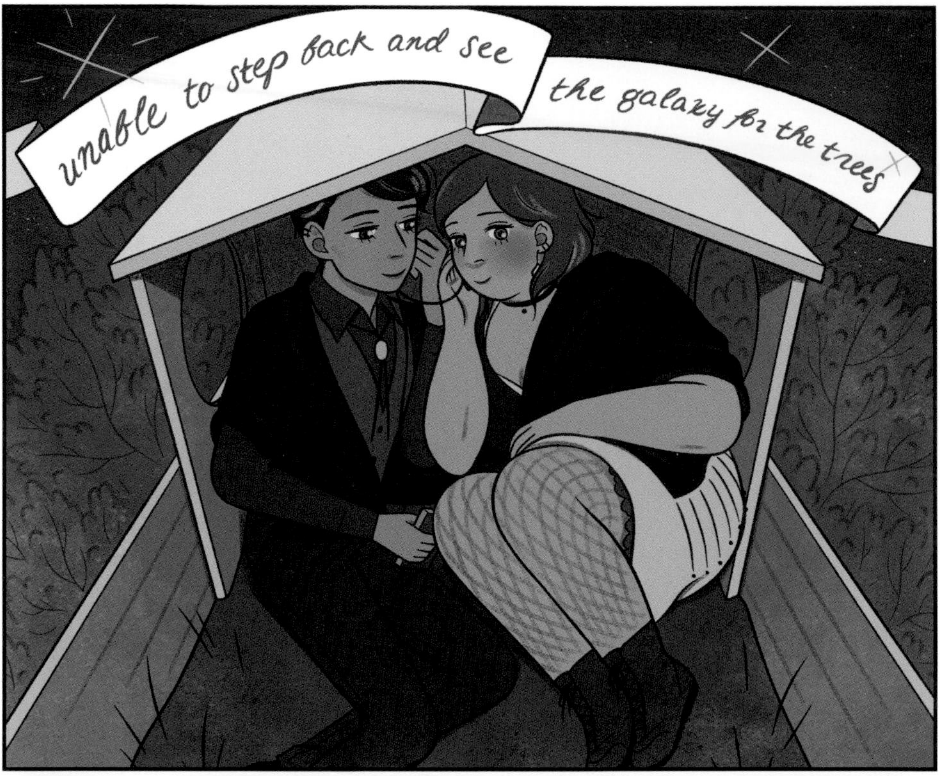
unable to step back and see
the galaxy for the trees

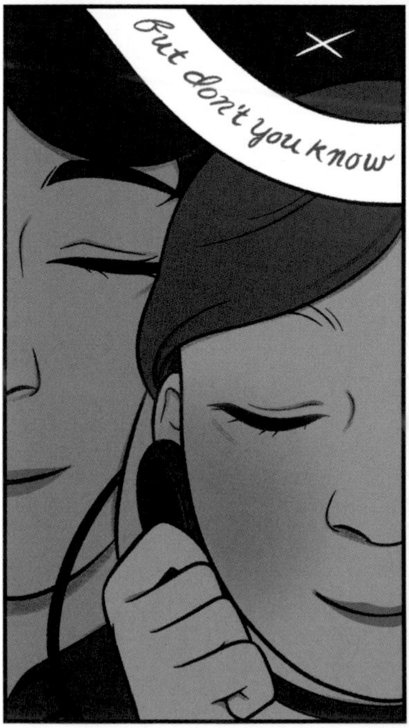
But don't you know

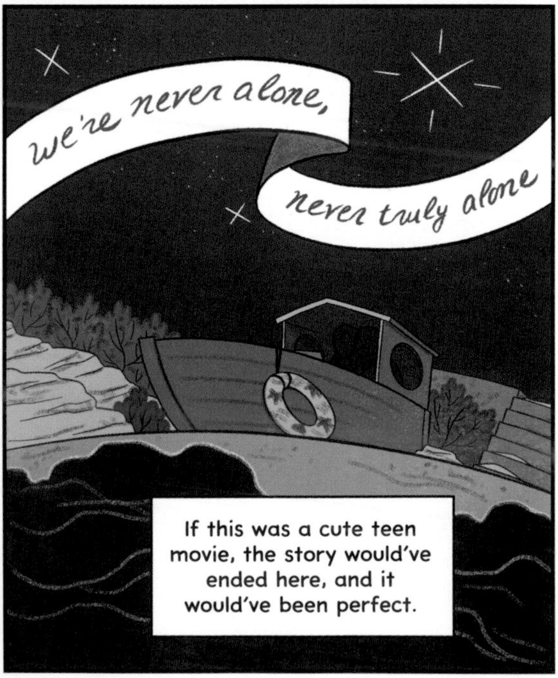
we're never alone,
never truly alone
If this was a cute teen movie, the story would've ended here, and it would've been perfect.

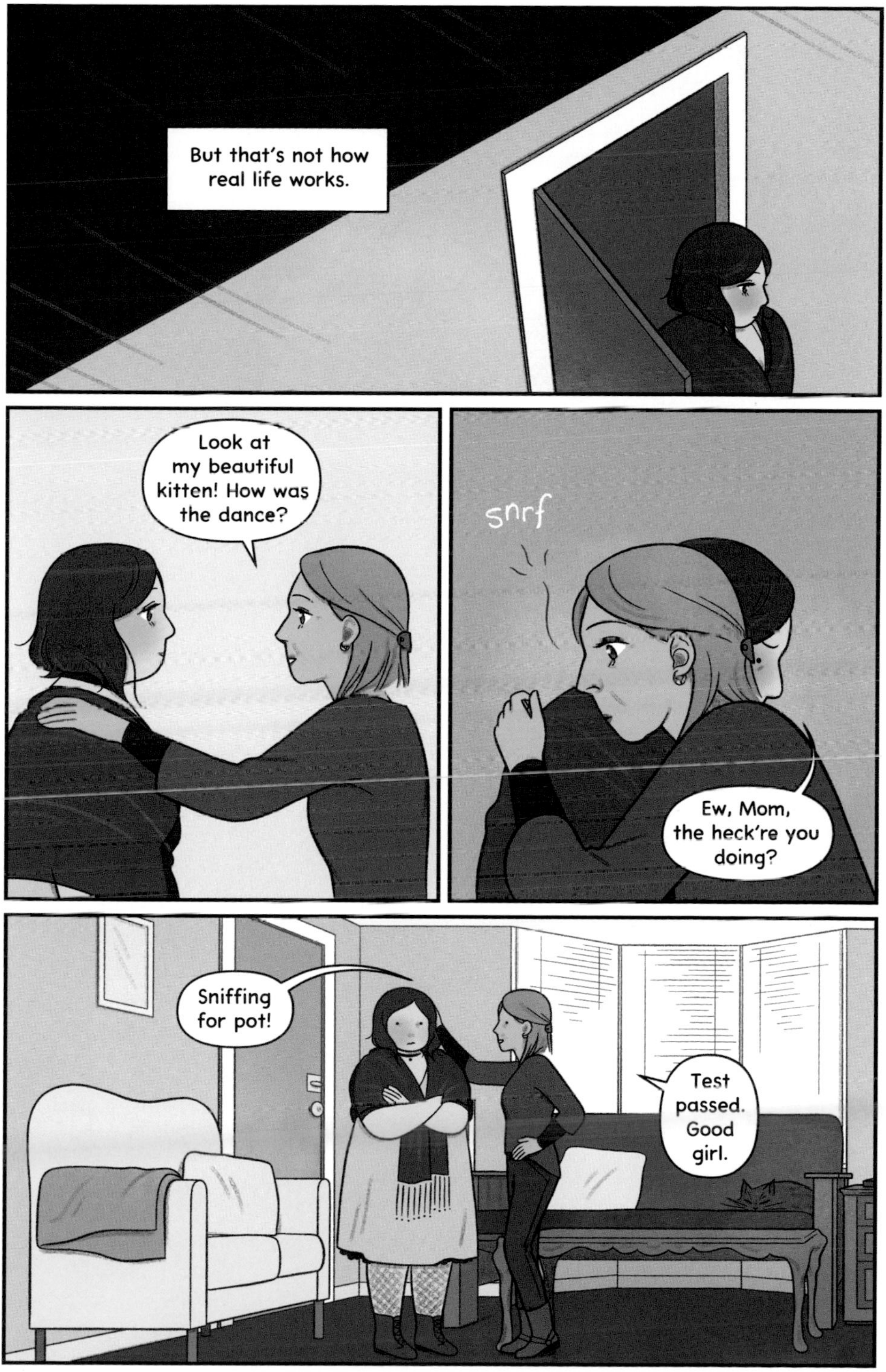

But that's not how real life works.
Look at my beautiful kitten! How was the dance?
snrf
Ew, Mom, the heck're you doing?
Sniffing for pot!
Test passed. Good girl.

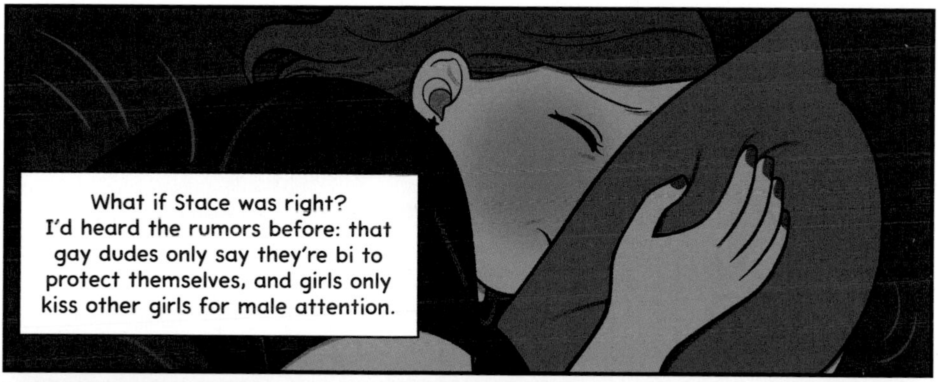
What if Stace was right?
I'd heard the rumors before: that gay dudes only say they're bi to protect themselves, and girls only kiss other girls for male attention.

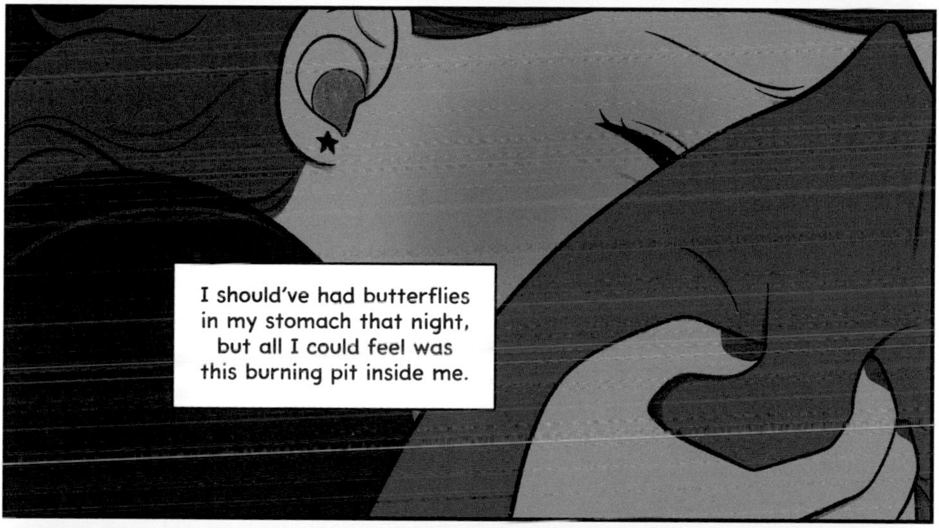
I should've had butterflies in my stomach that night, but all I could feel was this burning pit inside me.

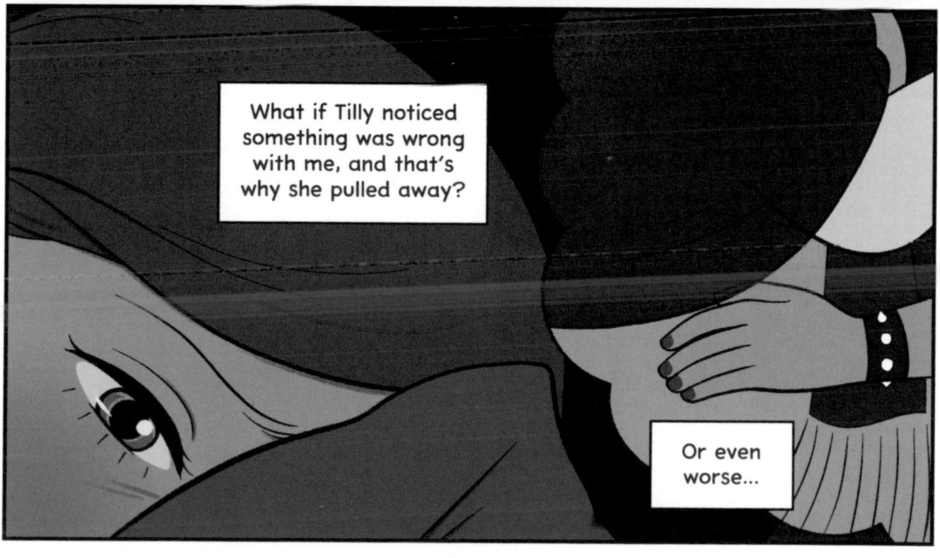
What if Tilly noticed something was wrong with me, and that's why she pulled away?
Or even worse...

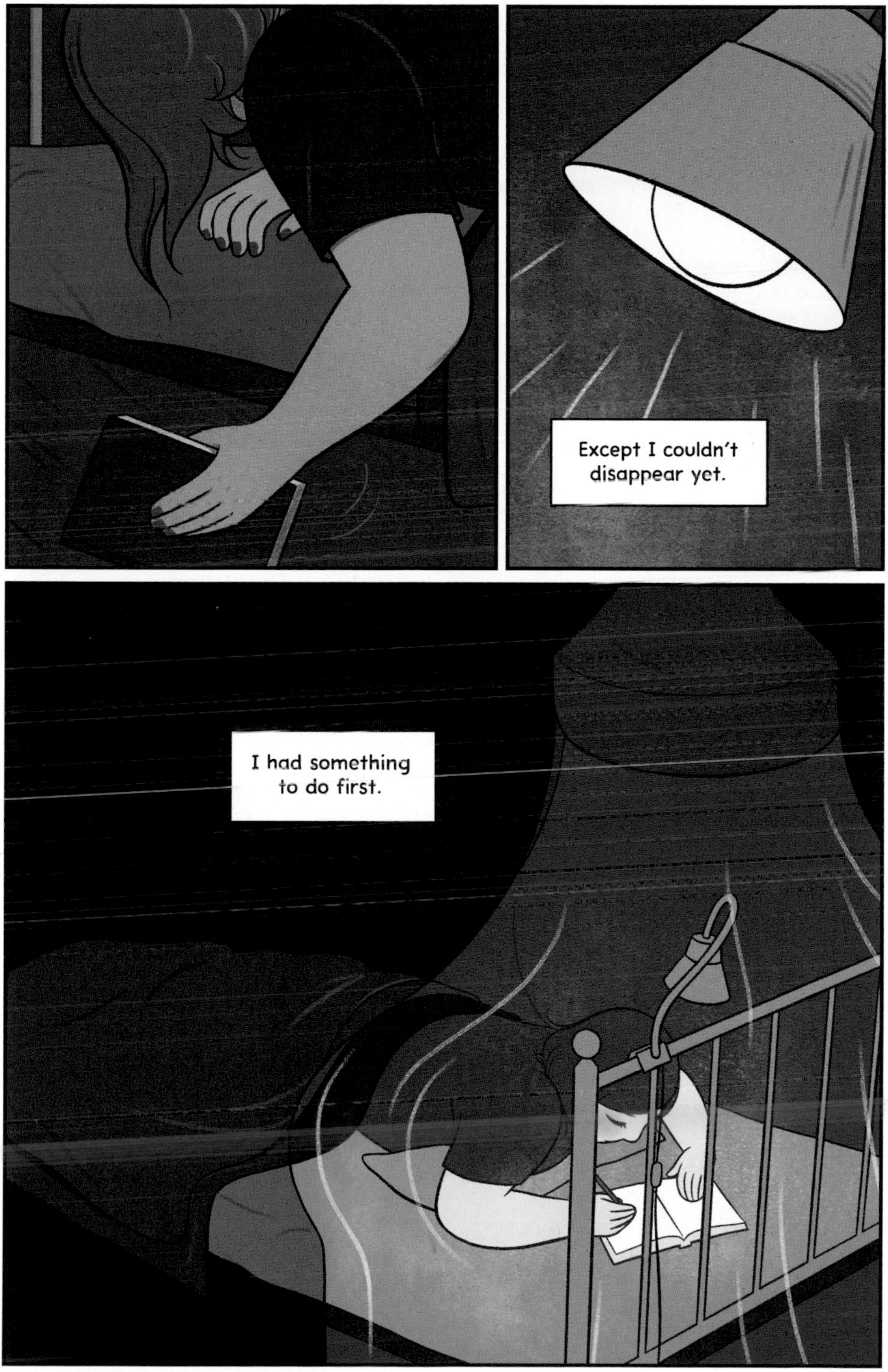
Except I couldn't disappear yet.
I had something to do first.

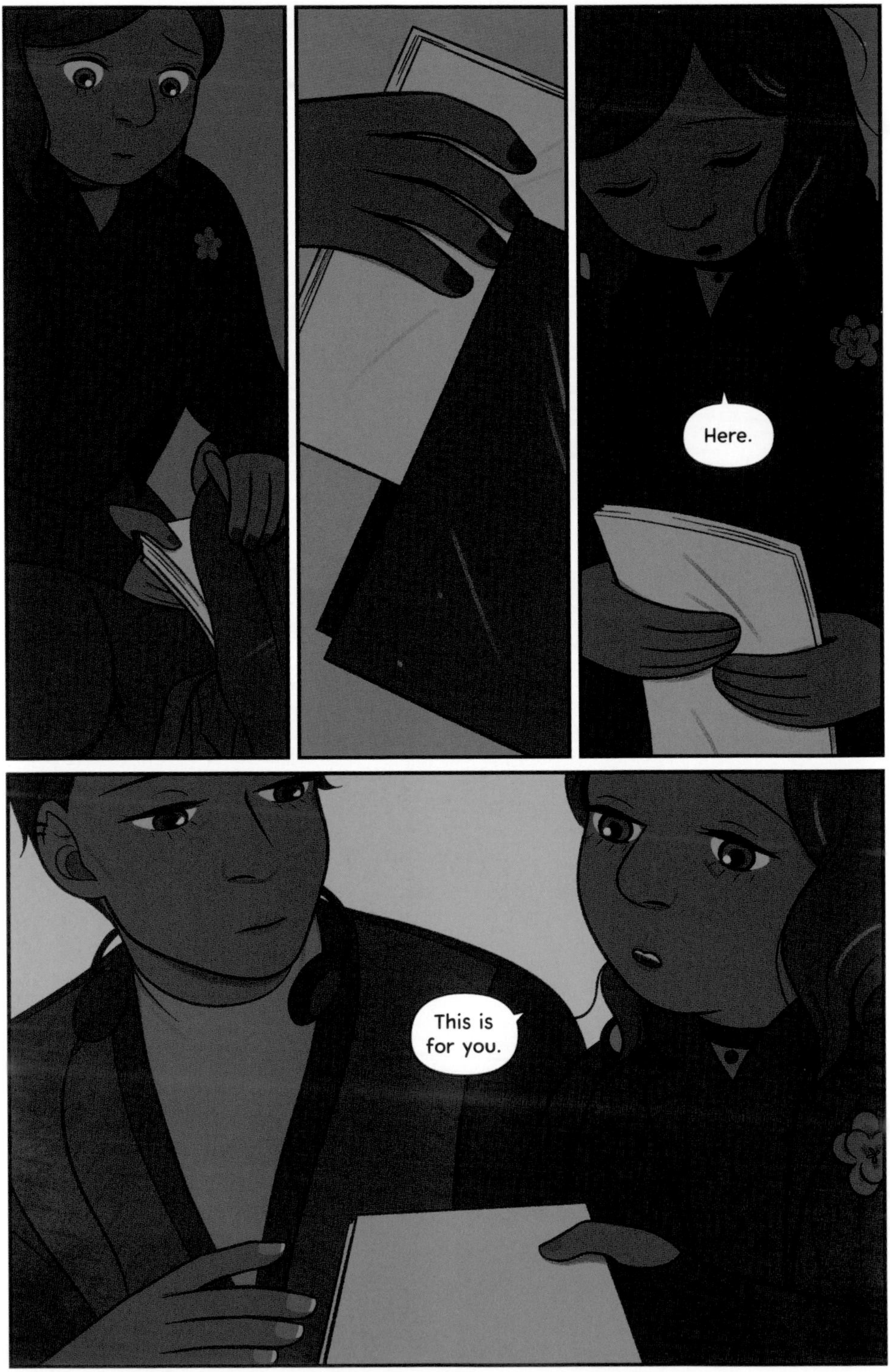
Here.
This is for you.

gutterglimmers III

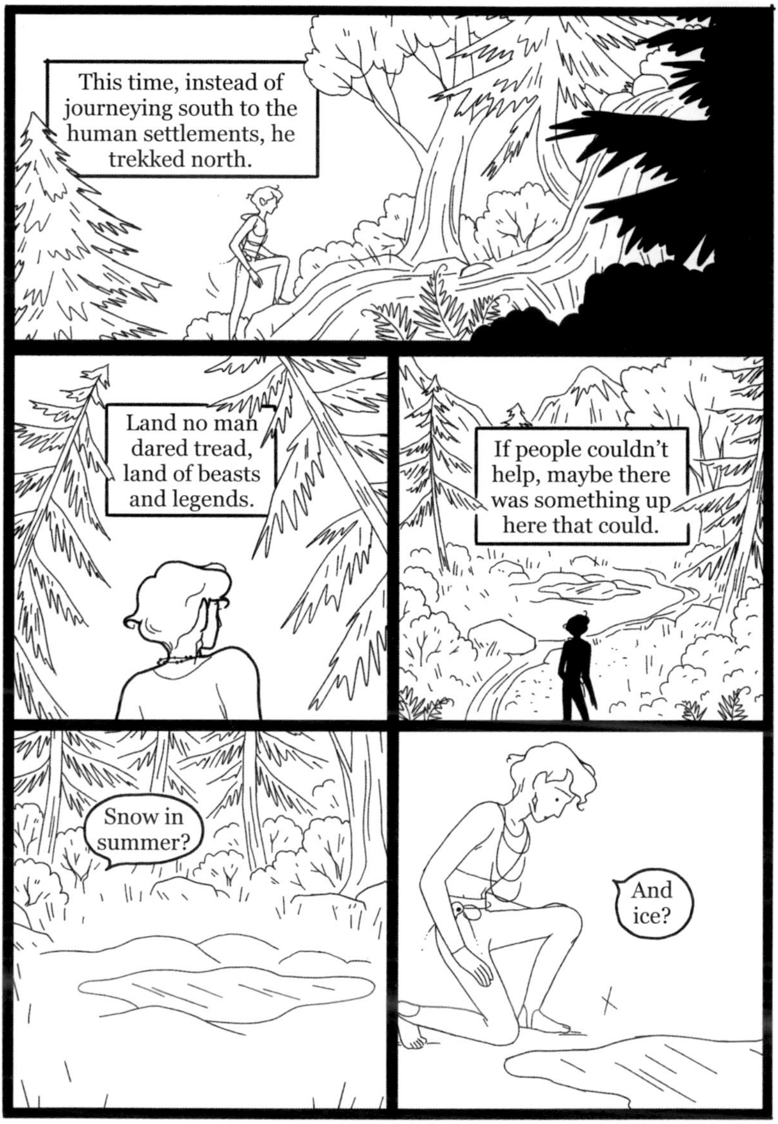
This time, instead of journeying south to the human settlements, he trekked north.
Land no man dared tread, land of beasts and legends.
If people couldn't help, maybe there was something up here that could.
Snow in summer?
And ice?

232

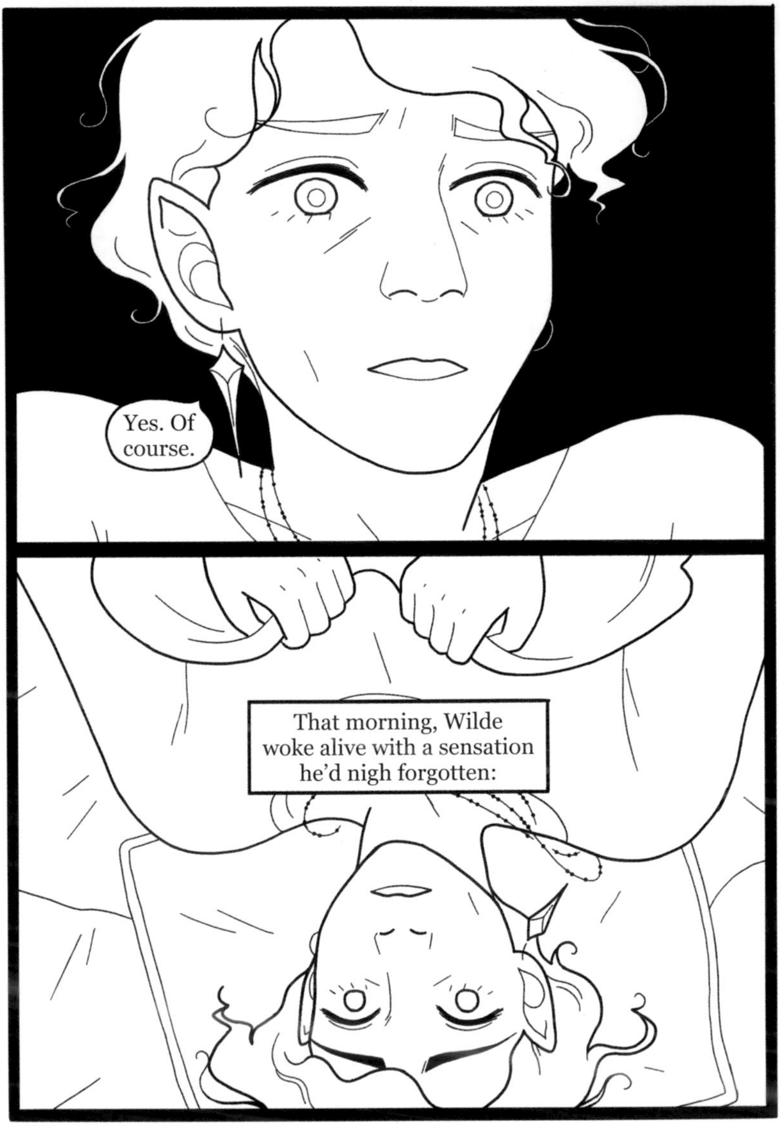
Yes. Of course.
That morning, Wilde woke alive with a sensation he'd nigh forgotten:

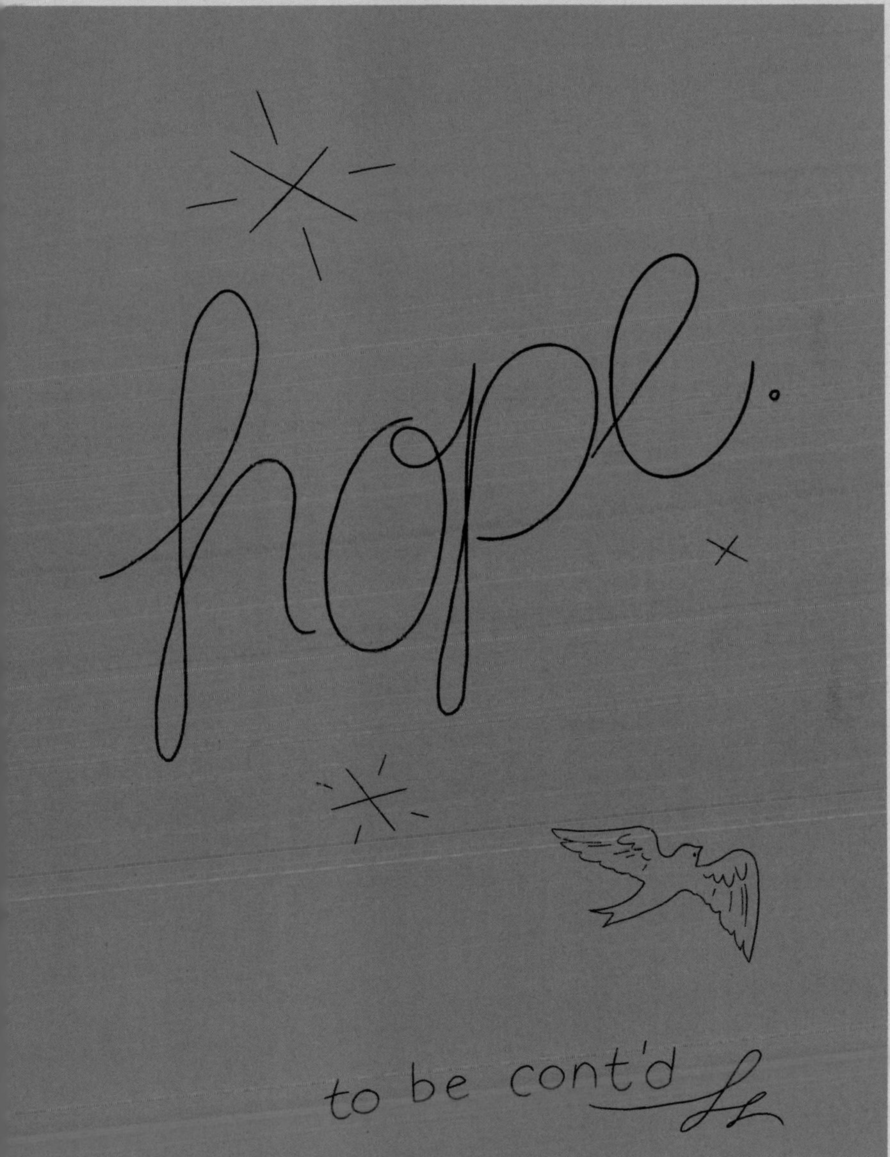
hope.
to be cont'd

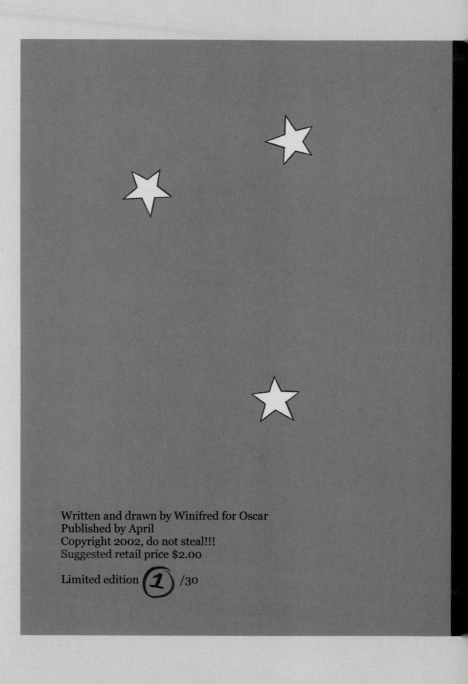

Written and drawn by Winifred for Oscar
Published by April
Copyright 2002, do not steal!!!
Suggested retail price $2.00

Limited edition (*1*) /30

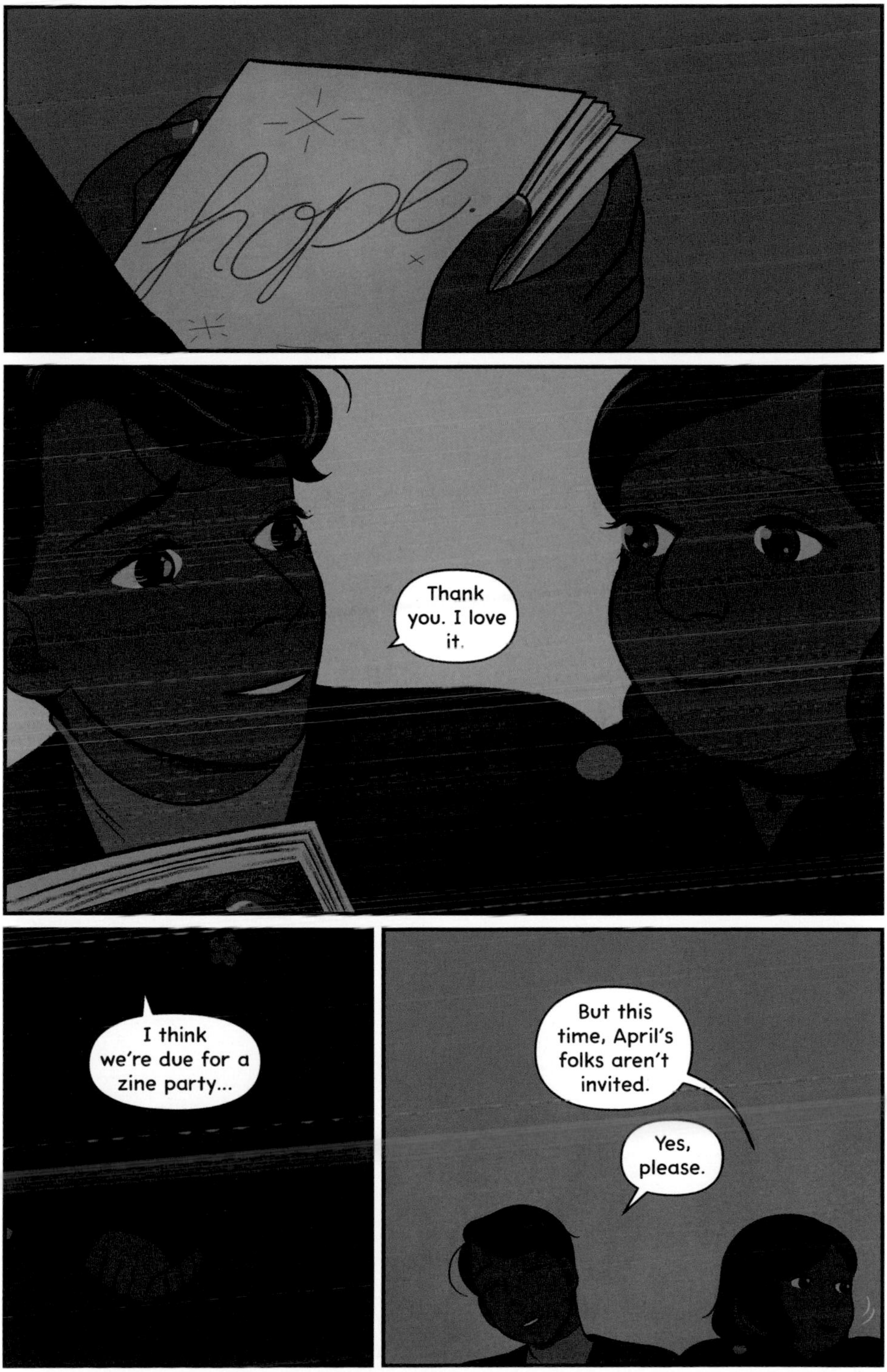
hope.
Thank you. I love it.
I think we're due for a zine party...
But this time, April's folks aren't invited.
Yes, please.

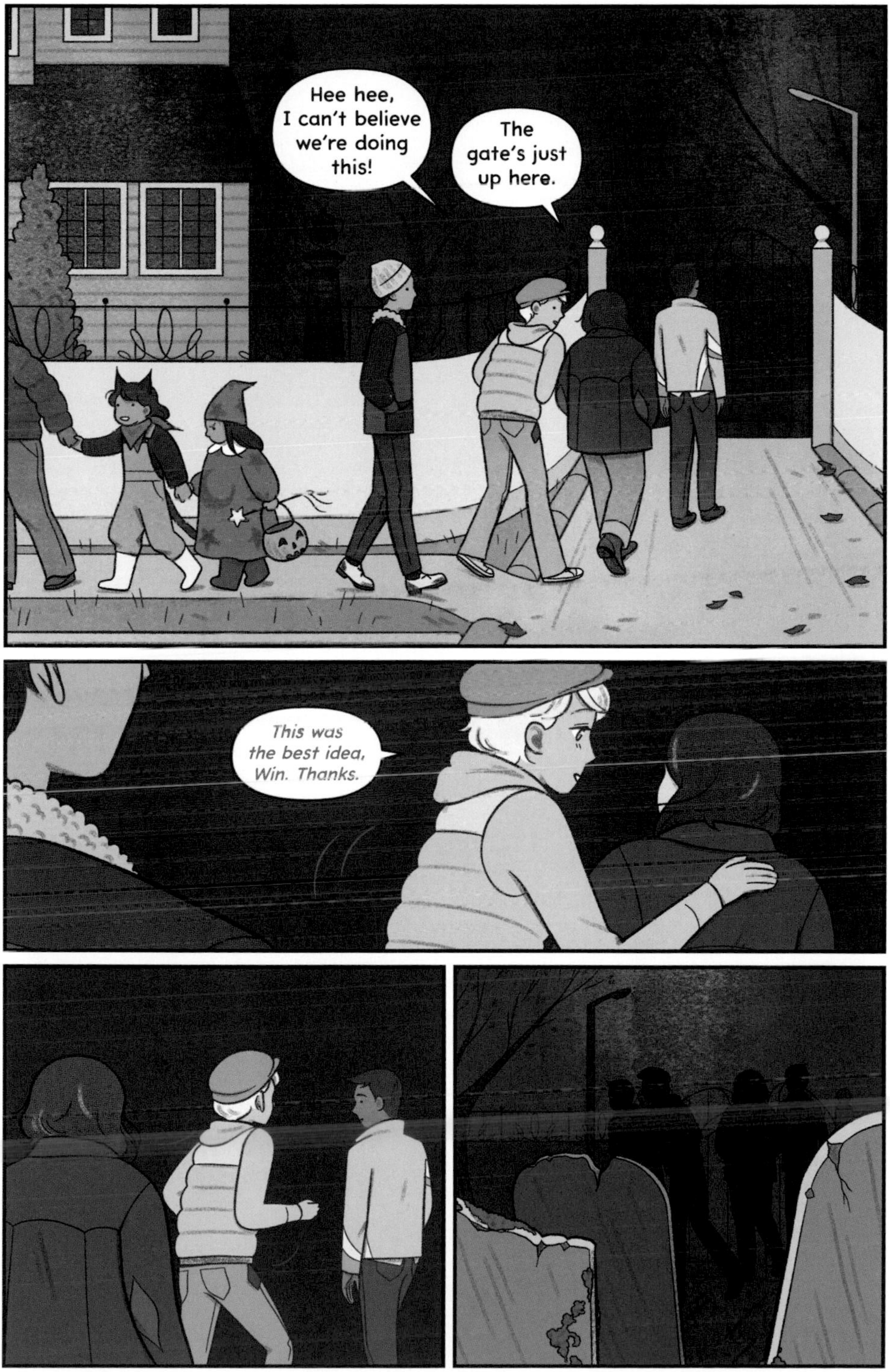
Hee hee, I can't believe we're doing this!
The gate's just up here.
This was the best idea, Win. Thanks.

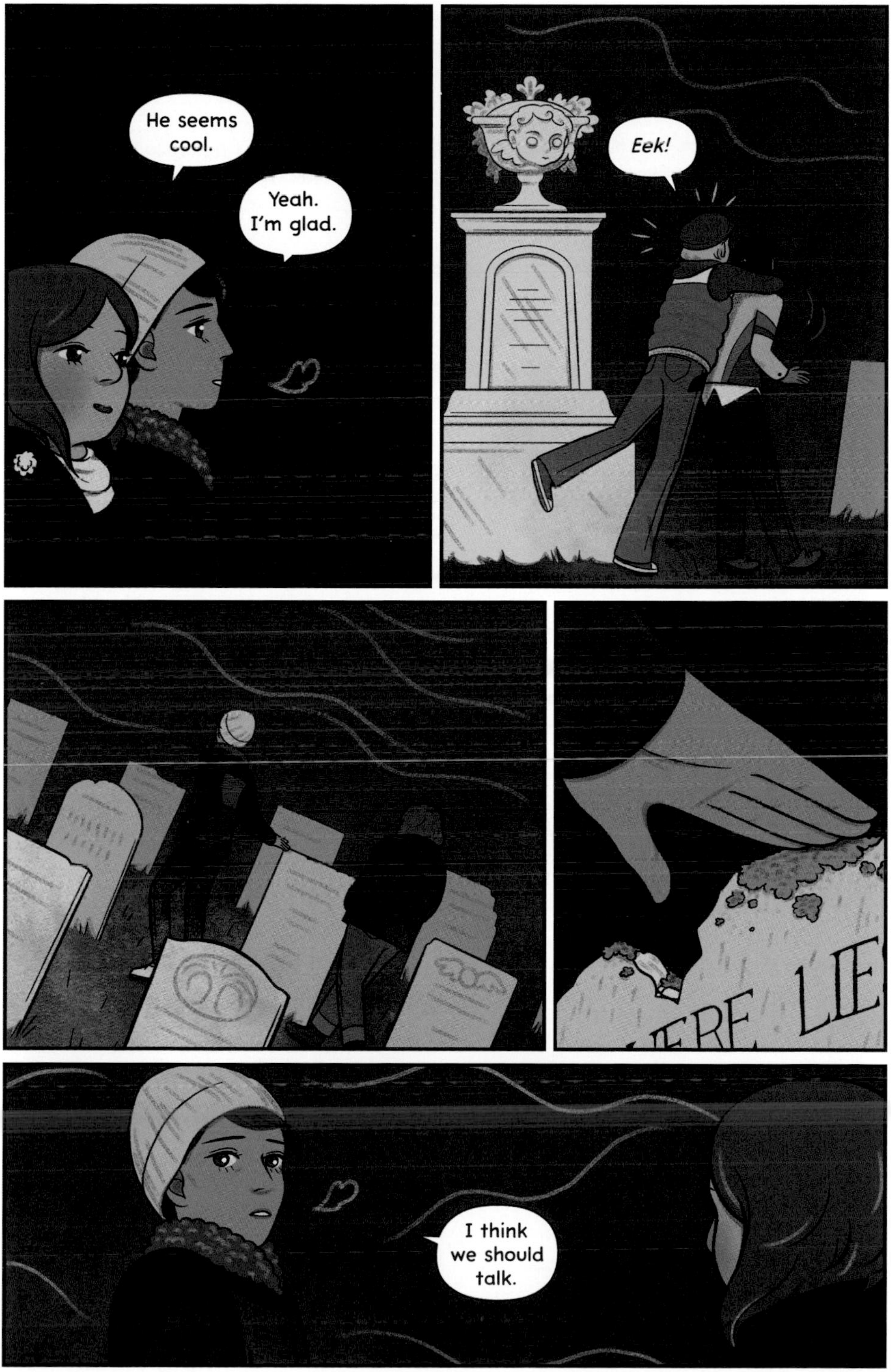
He seems cool.
Yeah. I'm glad.
Eek!
I think we should talk.

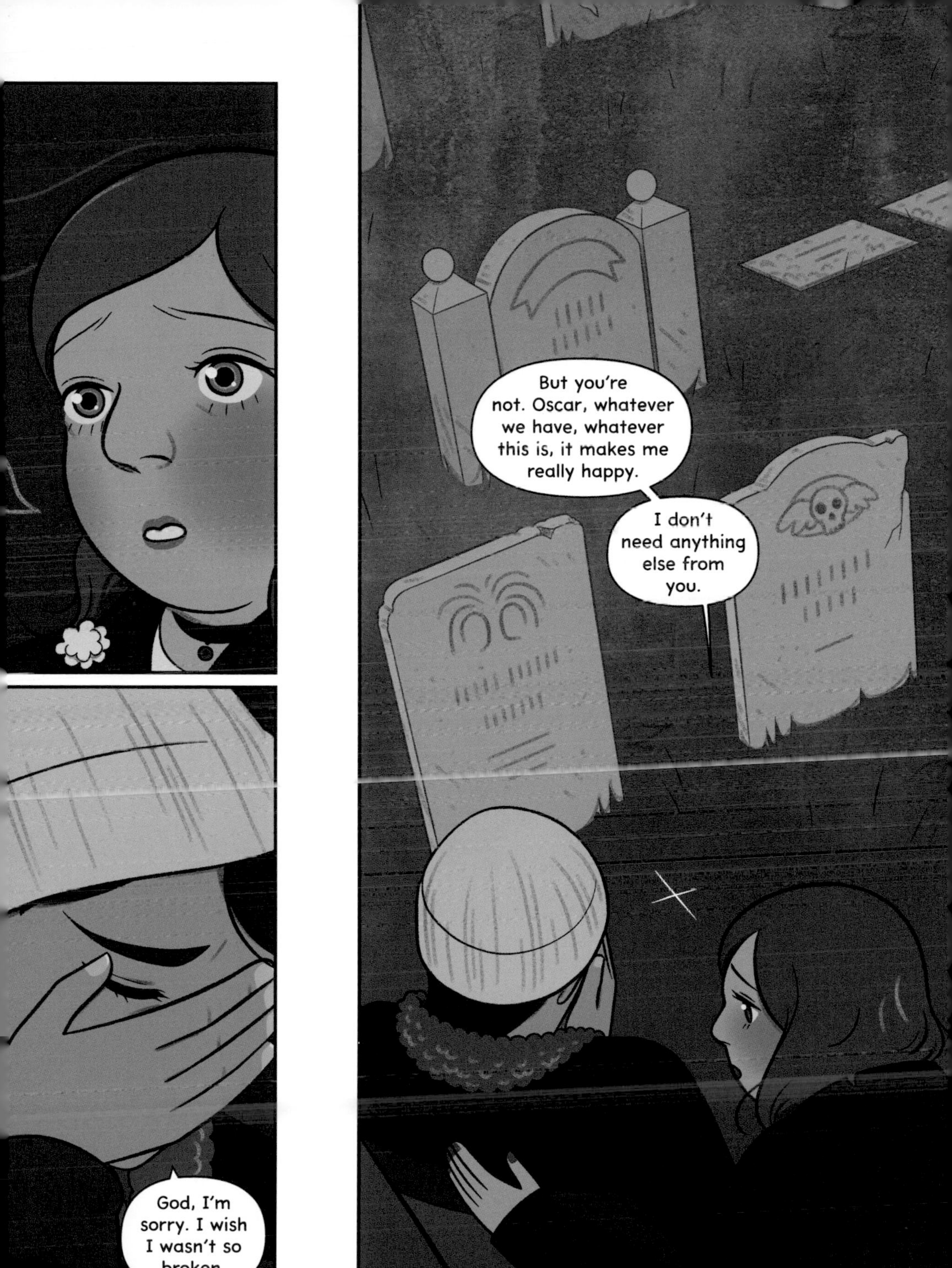
God, I'm sorry. I wish I wasn't so broken.
But you're not. Oscar, whatever we have, whatever this is, it makes me really happy.
I don't need anything else from you.

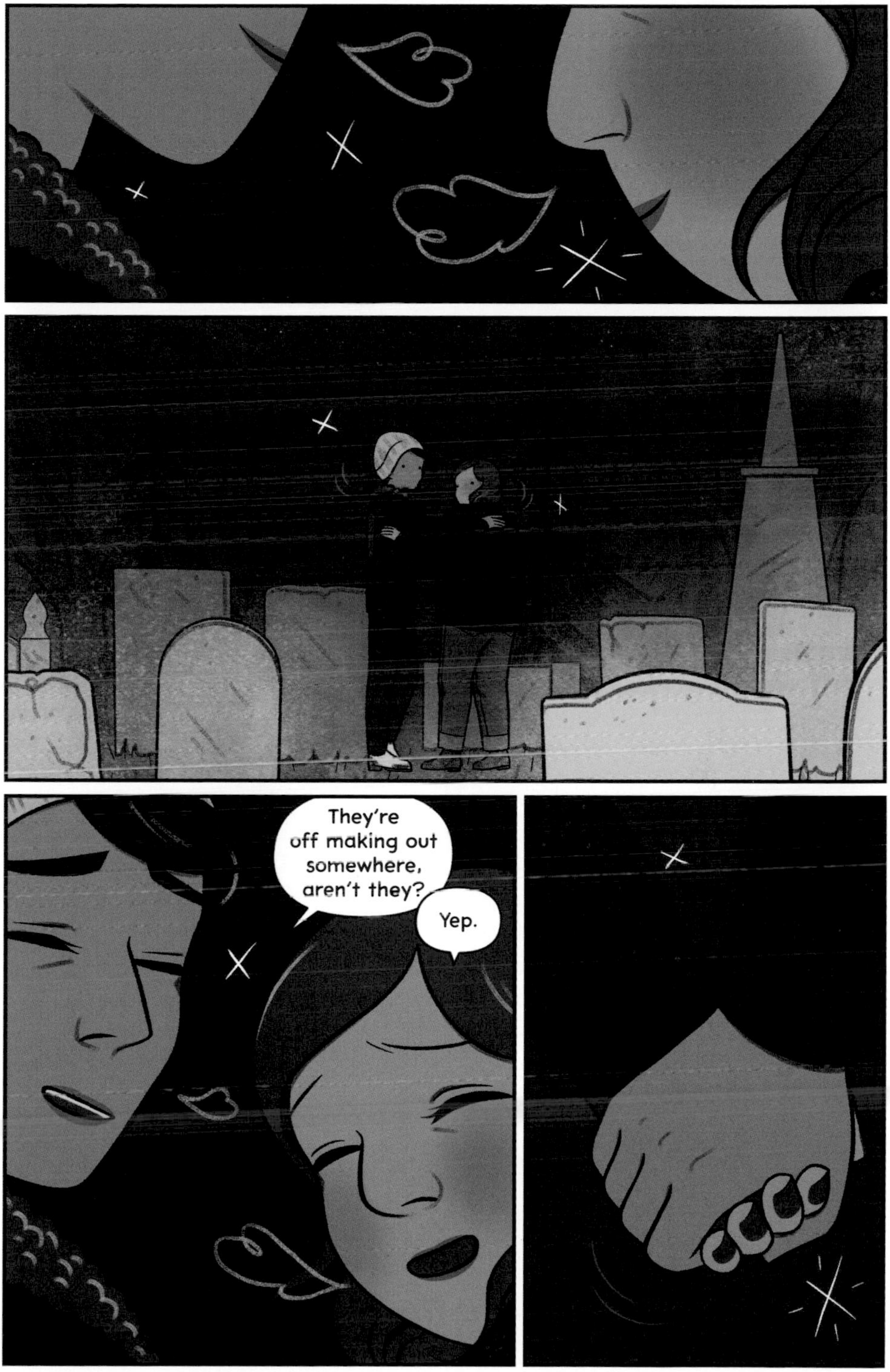
They're off making out somewhere, aren't they?
Yep.

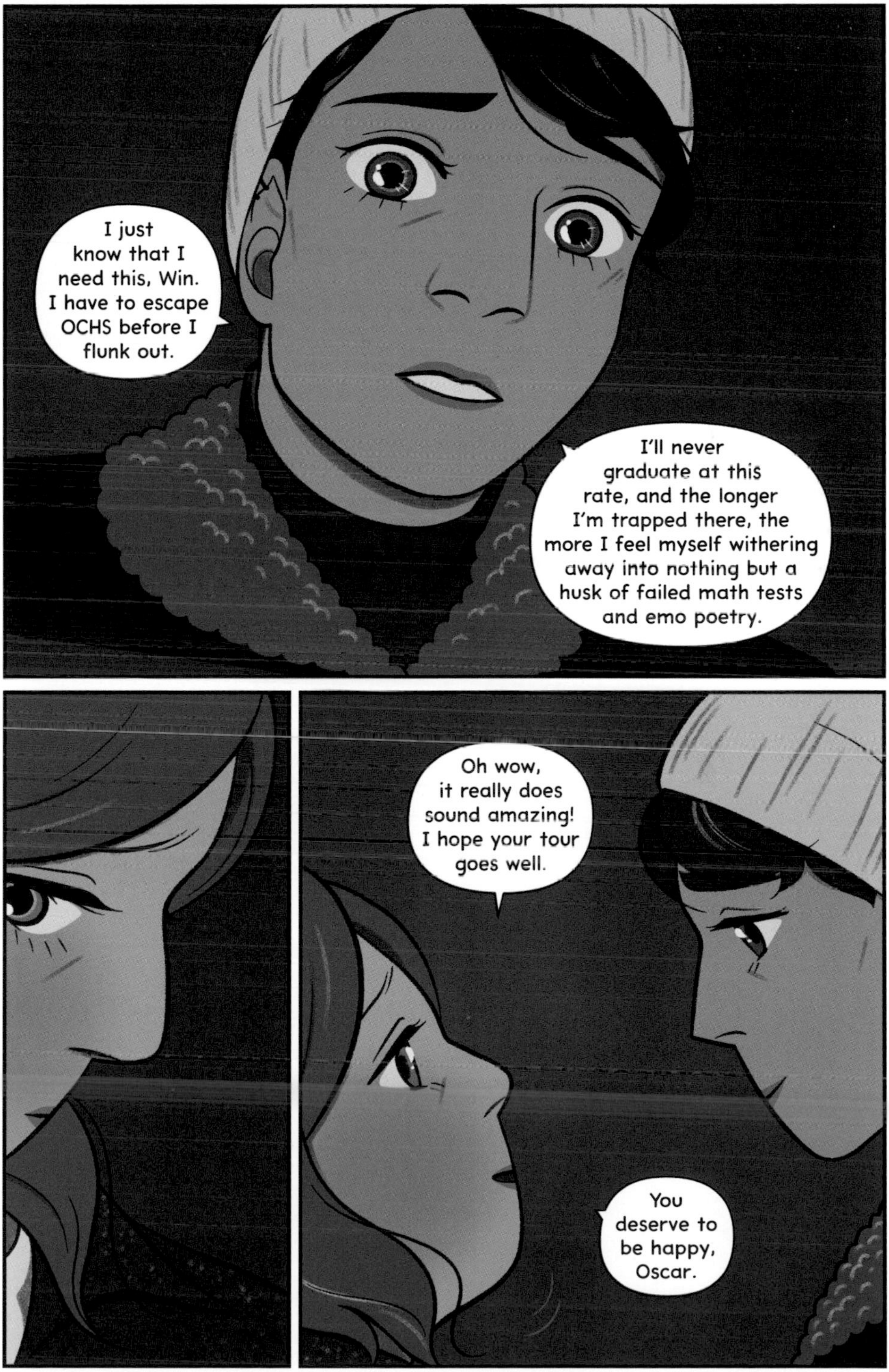
I just know that I need this, Win. I have to escape OCHS before I flunk out.
I'll never graduate at this rate, and the longer I'm trapped there, the more I feel myself withering away into nothing but a husk of failed math tests and emo poetry.
Oh wow, it really does sound amazing! I hope your tour goes well.
You deserve to be happy, Oscar.

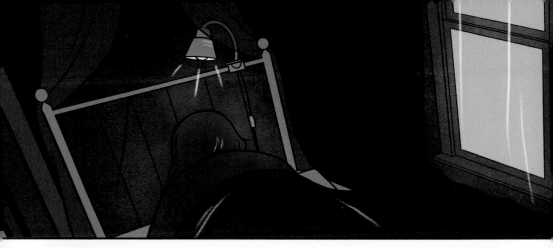

Ugh!

No wonder I couldn't come up with interesting stories. I was too much of a boring failure of a person to write anything different.

No wonder Oscar didn't want to be with me. No wonder he wanted to leave.

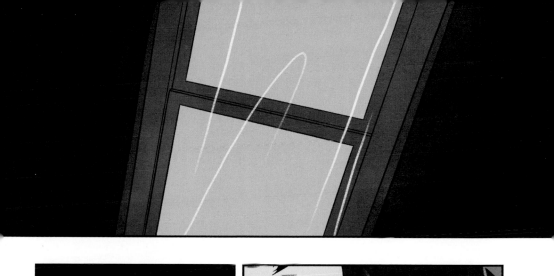

No. I wasn't so self-centered that I thought this was about me. He had a chance at happiness at a new school, and there was no way I'd begrudge him that.

But I knew how it went. There was no way our friendship could possibly stay the same if he left.

Just like what happened with Jayme and Jess. We hadn't talked in months.

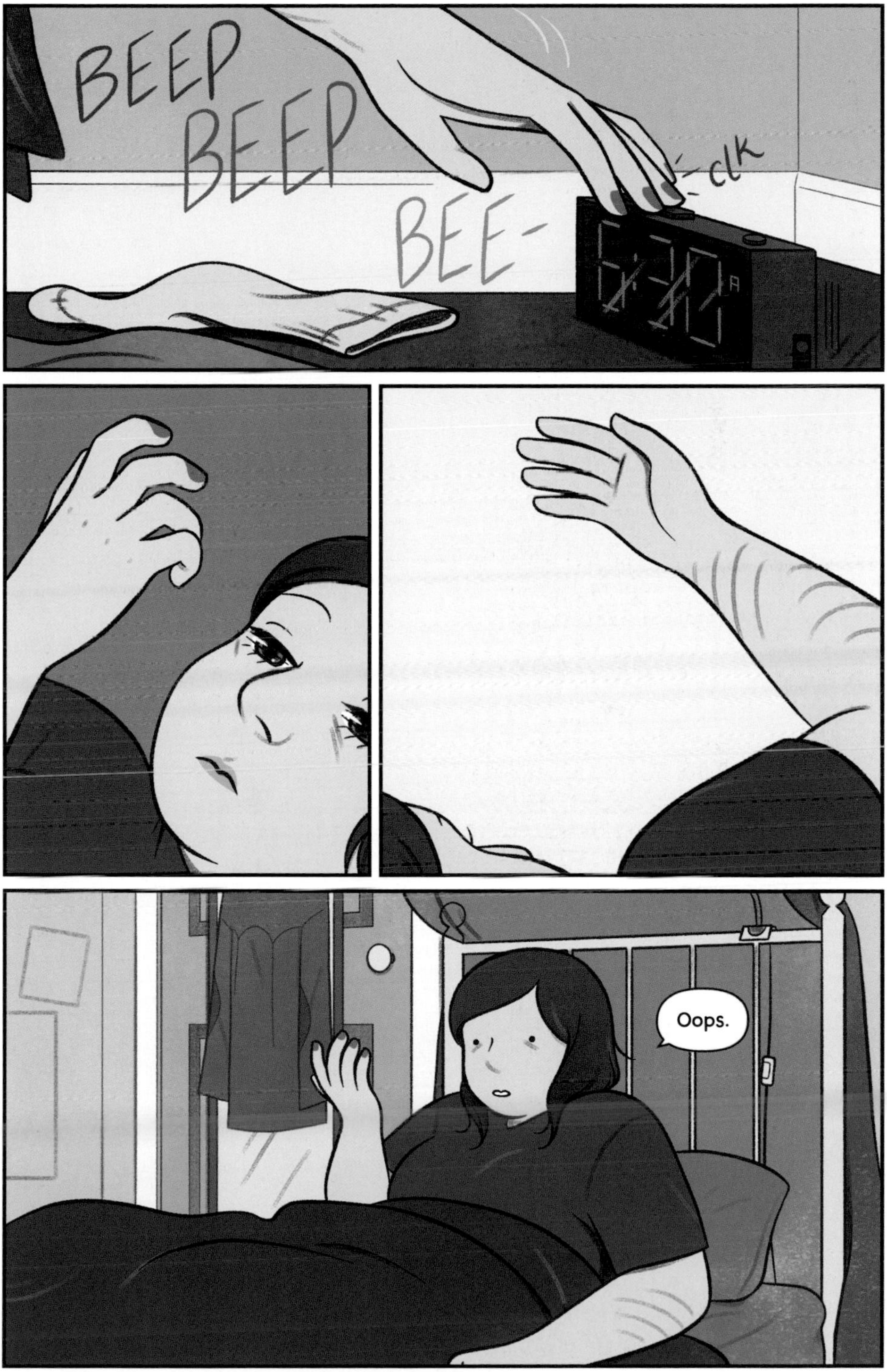
BEEP
BEEP
BEE-
clk
Oops.

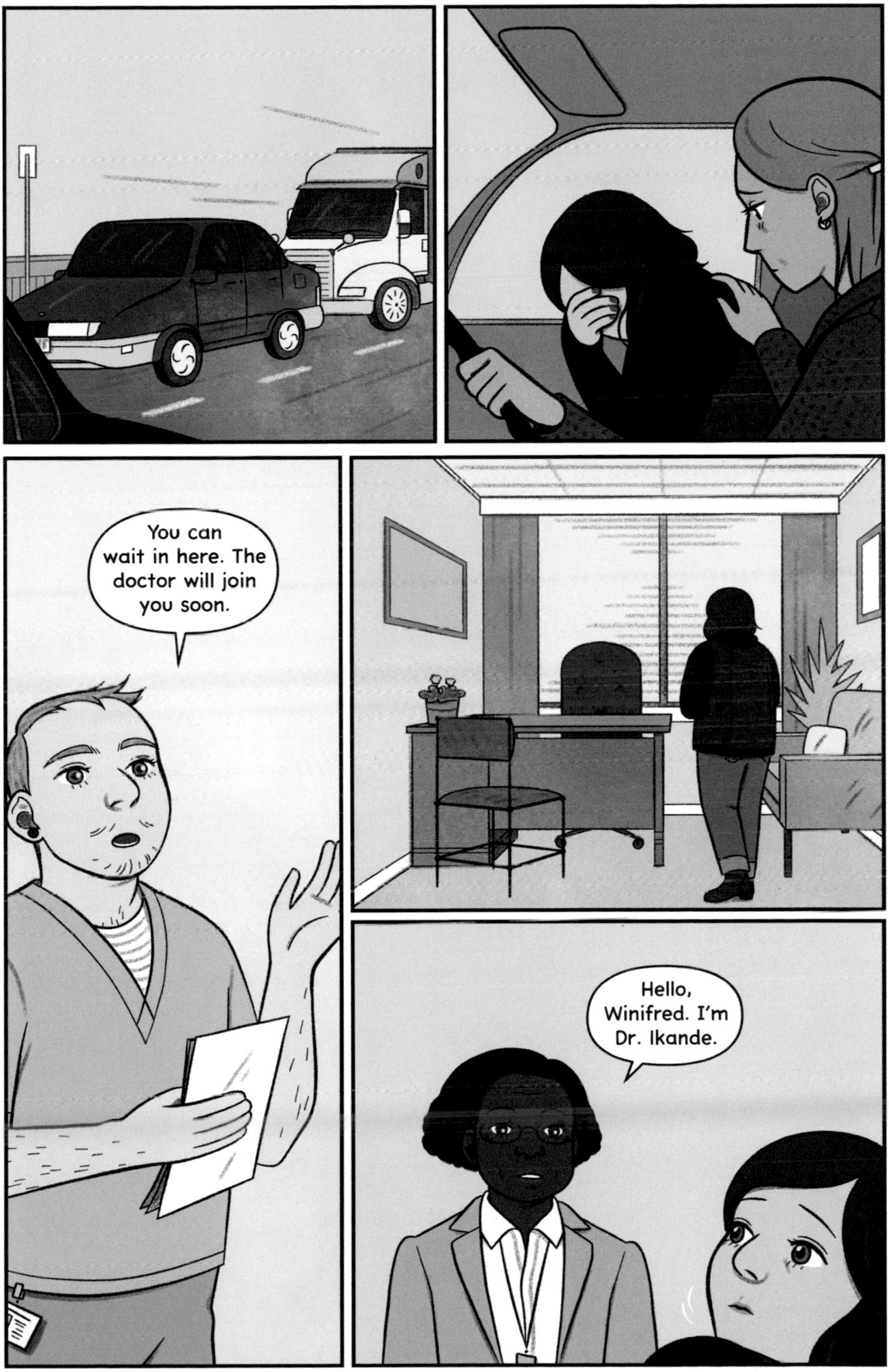

You can wait in here. The doctor will join you soon.
Hello, Winifred. I'm Dr. Ikande.

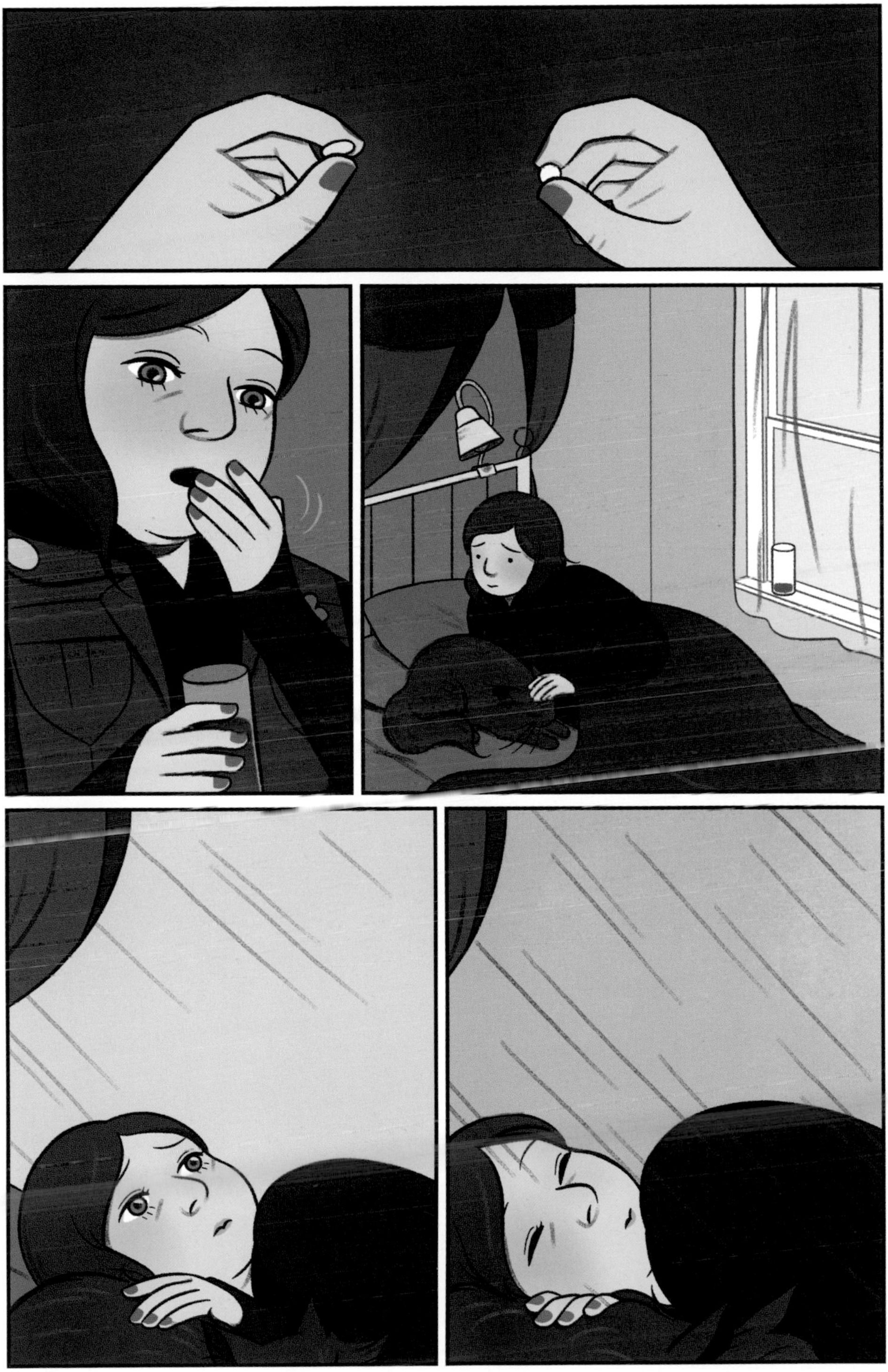

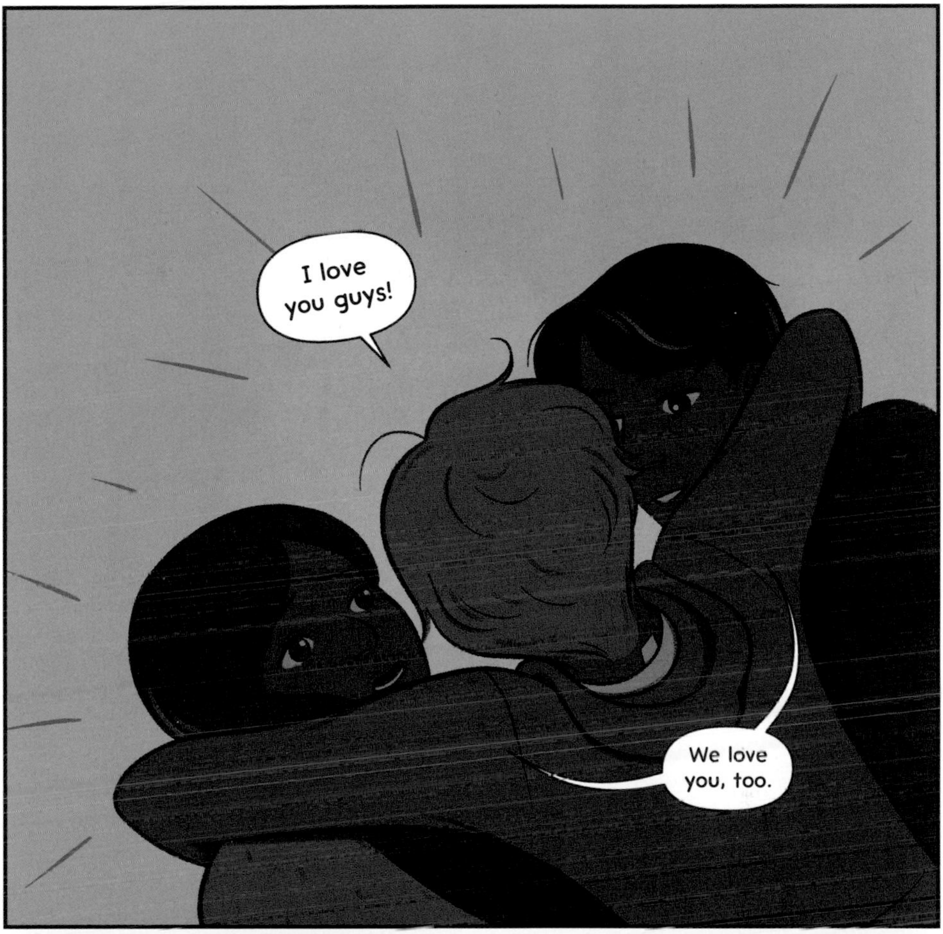
I love you guys!
We love you, too.

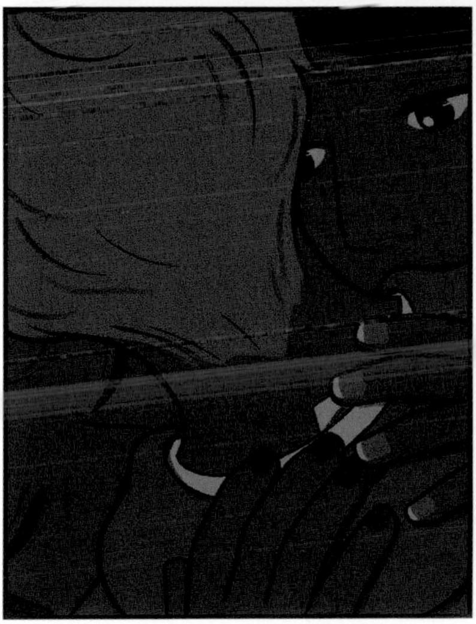

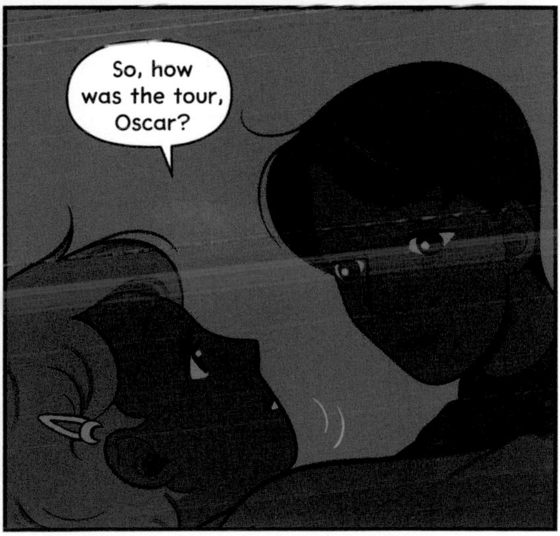
So, how was the tour, Oscar?

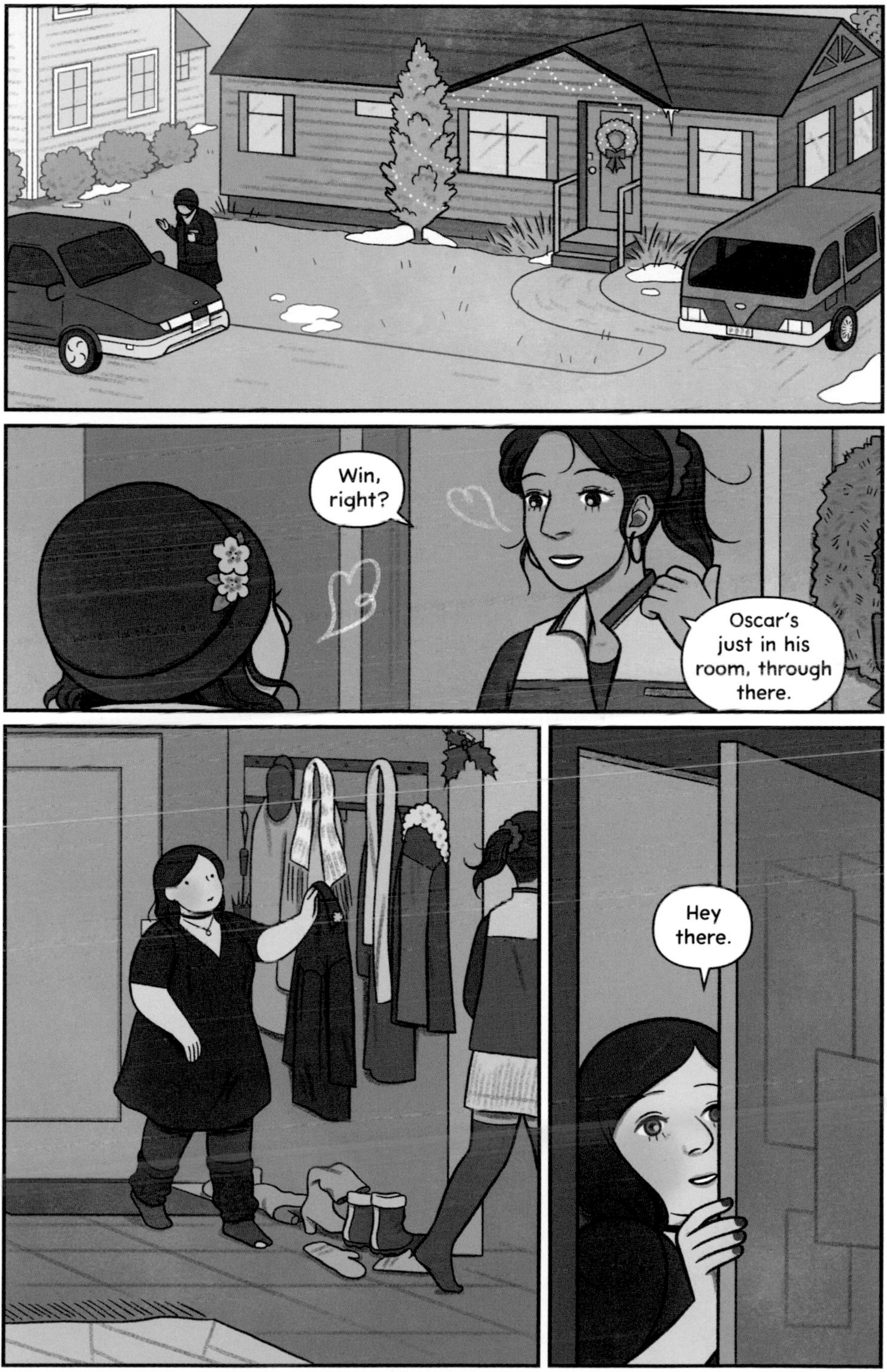
Win, right?
Oscar's just in his room, through there.
Hey there.

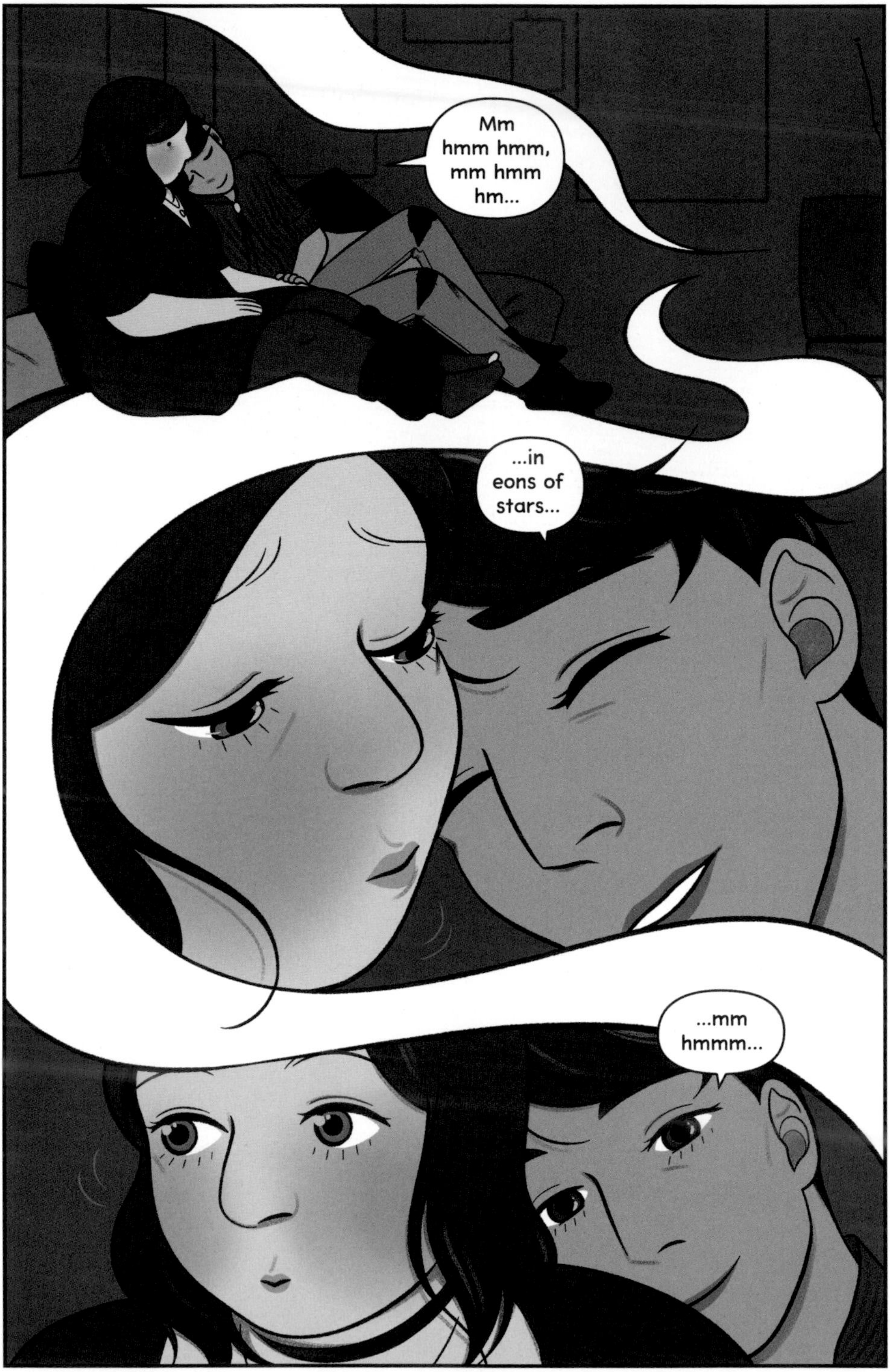
Mm hmm hmm, mm hmm hm...
...in eons of stars...
...mm hmmm...

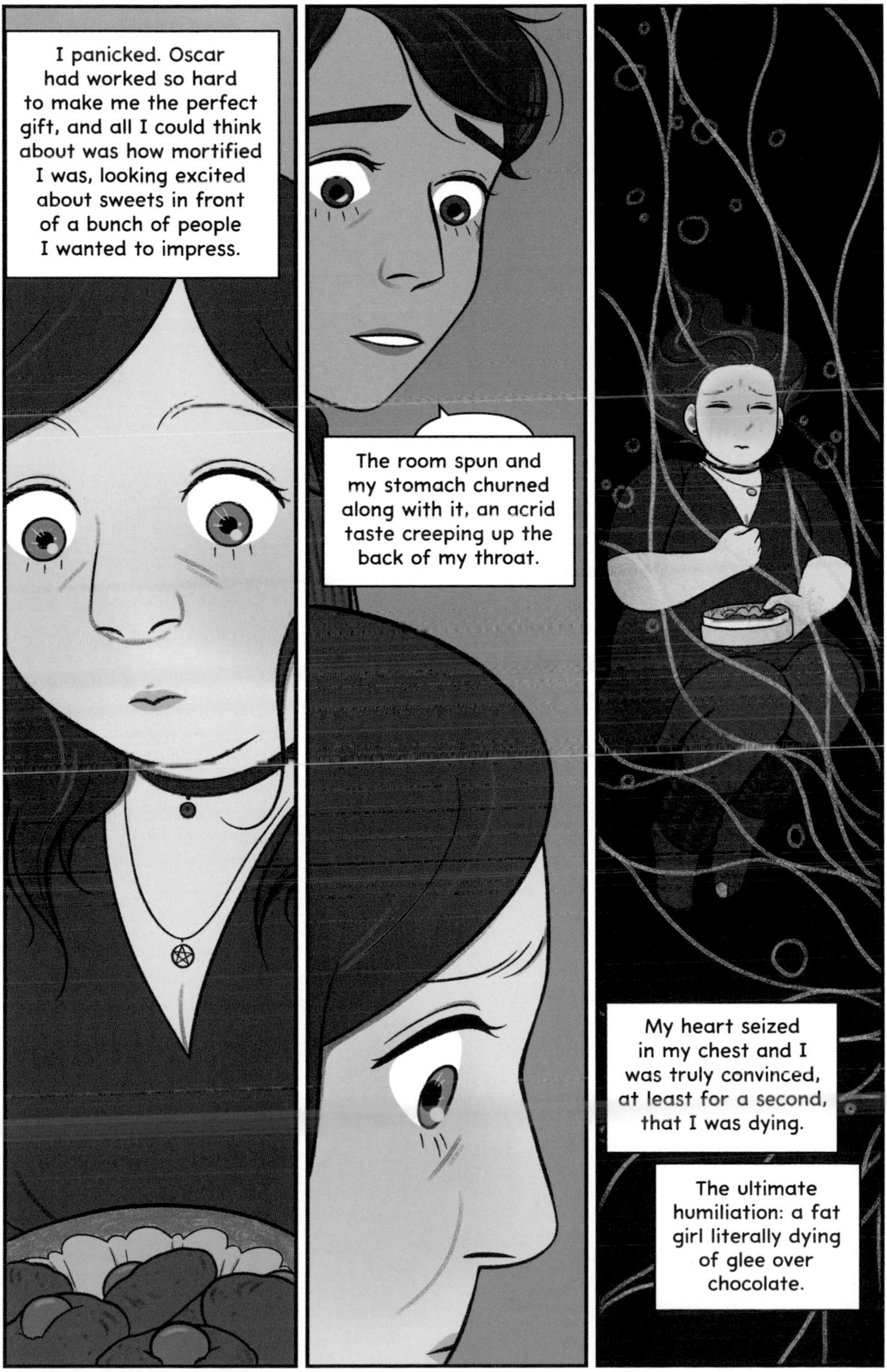
I panicked. Oscar had worked so hard to make me the perfect gift, and all I could think about was how mortified I was, looking excited about sweets in front of a bunch of people I wanted to impress.
The room spun and my stomach churned along with it, an acrid taste creeping up the back of my throat.
My heart seized in my chest and I was truly convinced, at least for a second, that I was dying.
The ultimate humiliation: a fat girl literally dying of glee over chocolate.

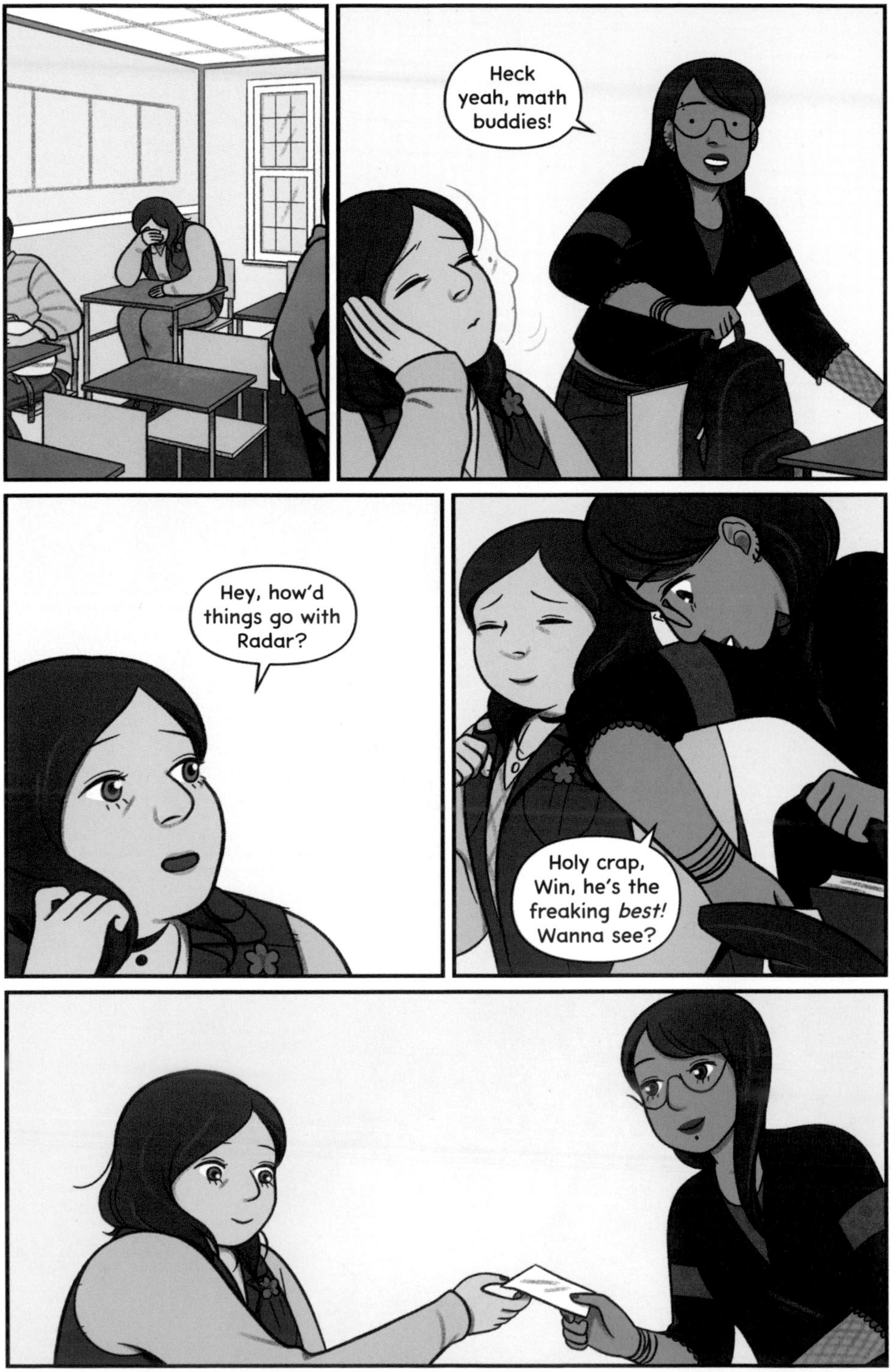

Heck yeah, math buddies!
Hey, how'd things go with Radar?
Holy crap, Win, he's the freaking *best!* Wanna see?

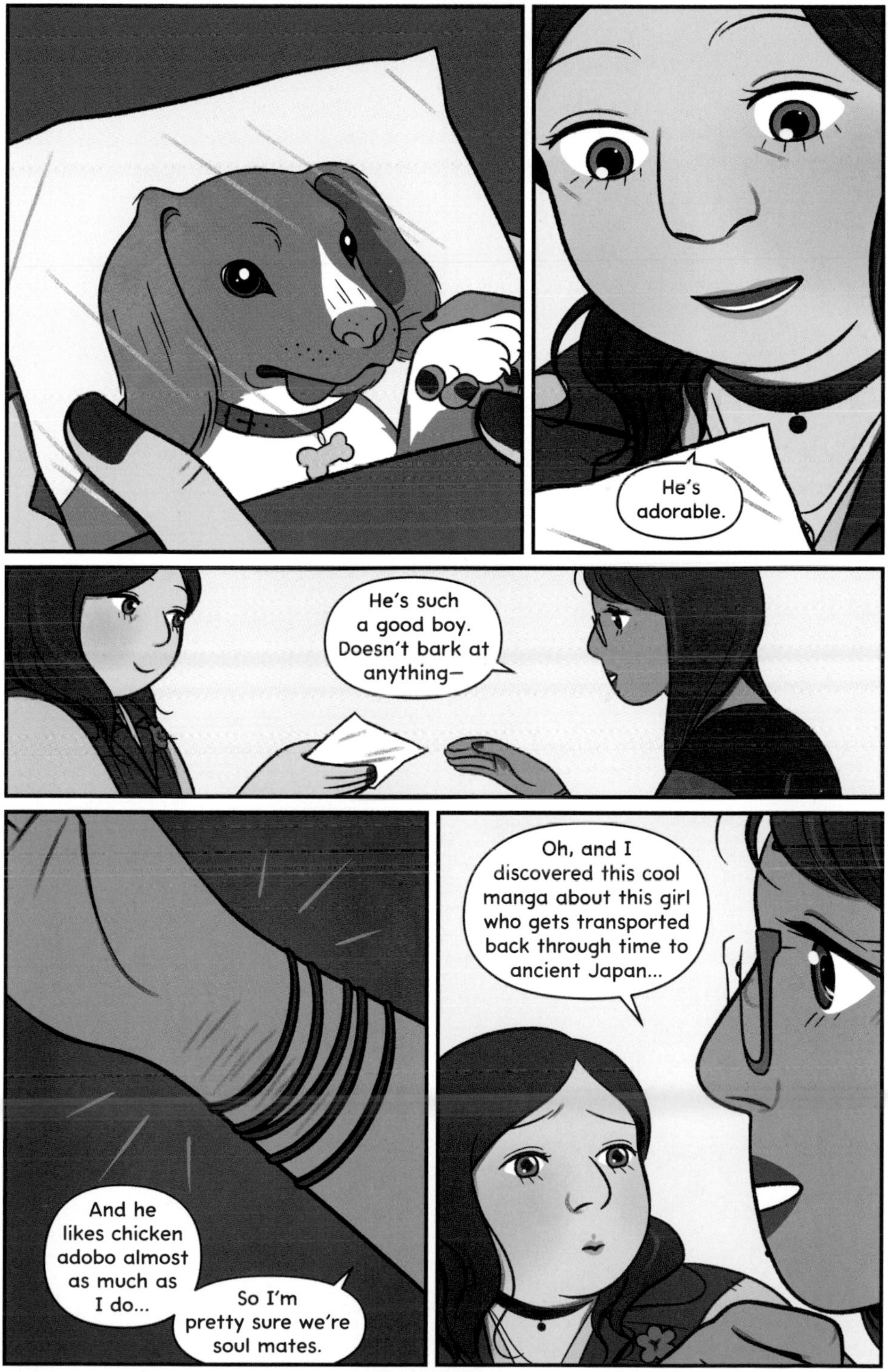
He's adorable.
He's such a good boy. Doesn't bark at anything—
Oh, and I discovered this cool manga about this girl who gets transported back through time to ancient Japan...
And he likes chicken adobo almost as much as I do...
So I'm pretty sure we're soul mates.

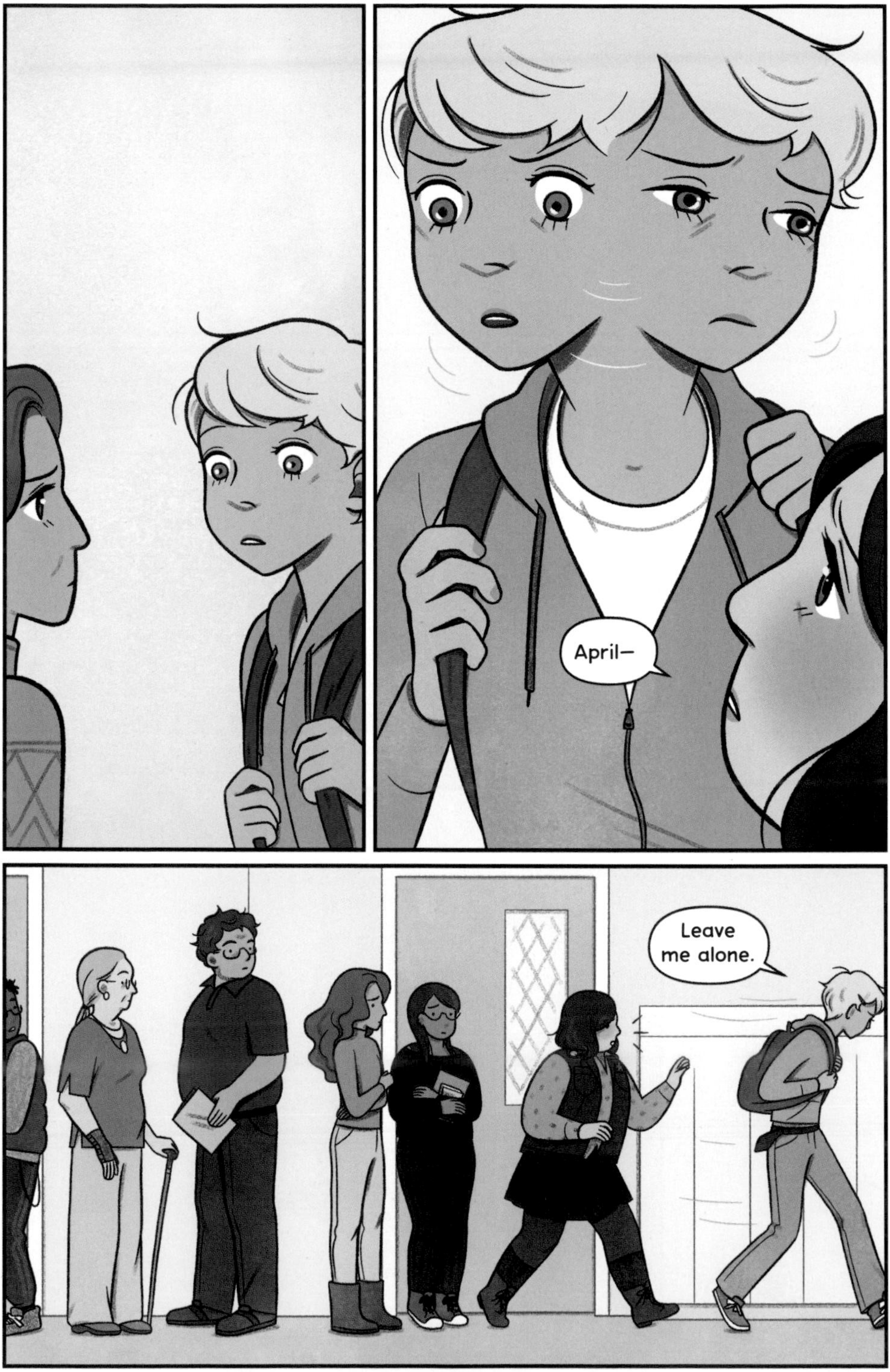
April—
Leave me alone.

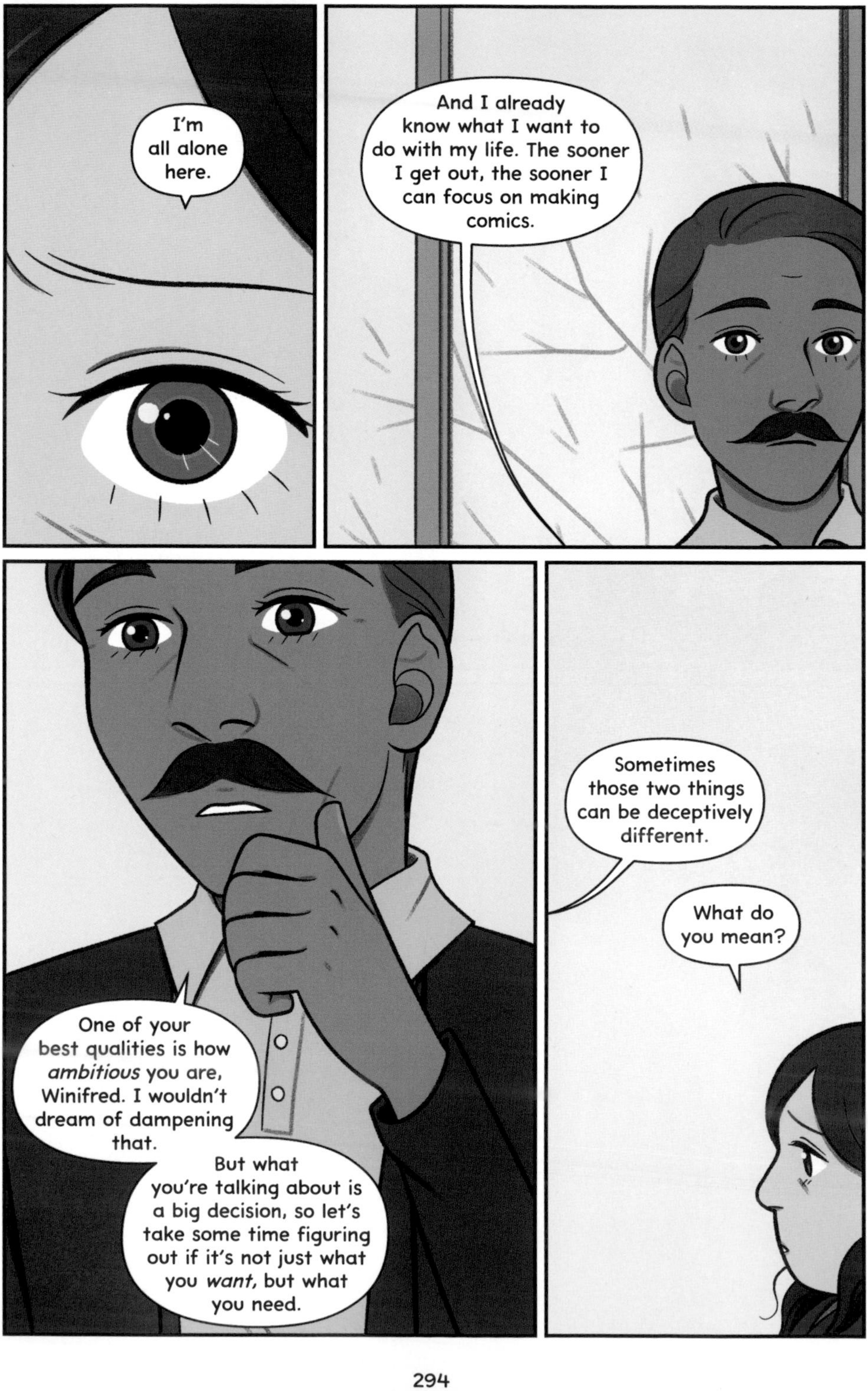
I'm all alone here.
And I already know what I want to do with my life. The sooner I get out, the sooner I can focus on making comics.
Sometimes those two things can be deceptively different.
What do you mean?
One of your best qualities is how *ambitious* you are, Winifred. I wouldn't dream of dampening that.
But what you're talking about is a big decision, so let's take some time figuring out if it's not just what you *want,* but what you need.

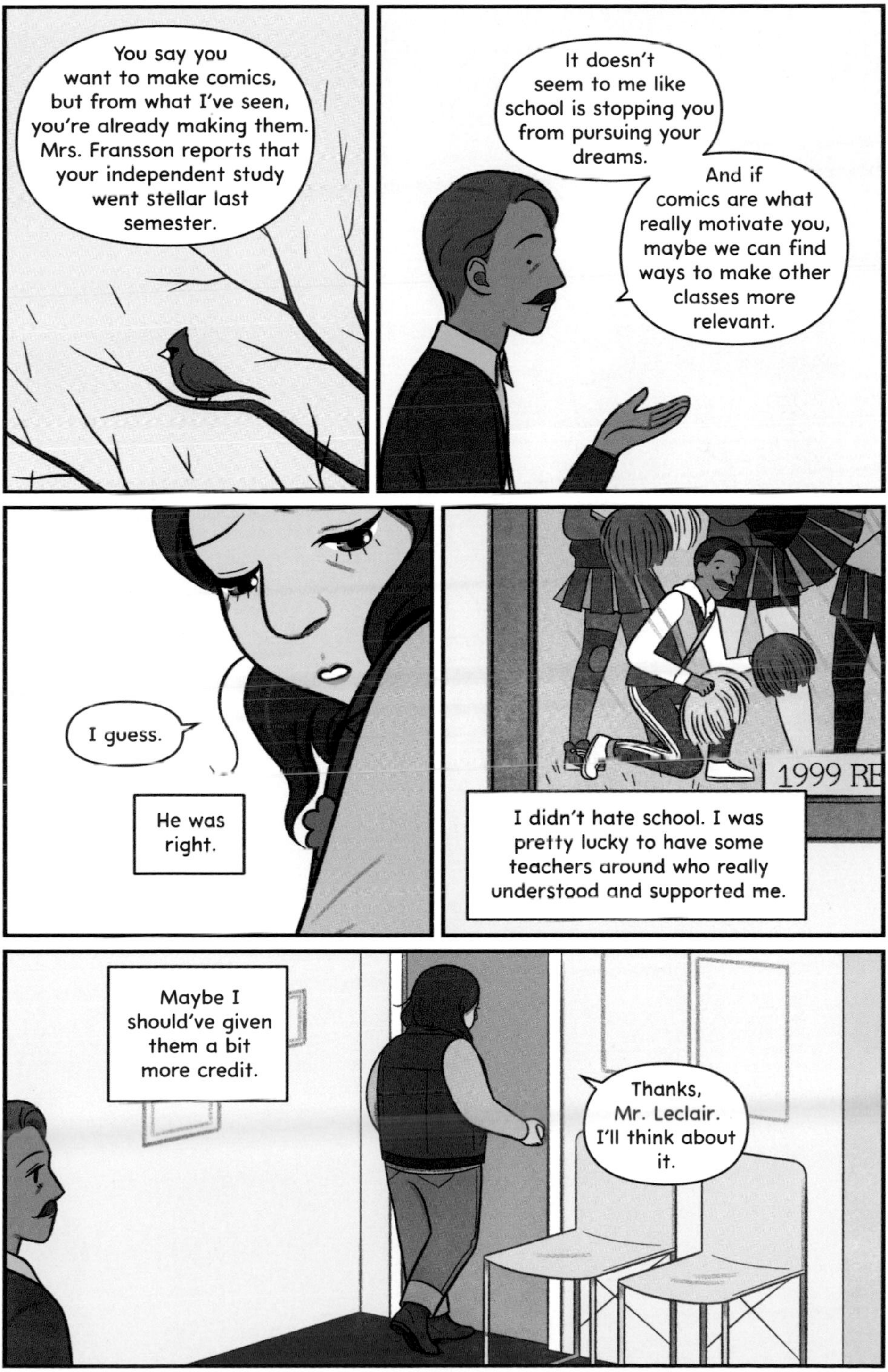
You say you want to make comics, but from what I've seen, you're already making them. Mrs. Fransson reports that your independent study went stellar last semester.
It doesn't seem to me like school is stopping you from pursuing your dreams.
And if comics are what really motivate you, maybe we can find ways to make other classes more relevant.
I guess.
He was right.
1999 RE
I didn't hate school. I was pretty lucky to have some teachers around who really understood and supported me.
Maybe I should've given them a bit more credit.
Thanks, Mr. Leclair. I'll think about it.

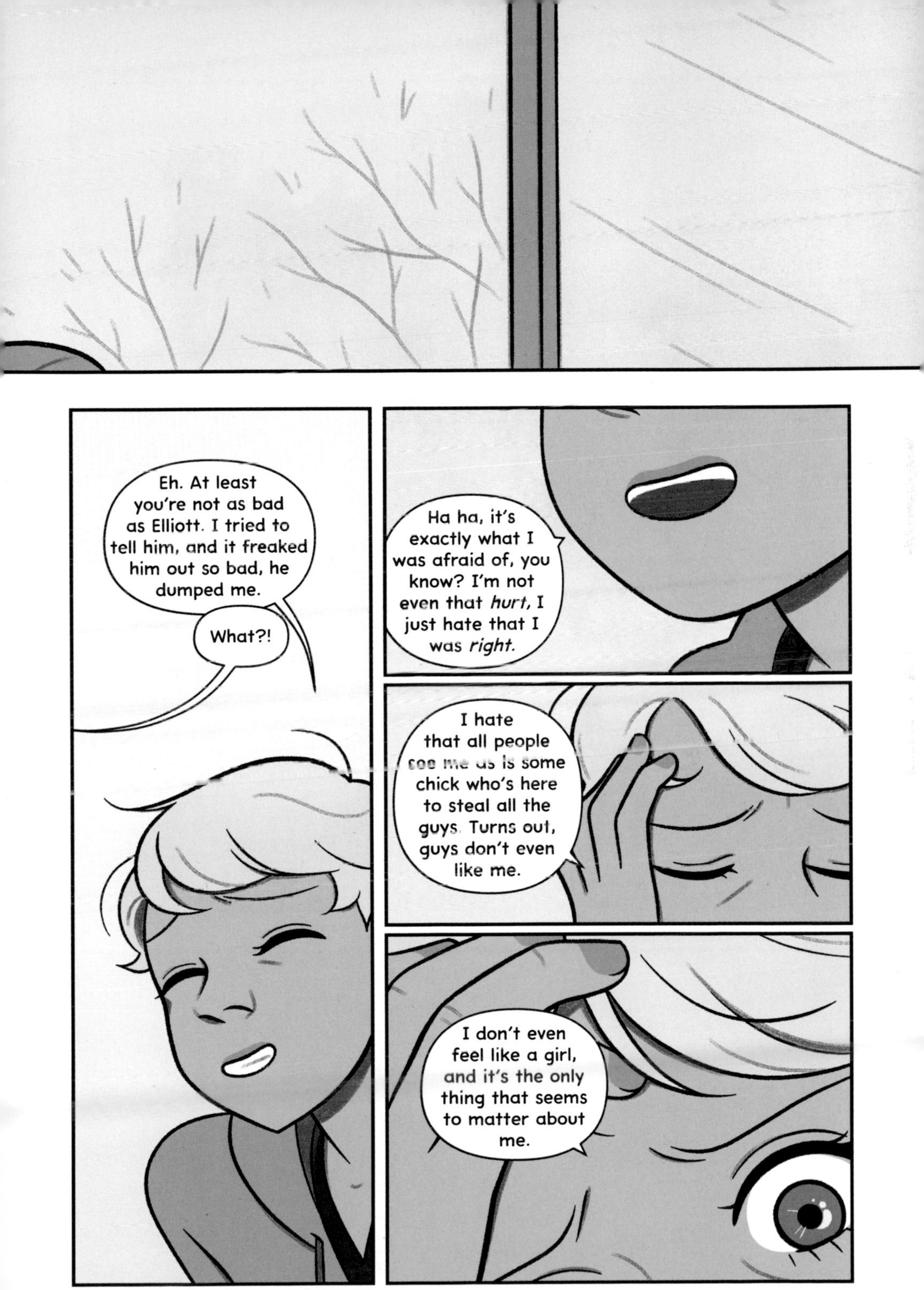
Eh. At least you're not as bad as Elliott. I tried to tell him, and it freaked him out so bad, he dumped me.
What?!
Ha ha, it's exactly what I was afraid of, you know? I'm not even that *hurt,* I just hate that I was *right.*
I hate that all people see me as is some chick who's here to steal all the guys. Turns out, guys don't even like me.
I don't even feel like a girl, and it's the only thing that seems to matter about me.

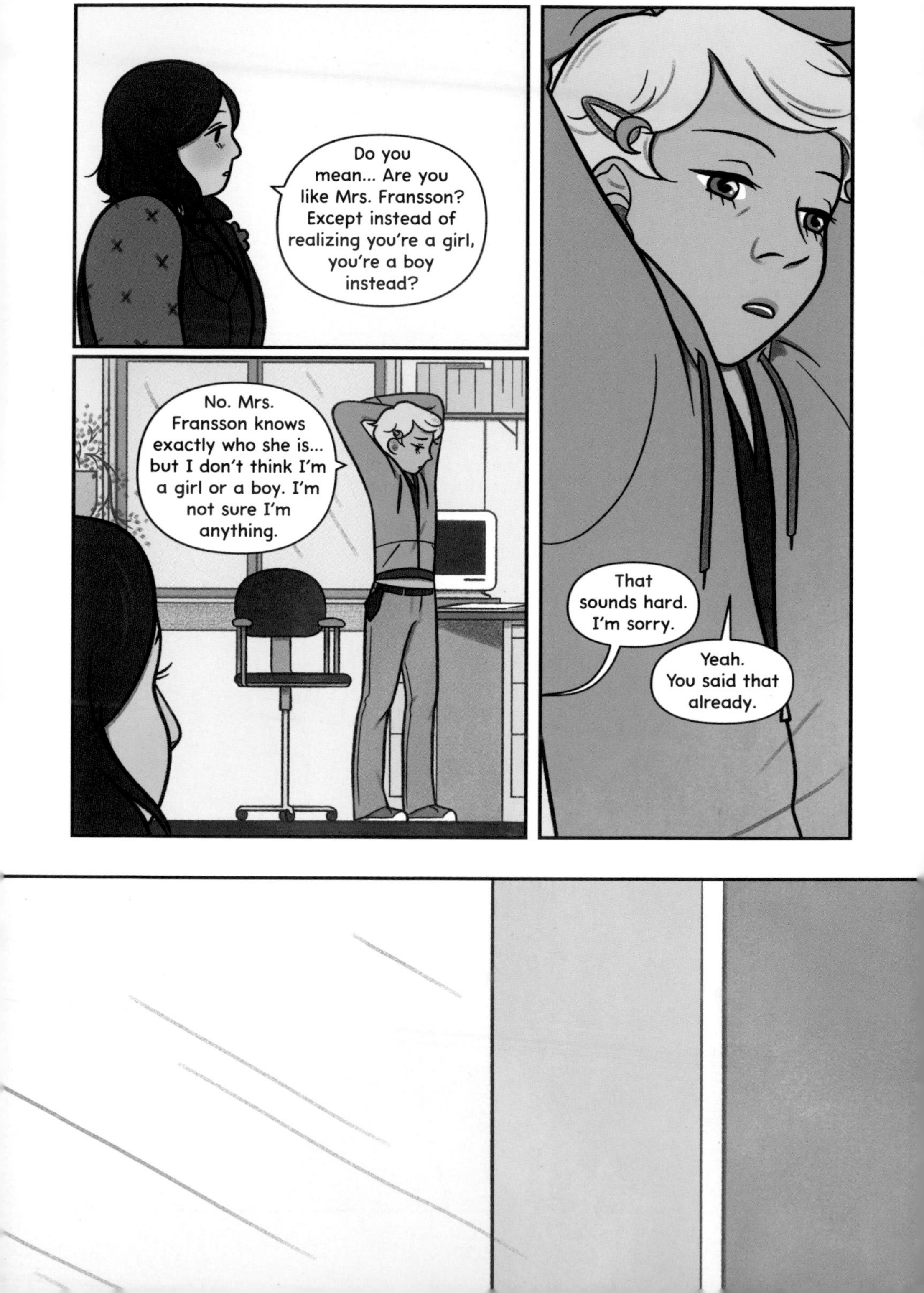
Do you mean... Are you like Mrs. Fransson? Except instead of realizing you're a girl, you're a boy instead?
No. Mrs. Fransson knows exactly who she is... but I don't think I'm a girl or a boy. I'm not sure I'm anything.
That sounds hard. I'm sorry.
Yeah. You said that already.

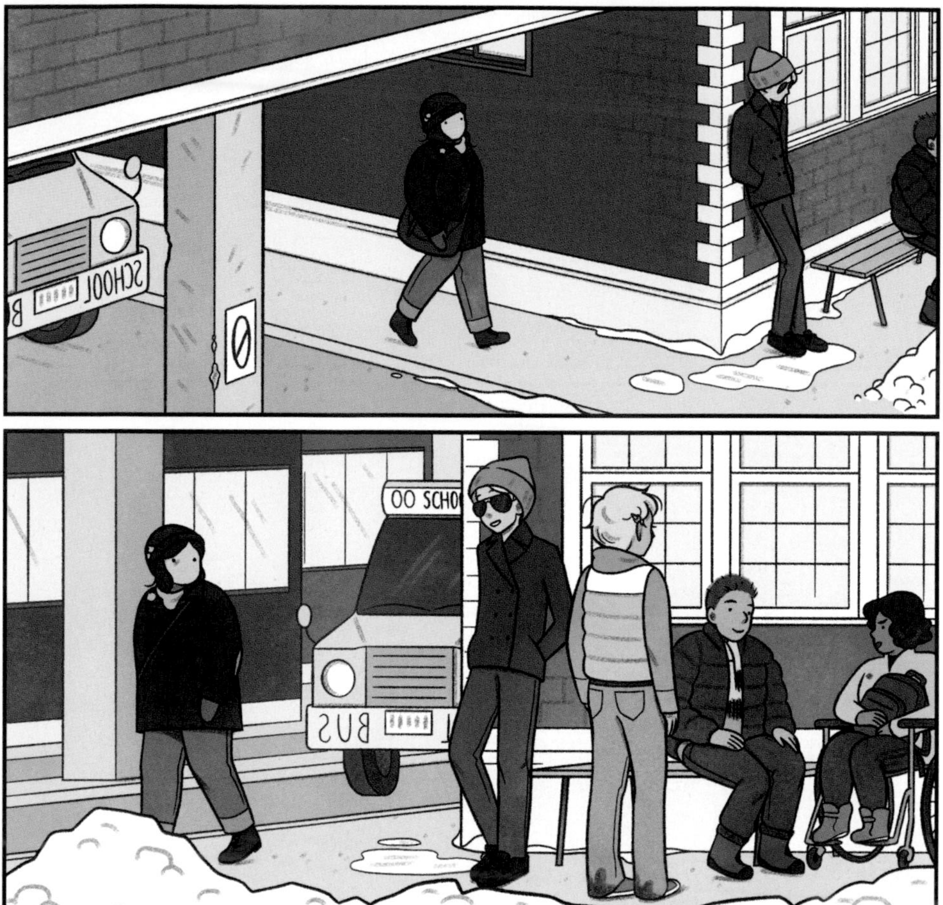
OO SCHO

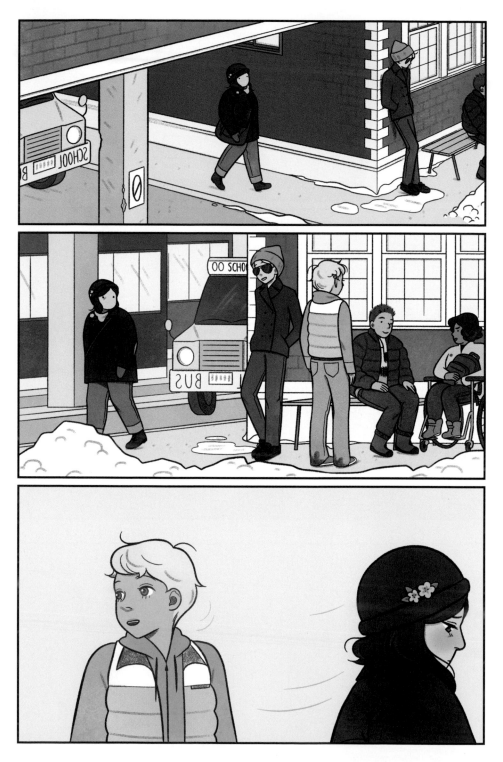

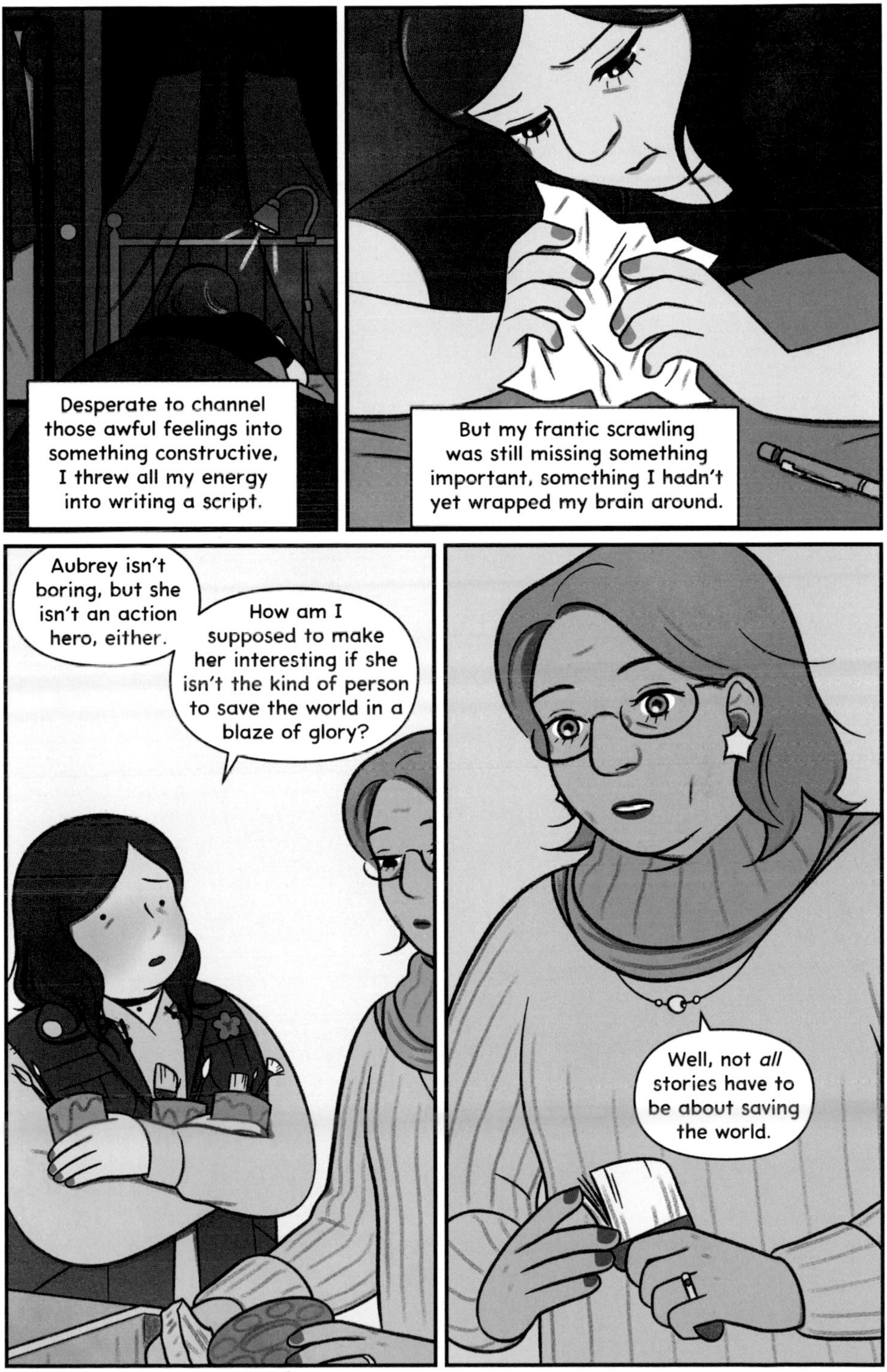
Desperate to channel those awful feelings into something constructive, I threw all my energy into writing a script.
But my frantic scrawling was still missing something important, something I hadn't yet wrapped my brain around.
Aubrey isn't boring, but she isn't an action hero, either.
How am I supposed to make her interesting if she isn't the kind of person to save the world in a blaze of glory?
Well, not *all* stories have to be about saving the world.

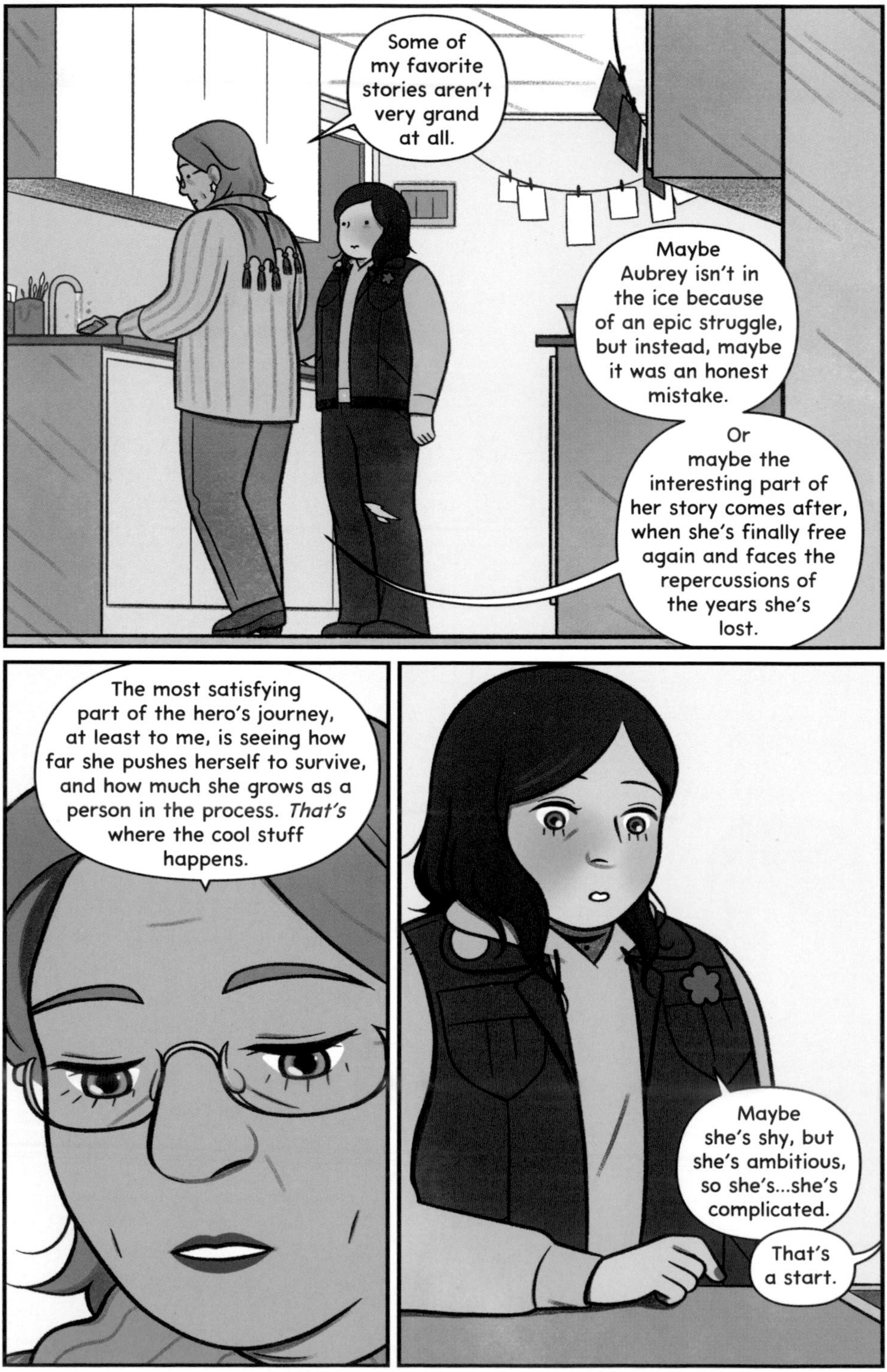
Some of my favorite stories aren't very grand at all.
Maybe Aubrey isn't in the ice because of an epic struggle, but instead, maybe it was an honest mistake.
Or maybe the interesting part of her story comes after, when she's finally free again and faces the repercussions of the years she's lost.
The most satisfying part of the hero's journey, at least to me, is seeing how far she pushes herself to survive, and how much she grows as a person in the process. *That's* where the cool stuff happens.
Maybe she's shy, but she's ambitious, so she's...she's complicated.
That's a start.

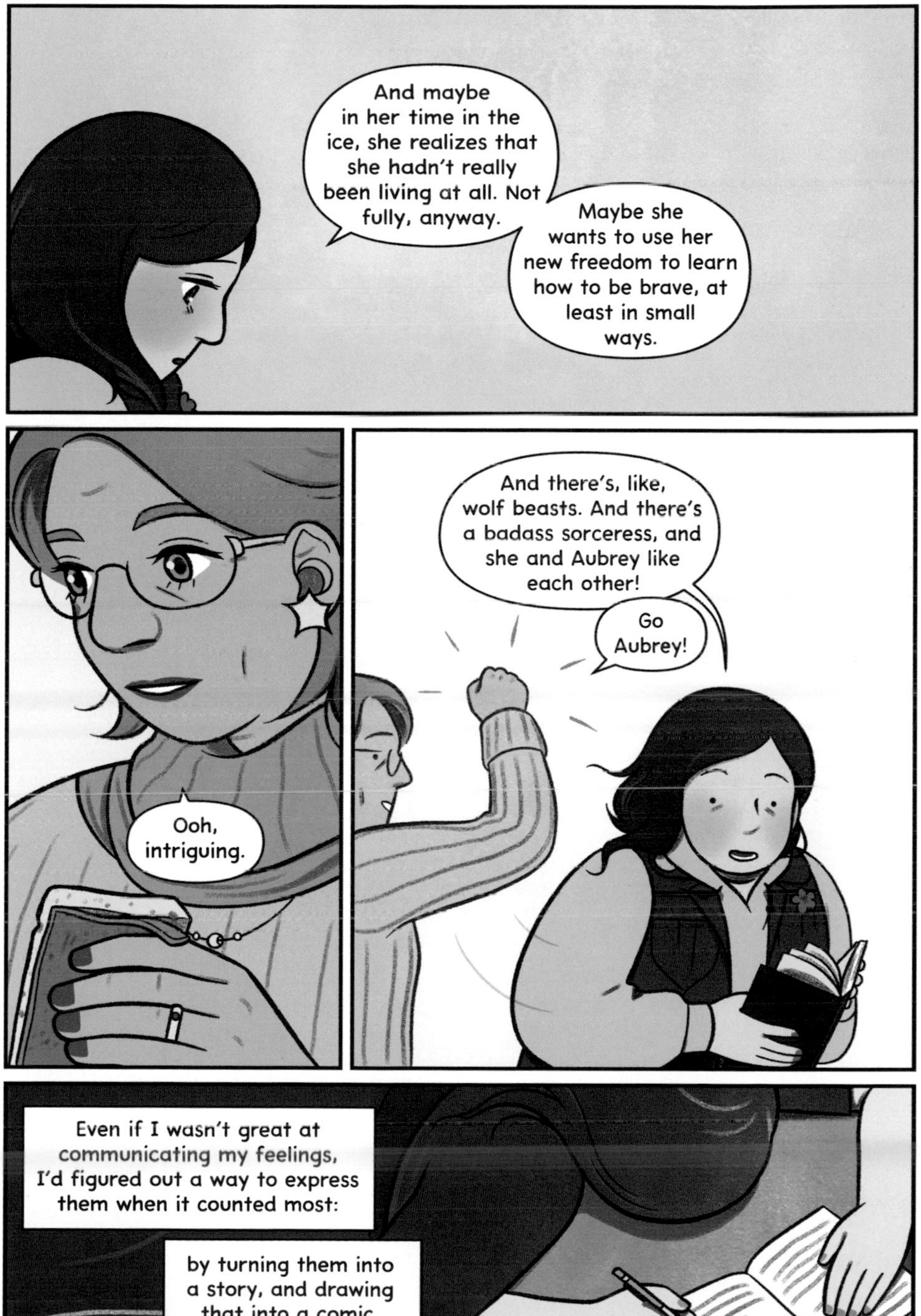
And maybe in her time in the ice, she realizes that she hadn't really been living at all. Not fully, anyway.
Maybe she wants to use her new freedom to learn how to be brave, at least in small ways.
Ooh, intriguing.
And there's, like, wolf beasts. And there's a badass sorceress, and she and Aubrey like each other!
Go Aubrey!
Even if I wasn't great at communicating my feelings, I'd figured out a way to express them when it counted most:
by turning them into a story, and drawing that into a comic.

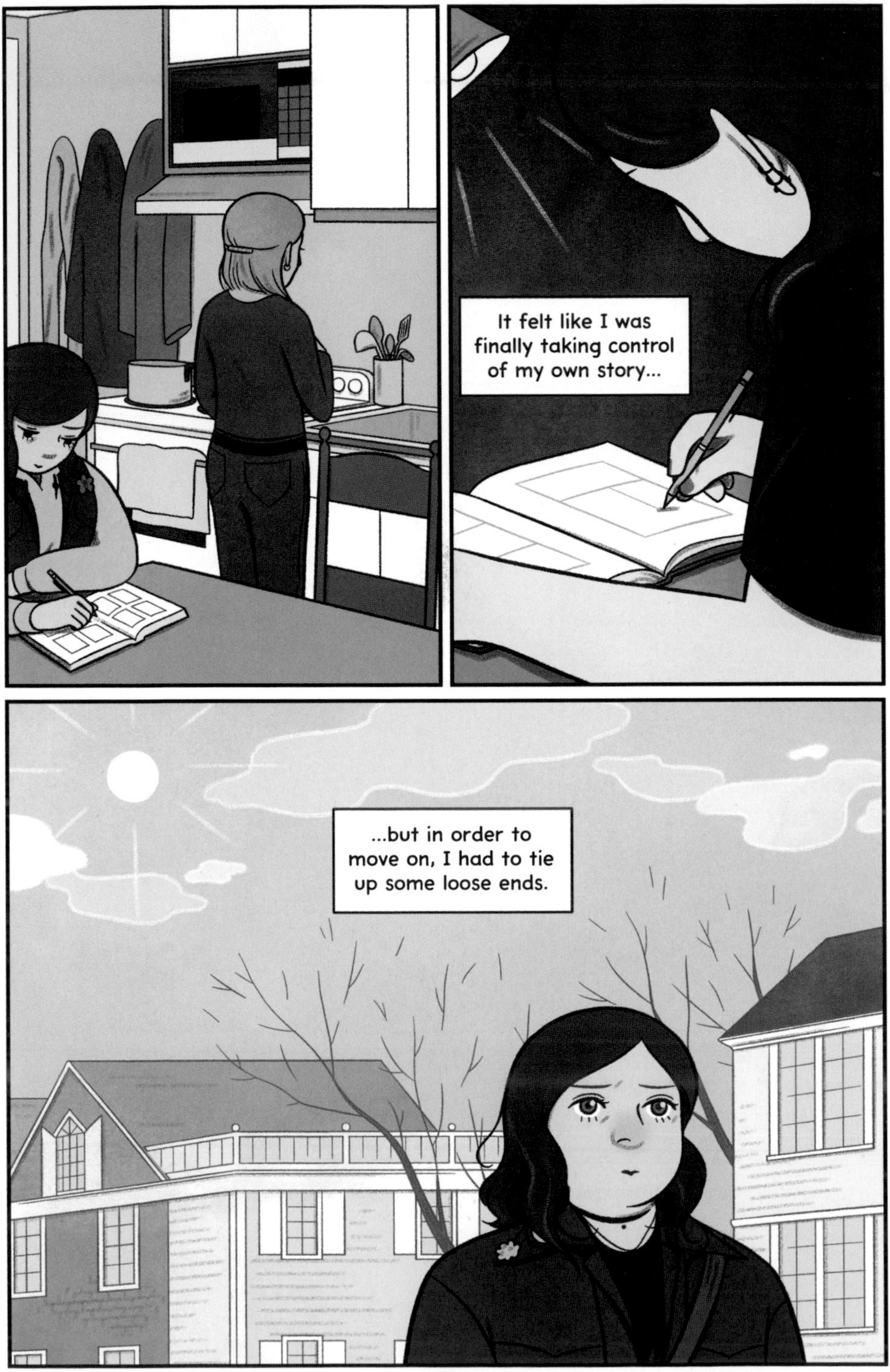
It felt like I was finally taking control of my own story...
...but in order to move on, I had to tie up some loose ends.

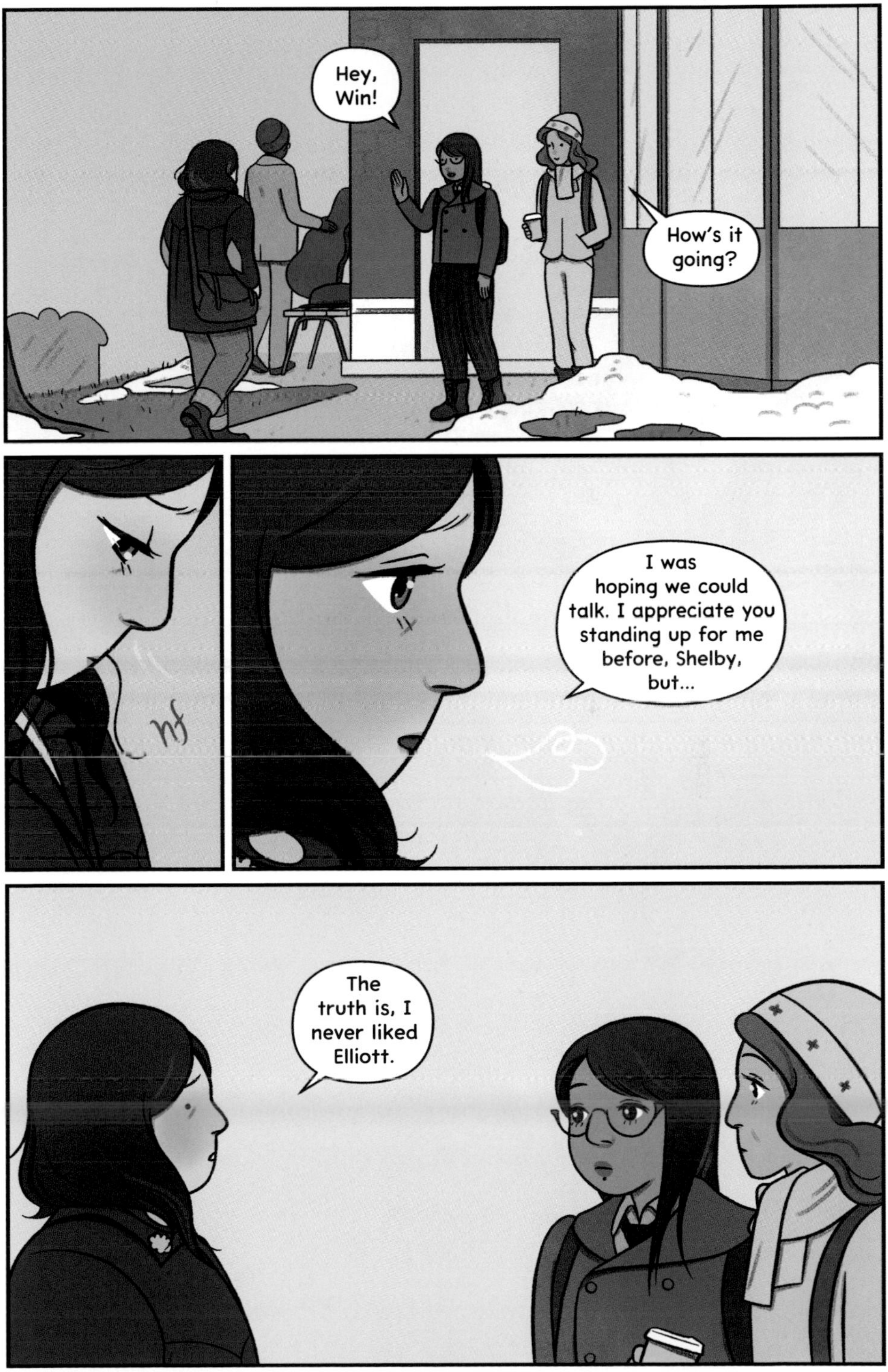
Hey, Win!
How's it going?
I was hoping we could talk. I appreciate you standing up for me before, Shelby, but...
The truth is, I never liked Elliott.

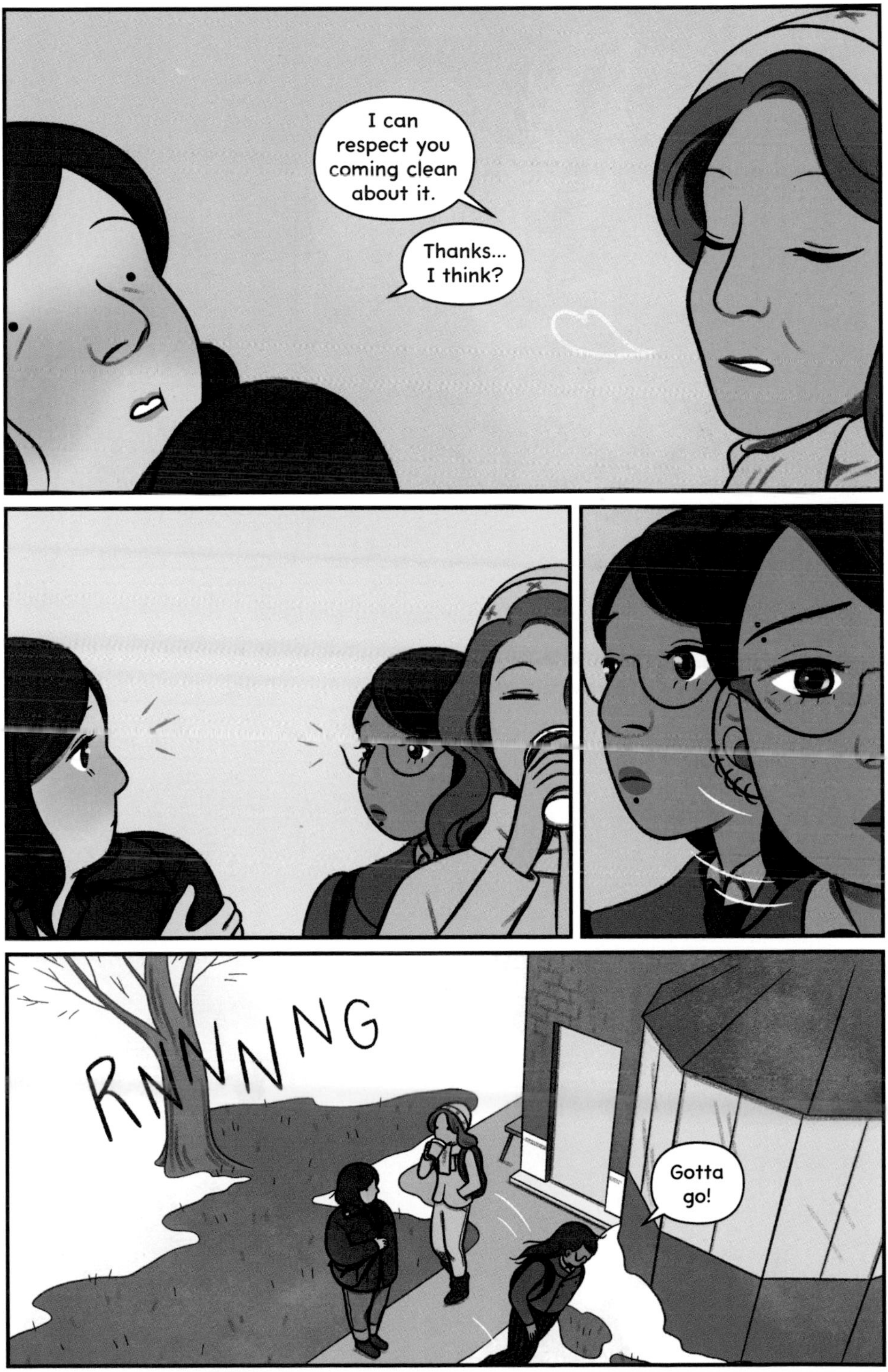
I can respect you coming clean about it.
Thanks... I think?
RNNNG
Gotta go!

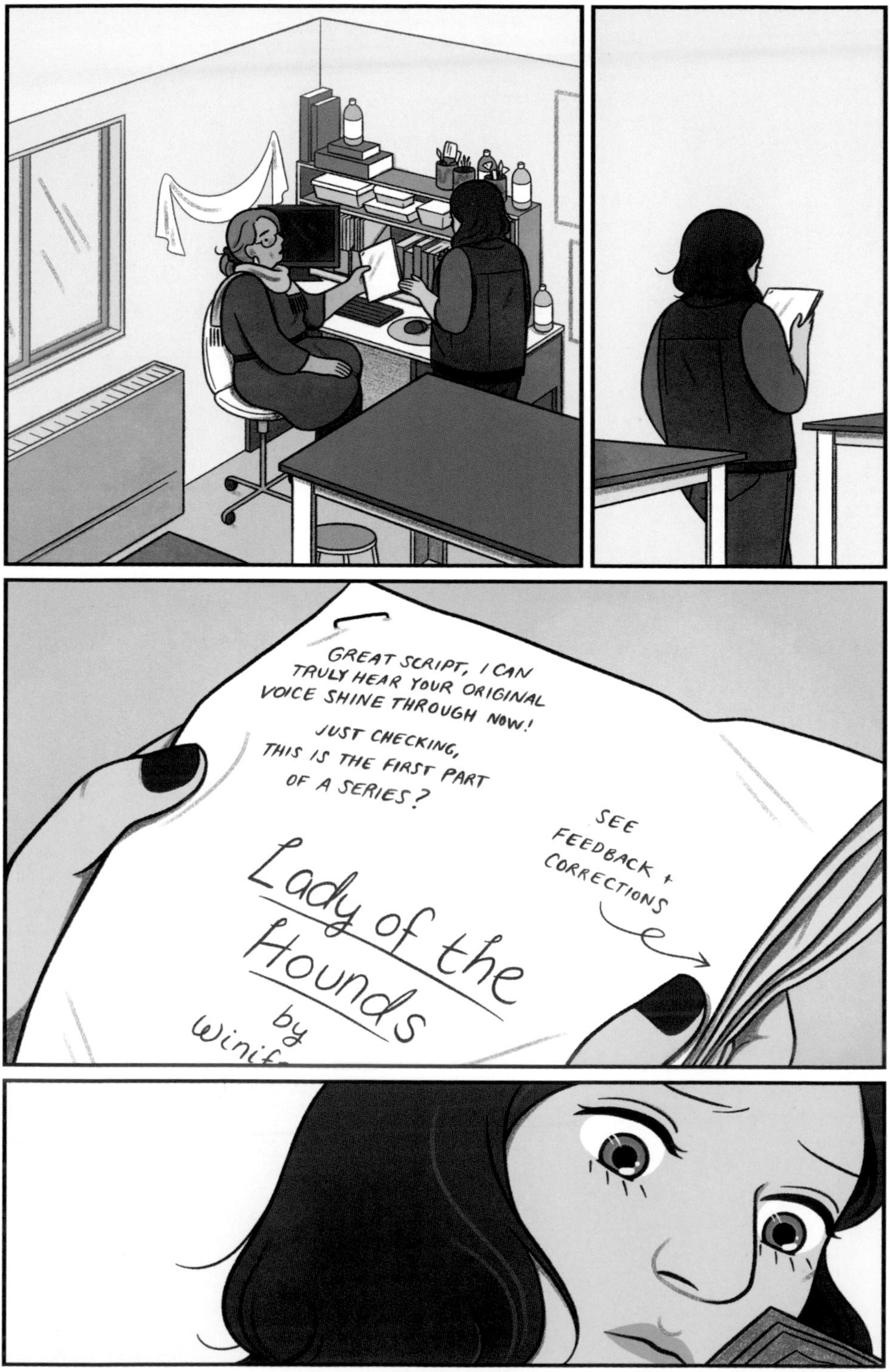
GREAT SCRIPT, I CAN TRULY HEAR YOUR ORIGINAL VOICE SHINE THROUGH NOW!
JUST CHECKING, THIS IS THE FIRST PART OF A SERIES?
SEE FEEDBACK + CORRECTIONS
Lady of the Hounds
by

I'm not proud of my brief career as a stalker, but I took the long way home more than once just so I could walk by Oscar's new school.

Each time, I thought I had the guts to go in looking for him...

But it turns out that was an awfully tall order for someone who was only just learning how to be brave in the smallest of ways.

And even if I found him, what would I have said?

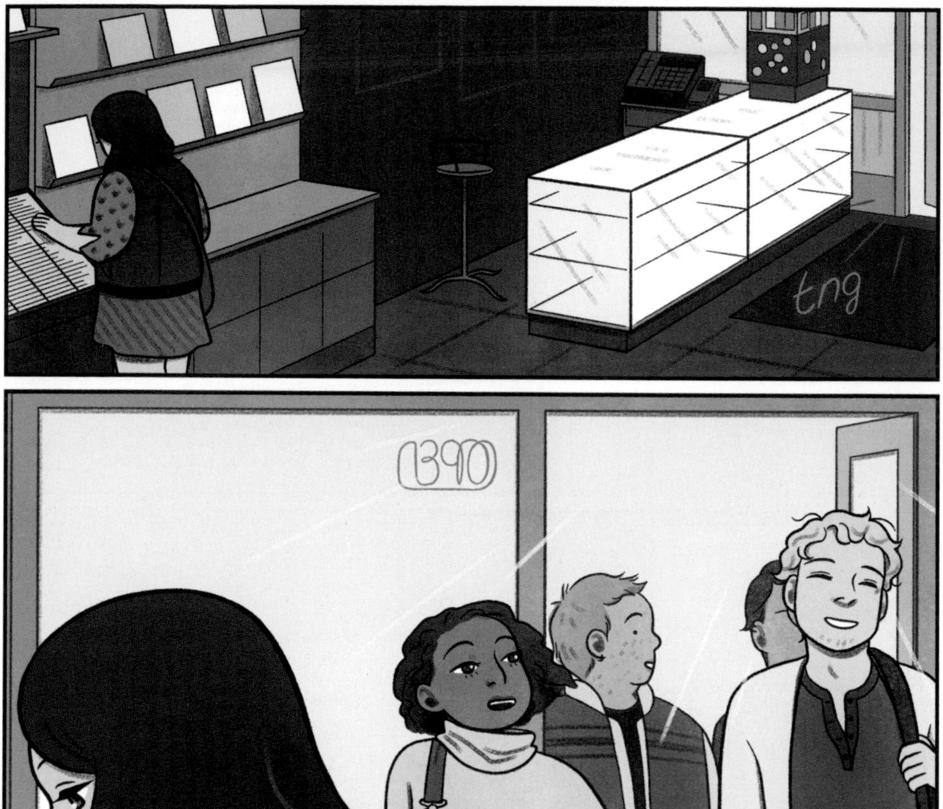
tng
1390

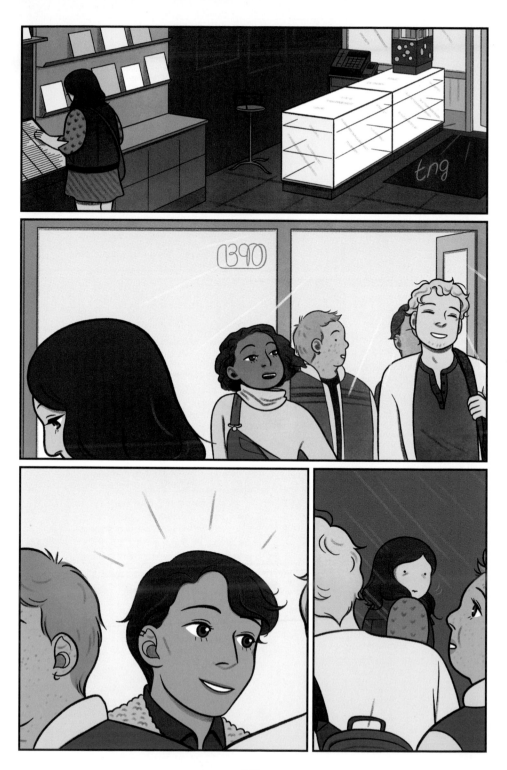

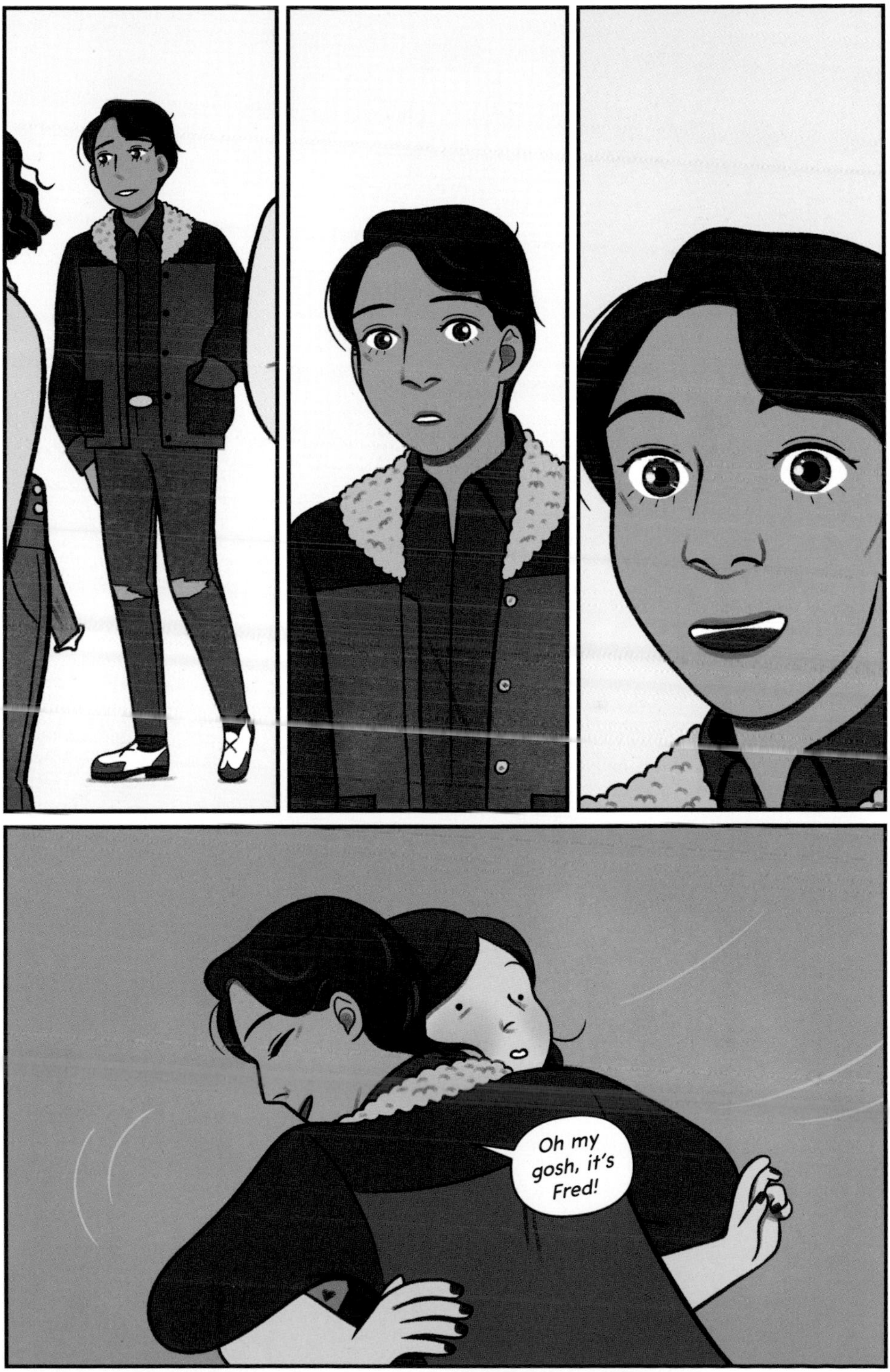
Oh my gosh, it's Fred!

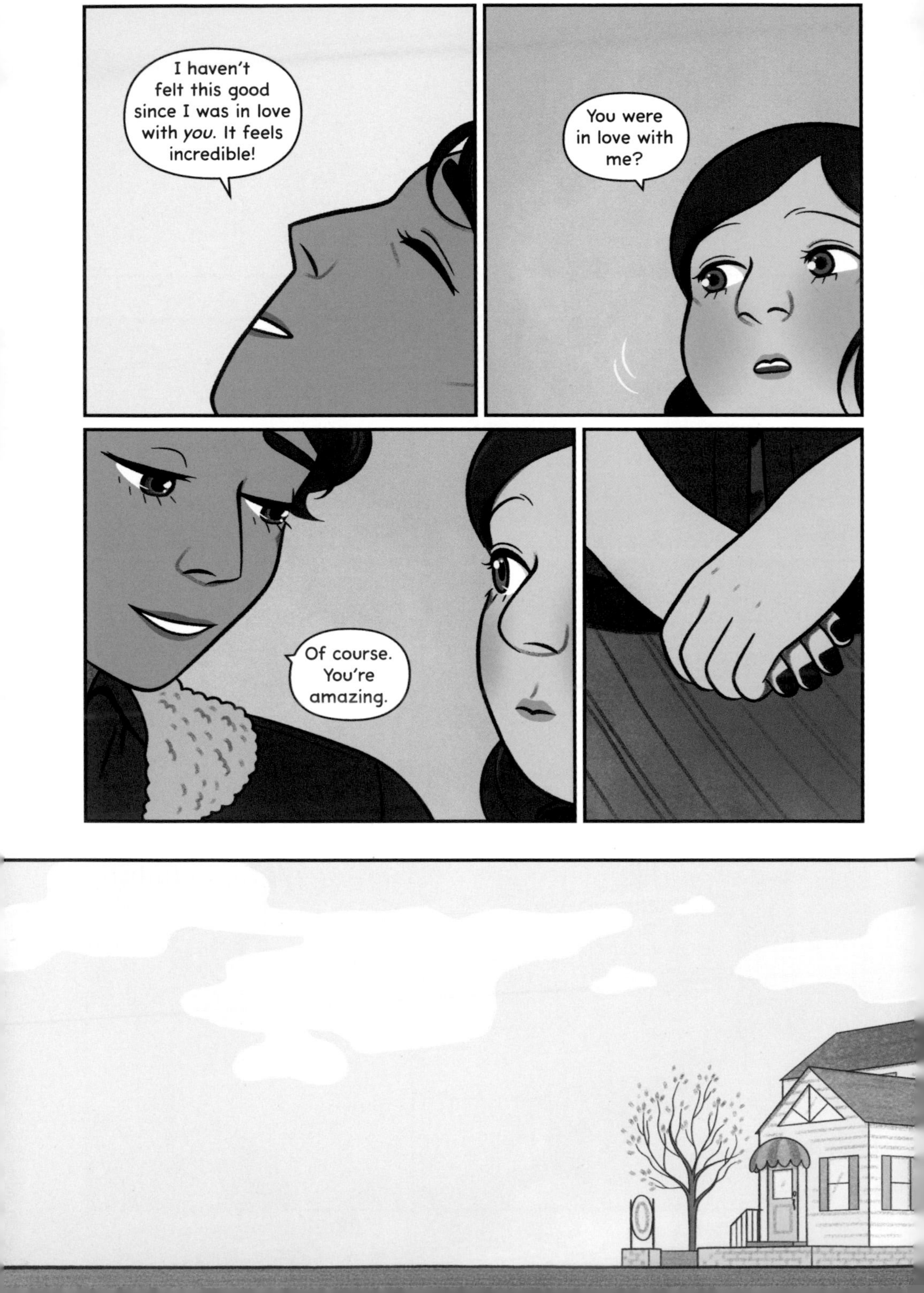
I haven't felt this good since I was in love with *you*. It feels incredible!
You were in love with me?
Of course. You're amazing.

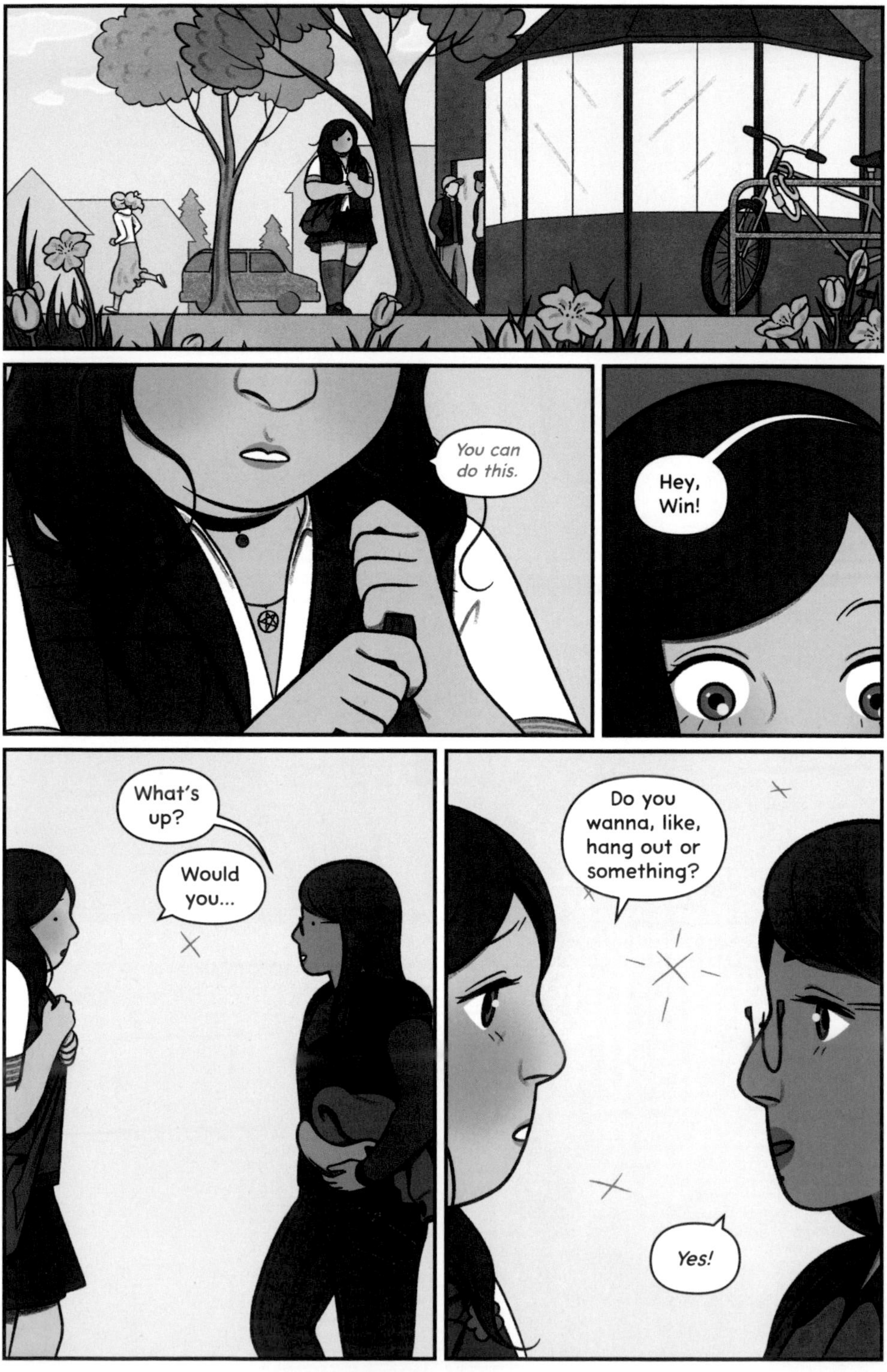
You can do this.
Hey, Win!
What's up?
Would you...
Do you wanna, like, hang out or something?
Yes!

gutterglimmers:
LADY OF THE HOUNDS

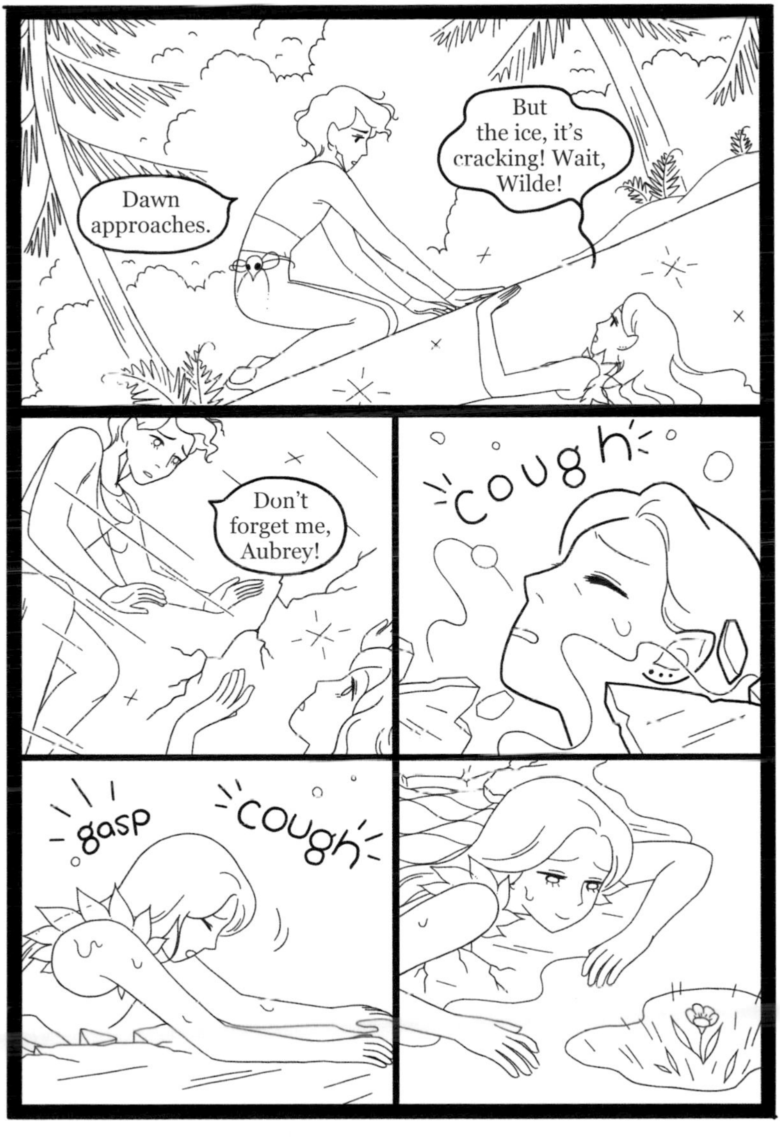
Dawn approaches.
But the ice, it's cracking! Wait, Wilde!
Don't forget me, Aubrey!
cough
gasp
cough

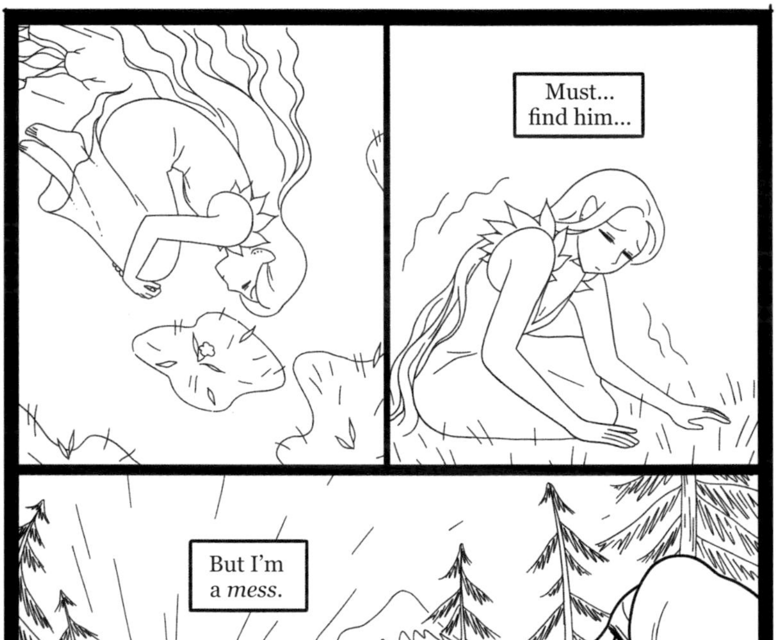
Must... find him...
But I'm a *mess*.
How could I possibly save Wilde when I can barely help myself?

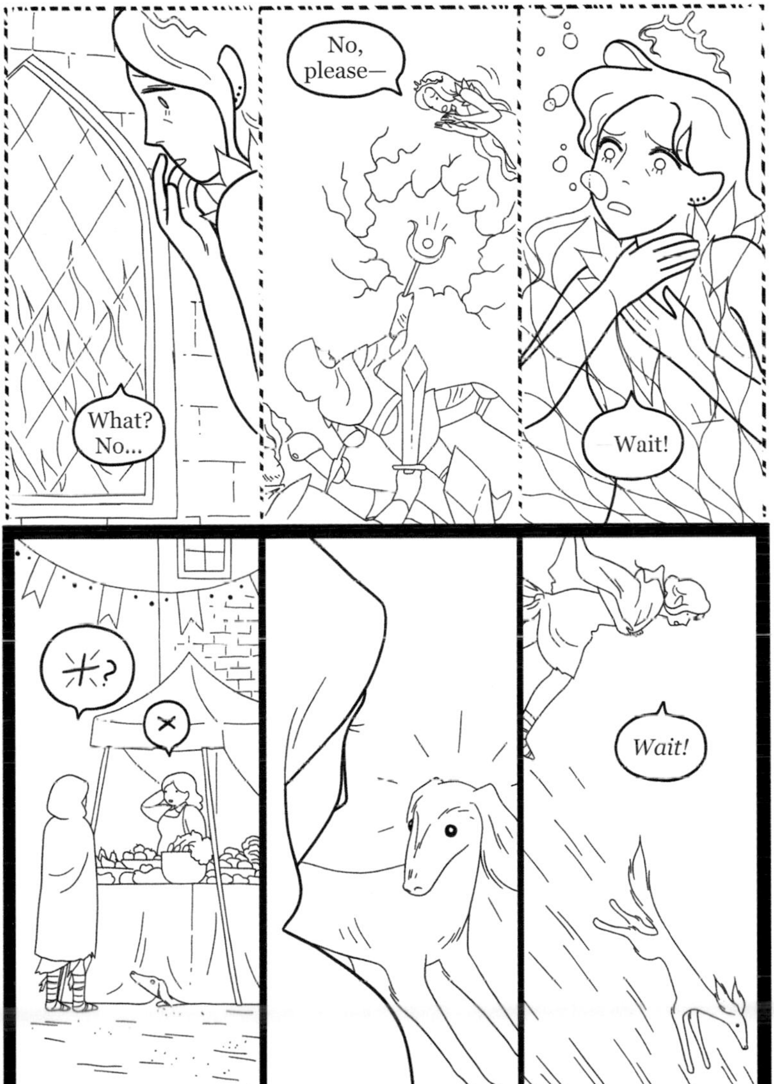
What? No...
No, please—
—Wait!
Wait!

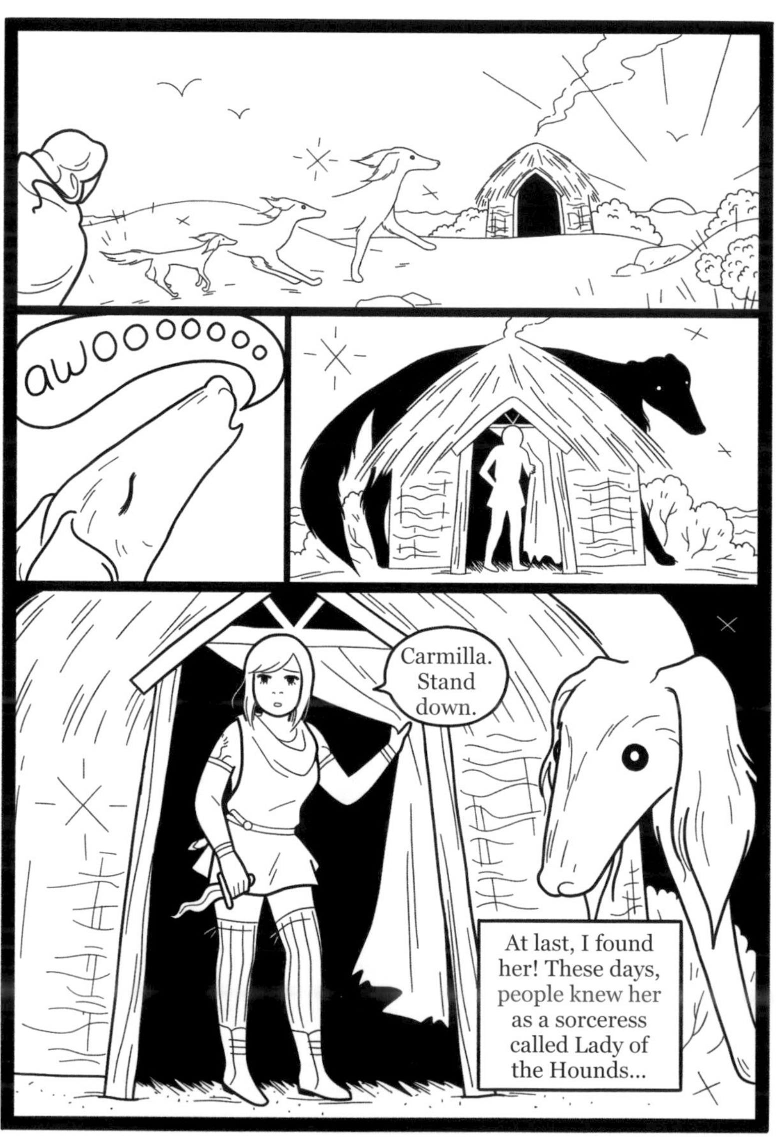
awoooooooo
Carmilla. Stand down.
At last, I found her! These days, people knew her as a sorceress called Lady of the Hounds...

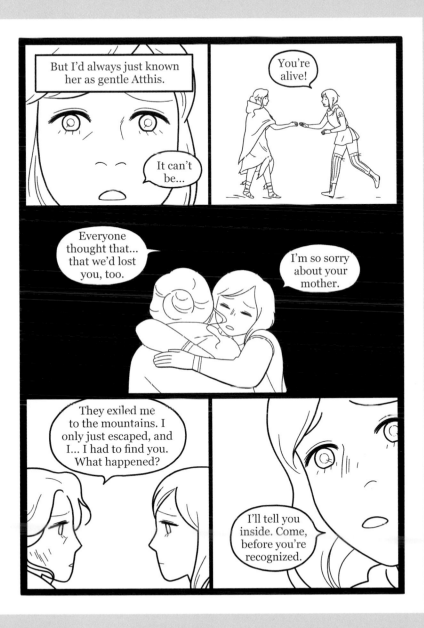

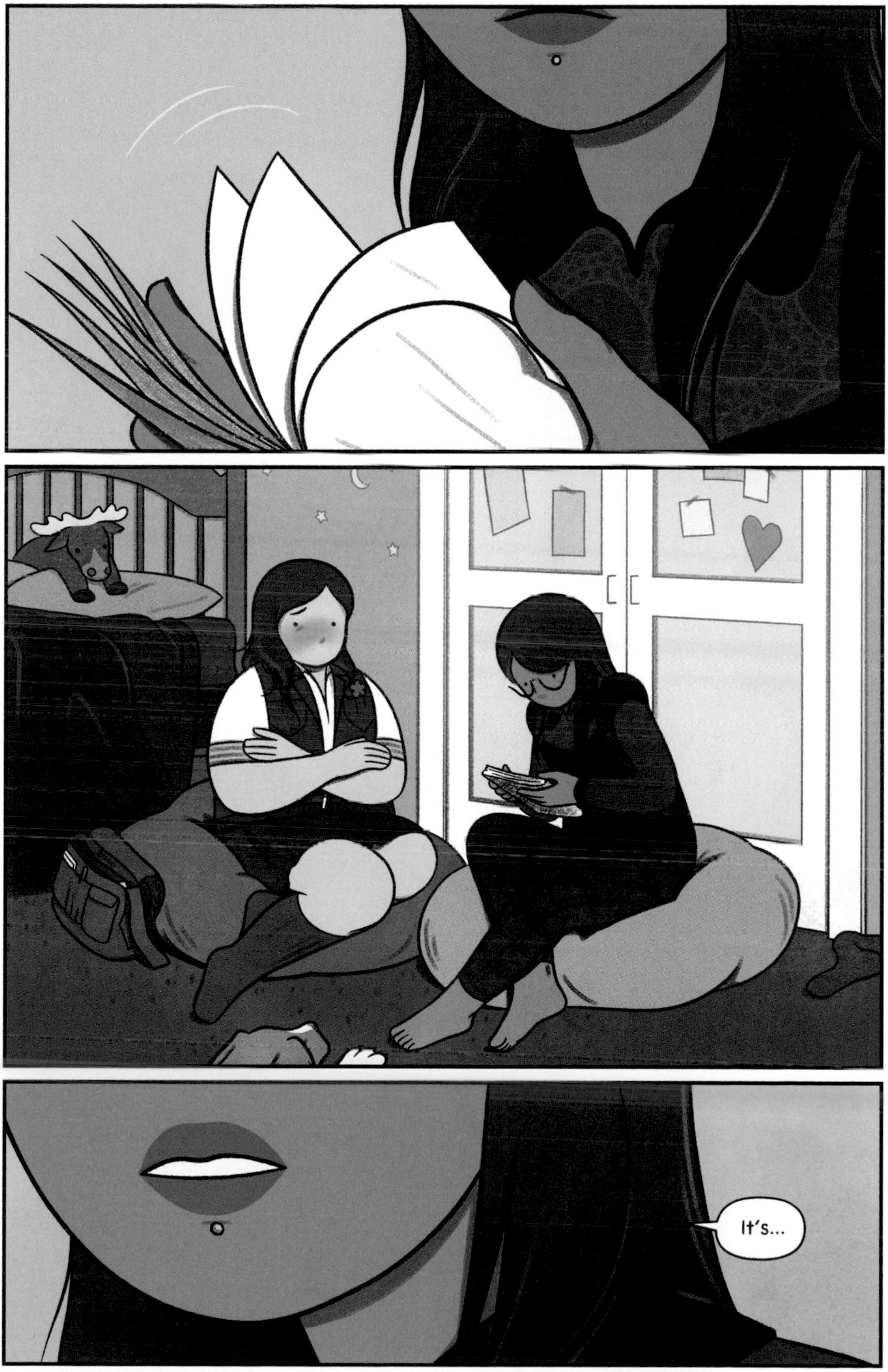
It's...

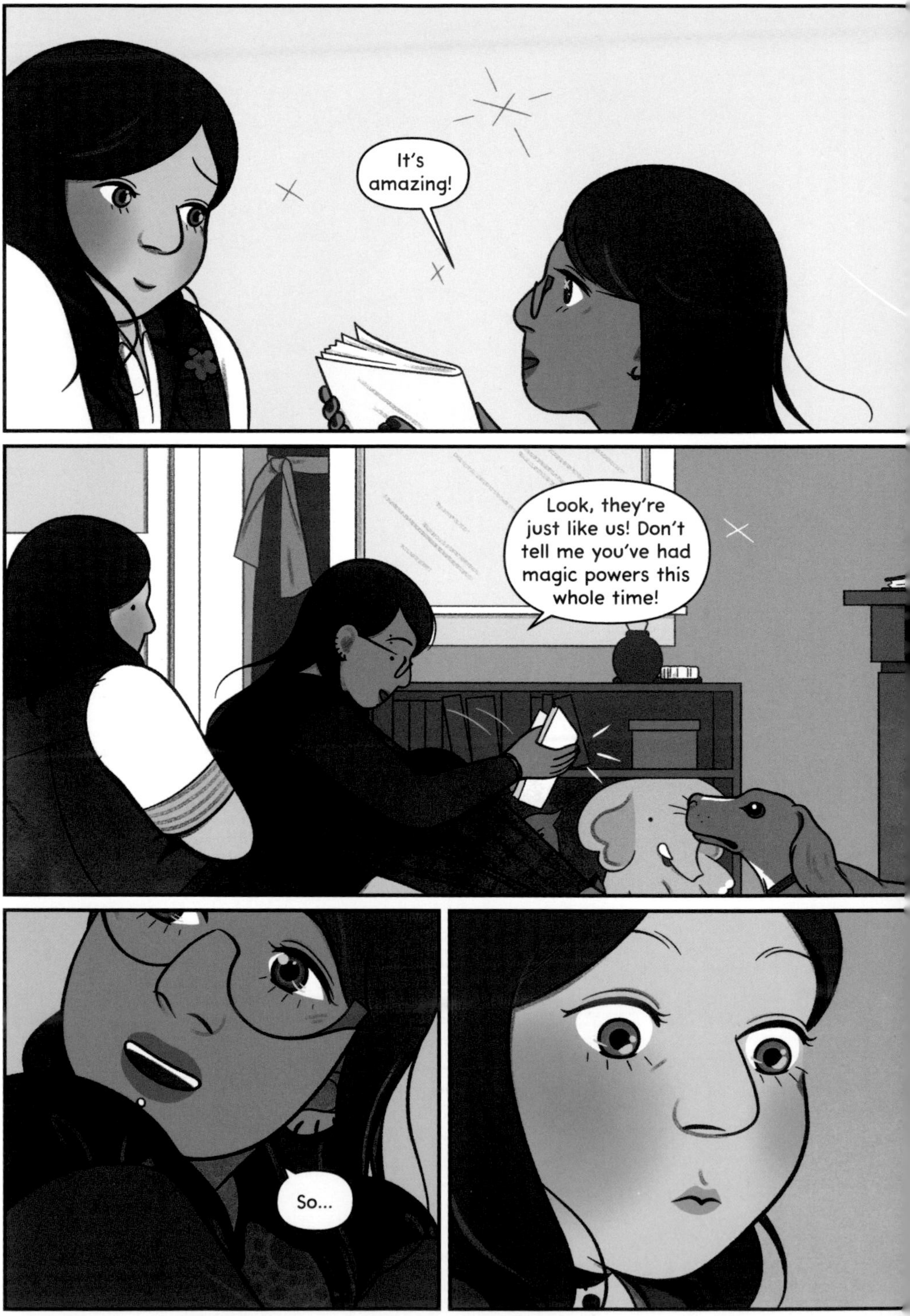
It's amazing!
Look, they're just like us! Don't tell me you've had magic powers this whole time!
So...

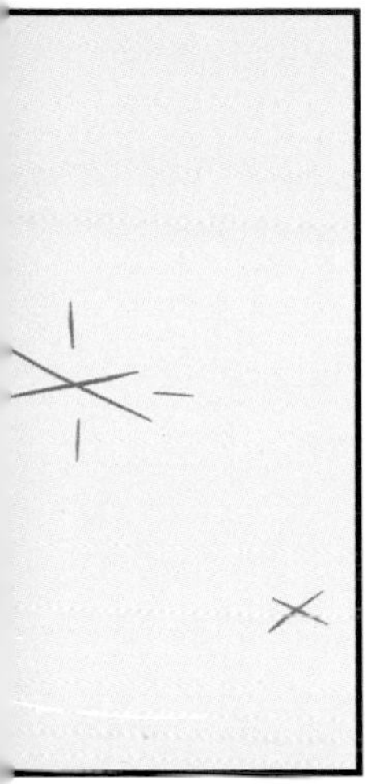

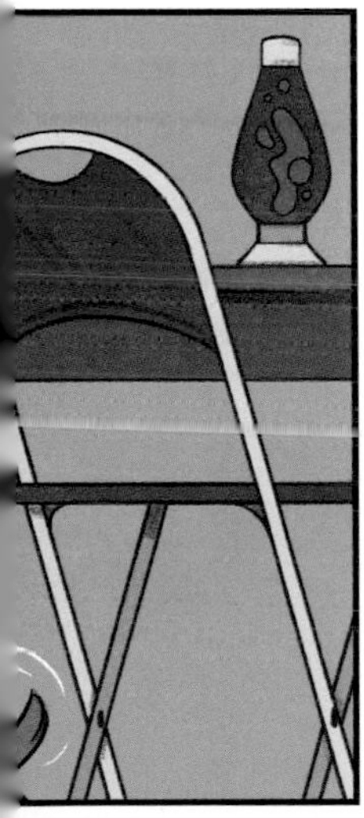

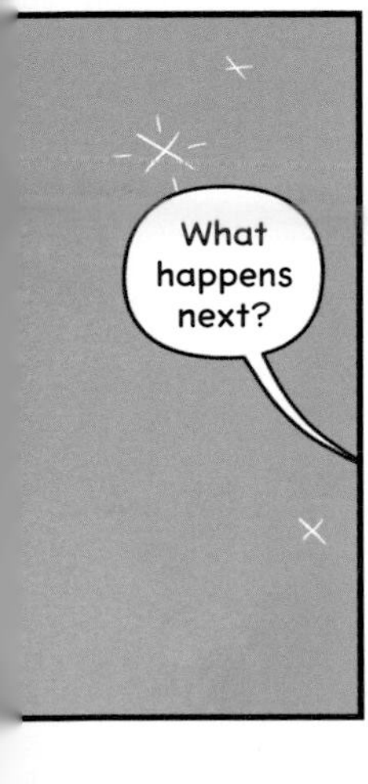
What happens next?

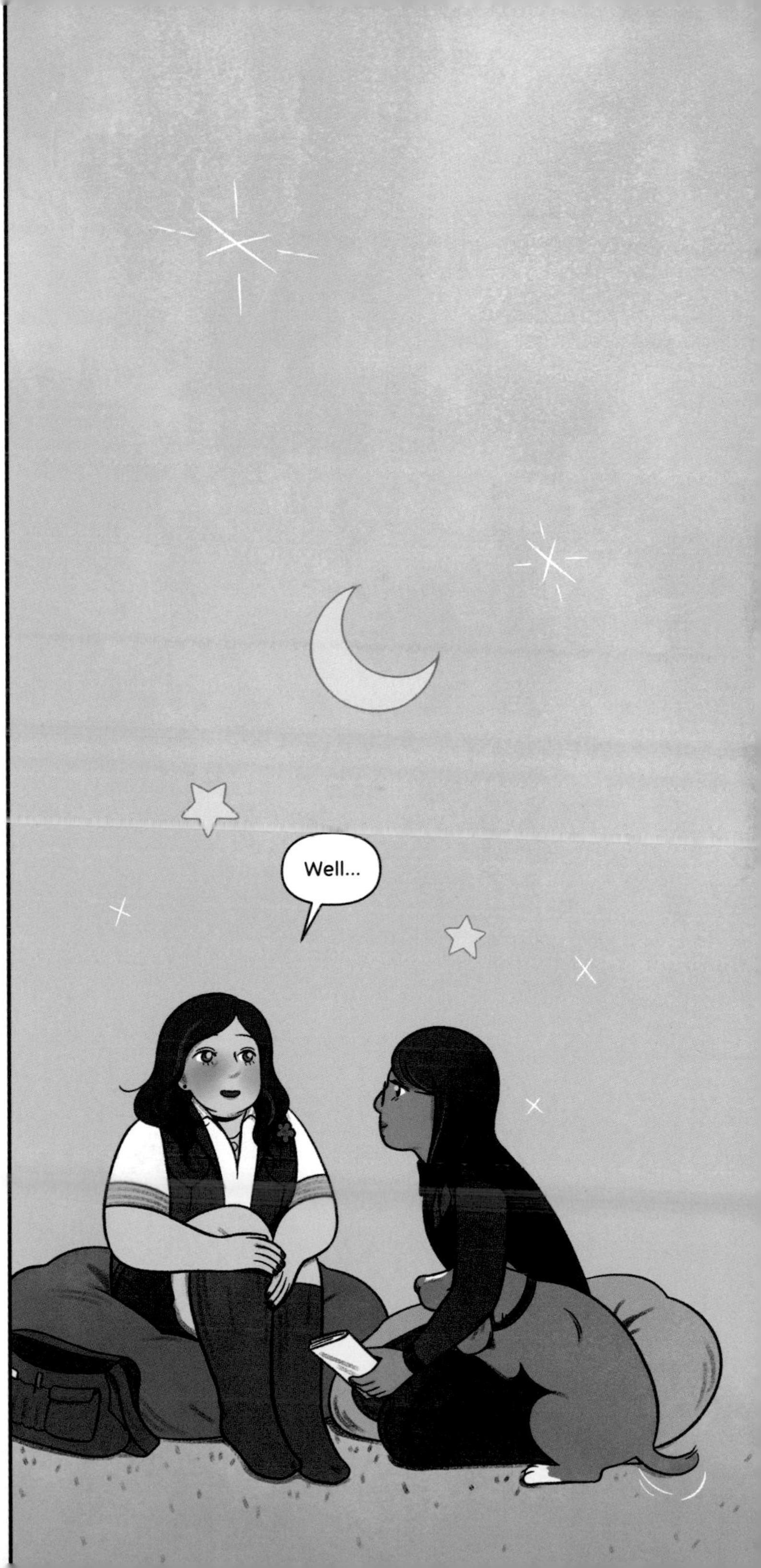
Well...

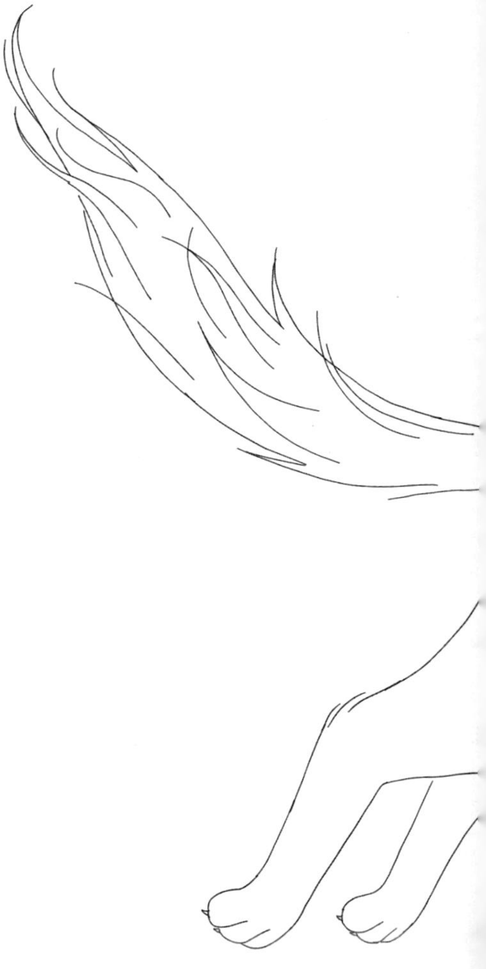

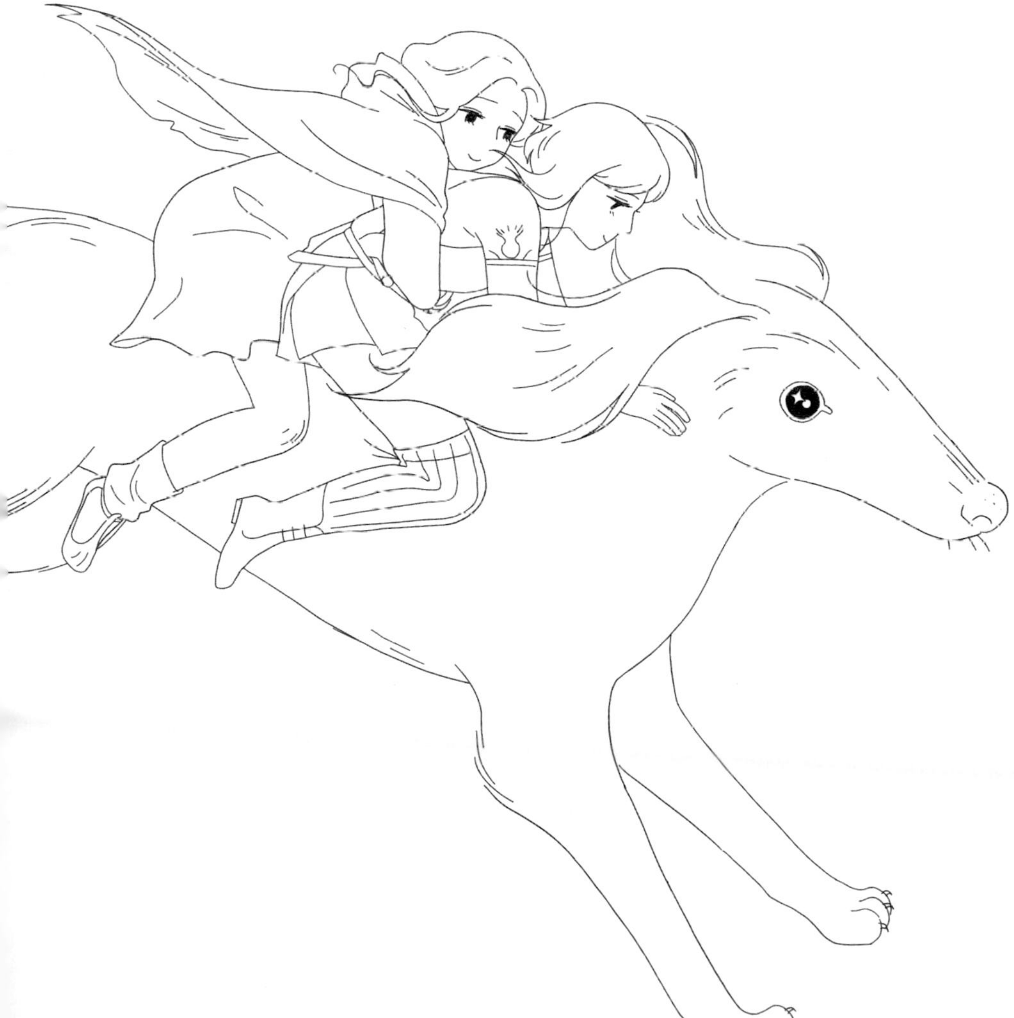

acknowledgments

Heartfelt appreciation for my understanding spouse, my family, and my friends. I couldn't make books without your care and support. I love you.

author's note

The Greatest Thing is a fictional story inspired by some experiences I had in high school. Characters like Oscar and April aren't exact replicas of my friends from that time but rather new creations that encapsulate meaningful impressions left on me by people I loved as a teenager.

But Winifred is just me, as much as my flawed memories allow. Her feelings and successes and mistakes are all things I went through when I was fifteen myself. This is my story as much as it is hers.

This book is my gift to the young me, to Win, and to anyone like her. I hope that if you feel alone, this story can be there for you but also that you find glimmers of hope in your own life. You deserve happiness. It just might take some time and effort to get there sometimes. And you're never as alone as you think you are.

resources

If you ever feel hopeless or you notice someone else is struggling, please seek help. Talk to your friends, confide in an adult you trust, and reach out to organizations who understand your situation.

The Trevor Project, thetrevorproject.org

> Trevor offers trained counselors and peer support for LGBTQIA2S+ youths in the form of a telephone hotline, texting and chat options, and a specialized social network. Their website features a robust assortment of resources for all sorts of related issues, including questions you may have about mental health and managing life at school.

National Suicide Prevention Lifeline, suicidepreventionlifeline.org

> NSPL provides a confidential telephone hotline and online text chat to support people who are in distress or who need resources to help others. They offer Spanish-language and d/Deaf-accessible options.

National Eating Disorders Association, nationaleatingdisorders.org

> NEDA includes a support hotline, text chat, online text chat, and listing of resources to help people find treatment for eating disorders.

A quick internet search for your region plus keywords relating to your problems can help you find local support groups and organizations who may be able to offer more specialized, face-to-face assistance.

But it's also important to know that if you or someone you know is ever in serious distress and needs urgent help, you should call 911 or seek other emergency/crisis services right away.

Take care. You are loved.

my zines

My guidance counselor made good on his promise to motivate me with comics. I still wanted to graduate early, but I had floundered in chemistry and dropped it to save my GPA, which meant I needed to make up an entire year in science. My counselor found me a spot in an experimental class, where a teacher was helping struggling students find passion in science with interest-based projects. They even agreed to let me double up for an entire year of credit in one semester.

Burnouts played with fire, cheerleaders learned about exercise biology, and then there was me. My teacher introduced me to the woman who ran the printing press for the school district, and she spent the semester teaching me how offset lithography works. I wrote and drew comics in my independent study in art, then in science class I made big metal printing plates for my zine and ran them through the press. My local comic shop, Casablanca Comics, invited me to sell the final product. It meant everything to me that people took me seriously as a cartoonist, and I continued making comics afterward, turning back to photocopying after class ended.

I was able to finish high school a semester early but still stopped by every other Friday until graduation to help edit the literary magazine. I spent that spring working weekends to save toward college and spending weekdays developing my drawing and writing skills. I got to treat my passion like it was my job for those few months, and that set me up to become the author I am today. Here's a peek at the zine I made for that class!

I'm forever grateful to Mr. L, Mr. M, Ms. C, Rick, and all my art teachers.
Your encouragement made such a difference.